THE SUN WILL
SHINE TOMORROW

CANCGUGO

Also by Maureen Reynolds

Voices in the Street

The Sunday Girls

Towards a Dark Horizon

MAUREEN REYNOLDS

THE SUN WILL SHINE TOMORROW

Black & White Publishing

First published 2008
by Black & White Publishing Ltd
29 Ocean Drive, Edinburgh EH6 6JL

ISBN: 978 1 84502 142 9

3 5 7 9 10 8 6 4 2 08 09 10 11 12

Copyright © Maureen Reynolds 2008

The right of Maureen Reynolds to be identified as
the author of this work has been asserted by her in accordance
with the Copyright, Designs and Patents Act 1988.

A CIP catalogue record for this book is available
from the British Library.

Typeset by Ellipsis Books Ltd
Printed and bound by MPG Books Ltd

I dedicate this book to Grandad Dwyer,
my mother Molly and
brother George.

I

It was May 1941 and Rosie was expecting a baby. It was an event which filled our family with dread and consternation – except for Rosie and Lily who were both delighted.

We all remembered Mum who had died almost ten years ago after giving birth to Lily. Because of this tragedy, we were all deeply worried – especially Dad. After all, Rosie was forty-five and this was her first child. Rosie's mum, Alice, and our granny didn't discuss it when we were in the house but I knew they weren't happy about it.

Dad, as usual, did his head-in-the-sand act and didn't talk too much about it but I knew he was also desperately worried about Rosie's well-being. As for me, well, I just hoped and prayed that, should anything go wrong, he wouldn't go back to his old ways of drinking away his sorrows.

In the two months since their marriage, Rosie had been a tower of strength and comfort to him and I hoped he would be the same for her. We were all still living in the same house on the Hilltown, the house we had before Dad's marriage, but it was becoming really cramped now that Lily was growing up fast.

I had been looking for another place for Lily and me but now this bombshell of Rosie's pregnancy had put an end to that. She needed my help because she was suffering from the most horrendous morning sickness as well as midday sickness and afternoon sickness. She had lost some weight before her marriage but she now looked thin, grey-faced and drawn. To say I was alarmed was an understatement.

I still had my job at Connie's newspaper shop but before going off in the early morning, I would get Dad's breakfast and see him off to work with his dinner-time piece box. I hated his look of relief as he set off through the door and I wondered if all men looked like this during their wives' pregnancies.

Rosie did try her best to get up before he left for work but she was no sooner on her feet when a feeling of faintness and nausea swept over her, making her slump back on the bed. When this happened, I made her lie still and drink a cup of tea with a Rich Tea biscuit. But, within a few minutes, she was sick. As I held the bucket under her grey, sweating face, I felt my own stomach heave but I tried to be strong for her sake. So I concentrated my gaze on the wallpaper while she was being sick.

Lily would stand wide-eyed at the door but I told her to get dressed for school as there was nothing she could do.

Afterwards, as Rosie lay prostrate on the bed, I would go around with a pail of water and Dettol and try to mask the ever-present smell.

Even Lily's usual robust appetite had waned a bit in this atmosphere, I noticed. Fortunately she was now able to go to school herself which was one chore less for me. We would leave Rosie to go back to sleep while we made our way to the shop. Connie would give Lily small jobs to do before she set off for school.

Connie tried to be cheerful when Lily was around but, like everyone else, the memory of Mum's death was on her mind as it was for all of us.

'Well, Lily, how are you today?' Connie asked as she handed over a pile of comics. 'You can put the names on these so the paper girl can deliver them.'

She gave me a look and whispered, 'How's Rosie?'

Lily, with her sharp little ears, overheard. 'She's terrible, Connie. Ann had to hold the bucket because she was awfully sick and, although Ann cleans the house with Dettol, we can still smell it.'

Connie gave me a look which meant we would discuss it later

but it wasn't to be. All our neighbours and a lot of the residents of the Hilltown had heard the news and they weren't slow in coming forward with all kinds of advice. Even Joe, who was one of Dad's oldest pals, made a daily comment on the dangers of older mothers. Still, it made a change from his daily, doom-laden accounts of the war.

'I aye mind one of my neighbours who had a late bairn and there was something wrong with him,' he said, touching his head. 'You know – mentally.'

Connie was annoyed. 'Thanks for sharing that with us, Joe. You've made Ann feel so much better.'

'Och, I don't want to alarm the lassie but I'm just telling it like it was. It's not a good thing to have a late bairn and I don't care if I say it.'

It was a relief when Lily was away to school. She, at least, wouldn't have to listen to these tales of doom and gloom.

'How's your dad coping with it?' Connie asked.

'In his usual way – by not talking about it. By the time he gets in at night, Rosie is feeling a wee bit better. Still, maybe that's a blessing because I know he's worried sick by the thought that it might happen to us again – that we might lose Rosie.'

Connie sounded morose. 'And there's this awful war to worry about too. Things look bad for us with the Jerries overrunning everything and America not coming into the conflict to help us.'

'I wonder what Rudolf Hess wanted when he flew into Scotland?' I asked.

Connie was cynical. 'The papers are saying it's either a peace treaty or that he's a mental case. Still, it's a strange situation and the papers aren't saying what he wants.'

Halfway through the morning, Connie let me run home to check on Rosie. I found her lying on top of the bed and I saw by the bucket at her side that she had been sick once more. She looked dreadful and I saw she had been crying.

Wiping her face, I asked her, 'What's wrong, Rosie?'

She tried to sit up. 'Ann, I'm such a wreck. What does Johnny think when he sees me like this?'

I was annoyed by her worries about my father and I told her
so. 'You've got to think about yourself, Rosie. You're the one that's
suffering – not him.'

'But you remember when he was married to Margot. Remember
how attractive she was.'

Margot – I hadn't given her a thought in ages but I could
understand Rosie's torment in the comparison. Dad had certainly
been taken in by the glamorous widow a few years earlier and he
had married her – a marriage that, fortunately for him, had been
a bigamous one on her part.

'I hear she didn't get a long sentence for the bigamy, Ann, and
maybe she's back as glamorous as ever.'

Poor Rosie. I knew Dad had been glad to be rid of Margot
but I also knew he was a bit of a fool over good-looking women.

'Look, Rosie,' I said, 'tonight, before he comes in, I'll put some
make-up on your face and you can wear something nice. What
do you think?'

She smiled weakly before retching painfully over the bucket.

I felt quite grim when I did the shopping in the afternoon and
standing in the endlessly long queues didn't help my mood. Just
about everything was on the ration and it was becoming more
difficult to feed a family. Still, I was lucky to get a marrowbone
from the butcher which meant I could make a big pot of soup
that hopefully would last a few days.

Lily and I usually went to our grandparents' house in the
Overgate every evening so that Dad and Rosie could have a little
time on their own. That evening, before his return, I put some
rouge on Rosie's grey cheeks and applied a little slick of lipstick.
It didn't really help but her blue frock made her look a bit
better. And there was the appetising smell of soup in the house
which made Dad's eyes light up when he walked through the
door.

He gave Rosie a quick kiss. 'You're looking better, love.' Glancing
at the pot on the stove, he said, 'What a smashing smell of soup.
I'm starving.'

Men, I thought.

Fortunately bread wasn't rationed so I had a whole loaf cut up to go with the soup but I noticed Rosie hardly ate a thing.

Later, Lily and I set off for the Overgate. While Lily went off to play with her friends, I sat in the kitchen with Granny and Alice who was Rosie's mother as well as being Granny's neighbour.

Alice was worried about her daughter. 'How is she today, Ann?'

I didn't know what to say as Rosie had warned me not to worry her mother or indeed anyone. I told them she was fine in spite of the sickness.

Alice shuddered. 'That morning sickness is a damned awful thing. It fair brings you down.'

Granny agreed. 'Aye, it is, Alice, and some poor folk get it worse than others. Some don't even get it at all but poor Rosie is unlucky to have it so bad.'

At that moment, Hattie arrived. My aunt, Dad's sister, looked as elegant as usual in spite of the clothes rationing but this was because she'd had such a fabulous wardrobe before the war.

Alice was on the verge of leaving when Hattie arrived and she couldn't be tempted with another cup of tea. 'There's a programme on the wireless, Nan. I want to listen to it so I'll see you tomorrow.'

Hattie twisted her face into a grimace as she pulled off her gloves. 'And how is the little mother today, Ann?'

Before I could answer, Granny leapt in with a sharp word. 'Don't speak about Rosie like that, Hattie. It's not her fault she's ill.'

Hattie flared up. 'I'm not running Rosie down. It's that stupid brother of mine.' She glared at me. 'Your father! What in heaven's name made him want to become a father again at his age? And Rosie is forty-five which is no spring chicken in the motherhood stakes.'

We were all used to Hattie's outbursts in the family and normally we took her statements calmly. Still, Granny was annoyed. 'Well, I expect it wasn't planned, Hattie, but these things happen. Rosie did tell Alice she thought it might be the change of life but it wasn't.'

A cold shiver went through me as I recalled hearing the same excuse given by my mother during her pregnancy ten years ago, before giving birth to Lily and dying from a haemorrhage a few hours later.

Hattie was still annoyed at what she saw as recklessness on Dad's part. 'Well, all I'm saying is this. Let's hope Rosie comes through this and that both she and her baby are well.'

Granny stayed silent and didn't look at me which made my heart grow cold. I could always depend on her to cut through Hattie's statements and denounce them as rubbish but I knew this time even she wasn't a hundred per cent happy or certain about Rosie's outcome.

I felt I had to add something positive. 'Rosie and Dad are both delighted by her condition and so is Lily.'

Hattie gave me a pitying look. 'They would be, wouldn't they? A first-time mother, a stupid husband and a little girl who doesn't know any better.'

I gave up. There was no way of coping with Hattie when she was in this mood. I changed the subject.

'I haven't seen Maddie or Daniel since last week. How are they?'

Hattie's face brightened at the sound of her grandson's name. 'Daniel is growing bigger every day and Maddie sends her love. She says you must visit her soon although she knows you're busy with Rosie.'

Granny appeared with more tea. 'Is Maddie more settled now, Hattie?'

Hattie gave a sigh of relief. 'Oh, she is, thank goodness. Ever since she had the letter from the Red Cross saying Danny is a prisoner of war, she has settled down to wait till the end of this awful war. She sent a letter by return to the Red Cross to let Danny know he had a son but we don't know if he got it. There hasn't been any more word back.'

I well remembered Maddie's state of mind at the end of 1940 when Daniel was born. Danny had been in the Dunkirk retreat and had been reported missing, presumed dead. I recalled the rejoicing when the letter arrived saying he had been very badly injured but was alive in a German hospital.

Lily then bounded in and it was time for us to leave. As we walked along the busy streets, the sun was dipping low behind the tenements of the Hilltown. I was dreading going back to the house. What if Rosie had been sick again? She would have hated Dad to have been a witness to her distress. What should have been a happy event was fast turning into a family melodrama, full of doom and gloom.

But, when we reached the house, I was pleased to see her sitting by the wireless, chuckling at a comedy show. Although she still looked grey and haggard, this was an improvement. Dad had gone to bed which was also a relief. Maybe Rosie was getting better.

Later, I lay awake in bed, listening to Lily's deep breathing as she slept the sleep of the innocent. The sky outside the small window had darkened but my mind was too alert to sleep. All the worries were like a jumbled mass in my brain. Maddie and my cousin Danny. How was he managing so far from home. And little Daniel. Would he be grown up when this war finally ended? Then there was Rosie and the baby and Joe's words about late mothers and mentally impaired children. I silently cursed Joe for his sweeping remarks and I vowed I would tell him tomorrow not to say another word.

The next morning, just after Dad departed, Rosie was violently sick. She sat on the side of the bed with her arms crossed over her stomach and her sweat-stained nightdress clinging to her thin body.

She was also crying. 'Ann, I feel terrible.'

'That's because you've hardly had anything to eat, Rosie. You're trying to be sick but there's nothing to come up.' Oh my God, I thought, what do I know about it? 'Look, you lie down and I'll make you a cup of weak tea.'

Lily had wandered through and she was crying as well. 'Will Rosie be all right, Ann?'

'Get dressed, Lily, and have your breakfast then go down to the shop and tell Connie I'll be a wee bit late this morning.'

She nodded but still gazed wide-eyed at the open door of Rosie's room.

After she had gone, I took a basin of lukewarm water through and gave Rosie a sponge down and gave her a clean nightgown to put on. Her face had a grey, clammy look and I was really worried about her

'Rosie, I'm going to send for a doctor,' I said firmly.

She tried to protest but was too weak even to sit up. I ran down to the shop and asked Connie if I could phone for a doctor. We didn't have our own doctor because it was expensive to call one out. This meant we didn't use one very much, relying instead on home-grown cures. Still, I knew Connie had a doctor and I could ask him to call in and see Rosie. At the shop, Connie said she would hurry round and phone him from her flat.

Doctor Bryson was a small bustling man with a bald head and wire-framed specs. He hurried into the house like a small beetle, his voice deep and brusque. Connie had mentioned Rosie's pregnancy to him over the phone and, when he came in, he found Rosie sitting on the edge of the bed.

He sat down beside her and took her temperature before giving her a quick examination. I stood inside the door with my heart thumping painfully, frightened of what he would say.

'How far on is your pregnancy?' he asked Rosie.

'About six weeks, Doctor.'

'This is your first child? And you're aged forty-five ?'

Rosie nodded.

The doctor stood up and put his stethoscope away in his large black bag. 'Well, I have to say you are a strong, healthy woman and, although forty-five is a bit old to be having a first child, it's not uncommon. Your problem, Mrs Neill, is that you are very unlucky to suffer from extreme morning sickness but this is nothing to worry about. You will feel a lot better after three months.'

Rosie looked unconvinced. 'I don't think I'll ever feel better, Doctor.'

'Yes you will. In a few weeks' time, this will just be an unpleasant memory.'

I paid him and he disappeared through the door, still bustling with his black bag banging against his leg.

Then Alice appeared. She looked worried. 'I saw the doctor, Ann. Has something happened?'

I repeated what the doctor had said but my words were interrupted by the sound of Rosie retching.

'If the doctor is right, Alice, then Rosie has another six weeks of this,' I said.

I left Alice with her daughter and went to work. Connie was full of sympathy and wanted to know what had happened because it wasn't every day I sent for a doctor. But we couldn't discuss it properly because Joe was in the shop.

Connie had obviously warned him because he didn't mention Rosie or her age. Instead he was full of Rudolf Hess's flight to the Duke of Hamilton's estate.

'There's something in the wind,' he said, lighting up one of his home-made cigarettes. 'A Nazi like that doesn't fly hundreds of miles just to say hello. I bet Hitler wants to make peace with us.'

I let his words wash over me but Connie was eager to keep the conversation going. She said, 'What do you think about the call-up for women, Joe?'

Joe was all for it but he got me worried again when he said, 'I expect you'll be called up, Ann – you being a young single woman.'

I looked at him in alarm but Connie laughed. 'Ann can't go because she has her sister to look after. She might not be married but she's got more responsibilities than some who are.'

After Joe had gone, I asked Connie if this call-up would include me but she said no. It would only be women and girls who had no ties – women who could move to the munitions factories or work on the farms in the Land Army. To be honest, by dinner time I was totally washed out and thinking once more what a terrible world this was. I wondered if the sun would ever shine on us again.

That evening, Dad was almost beside himself with worry when Rosie mentioned the doctor and even the doctor's reassuring words didn't make him feel any better.

I went to bed early as I wanted to write to Greg, my fiancé. He was working in a place called Bletchley Park in England, in some office doing war work, he said. He hadn't passed the medical for the armed forces because of his bad leg but his letters were full of news about days spent being busy and I know he enjoyed the routine and the work. It was all a bit hush-hush but then so was everything in these traumatic times.

I had mentioned Rosie's pregnancy in one of my letters but I didn't want to be all gloomy tonight and give him all my worries and woes so I tried to keep the letter as cheerful as possible – not an easy task.

His letters were full of chat about the people he worked with and how lovely the countryside was where he was stationed. 'The war seems so unreal in a lovely peaceful place like this,' he wrote. 'Yet we can hear the muffled sounds of the planes as they drop their bombs on London and the night-time sky is often fiery red with all the blazing buildings. It's terrible to think about it.'

I dashed off a quick letter before I spent another sleepless night. I was hoping to look for somewhere else to stay but I felt I couldn't abandon Rosie just now. She needed help with the house and the shopping and I was the only one close enough who could do it as Granny and Alice were unable to rush around looking after her. All these jumbled thoughts went round in my brain again – the worry and uncertainty of the war and thinking about Danny and Greg. Would they ever come home again?

I fell asleep around dawn only to be wakened a couple of hours later by the usual sounds coming from Rosie's room. I stumbled wearily towards the door, feeling as if I had the entire weight of the world on my shoulders. Still, the next day was Saturday. On Saturday and Sunday Lily and I normally stayed away from the house. Dad and Rosie needed some time on their own so we would head for the Overgate.

On the Saturday afternoon, Granny had a visit from Minnie and her son Peter. I hadn't seen her for a while and it was great to catch up with all the news. Minnie and Peter had been lucky to escape from the Clydebank bombing last year and they were now back staying with her mother while her husband was away in the army.

What a strange man-less society we are, I thought – women and children and older men only. As Greg said, an unreal world.

Minnie said, 'I'm looking for a house, Ann. It's terrible living with my mother and she's getting worse.'

Granny was sympathetic. 'Is she still cleaning the house from top to bottom, Minnie?'

Minnie looked grim. 'Aye, she is but it's getting worse. The other night Peter was playing with a pencil and she started wiping the floor around him, saying he'd put pencil marks on the linoleum. She sloshed so much disinfectant water around him that he was soaked and smelling of San Izal for ages. I'm sure she's going daft with all this cleaning.'

'What will you do, Minnie?' I asked.

She shook her head. 'I wish I knew.'

Suddenly the door opened and Bella, Granny's sister, appeared. On seeing her, Grandad said he needed some more tobacco and he hurried off.

Granny was appalled by his behaviour but fortunately Bella didn't seem to notice.

Bella said, 'I couldn't help overhearing that you're looking for a house, Minnie. Is that right?'

Minnie nodded.

'Well, the house next door to me is becoming empty next week. The old wife died, poor soul, but if you go down to the factor in Reform Street you'll maybe get it.'

Minnie was overjoyed. 'I'll go and see them first thing on Monday morning. Thanks, Bella!'

Bella tried not to look like Lady Bountiful but couldn't. 'Och, that's all right, Minnie. We know what a dragon your mother is with the washcloth.'

Bella lived in Cochrane Street, one of the highly populated streets that formed the 'Crescent' area situated beside the very busy Lochee Road. It was also near the Hawkhill where Minnie's mother lived.

Bella then turned her attention to me. 'You might have to join up, Ann – you being a single lassie with no bairns. The papers are saying that you'll get sent to the munitions factories or you can join the Land Army. What would you like?'

Before I could answer, Granny butted in. 'Ann has Lily to look after. How can she go to some munitions factory or anywhere else for that matter?'

Bella sat in the best chair like a fat Buddha and shook her head. I was always fascinated by the way her heavy jowls wobbled like a plate of jelly. She continued. 'Doesn't matter about a sister, I don't think. Ann will have to go if she's told.'

More worries, I thought. Was there no end to them? Also, although I wouldn't say anything to Bella, I wished she had mentioned the empty house to me. But maybe she didn't know I was looking for one. And I certainly didn't begrudge it to Minnie who had been through so much in the last few months, coming out of the shelter in Clydebank to discover the entire area completely flattened and everything gone except what they were wearing. It had been a traumatic time for her and little Peter.

Bella was now on the subject of Rosie. 'What a pair of daft beggars they are, having a bairn at their time of life. Still, your father was aye a bit stupid, Ann.'

Granny glared at her but she went gaily on, 'And I hear Rosie is sick every morning, noon and night. That can't be right. There must be something wrong with her to be aye so ill.'

'It's never stopped you, Bella,' said Granny acidly. Bella either didn't hear or else she pretended to be deaf.

I tried hard not to laugh. Bella was our family hypochondriac and here she was running down Rosie who had just cause for her sickness. But there was no stopping her when she got going in a character assassination.

'Rosie has the shape that'll run to fat. I bet she'll be like a house end by the time the bairn's born.' This was rich coming from her. There was the well-known family joke about the time she got stuck in a chair at home and it had taken three young men to pull her free.

Minnie got ready to leave and, to our relief, so did Bella. Minnie said she would let us know about the house and they all departed.

I said to Granny, 'I'm looking for a house as well, Granny. It's not fair on Rosie and Dad having Lily and me hanging about – especially after the baby's born. I wish I'd heard about the empty house next door to Bella.'

Granny laughed.

I looked at her.

'I hope in one way that Minnie doesn't get it. Imagine living next door to Bella with all the world's ailments. I think living with a house-proud mother would be better than that.'

Later, Lily and I left. We made a detour through Dudhope Park where Lily played on the swings. The sun was warm and the sky a cloudless blue. I sat on the grass, alone with my thoughts. I imagined hundreds of planes flying across with their cargoes of exploding bombs and I began to shiver in spite of the warmth. We were lucky here in Dundee. Although a few bombs had fallen, we didn't have to contend with anything like the people in London, Glasgow and Coventry had – and Clydebank, come to that.

It was indeed, as Greg had described it, an unreal world. Yet this unreality had violence and death breathing round its edges. For the moment, it had missed us but our turn would surely come. Another thing – what if I did have to go away to a factory somewhere? What would happen to Lily?

As if she read my mind, she hurried over from her swing to sit beside me. We sat and watched a large bumblebee settle gently on a nearby flower.

Lily turned to look at me. 'Is Rosie going to be all right, Ann?'

'Of course – she'll be fine,' I said.

Lily didn't look happy.

I said, 'Rosie's just going through a bad stage just now but she'll get much better in a wee while.'

Lily thought about this for a moment then looked at me with anxious eyes. 'It's just that Jean McBean was saying things about Rosie when we were playing.'

'What did she tell you, Lily?'

She seemed on the verge of tears. 'She says Rosie is going to die – just like Mum.'

I was angry but I knew comparisons were being made over the two women. I took her hand. 'Well, Rosie's not going to die, Lily – I promise you,' I said and this seemed to cheer her up.

I wondered what was waiting for us at the house. Was Rosie feeling better? Or worse? And I was mentally kicking myself for making a promise – a promise which I sincerely hoped would turn out all right but, to be honest, it was one I wasn't a hundred per cent sure about.

2

Tuesday afternoon was my usual day for doing the weekly laundry at the Meadows wash-house. I was feeling tired and hot and not looking forward to the next few hours in the hot, steamy building. Up to a few weeks ago, I had only my grandparents' washing to do along with my own and Lily's but, with Rosie feeling so ill, Dad had asked me if I could maybe do their laundry as well.

I trundled the little pram, with the huge basket perched on top, through streets that were dusty and hot in the lovely sunny weather. The sun beat against the pavements and I felt its heat on my bare legs. Just before reaching the steep hill that led to the wash-house, I suddenly felt so weary that I had to stop for a moment. I stood beside the row of large houses that lined Dudhope Street. These were houses that were mainly owned by doctors and their families. The lovely houses had gardens that swept down towards the street. Because of the rationing, these gardens were now planted with vegetables but there was still a patch or two of flowers.

I stood and watched a fat bumblebee land on one bloom, its droning filling the air, and I was reminded once more of the war and the clarion sound of the eerie siren that heralded an air attack. As I stood looking at the gardens, I thought, not for the first time, of how far away the war seemed to us.

Then it was on to the wash-house which was even hotter than I imagined. Still, I had no choice but to get started on the dirty washing. The large expanse of green meadow that lay behind this building was full of chattering women and lines of clean laundry flapping in the gentle breeze. The scene was a kaleidoscope of colour and noise – a truly rural scene in the middle of this grimy, industrial city.

I divided the washing into three separate bundles – that way I wouldn't get mixed up when it came to deliver Granny's bundle at the Overgate – and, for the next few hours, I scrubbed and scraped the clothes against the side of the ribbed washboard, rubbing Sunlight soap into the neckbands and cuffs of Dad's shirts which were really grimy.

The building was very quiet that day. No doubt most of the women were out in the sun and there was only a muted, droning sound of muffled words being filtered through the hot, steamy air – not unlike the sound of the bumblebee, I thought.

By four o'clock, I was finished and glad to push my pram out into the open air. I was turning out of the narrow track on to the main road when I saw Maddie and Daniel. She was pushing him in his large Silver Cross high pram and she looked as worn out as I did.

She waved when she saw me. 'Hullo, Ann. I went to the house to see you and Rosie told me you were doing the washing.' She fell into step beside me.

Maddie, with her regal-looking pram that looked fit for a prince, had a golden-haired baby sitting up under the cotton canopy with its cream fringe. Meanwhile my tatty old pram held the huge wicker basket with the washboard tied on top.

Little Daniel was smiling at all the trees in the gardens, holding out a chubby hand in their direction.

'You're getting bigger every day, Daniel,' I said, leaning over to kiss the top of his fair hair.

I was constantly amazed at how little he looked like Danny, his father – except, perhaps, for his blue eyes. He certainly didn't have his father's bright red hair.

Maddie swept her blonde hair away from her face and I saw it was as damp with perspiration as mine was.

She laughed. 'How you can manage to do a huge pile of washing like that I'll never know, Ann – especially in this weather.'

'Someone's got to do it, Maddie. Rosie isn't well enough just now. Still, things will get better when she's back on her feet.'

'Rosie looked terrible when I called at the house, Ann. I think she had been sick. Her face looked grey and drawn.'

I didn't tell Maddie that this was how she looked every day. Instead, I said to her, 'You were awfully sick all the time when you were expecting Daniel?'

Maddie nodded. 'Not just first thing in the morning either. It lasted till early afternoon but it does pass after a few months. You remember how ill I was, Ann? Is Rosie like that?'

'No, she's sick all day and night. Everything she eats or drinks seems to come up. It's terrible, Maddie. Still, the doctor doesn't seem to think there's anything wrong.'

'That's a shame because it's bad enough being sick in the morning without it happening all day.' She stopped. 'Are you going home now?'

I shook my head. 'No, I'm going to the Overgate first to leave Granny's washing then I'll head for home.'

'Then I'll walk with you as far as that, Ann, as I've got to get home and feed Daniel. He's now getting rusks with hot milk for his tea and I'm slowly starting him on solids.' There was no disguising the motherly love in her voice but when she spoke again it was with sadness. 'I just wish Danny was here to see his son, Ann.'

I nodded but daren't speak. I knew I would burst into tears at the thought of Danny being in a prisoner of war camp somewhere strange and alien but I didn't want to upset Maddie. I remembered the terrible time before Daniel's birth when everyone thought Danny was dead – killed at Dunkirk. But, by some miracle, he had only been injured and put in a civilian hospital in Germany. It had been months before the Red Cross had found this out and informed Maddie.

She was still speaking and I realised I hadn't heard a word she'd said. She stopped and looked at me. 'The war could go on for years and years and Daniel will grow up and never know his father. What a terrible thought, Ann.'

She needed to be reassured. 'Och, this war will be over sooner than you think, Maddie.' Now why had I said that? I had the talent for coming out with statements that were based on thin air.

'Do you think so? I heard it could last another twenty years.'

'No, Maddie, I don't think it'll be as long as that. I'm not saying it'll be over tomorrow but in a couple of years I'm sure we'll be at peace with Germany.' There I go again, I thought – Crystal Ball Annie. Still, she looked relieved and that was the main thing.

'The reason I've come to see you today, Ann, is to ask a favour. My sister Joy has got this big box of paints and all sorts of artist's equipment from an old uncle of mine who used to be a painter. Well, Joy was wondering if Lily could come and stay for the weekend at the house. They could paint away to their hearts' desire.'

'Oh, Lily will love that, Maddie. You know how much she likes to paint and draw – just like Joy.'

Lily and Joy were the same age. Both girls had been born on the same day and they had been friends since their toddler days – even though Joy was at a fee-paying school and mixing with the children of well-off parents.

By now, we had reached the Overgate. 'Do you want to bring Daniel up to see Granny?' I asked.

'Yes, I do.' She unbuckled Daniel's reins and we left the two prams against the wall of the stiflingly hot close.

Granny was with Alice and the two women were delighted to see the baby.

'This will soon be you, Alice,' said Granny, holding Daniel on her knee while I put the kettle on. I was so parched I could gladly have drunk a small stream dry.

Alice looked weary. Her thin face was deeply lined with furrows that had been made worse with all the worry over Rosie. 'Well, Nan, I'll just be glad when it's all over I can tell you,' she said.

After our tea, I hung Granny's washing on the kitchen pulley. The houses in the Overgate didn't have the luxury of drying greens which meant everything had to be hung up inside – a huge pity when the weather was as glorious as this. Our house had a small, postage-stamp-sized drying green which, although a bit inadequate, was at least better than nothing at all.

Maddie and I then left but, before pushing our prams in different directions, Maddie said, 'I would really like you to come for the weekend as well, Ann. Do you think you can leave Rosie?'

'Aye, I can, Maddie. We try and leave Dad and Rosie on their own at the weekend so that will be great.'

Her face lit up. 'Come on Saturday and stay until Sunday. We can have a good gossip while Lily and Joy play with their paints.'

'I'm looking forward to it already, Maddie,' I said. 'But, for now, I'll have to get this washing pushed up the Hilltown and get it dried in this lovely sun.' I looked at Daniel. 'Cheerio, wee pet – I'll see you on Saturday.'

He gave me a toothless smile and waved his chubby arms at people passing by.

'Ann . . .' Maddie hesitated. 'I'm thinking about you having this awful load of washing every week. Do you think I could give you a hand? Or ask Hattie to help? She does our laundry at home.'

It was nice of Maddie to offer but I tried not to burst out laughing. As offers went it was one of the more hilarious ones. Hattie? Do our washing? Heaven forbid. She might do Mrs Pringle's washing but that was because she was their housekeeper. And I happened to know they sent most of their things to the laundry which meant it would only be the small items that Hattie washed.

I had a mental picture of Hattie, immaculately dressed, struggling up the steep slope with our shoogly old pram with the basket placed on top. I almost had a fit of the giggles. However, I managed to keep a straight face. 'That's really good of you to offer, Maddie, but I'll manage – thanks.'

Lily was at home when I reached the house. She had made

some tea and toast for herself and Rosie but Rosie was now in her room being sick.

Lily was almost in tears. 'I should never have made it for her, Ann. It just makes her ill again.'

I put my arms around her. 'It's not your fault, Lily. It's just something that happens to some women when they're expecting. Anyway, I've got good news for you.'

Her eyes widened. 'What is it?'

'Joy wants you to go over to her house on Saturday and do some painting with her.' I told her of the uncle's gift. 'I'm going as well and we are staying over till Sunday.'

Lily was so delighted that even the sight of poor Rosie coming out of the bedroom couldn't dampen her spirits.

'Rosie, we're going to the Perth Road on Saturday to paint with Joy, and Ann's going to have a good gossip with Maddie. We're staying till Sunday.'

Rosie tried to look pleased for her but she merely looked ghastly.

I went over and made her sit down. 'I'll not go if you need me here, Rosie,' I said.

She shook her head. 'No, no, Ann, just you go and enjoy your-self – I'll be fine.'

'You'll have Dad for company so at least you'll not be on your own, Rosie.'

She wiped her eyes and looked over to where Lily was standing. She shook her head and I knew she didn't want to speak in front of her.

'Lily, will you run down to Connie's shop for the evening paper please?'

After she left I asked Rosie, 'Now what's all this about? Is it Dad?'

As if a dam had burst, the words came tumbling out of her mouth. 'Och, it's not his fault, Ann. He's really worried about me. After what happened to your mum, he thinks the same thing is going to happen to me.'

'Well, it's natural for him to be worried about you, Rosie.' I didn't tell her that the entire family was worried about the same thing.

Her hands were on her lap and she kept twisting them, unsure whether to go on. Then she said, 'It's just like this, Ann. I hardly ever see him. He goes for his pint after work on a Saturday. He comes in for his tea and then he goes out for another three hours. Then on Sunday he goes to see Joe for another four hours.' She looked at me with red-rimmed eyes. 'I think he's seeing another woman and who can blame him when I'm aye feeling lousy and looking like a washed-out rag?'

I was so angry with my father that I had a strong impulse to charge down the road and meet him coming from his work. Then I saw Rosie was looking for reassurance. 'Listen to me, Rosie. I don't think there is another woman – it's just your mind playing tricks because of the baby. But, as for him going out, well, that's just Dad all over. He could never face anything distressing and the thought of you going the same way as Mum is enough to send him daft. Still, you have to be firm with him and not let him off with it. I mean it's not as if this baby is all your own doing, is it?'

She nodded weakly. 'Oh, Ann, I wish I could be firm but at the moment I feel about as firm as a half-set jelly.'

I laughed at this thought and she joined in. By the time Lily arrived back, we were both laughing and I was grateful to see Lily's little face beam with joy. Whatever was bothering Rosie was now gone, she thought. If only . . .

I made up my mind to stay with Rosie and let Lily go on her own to see Joy but on the Saturday I was surprised when Rosie said she would come as far as the Overgate with us.

'Will you be all right?' I asked her.

She looked grim. 'Let's just say I'm as well being sick in my mother's house as here.'

I left her in the capable hands of Alice and Granny and set off for the Perth Road. The weather had turned slightly cooler but it was still bright and sunny.

As always, when visiting Maddie's house, I was struck with

how lovely it was. Because of the 'Dig for Victory' campaign, the garden seemed to be full of vegetables instead of flowers. The lawn was still in place and it swept down towards the river which sparkled in the sunlight and was capped by white-tipped waves.

Joy and Maddie came to meet us and Lily was soon whisked away to look at the wonderful painting gift.

'Wait till you see it, Lily,' said Joy. 'We can paint hundreds of pictures with it.'

Lily's face was a delight as she tagged behind Joy.

Mrs Pringle appeared and watched them go. 'Heavens, I hadn't noticed how little Joy has grown. Lily is such a lovely tall girl while Joy is quite tiny.'

It was true. Joy, who had always been so much tinier and more fragile-looking than Lily, was still small and doll-like with her very fair hair and blue eyes. She was wearing a lovely floral summer dress and she made poor Lily look positively gargantuan. Still, I was glad now that I had managed to get her a new dress and sandals.

Daniel was asleep in his cot but Maddie said she would wake him soon. We moved into the lounge and it was as gorgeous as ever. My mind went back to the end of 1931 when I had first seen this room and fallen in love with it. Although it had been decorated since then, the curtains, carpet and lamps were all in matching and toning shades of apricot. It was similar to being in a warm and golden bubble.

Thankfully, Hattie wasn't working. It would have broken her heart to have us as guests. She was so snobby it was unbelievable.

I went with Maddie to her room under the eaves. It at least hadn't changed since my last visit – except for the blue cot which sat beside the open window.

Wearing only a terry nappy and lying blissfully asleep was Daniel. Maddie and I sat down beside the open window and talked about past times and how happy we had all been before the war. In fact, that wasn't quite true in my case. I had too many unhappy memories from under the gaze of Miss Hood, the ousekeeper at Whitegate Lodge. She had been really evil towards me. Still, this was compensated by the kindness from my late employer, the lovely Mrs Barrie. I often thought about her. Alas she was now dead, as was Miss Hood. Another person who had been good to me was the cook, Jean Peters. I made a mental note to visit her soon.

But I didn't mention these thoughts to Maddie. I didn't want to spoil this golden day so I sat and looked at the river while Maddie chatted on.

'I see the government is calling up young women, Ann – between the ages of twenty and twenty-one. You'll be hoping your age group doesn't get sent to the munitions factories.'

She made me sound like Methuselah and I had to smile. I was almost twenty-five but it was all very worrying.

'I can't go and leave Lily on her own. Granny could maybe look after her but she's not so able these days. As for Rosie . . .' I let the question hang in the air.

Maddie nodded sympathetically. 'I know what you mean, Ann, but maybe it won't come to anything. Anyway, there's maybe some job you can help out with as well as the paper shop.'

'I've thought about that and maybe I can do something in the Home Guard in the evenings – fire watching or something like Dad does.'

'Mum and I do a few days with the Red Cross, Ann, raising funds and generally helping out. If a lot of casualties come back from the battlefields, then I may have to go back to nursing.' She stopped and wiped her hand over her eyes. 'It's a terrible world, isn't it? Babies and children all growing up without their fathers and goodness knows when they'll ever see them again.'

I was saved from answering this thorny question by a loud wail from the cot. Young Daniel was back from the world of sleep.

I was amazed. 'Does he always make that racket, Maddie?' I said with a laugh.

She looked at her son with a rueful smile. 'Of course you do, don't you, Daniel?'

We went downstairs to give him his tea. Joy and Lily were in the garden with the paints and Mr Pringle, who had just arrived back from the office, was admiring their work.

'They're very good paintings,' he said, throwing himself down on a chair while making a face at his grandson. Daniel responded by blowing a big, wet kiss in his direction.

Mrs Pringle was in the kitchen and a wonderful smell of cooking wafted through. I went to see her and asked if I could maybe help her but she told me to relax and enjoy my visit.

'Maddie tells me that Rosie isn't keeping very well, Ann. At least she's got you and your Dad to look after her. Still, we think you do too much hard work so try and cut down, will you?'

I promised but I didn't believe myself.

I had brought along some tea, sugar and butter. With everything on the ration, people could no longer afford to feed another two mouths from the meagre allowances. However, Mrs Pringle wouldn't hear of taking them. 'Not at all, Ann. It's a pleasure to have you both here. We were lucky before the war in buying lots of things in bulk which means, except for fresh meat, fish and eggs, we still have some spare stores. Still, if the war goes on for much longer then even these will be used up.'

We all sat round the table in the dining room. I had warned Lily not to eat too much but as it turned out, Mrs Pringle filled our plates with so much that it would have been a waste of food to leave anything behind. Not that this bothered Joy because, as usual, she merely picked at her food. She was eager to get back out in the garden with the paints.

'Lily and I are going to be painters when we grow up, aren't we Lily?'

Lily nodded cheerfully between mouthfuls of a delicious pie.

'When we leave school we're going to go to an art college and become famous painters, aren't we, Lily?'

Mrs Pringle said she should eat up her food in case she ended up starving in some garret. 'Look at Lily – see what a great eater she is? You should be the same.'

Lily looked at Joy and they both burst out laughing.

Later, after Maddie, Lily and I bathed Daniel and put him to bed, we all sat in the lounge with the sun going down over the river. The entire room was bathed in this golden glow and once again I felt this strange affinity with this wonderful house.

The two girls went outside to try and paint the lovely sunset while we sat with a glass of sherry and listened to the wireless. We sat and listened to the stark news that Germany had invaded Russia in spite of having a peace pact with them.

'So much for siding with the Germans,' said Mr Pringle. 'I think Hitler and his cronies would go against their own mothers.'

We all agreed. Hitler seemed to be invincible and where did that leave us? At war and alone against the Nazis.

Later, Maddie and I got ready for bed in her room. She said, 'I've been meaning to ask you something, Ann. Do you think you and Lily could stay in the flat at Roseangle? I haven't been back since the night Daniel was born and Dad says it needs someone in it during the winter months. To keep it aired and warm.'

I was overcome. 'Oh, Maddie, that would solve our problems when the baby comes. I feel we should let Rosie and Dad and the baby to have time to themselves so, yes, we'll look after it.'

I tried to make her accept rent for it but she said no – we were doing her the favour.

'Of course we can't go till Rosie has her baby. That will be in December, Maddie. Is that all right?'

'Yes, that's fine. It'll be a relief during the worst of the winter months to know someone is looking after it.'

We lay in bed for ages, giggling over past events but keeping pretty quiet in case Daniel wakened up.

'He usually sleeps quite well but sometimes he can bawl the house down. Dad says he must have the Pringle lungs because Danny and Hattie and you all have soft voices.'

But Daniel slept all night – even when the siren went off around four o'clock and when the all-clear sounded an hour later.

Maddie said, 'That will be some other poor people bombed out of their houses. Why is it such a relief when it isn't our houses?'

'That's just human nature, Maddie. Somebody gets hit but thank the Lord it isn't us.'

On the Sunday, the weather was just as glorious so we had a lazy day out in the garden and watched the girls' frenzied attempts to capture a colourful butterfly on paper. Then the lovely weekend was over.

As we made our way back to the Hilltown, I was heading home with a heavy heart. I couldn't speak for Lily but I was dreading it. I wished Dad would face his responsibilities and not bury his head in the sand. Rosie needed all the help she could get and was he helping? No, he was not.

I knew Rosie worried about little things but she would have to be tough with him. I made up my mind, as we walked through the still-warm streets that Sunday evening, to have a good talk with my father.

Lily was carrying her paintings home and I had promised to get some of them framed as they were very good. She must have picked up some of my tension because she blurted out, 'I loved being at Joy's house. I hope Rosie isn't sick when we get back.'

'She can't help it, Lily, so we'll just have to put up with it for a wee while longer.'

I hadn't wanted to mention the flat at Roseangle but I thought it might cheer her up. 'Can you keep a secret, Lily?'

She turned her dark, serious eyes to me. 'Cross my heart.'

'When Rosie has her baby in December, you and I are going to live in Maddie and Danny's house – just for the winter but isn't that wonderful?'

Lily was over the moon but I warned her not to say anything. 'I don't want Rosie to think we're abandoning her and Dad.'

Full of high spirits at the thought of the future, we reached the house.

Rosie was sitting with Dad and it looked as if they had had a row. My heart sank.

Lily ran over to them with her paintings and, although they both tried to look cheerful and interested, I knew there was something wrong. After Lily went to bed, it all came out. Dad's unit of the Home Guard were going on a training course.

Rosie's voice was strained. 'And it's in the Orkney Islands, Ann – the other end of the country.'

'Can you not get compassionate leave, Dad?' I asked. 'Rosie needs you here with her.'

'No, I can't. There's a war going on and we have to be fighting fit when Hitler decides to invade so I have to go.'

Rosie looked dejected while I was appalled by the look of relief on his face. We might be at war with Germany but my father was grateful for the chance to escape from his pregnant wife. I was sure of that.

3

Dad left for Orkney in the middle of July. It was a damp misty day full of grey skies and grey emotions. His train was in the late afternoon and just before leaving with him, Rosie took another violent spate of sickness which left her weak and almost gasping for breath. When Lily and I arrived at the house from Granny's, Dad looked stunned. He was holding her in his arms and his small suitcase was sitting at the door.

Rosie had her coat on and I hurried over to take it off. It was the coat she had bought for her wedding and I knew she wouldn't want to stain it.

Dad stood up as I approached and he looked almost as ill as his wife. 'I'm not going, Rosie. What kind of husband am I to even be thinking of leaving you?' he said.

Rosie looked relieved and, to be honest, I'm sure I did too. Then, to my utter amazement, she said, 'You've got to go, Johnny. As you said, it's wartime and thousands of women are struggling to survive while their men are away.'

I didn't look at Dad – I was too frightened of seeing even the smallest trace of relief on his face. If I had, then I think I would have lashed out at him. But, if Rosie wanted her husband to go away to his training camp while she bravely carried on, that was her decision.

Dad said, 'Is that what you want me to do, Rosie?'

She nodded weakly then added, 'Mind you, I don't think I'll make it to the station with you but Ann can go with you and maybe Lily will stay here with me.'

Lily didn't seem too pleased by this but she was too well mannered to contradict Rosie, especially when she was so ill. So Dad and I set off for the station. I couldn't imagine his feelings but my head was spinning with a hundred questions and I could feel the unspoken words between us.

The station was full of soldiers and their kitbags and they swarmed all over the platform. An air of tension hung over the place, like a thunderstorm waiting to break. I could feel the air crackling with emotional goodbyes.

I could see no passenger arrivals at the station, only departures. These men and a smattering of women were all going away. Some, like Dad, to a training camp for a month but most of the younger men were going away to goodness knows where or for how long. As for the young women, were they being sent to the farms or the factories? My heart sank when I saw them. Would I be the next one standing on this platform? Would I be saying my goodbyes to Lily and Rosie and my grandparents?

Then Joe appeared. He had come to see Dad off but was surprised by the non-appearance of Rosie. His face was full of sympathy for he also remembered Mum but thankfully he said nothing. He handed Dad one of his homemade cigarettes and both men lit them up, the blue smoke spiralling in a foggy haze towards the cavern-like roof.

Joe said, 'We never thought we would see this all over again, did we, Johnny? Another bloody war with Germany.' He drew deeply on his cigarette and scowled at no one in particular. 'We were a lot younger than some of these laddies when we went to fight in the Great War.'

Dad agreed. 'You're right, Joe, and now another generation of youngsters have to sacrifice their lives. What an awful world they've inherited and I'm glad to say I'm grateful I've got two lassies instead of laddies.'

I was almost in tears. I know Dad and Joe and thousands like them had survived the chaos and carnage of the last war but millions hadn't and it was all happening again.

Joe said, 'Aye, we thought the invasion would come last year but, now that Hitler has decided to break his pact with Russia, then maybe we're a bit safer.'

Dad shook his head. 'The invasion can still happen, Joe. Hitler thinks he can reach Moscow pretty quickly and then it'll be our turn. That's why these training programmes are going ahead.' He stubbed out his cigarette. 'Are you still doing your fire-watching, Joe?'

Joe nodded. 'I'm lucky that I've not been sent on any training courses but the fire-watching keeps me busy. Some nights it gets a bit boring but I expect the fire-watchers in Clydebank, Coventry and London would be glad to be bored. Heavens, they must be run off their feet with all the incendiary bombs.'

I found all this talk of war so depressing. There seemed little point in discussing Hitler's motives or possible invasions – either it would come or it wouldn't. To be honest, at that moment my main worry was Rosie – she wasn't getting any better and she was almost four months gone.

Thankfully a loud distorted voice echoed from the tannoy and all the soldiers gathered up their kitbags. They waited with a multitude of expressions for the train to arrive.

Dad looked tired and his face was strained with worry. 'Ann, you'll look after Rosie?'

I nodded.

He seemed embarrassed and awkward. 'You think I'm a coward running away from Rosie at this time, don't you?'

I felt a mixture of emotions and didn't know what to say.

'You think that, don't you?'

'No, Dad, but I think Rosie needs all the help she can get at this time.'

He nodded and, to my horror, I saw his eyes were wet. 'I know but it brings back all that terrible time when your mum died. I can't help it. I keep thinking the same thing is going to happen all over again and I don't think I can take that, Ann.'

I gave him a hug. 'It'll not happen again, Dad, so don't worry. I'll look after Rosie and so will Lily. Anyway, you're just away for a month.'

The train was approaching. When it stopped, he grabbed his bag and boarded the train which stood like a giant Titan guarding the gates of the gods. Then it slowly moved away with a huge spurt of sooty steam and a mechanical clanking noise. It was like the wailing of a soul in torment.

Joe had tactfully moved away but he now came and stood beside me and we both waved to no one in particular. The train was so overcrowded that there was no room to stand at the windows and make long farewells like they did in the Hollywood pictures whose stars played at make-believe war which was a thousand light years away from the real world.

Joe and I moved out into the street and it was as grey as ever. Joe sniffed the air. 'I think the sun's going to shine tomorrow, Ann.'

'Oh, I hope so, Joe!' And I didn't just mean weather-wise.

'Your Dad's worried about Rosie and I hope everything goes well for them this time.'

I couldn't bear all this talk about Rosie's impending death and my voice was firm when I answered, 'Rosie will be fine when she gets over this awful sickness, Joe. Honestly, she'll be fine.'

As we parted at the foot of the Hilltown, I once again cursed myself for my crystal-ball attitude. Yet someone had to be optimistic for Rosie's sake.

When I reached the house, Lily was sitting with her books and crayons. She looked relieved when she saw me and she said Rosie was lying down.

'Has she been sick again?'

She shook her head.

I peeped into the small bedroom and saw that Rosie was asleep. 'I have to get some messages, Lily. Do you want to come?'

She was on her feet in a flash.

When we reached the butcher's shop further down the hill, we were both dismayed to see a large queue. It was just the way of life now and no one could do their shopping in a hurry these days. Everything was done by standing around – rain or shine.

We joined the end of the queue. 'I hope you're not too disappointed at not seeing Dad off,' I said.

'Well I am a bit but somebody had to stay with Rosie. Anyway, he's just away for a month so we'll see him soon.'

'Aye, we will,' I said as the queue shuffled slowly forward.

Rosie got a letter a few days later and she read it out. 'Your dad says the island is windswept but lovely. He's in a camp somewhere on the island but he can't say where for security reasons. He's missing us and counting the days till he's home.' She scanned the page and I saw her blush. 'The rest is a bit personal so I'll not read it out.'

She seemed quite happy about his absence. We knew we were living in difficult times and Dad had to go – he had no choice. But, unlike the fighting men on the battlefields, he would soon be home.

Rosie was still being sick but I had become used to this routine and I prayed it would all end soon.

On the Sunday, Alice came to the house as usual so Lily went to the Overgate and I went to Lochee to see Kit and George.

The street was busy with children playing when I arrived. A group of girls had just chalked numbered boxes on the pavement and were busy jumping from one number to the next. Another group was playing with a length of washing rope which they used for their skipping games.

Kit and George were in the house along with their son, Patty. Kit had told me earlier that they were dreading him getting his call-up papers. He was eighteen and working as an apprentice welder in the Caledon Shipyard. Patty had always been a delicate child, suffering from asthma from a young age.

As Kit was making the tea, she said, 'We're hoping he doesn't pass the medical if he gets called up but maybe the fact he's doing his apprenticeship in the shipyard might help. It's a reserved occupation.'

I felt sorry for her and all the mothers who had young sons.

The thought of them going off to war was horrendous but Winston Churchill had said the country needed every man and woman to be prepared to fight for freedom. It was all stirring stuff but that didn't help the families.

There had been no more word about Danny since the Red Cross letter saying he had been injured at Dunkirk but it was likely that he was in some prisoner of war camp in Germany.

Kit seemed tense and her face was white and strained. 'I often think about Danny and hope he's keeping fine. Now it looks like it might be Patty's turn to go.'

She turned her tired eyes in my direction. 'I just hope this awful war is soon over and everyone can get their laddies back again.'

George sat in silence, just nodding at her words.

I told her about Dad being away for a month and how Rosie was coping. 'I just hope she gets over this terrible sickness, Kit. It's making her feel run down.'

Kit was sympathetic. She asked me, 'Have you tried giving her a cup of tea and a dry biscuit before she gets up?'

'I've tried lots of things, Kit. All the old wives' tales and a few more for luck but nothing seems to help her. She manages to eat and drink something then it all comes back up. It's horrendous and I think she's getting thinner. She's getting no nourishment at all.'

Kit said, 'Well, the old wives' tales do say that the bairn is getting the nourishment it needs but at the expense of the mother so let's hope she gets better soon. She's certainly unlucky to be still sick after the three-month mark.'

I nodded but could add nothing else to the saga, not having been in the motherhood stakes myself. And, quite honestly, Rosie's state was putting me off ever becoming a mother.

I was on the verge of leaving when Kathleen came in with her little girl, Kitty.

Kit's face lit up like a beacon when she saw her granddaughter. 'Hullo, my wee pet! Are you going to stay with your granny and grandad?'

Kitty nodded. Her blue eyes full of mischief. She was clutching a huge doll which she placed on the couch. 'Mummy says I can stay here and put my dolly to sleep.'

Kit produced a small blanket from the toy box and Kitty busied herself with it, fussing over the doll and speaking to it as if it was a real child.

I looked at Kathleen and once again was amazed by her beauty. Her skin looked translucent and fragile against her bright auburn hair. She was every bit as good-looking as Rita Hayworth, I thought. She had a job in a shop in the town. Hunter's outfitters in the Wellgate was a large department store and I had seen her behind the hosiery counter looking smart and lovely in her dark, sober-looking dress. Now of course, with the clothes on the ration like every other commodity, the shop wasn't as busy as it was before the war but it still got its share of customers.

No one mentioned her husband Sammy who had also been injured at Dunkirk, and who, by some strange coincidence, was also a prisoner of war like Danny. I knew Kathleen was going to end this marriage after the war because of Sammy's behaviour. As far as Kit and George were concerned it couldn't come soon enough and I remembered only too well the bruises he had inflicted on Kathleen before he left.

Patty arrived and I was struck again by his fragile-looking air which I think was caused by his ivory coloured complexion which looked so pale against his red hair. Apart from his asthma with left him breathless at times, I don't think he suffered from any illness but hopefully he would remain at the Caledon Shipyard.

Kathleen stood up when her brother came in. 'I'm ready, Patty.' She turned to her mother. 'We're going out for a wee while but we'll not be long.'

After she left, the subject of her marriage was raised. 'That toerag Sammy Malloy had better not come creeping back here to her when this war is over,' said Kit. 'Kathleen wants to make a new start without him. We thought she would end up with that boy Colin Matthews but he's also been called up. Still maybe it's just as well because she is still a married woman and you know how folk talk, Ann.'

Before the war, Colin was a clerk in Mr Pringle's office. Kit told me at the time that they were just friends – companions at the pictures or a couple of dances – but Kit was right to be concerned.

George said, 'She is still a married woman, Kit, and she should mind that. Why she ever got married to Sammy is a big mystery but she was aye headstrong and doing her own thing.'

I wondered where Ma Ryan was. She was normally to be found in Kit's house.

'Where's Ma today, Kit?'

Kit grinned. 'She's over at my sister Lizzie's house. Lizzie has hurt her back so Ma is looking after her. Poor Ma, I heard that Lizzie had her dusting and cleaning all week and Ma is threatening to go on strike. She says she doesn't have to lift a finger when she visits me so why should she have to spring-clean Lizzie's house.'

I laughed but was a bit disappointed. Ma was said to have the sixth sense and she had given me a couple of warnings in my life. I was hoping she would tell me if Rosie was going to be all right. Still, knowing Ma, she might not. I remembered how she told me years ago that she didn't get feelings about some people and that she didn't interfere in matters concerning her own family.

It was time to go. Kit made me promise to come back soon and I said I would. The tramcar was busy, no doubt with people on their way to visit friends and relations on the only work-free day of their week. I sat in the tram as it meandered its way through the grimy and busy streets, all full of children playing in the warm sunshine.

My head was full of jumbled-up thoughts. I hadn't heard from Greg in over a week. I put my hand to my neck and felt the ring hanging from its chain – my engagement ring. Would there be a wedding? I wondered. Oh, I hoped so with all my heart, after this war was finished – whenever that would be. Hopefully not when I was seventy.

It would soon be Lily's birthday and Joy's – their tenth. How big she was growing and soon she would be out of my life, but not just yet thankfully.

Then there was the awful daily problem of Rosie. Would she ever get better?

By the time I reached my stop, I had a splitting headache which wasn't helped by meeting Alice on the stairs.

She just shook her head at my unasked question. 'She's not had a good day, Ann. I'll be glad when your dad gets back from his training camp.'

I echoed that sentiment.

The following morning, Joe was full of the Russian invasion. I often wished he wouldn't talk so much about the war and I suspected that Connie felt the same but there was little we could do against his non-stop chatter.

'I see the Jerries are making good headway in Russia,' he said morosely, before brightening up a bit. 'Still, Napoleon couldn't conquer Russia so let's hope Hitler's henchmen have the same fate. It's the bad winters that get them over there. Twenty or thirty degrees below freezing would make your fingers fall off,' he added cheerfully.

'But it's just July,' said Connie. 'Surely Russia doesn't get cold weather for months yet?'

'Aye, but Russia is a vast country, Connie. The German Army can't conquer it in a week. No, you wait and see. They'll still be fighting in the winter and that'll sort them out – just like Napoleon.'

Then the three girls arrived – Amy, Edith and Sylvia. As usual, they were full of fun as they bought their normal cigarettes and sweeties.

Joe gave them a stern look. 'Are you lassies not getting called up for war work?'

Sylvia looked at him in surprise. 'No, Joe, we're working in the mill and doing our share for the war effort.'

On that note they all departed, laughing.

Joe looked disgusted. 'War work indeed. They spend their days laughing and joking and buying sweeties.'

'Well, as long as they've got their sweetie coupons that's all that matters,' said Connie, winking at me.

After he left, she said, 'It's a wonder folk need to buy a paper round here with Joe the oracle spouting forth.'

That was true – where would we be every day without our running commentary on the war front? It was as if he was on the spot, telling it like it was.

It was Lily's birthday at the end of the week and I planned to take her to see Jean Peters at the Ferry but before I wrote my letter to Jean, Mrs Pringle invited us to a party for Joy at the Perth Road.

'It won't be a big party, Ann,' she'd said, 'because of the rationing but it will be a day out for Lily and you. Please bring Rosie if she feels up to it and your granny and grandad.'

Once again, the weather was lovely and warm as Lily and I set off. Rosie had initially been delighted with the invitation but, during the morning, she didn't feel well and had to lie down. As for Granny, well, she would also have come but Grandad had a bad cough and she didn't want to leave him.

I was in a quandary about leaving Rosie alone but she insisted I should go with Lily and have a good time. 'After all,' she said, 'it's her birthday and she's looking forward to her party.'

Lily had grown out of her summer dress so I had to take the hem down and sew a row of colourful rickrack braid along the edge of the hem. How strange it was that Lily was growing so tall while Joy never seemed to grow an inch. Still, maybe she would get a spurt of growth later.

Lily was unhappy about the altered dress.

'Well, there's nothing we can do about it, Lily. We need clothes coupons for everything and you'll soon need new school clothes so the coupons will have to be kept for them.'

I would have loved to give her a new dress for her birthday but we were now living in austere times. Although the threat of invasion was fast receding, the ships in the Atlantic were still being sunk by the German U-boats. An even tighter grip was being put on the rationing system and we were all thankful for the unrationed bread and potatoes which filled us up.

Hattie was at the house with Mrs Pringle and Maddie when we arrived. Daniel was sitting in his pram in the garden and Joy and Lily ran out to play with him.

Maddie looked lovely and cool in a thin cotton dress and her hair was tied up with a blue ribbon, the exact colour of her eyes. I knew this was an unconscious act on her part because she was not pretentious but the effect was lovely and elegant, to say the least. I felt so dull and insipid beside her with my five-year-old frock and sensible-looking sandals. Yes, I had to admit that some women were just born elegant.

Maddie was one and Hattie was another. She was dressed in a lovely soft grey jersey wool dress which clung to her still-slender figure. Her hair, although still dark, now had a few flecks of grey which enhanced her face. Lucky Hattie, I thought, she's not dowdy like her niece.

The table was set with sandwiches and some homemade little fairy cakes plus a small birthday cake with both Joy's and Lily's names piped on the top with watery-looking icing.

Lily was entranced by this and, although the cake was too small to hold ten candles, Mrs Pringle had put one candle at either end for the girls to blow out. Joy didn't want to blow hers out so Lily got the pleasure of blowing both candles.

I overheard Joy telling her mother, 'I'm not a baby any more – I'm ten.'

Mrs Pringle caught my eye and we both smiled while we watched the still babyish Lily, her eyes aglow and her cheeks puffed out with the effort of blowing two candles out.

Later, Maddie, Daniel and I went for a walk along the Esplanade. It was turning into another lovely evening and the river was calm and streaked with gold. Across the river we saw the houses nestling amongst the trees. A few of the windows caught the western sun which turned them into sparkling jewels.

Maddie sighed. 'It's hard to believe we are at war on such a lovely day as this.'

I agreed.

'How are Granny and Rosie, Ann? It's such a shame they couldn't come to the party.'

'Granny's fine although Grandad has a bad cough. It's his pipe smoking, Granny says, but he'll not give it up. She didn't want to leave him but she would have come if he had been feeling better. As for Rosie . . . well, what can I say? She's still the same and we're counting the days till Dad gets back.'

Maddie stopped and gazed at Daniel who was fast asleep in his pram. 'She's been very unlucky to still have this sickness. I was well over it by three months, thankfully.'

'Rosie is four months now and it doesn't look like it's going to stop. Poor soul.'

We walked back to the house. Hattie had gone and Mrs Pringle asked if Lily could stay the night with Joy. They both wanted to paint.

'I haven't brought a nightdress, Mrs Pringle,' I said.

Maddie's mum said that wasn't a problem. 'We'll find something for her to wear, Ann. We'll bring her home tomorrow morning before we go to the church.'

I wouldn't hear of them putting themselves out. 'Oh, no, Mrs Pringle, I'll come and fetch her.'

So it was arranged that I would collect Lily at the church which was the same church that Maddie was married in, St Andrews at the foot of the Wellgate.

As I walked home, I thought Mrs Pringle would think we were heathens. We didn't belong to a church so I made a mental note to take Lily to Bonnethill Church which was a mere hundred yards from our house. She could join the Sunday School and, quite honestly, I knew of a lot of people in my life who could use a few prayers. As I walked towards the house, I was glad I had made that mental commitment. I would ask Lily and, if she agreed, we would go next Sunday.

Rosie was crying when I got in and a letter was hanging from her white fingers.

My heart sank. 'Rosie, what is it?' My voice sounded harsh with worry.

She looked at me, her face puffy, her eyes red-rimmed with

crying. 'I got this letter today. It's your dad – he's had a bad accident and he's in hospital in Kirkwall.'

I thought I was going to be sick but Rosie beat me to it. I took the letter from her lifeless fingers. Written by one of Dad's friends, it was quite short and read:

Dear Rosie,

Johnny fell down a cliff on Thursday and has a suspected fractured skull which means he'll be in hospital for a while. He won't be coming home with the rest of us but the doctor is keeping an eye on him. Ann will look after you till he gets home.

Love J

(Written for Johnny by Bill)

Rosie was back at my side. 'What does a while mean, Ann? Is that weeks or months?'

I gave her a hug. 'Och, he'll be back soon so don't worry, Rosie.'

She looked relieved and I felt guilty. 'It's not like we can go and visit him, Ann – he's hundreds of miles away.'

I agreed. 'You'll just have to keep in touch by letter, Rosie – at least for the next few weeks.'

The lovely day I had spent with Maddie and the Pringles was now just a memory. And why was I reassuring Rosie when I hadn't a clue how long Dad would be lying in hospital? Crystal Ball Annie again – when would I ever learn?

4

It was mid August when Rosie woke up one morning and she wasn't sick. We thought it was a fluke but, when a week went by without the terrible feelings of nausea, she began to look forward to the future.

'I can't believe it, Ann – I feel super.'

I had to admit she looked it. Her skin had a youthful bloom and her hair, which had been so limp and lifeless, was now thick and shiny.

Even Lily noticed the difference. 'Rosie's looking beautiful, isn't she, Ann?'

Indeed she was. She also regained some of her old energy which manifested itself in a burst of house cleaning which both surprised and delighted me.

Still, there was one blot on her new horizon – Dad. He was still incarcerated in a hospital in Orkney and, although the skull fracture had been diagnosed as a hairline fracture, he was still recuperating. Rosie was beside herself with worry. As the days passed, she became more fretful and I began to worry about her. I couldn't believe we had finally got rid of one worry only to be confronted with another one.

She said, 'I wish he could get home to recuperate. He's miles away with no visitors.'

Maddie came to tea on the Sunday and, while I was setting the table, Rosie was telling her all the worry over her husband.

'What a pity he couldn't get transferred back here, Maddie. It would make such a difference to us all.'

Maddie nodded sympathetically and Rosie seemed to cheer up. 'Still, I'm not as badly off as you, Maddie. At least Johnny isn't in a prisoner of war camp in some foreign country. Mind you, as far as I'm concerned, with all the restrictions on travel, he might as well be in a foreign country – after all, Orkney is practically in Norway.'

That wasn't true but Maddie hid her smile. She knew Rosie was unhappy about her husband's health.

Later on, as Maddie and I walked back along the road, she said, 'I think I'll ask the Red Cross if they can help to get your dad home. Maybe if there's another training group coming up then your dad could get a lift in their transport.'

I was overcome with gratitude. 'That would be great, Maddie – especially for Rosie. She's just got over one hurdle and now she's faced with another one.'

Maddie said she would help all she could and she hurried towards the house to see to Daniel. Her mother was looking after him to give her a couple of hours off.

I didn't mention Maddie's suggestion when I got home. After all, it was only a thought and Maddie's plan might not succeed. There was no sense in upsetting Rosie. I didn't want her getting her hopes up only to be dashed at the last moment.

Rosie decided to buy a maternity smock. 'Just something bright for when Johnny comes back,' she said.

I went with her to Hunter's department store in the Wellgate. It was a lovely hot summer afternoon at the end of August. We were glad to be out of the heat and inside the cool, dim interior of the store. Long wooden counters ran the full length of the walls and everything was hushed. It was like being in a cathedral.

I spotted Kathleen at the far end of the hosiery counter. She didn't see us but I decided to try to see her before leaving.

There wasn't a huge selection of smocks due to the wartime shortages but Rosie didn't seem to mind. She had spotted the one she wanted right away. It was a lovely deep-blue cotton one, very plain but it suited her complexion and also made her seem slimmer.

The assistant put the money in a small tin canister and pulled a wire. The container then shot across the store to the cash desk before returning with Rosie's change.

We made our way towards the front door but I still wanted to see Kathleen. I stopped. She was deep in conversation with an elderly man who looked very aristocratic with his well-cut and expensive clothes. He had a small, well-trimmed white beard and he looked like the late George V.

Rosie stood waiting for me but I didn't want to interrupt Kathleen's conversation so we left.

'Who was that man talking to Kathleen?' asked Rosie. 'He's really handsome in an old kind of way, if you know what I mean.'

I was thinking the same but at the back of my mind I felt I knew him. I just couldn't think where or how I knew him.

We stopped at the grocer's shop to get the weekly rations and were dismayed to see a large queue.

Rosie gave a huge sigh. 'I wish we were back in the days before the war when there wasn't all these queues. And this smock cost me some of my coupons which I'm trying to save up for when the baby comes. He or she will need baby things and I'll have to start again from scratch. Quite a lot of the families in the street have other children which means they've lots of cast-offs but we don't have anything like that.'

That was true. Lily was born in 1931, ten years ago, and all her baby clothes had long since vanished, cannibalised to make something else from the wool and material.

I kept thinking about Kathleen and the man. They had looked very intense in their conversation. The man's identity still eluded me although the more I thought about it, the more I realised I knew him. It was just before falling asleep that night that I remembered where I had met him – Maddie and Danny's wedding.

He had been the photographer and a high-class one at that. He had his studio in a posh-looking, stone building at the foot of the Perth Road. He didn't have a window full of photographs extolling his wares. No, all he had was a well-polished plaque with his name and occupation. He didn't quite say he was a photographer to the rich but he was very high-class and, whatever it was that he wanted with Kathleen, she was seemingly considering it – at least I thought so judging from the look of concentration on her face.

Now that Rosie was blooming with health, Lily and I were eager to get into our new abode – Maddie and Danny's flat. Lily was forever speaking about it and I had to warn her, 'You're not to keep speaking about it, Lily – especially in front of Rosie as we can't leave her till Dad gets back.'

The next morning in the shop, Joe was doing his usual commentary on the German Army's trek into Russia. His face would beam every morning when he read the headlines. 'Aye, they'll have to retreat when the winter comes in,' he said. 'The Jerries will find it's no picnic in Moscow.'

Personally, I was growing weary of the war and all the queuing for food and the never-ending problem of making meals with fewer and fewer ingredients. In fact, there had almost been another war at the butcher's shop that afternoon when one customer had discovered her whole meat ration was used up for that week.

'How am I supposed to feed my man and three hungry bairns if I've no meat coupons left?' she hollered in front of a dozen women who all agreed with her.

The butcher looked embarrassed but said there was nothing he could do. 'You'll just have to make a big vegetable pie with loads of tatties,' he said. His unhelpful suggestion was met with a dozen scornful remarks.

'A vegetable pie with no carrots or onions – just neeps and tatties? What kind of a meal is that for a growing family?'

A wee woman at the back came up with a suggestion. 'I always flavour my chunks of turnip with Bisto and it looks like chunks of steak.'

The butcher looked relieved. 'There you go, then. What a great tip.'

The customer gave him a withering look and he retreated to the back shop before coming back a moment later with three slices of corned beef.

'There you are, missus. I'll let you have this from next week's coupons and don't say I'm not good to you.'

Of course everyone in the queue wanted some corned beef as well and, when I left the shop, the butcher looked shell-shocked.

I knew life was difficult for everyone – shopkeepers and customers alike. I was used to hearing snippets of conversation from the women who came into the shop.

'It's all right for some folk who get more than their fair share. It's not coupons that counts but who you know.'

Well, we all knew that was true. A thriving black market existed but, like all illegal things, I often wondered if it suffered from myths and exaggeration. After all, we were always hearing about someone who got an extra bag of sugar or butter or sweeties but it was never anyone we knew. It was always this mythical person – the person who knew all the sources and had the money to buy these illegal items.

Then, at the end of the month, Maddie arrived at the house with great news. 'Mum was asking at the Red Cross about your dad and the wonderful news is that a training group is going to Orkney next week. If your dad is allowed out of hospital, they'll bring him back.'

Rosie was visiting her mother but, when she heard the news, she was overcome with excitement. So much so that I had to make her lie down to recover.

Maddie warned her, 'Of course, it's not fully settled yet, Rosie, but Mum thinks the group will go. Then you have to consider that the hospital may not let Mr Neill out. It all depends on how well his injury has healed.'

I was immediately brought back to earth. There were so many ifs and buts but Rosie refused to be deflated. In her mind, Dad was already home.

As it turned out, the training group was held up for another week but they eventually set off. Dad then told Rosie the hospital was reluctant to let him go but they would if the transport was suitable.

I confided in Connie. 'I just hope Rosie's not disappointed. Army convoys are usually bone-rattling trucks and the hospital won't let Dad out in one of those.'

Connie said I should look on the bright side. 'Och, well, even if he doesn't get home straight away, at least Rosie is keeping fine now and her time is going in.'

It certainly was and I couldn't believe how fast the year was flying by.

Dad arrived home on a misty Sunday in September. Much to his disgust, he was carried upstairs on a stretcher. As soon as the two stretcher-bearers left, he got up and walked through to the kitchen.

He looked at his wife in disbelief. 'Rosie,' he said, 'you're looking beautiful.'

Rosie blushed like some love-struck sixteen-year-old. 'Och, away you go, Johnny!'

'No, I mean it – you look radiant.'

We had planned a welcome-home meal for Dad. I'd made a huge pot of soup and we had saved up our meat ration that week so that Dad could have a whole pork chop to himself.

Later, he told us about his accident. 'We were climbing up this cliff when the rope broke and I fell on to a ledge – which was lucky for me because I would have fallen another hundred feet or so and probably been killed.'

Rosie went white. 'Don't speak like that, Johnny – don't tempt fate.'

He laughed. 'Well, I'm back home now and that's all that matters. I expect I'll be off work for some time but Mr Pringle has asked me back to the fruit warehouse a couple of days a week and he says it's nothing strenuous.'

Rosie was unsure of this arrangement. 'Should you not be resting, Johnny?'

'Och, I've been resting since July, Rosie. I want to get back to work but I'll have to leave the Caledon Shipyard. Still, John

Pringle's offer is great because I can do some paperwork for him and also give him a hand.'

Although Rosie was still unsure of this arrangement, she readily agreed. Anything to keep him happy and she also knew he would get restless being in the house all day.

John Pringle, who was Maddie's uncle, was well known for being a good employer and Dad was glad to be going back there. Because of the war, fruit coming from all parts of the world had virtually stopped and John Pringle had had to let some of his staff go. He had promised to reinstate them when the war was over. Because of this, Dad had got a labouring job at the Caledon Shipyard. As for the Home Guard . . . well, it looked doubtful if he would ever be able to return there.

The following week, Lily and I moved to the flat at Roseangle. Maddie was quite happy for us to move in earlier than planned. It was a cold autumn evening when we moved in but we soon had a lovely fire in the grate and had put the kettle on for our tea.

Lily lay back on the hearthrug. 'I love this house, Ann. When I grow up, I'm going to buy a house like this for you and me.'

I laughed. 'What happens if you get married?'

She made a face. 'I'm never going to get married. I'll just stay with you forever and ever.'

I smiled and wondered what Greg would say to that arrangement. As soon as the war was over, I hoped we would get married – it was just a question of waiting.

We had our tea by the light of the fire, sitting by the window and gazing at the ever-darkening sky and the river which was tinged a grey gunmetal colour in the gathering dusk. Once again, I was struck by the peacefulness. Miles away people were being killed or captured and we were gazing at a river with its changing moods.

'There's one thing,' I told Lily, 'we're not using Maddie and Danny's room. I think we'll keep that door shut as it's their private room.'

Lily was puzzled. 'Where are we going to sleep, Ann?'

I pointed to the sofa. 'This is a bed settee. We can sleep on it.'
This pleased Lily. 'Can I pull it out?'

'Aye, you can and you can also put it away in the morning.'

Another thing I was going to do was put all the wedding presents away. Things like their crystal glasses and vases and their
wedding china. I was so afraid these things would get broken, no
matter how careful we were.

So I saved up all the newspapers that week and Lily and I
carefully wrapped all the lovely ornaments and other wedding
gifts. We placed them in a large trunk that we'd found in the
lobby cupboard.

Another bonus was Hamish the stag. Lily had grown quite
fond of him and she regularly hung her coat and schoolbag on
his ample antlers.

I was beginning to worry about Greg who normally wrote faith-
fully every week but I hadn't received my usual letter. I was beginning to think that he was ill or, even worse, that he was no longer
interested in me. Still, life had to go on and I put it firmly from
my mind. I was still writing to him and I gave him the new address
plus all the news on the home front.

One day, we had a visit from Minnie and Peter. She was suit-
ably impressed by the house – especially the view from the window.
'Oh, I could gaze at that scene forever,' she said.

Meanwhile Peter was more interested in Lily's crayons and
comics.

Minnie and I sat looking at the view and sipping tea. It was
very soothing.

I asked her if she had any news of her husband but she shook
her head. 'What's worrying me is that, if he does get some leave,
he'll not be able to find the house in Clydebank.'

'Speaking of houses, Minnie, did you get that house next door
to Bella?'

'No I didn't. Seemingly it was already taken when Bella mentioned
it although she didn't know that. But I have a chance of another
house in the Hawkhill next month. The old woman has had to go
into hospital and the rumour is she won't be coming back to live

in her house. Mum's had a word with the factor and he says if it becomes vacant, I can have it.' She sighed. 'It's not before time I can tell you, Ann. My mother is driving us up the wall with her constant nagging at wee Peter. He can't pick up a pencil but she's wiping the floor with a wet cloth. I spilt a cup of tea the other night and to hear her moan you would think I'd committed a murder. Mind you,' she said darkly, 'I might just murder her.'

Lily looked at her with alarm but, when we laughed, she looked relieved.

Meanwhile, back in the shop, Joe was still harping on about the Russian front and I think that Connie was becoming tired by all the talk of war.

'Have you nothing cheerful to tell us, Joe?' she asked. 'It'll soon be Hogmanay and we can say cheerio to another dismal year.'

Joe looked sceptical. 'Hogmanay? That's another five weeks away.'

Connie was unrepentant. 'Well, I'm looking forward to it.'

Then Greg's letter arrived and its contents filled me with delight.

I told Lily, 'Listen to this. Greg's managed to get a forty-eight-hour pass for the sixth and seventh of December. He'll get the train and I've to meet him at the station on Saturday evening. We'll not have very long together but it's better than nothing. Isn't that wonderful?'

Lily's eyes were glowing. 'Oh, that's great, Ann. Will you be getting married then?'

I laughed. 'I don't think so, Lily – there won't be enough time.'

I spent the following week in a frenzy of excitement. I went through my meagre wardrobe, wondering what to wear at the station. I was determined to look my best as I wanted to knock Greg over with my beauty. On the other hand, while studying my reflection in the mirror, I decided that a smart outfit would have to do the trick as beauty was out of the question.

Connie noticed the spring in my step and she was pleased for me. I knew I was fortunate to have Greg coming home, even if it was for such a short time – unlike the thousands of men in the army, navy and air force.

Connie said one morning, 'If you don't mind wearing something of mine, Ann, I've got this lovely suit I bought before the war and you're about the same size I was then. You can borrow it if you want.'

I didn't think I would want to do that – it was probably something frumpy. However, I also didn't want to hurt her feelings so I said I would go to see her that evening.

Connie's flat was in Stirling Street. The close was clean and well maintained and Connie lived on the top floor. In spite of all the wartime shortages, she had a good going fire and she made a pot of tea and a plate of toast. A small pot of marmalade stood beside this plate and I was impressed.

'Marmalade, Connie? You must have saved up lots of coupons for that.'

She smiled and shook her head. 'No, I didn't buy it. I used to make lots of jam and marmalade before the war and as a result I had a cupboard full of jars. Mind you, I'm down to my last couple of jars now.'

While I was savouring the tangy taste of the marmalade, Connie disappeared into her bedroom to get the suit. I tried to compose my face so it didn't register deep disappointment at what I thought must be a musty old costume. That's what made my delight all the more noticeable. The suit was lovely. The deep-blue jacket and dress had a quality that wartime clothes lacked. The 'Utility' label was on everything now and this meant the garment was cut to the bare minimum and there were no trimmings or nice buttons – just the bare bones of the garment.

'Go into the room and try it on – I think it'll fit you a treat.'

It did. I fastened the large chunky buttons of the jacket and I felt so comfortable in it. And the colour was marvellous. I stood in front of the large mirror on the front of the wardrobe and surveyed myself. I was suddenly transported back to Mrs Barrie's bedroom in the Ferry, to the day she gave me a gorgeous russet cashmere coat with the fox-trimmed cuffs and collar – the lovely coat that Hattie coveted and Miss Hood so callously burned.

I said to Connie, 'What can I say? If you don't mind me borrowing it for the weekend, I'd love to have it.'

Connie beamed. 'It looks lovely on you, Ann. Greg will be bowled over when he sees you – you mark my words!'

I lived the next few days in a frenzy of anticipation, barely able to sleep at night for the thought of seeing Greg again – it had been so long.

Saturday, 6 December duly dawned and I took Lily to the Overgate as I wanted to meet Greg on my own. His train was due in at five o'clock and it would be a very short reunion because he had to catch the three o'clock train the next day. Still, it was better than no meeting at all.

I was dressed early so I decided to pay a quick visit to the Hilltown to show Rosie my new suit. I had barely reached the stairs when Dad appeared. His face was red and he was agitated.

'Ann, thank goodness you're here. I was going to ask Connie to get you. Rosie's pains have started and she thinks the bairn's coming.'

'But she isn't due till the end of the month, Dad,' I said. 'Maybe it's just a false alarm but you better take her to the hospital as a precaution.'

He looked as if he was going to burst into tears. He wiped his face with a huge red handkerchief. 'I don't think I can take her to the hospital, Ann. I can't face the place after that unhappy time when your mum died there.' He was referring to the awful time when Mum had been taken there after haemorrhaging after Lily's birth – that terrible night of her death.

Dad was distressed. 'I can't go back there. What if the same thing happens to Rosie?'

'Can Alice go with her?'

He shook his head. 'Rosie wonders if you'll go with her.'

'But I'm on my way to meet Greg at the railway station, Dad. He's got this weekend pass and I was looking forward to seeing him again so much.'

Although outwardly calm, I was a mass of conflicting emotions. Please don't let me miss seeing Greg, I prayed to an unknown god. Of all the days to be born, I thought – on my big day, Master or Miss Neill had decided to enter this world. Perhaps this God was taking revenge on my earlier intention of taking Lily to the Sunday School – an intention that never materialised.

Then I felt contrite. Here was I being selfish while Rosie was sitting at home alone. What were her feelings? I wondered. A lot worse than mine no doubt – having her first baby at her age.

'All right, Dad, I'll go to the hospital with Rosie but what about Greg?'

Dad's face was a picture of relief. 'I'll meet him off the train and I'll tell him where you are.'

We hurried upstairs where Rosie was sitting on the edge of the chair, clutching her stomach. Her face was red and covered with perspiration in spite of the cold December day. She looked so pleased to see me that I felt I'd been really selfish.

'The pains are coming every ten minutes, Ann,' she said as a spasm of pain showed on her face.

Every ten minutes? Did we have time to get to the hospital? I wondered?

I helped her up from the chair and managed to get her coat and scarf on.

'Better wrap up well, Rosie. It's a nice day outside but it's a cold wind.'

Dad had obviously talked about his reluctance to go to the infirmary with her because she merely said cheerio.

Dad came down the stairs with us. 'You'll be fine, Rosie – I just know it.'

He gave her a quick hug and we set off along the road to the infirmary while Dad would be heading for the railway station.

Before he left us, he asked me, 'Can you stay with her, Ann? That is if you're allowed to. I know she'll appreciate it if she knows you're near at hand.'

Oh, great, I thought. How long did a labour last? A few hours, a few days, a week?

Rosie gripped my hand tightly and I said I would stay with her as long as she needed me.

I said, 'Tell Greg where I am and ask if he'll come and see me at the infirmary.'

He promised he would.

It was a journey I will never forget. Rosie had to keep stopping every few minutes to let a spasm of pain pass and I was frightened out of my wits. What if the baby should arrive here on this cold and windy winter street? I was never so glad to see the entrance to the infirmary and we made our way inside. The nurse on duty took all her particulars and led her away.

Before she left to walk along the corridor, Rosie turned to me. 'You will wait, won't you, Ann?'

I nodded. 'I'll stay in the waiting room, Rosie. Now just you think about yourself and the baby and I'll be here.'

The nurse looked quite nonplussed. 'Is your husband not with you, Mrs Neill?'

'No, Nurse, he wasn't at home but my stepdaughter kindly agreed to bring me in.'

It was a lie but I understood the reason for it. Rosie wouldn't want the infirmary or this cool-faced nurse to think her husband was some sort of moral coward. We all knew the reason for his phobia but maybe the nurses wouldn't understand. After all, they must be quite used to dealing with death. Maybe not every day but they couldn't use this excuse to stay away from their duties – even if they wanted too. No, I didn't think they would understand Dad and his fears.

I sat in the waiting room. It was beginning to fill up with visitors and, in my smart blue suit, I felt like an alien. I looked as if I got lost on my way to a wedding. I got some curious looks but on the whole most people were so absorbed or worried about their loved ones who were patients in the wards that they hardly gave me a passing glance – this smart stranger who looked like she had lost a ten bob note and found a sixpence.

What would Greg say? Every time in the past when we made our plans, something cropped up to change them. It seemed as if nothing had changed. There may have been a war on but I was still being pulled in different directions by my family.

Visiting time came and went and once again I was the sole occupant of the waiting room.

The lodge porter appeared. 'You can go home, Miss, and come back when the bairn's born.'

I shook my head. 'No, I promised I would wait.'

The sky outside was now dark and I stood in the infirmary grounds and gazed at the black expanse of Dudhope Park. The stars glittered in the black night sky and a bitterly cold wind was blowing from the east.

I wondered where Greg was. Surely Dad had managed to pass on my message. But, if he had, then surely Greg would be here by now and both of us would be sitting waiting for a new life to emerge.

At ten o'clock, I was still waiting when the lodge porter appeared. 'I'll have to close the doors soon. I don't think you can wait much longer, Miss.'

Then I'll just wait outside, I thought. Then Greg appeared and I ran towards him.

'Greg, I'm waiting for Rosie to have her baby.'

He looked quite grim but maybe he was just cold and miserable like me. 'So I've been told, Ann – just half an hour ago at my lodgings in Victoria Road.'

I was stunned by this blow. 'Half an hour ago?' I repeated, like a backward parrot. 'I sent Dad to meet you at the station to tell you.'

Greg's face looked grey. 'Your father went to the station but he forgot what time you told him the train was due in so he arrived late and I was long gone by the time I assume he appeared.'

Poor Greg. 'I don't know what to say. What a stupid thing to do!'

Greg seemed to cheer up. Perhaps it was my contrite apology. 'Oh, well, I'm here now.'

I tucked his arm in mine and we sat on the low wall at the edge of the park. 'I'm really sorry about this Greg but Dad was in such a panic about Rosie. You do remember I told you that my mum died in this infirmary – just a few hours after Lily's birth?' I felt choked up and was surprised that, even after all these years, I could still be reduced to tears by the memory of that terrible night.

Greg leaned towards me and wiped my face with his hand-kerchief. 'I remember it, Ann, and it is good of you to come with Rosie.'

'But I'm not with Rosie, am I? She's inside the infirmary and we're standing in the dark like a couple of idiots. Still, I did make a promise.'

Greg laughed. 'You're a stickler for keeping promises, aren't you, Ann?'

I tried to read his expression when he said this but it was too dark. I said, 'Is that a complaint, Greg?'

He squeezed my hand. 'Of course not! It's a compliment and it's one of the things I like about you.'

A warm glow swept over me and I felt so lucky to have such an understanding fiancé. I was on the point of saying so when suddenly two figures appeared out of the darkness, startling me with their presence. To my surprise, it was Dad and Lily.

'I couldn't wait in the house any longer and Lily was driving me crazy with all her questions so I thought we were just as well coming here. Has there been any news?'

'No, Dad, although the porter did say he would come out and tell me when the baby arrived.'

We made a strange little party, all standing in the darkness of a winter's night.

'I'm really sorry, Greg, for getting your train time mixed up,' said Dad. 'It was just all this worry with Rosie and the bad memo-ries this place holds for me . . .'

'That's all right – I do understand so don't give it another thought.'

I mentally thanked Greg for being so kind to Dad.

We all gazed over at the infirmary but it was also in darkness, every window covered with the blackout blinds.

Dad said, 'I think you should all go home and I'll wait here.'

It was midnight and I was thinking of Lily being out in the cold night air so I agreed. We had just stood up, our legs stiff with cold, when suddenly a figure appeared from the courtyard. It was the kindly little porter.

'I can only stay a moment,' he said, 'but the maternity ward has just phoned down to say Mrs Neill has had a boy. She was anxious to let you know because she knew your daughter was waiting.'

Quite honestly, I could have kissed him and Dad shook his hand. 'Thanks for letting us know – it was really good of you to come over.' He turned to us. 'A boy! Did you hear that Ann and Lily? You've got a baby brother.'

Lily was excited. 'What are you going to call him, Dad?'

'He's to be called after me – John Neill.' His voice was full of pride and, although I couldn't see his face, I could just imagine his expression.

'Congratulations, Mr Neill!' said Greg.

'Thanks, son! It's visiting time tomorrow afternoon so will we see you both here?'

Before I could answer, Greg said, 'My train is at four o'clock so of course we'll manage a quick visit to Rosie and John.' He turned to me and smiled.

Dad said, 'I'll have to spend the entire morning going round everybody with the news. Starting with Alice and Granny and Grandad. They'll be pleased it's all over.'

They weren't the only ones, I thought, and I said a silent prayer, hoping Rosie and the baby were both well.

Greg came to Roseangle in the morning and we went for a walk along the Esplanade. The river was choppy with white-tipped waves and a strong easterly wind blowing from the North Sea.

'I'd forgotten how cold it is up here, Ann,' said Greg. 'It's been a lovely warm summer down in England.'

'Do you like it down there, Greg?' My heart was thumping.

He nodded. 'Yes, I do. It's a bit like Trinafour with the hills – all lovely green countryside in spite of not being far from London. I also enjoy my work.'

'I see.'

He pulled me close. 'I don't want to stay down there, Ann. If you're not with me, that is. I want to be where you are.'

I was suddenly happy again as that cold finger of fear slowly dissolved in my mind. It was just my imagination that I was losing him – at least I hoped so.

The afternoon found us heading once more up the infirmary brae to join the long queue of visitors.

Because the visiting rules stated that only two visitors were allowed per bed, Dad and Lily set off for the maternity ward first. Lily was carrying a huge bunch of flowers that Connie had managed to get in her usual way. Greg and I sat in the now familiar waiting room.

'What kind of work do you do, Greg?'

He gave it some thought. 'It's all a bit hush-hush. It's just like working in an office but it's with the government. I sometimes curse this gammy leg of mine – I could have been in the army or air force by now.'

Greg's bad leg was due to a fall from a horse when he was a child. In fact, I'd first met him in this infirmary. Maddie had been doing her nursing training and she asked me to visit this lonely patient who lived far from home and didn't get many visitors.

'But you're still doing a good job, Greg. It's just as important as being on the battlefield.'

'Yes, well . . . maybe . . .' He sounded doubtful. 'Has there been any more word about Danny?'

I shook my head sadly. 'Nothing except for the letter from the Red Cross but at least Maddie knows he's alive and that's a blessing.'

Then Dad and Lily arrived back from the ward and handed us the two visiting tickets.

Rosie was sitting up in bed and she looked tired and pleased at the same time. She smiled when she saw us.

'How's the baby, Rosie? How's John?'

Her face lit up. 'He's a braw wee lad, Ann! He was nine pounds and one ounce and he's gorgeous.'

Even this simple statement seemed to take its toll and she lay back on the pillows. Still, her colouring was all right and it was only to be expected that she would be tired.

She managed to say a few words to Greg, apologising for taking me away his visit. 'And I hear that silly man of mine got the wrong train time.'

Greg laughed. 'Well, he did have a lot on his mind, Rosie.'

I gave her hand a squeeze. 'Well done, Rosie. Now we'll get away to let Dad have the rest of the visiting hour with you and I'll see you later in the week.'

We took Lily with us to let Dad stay with his wife and new son. We set off for the station, picking up Greg's small suitcase from Victoria Road on the way.

As usual, the station was full of people and we didn't have much time to speak. Lily went and sat in the buffet with a glass of lemonade while we said our goodbyes.

As the train drew into the station, Greg whispered, 'The next leave I get will be with a special licence to get married.' He laughed. 'Now mind and keep it free!'

The train pulled out of the station and I shouted after him, 'I promise, Greg – cross my heart!'

He called back, 'I'll hold you to that promise!'

Once again, I watched as he departed from my life. A few hours together, a lot of goodbyes then a parting – what a life!

Lily was still in the buffet and I sat down beside her with a cup of tea.

'Are you excited about Rosie's baby?' I asked her.

Her face lit up. 'Oh, I am, Ann, and his full name is John Alexander Young Neill. The Alexander Young is from Rosie's side of the family,' she informed me.

Welcome to the world, little John Alexander Young Neill, I thought. With a name that long, he had to be a success.

Alice and Granny were going to visit him the following day.

But the next day brought shattering news. I was in the shop when the news broke. The papers were full of it and Joe was almost apoplectic. Pearl Harbour in Hawaii had been brutally bombed by a devious Japanese Air Force and most of the ships of the American Navy now lay wrecked and useless. Sailors and civilians had also been killed in this unprovoked attack. America had finally entered the war, hot on the heels of John Alexander Young Neill entering the world.

5

Granny and Grandad were almost speechless with amazement, as I found out on my visit to the Overgate one cold day in January. Hattie had found herself a man friend – something unheard of in her life.

Granny's eyes were full of mischief as she told me about this new beau. 'She met him at the Pringles' house, Ann. He's a solicitor like Mr Pringle but his office was bombed in the Clydebank Blitz so he's come here to Dundee to carry on his practice and he has a wee office in the Westport.'

I couldn't believe it and neither could Grandad. He said, 'She doesn't know the first thing about him but she's fallen hook, line and sinker for him.' He sounded worried.

Granny chided him. 'Och, come on, Grandad. Let Hattie have her bit of pleasure. She's never looked at another man since Pat died and that was years and years ago.' Granny winked at me. 'I wonder if there will be a wedding?'

It all seemed so sudden to me. One minute he was in Clydebank and the next minute the Neill family was trying to marry him off to their widowed daughter.

Then Bella appeared and it seemed she was also in the picture as far as opinions went.

'She'll rue the day she gets married again, Nan – especially after all these years.'

Grandad scowled at her but said nothing.

Bella, unheeding of the dark looks, went on, 'I mean she's getting on a bit now. What age is she, Nan? Fifty-five?'

Granny nodded.

Bella smacked her lips at the anticipated gossip. 'Your family are all developing late in life, Nan. There's Johnny with a brand-new bairn at his age and Hattie cavorting with a man and acting like a young thing.' She then turned to me. 'Then there's you, Ann. When are you and your young man going to get hitched? You'll be another old bride – mark my words.'

Granny gave her an angry look and, although I was hurt by her remark, I was determined not to show it. After all, Bella was well known for her outrageous remarks. 'Well, it would be hard to get married just now, Bella,' I said with as much dignity as I could muster. 'After all, most of the men are fighting in the war and they're hardly hanging around waiting to be led up the aisle.'

Bella sniffed. 'Your young man was here a few weeks ago and what did you do about it? Nothing.'

Granny stepped in when she saw my face. 'Ann had to be at the infirmary with Rosie that weekend and fine you know it, Bella.'

Grandad, who'd had enough of his sister-in-law, said, 'I'm away for my tobacco.'

Granny called after him, 'Put on your warm scarf. It's a freezing cold day outside.'

But Grandad was away through the door and didn't hear her. Still, this interruption had stopped Bella's gossiping – at least for the moment.

'How's Rosie and wee Johnny?' asked Granny. 'I haven't seen them this week because Rosie says it's too cold to bring him out.'

I had left Lily at the Hilltown as the baby was a big attraction for her. She loved holding him.

'They're both fine, Granny, but Rosie is still a bit tired. Still, she says she's getting better every day and the baby is such a good bairn. He just eats and sleeps and Dad tells Lily he's just like she was – a sleepy wee glutton.'

Although Granny didn't voice it, we were all relieved when Rosie came safely through the birth. Although it had been a long labour, everything had gone well and the baby was thriving.

Bella suddenly thought of something. 'I hope if Hattie gets married she doesn't have a late bairn as well, Nan.' She sounded sarcastic.

Granny, who was fed up with Bella's remarks, said placidly, 'Well, that would be her business and nothing to do with anybody else.' Granny and I knew well that this wouldn't happen as did Bella.

There was a lull as Bella digested this snub.

Before she could think of another subject, I said, 'Rosie and Dad have sent me here to ask you all to the christening at the end of February. It's to be in the Salvation Army Citadel.'

Bella opened her mouth to say something but Granny got in first. 'Och, that's great. We'll all be there.'

'Am I invited?' said Bella churlishly.

'Of course you are,' I said, not repeating Dad's words of 'Don't invite that old battle-axe, Bella.'

'Also, if Hattie wants to bring her friend, that'll be fine,' I said, thinking about Dad's reaction to Hattie's presence, never mind the inclusion of this new man in her life.

'What about the Lochee crowd?' said Granny. 'Will they be coming?'

I nodded. 'I've sent Kit a letter because I didn't have time to go and see them before the christening and I also invited Maddie and her parents, Connie and Nellie and Rita, our old neighbours. It'll be a bit crushed in the house but we'll manage somehow. It'll not be a great christening meal because of the food shortages but Rosie thinks we can rustle up something.'

'Well, as long as she's got a bottle of sherry to wet the bairn's head, it should all go with a swing.' Bella obviously wasn't caring about sandwiches or a christening cake – as long as there was the booze.

Lily and I were still enjoying our stay at Roseangle. The flat was so peaceful and quiet. Lily did her homework after tea and

I liked to listen to the wireless – especially the cheery variety programmes and the dance music.

Afterwards, when Lily was in bed on the bed settee, I would write my letter to Greg, trying to sound cheerful while giving him all our news. I thought I detected a touch of annoyance in his letter since the night of Rosie's labour but I hoped and prayed I was wrong.

And there was now the forthcoming christening to help Rosie with. Alice had kept Rosie's christening robe. It lay in sheets of tissue paper in a drawer and Lily thought it was the most beautiful garment in the world. It was, except for one important thing – it was too small. There was simply no way it would fit the new baby so it was panic stations.

Dad couldn't understand what all the fuss was about. 'Can he not get christened in something else? Like his wee romper suit?'

Rosie had almost burst into tears at this suggestion and turned to me for help. 'What are we going to do, Ann? I wanted him to be a wee picture in his bonny white robe but it's not going to happen, is it?'

'Don't worry, Rosie – leave it with me. I'll ask folk in the shop. Maybe somebody has a bigger robe and they'll let you have a loan of it.'

She looked so grateful and I kicked myself for giving her hope. This was wartime and christening robes didn't grow on trees. Where on earth was I going to get one from? And more importantly, why couldn't I keep my big mouth shut?

Rosie was also fretting about the food and the size of the house. She ticked her list, muttering to herself, 'I make it about twenty people coming. How will we get them all into this wee room?'

She had a point. Once again she seemed to be on the verge of tears so I said to leave it with me. Afterwards, I thought I was well named – organising Annie.

I mentioned the problems to Connie the next morning but, although she was full of sympathy, she said she couldn't help. 'I've never been married and I've certainly never had any bairns so I can't help you out with a christening robe, Ann – I wish I could.'

Then Joe appeared with news from the war front. 'The Japs have surrounded Singapore, Connie. You know what that means?'

We both looked blank.

'It means that the devious Japs will overrun the whole of the Far East. They took over Hong Kong on Christmas Day and they'll now turn their attention to Australia and New Zealand. It'll all be under the thumb of the Emperor Hirohito instead of the British Empire.'

'That's terrible news Joe. Here's Ann and me worrying about a christening robe for a new bairn but what kind of world will he grow up in, I wonder?'

On that depressing note, the subject of the robe was dropped. It wasn't mentioned again all that week and I honestly thought Connie had forgotten about it but she hadn't.

By now, Rosie was almost having a fit of the vapours and threatening to cancel the christening all together. Something I'm sure Dad would have been grateful for but he wisely held his tongue – such was his love for his wife and new son.

Then, a week before the event, Connie said, 'I've been having a wee word with Mrs Chambers. You mind her son Davie used to be our paper laddie?'

I remembered. He was a lovely big lad and I had managed to get him some of Danny's cast-off clothes when his mother was in dire straits.

'What's Davie doing these days, Connie?'

Her eyes clouded over. 'Well, he had a good job in the shipyard but he's been called up and he's in the navy now. Mrs Chambers has got another house in Tulloch Crescent but I met her the other day and we got chatting. She's got on her feet since Davie started working and she doesn't have to wash stairs now. She's now got a good job as a dinner lady in Rosebank School and she loves it.'

Much as I loved to hear all the local gossip, I wondered where this conversation was leading. I hoped it wasn't bad news about Davie as he was a lovely laddie.

Connie was still chatting. 'Well, I ended up telling her all the Hilltown news – especially about your Dad and Rosie – and she was so pleased for them. Then I mentioned the christening and all the problems you were having – and what do you think?'

I looked puzzled because that was what I was. Truly stymied.

'Seemingly, when Davie was born, he was a big bairn as well. In those days, Mr Chambers was alive and working in a good job and they were quite well off. Well, to cut a long story short, Mrs Chambers had bought Davie this lovely christening robe and she's still got it. And, hey presto!' said Connie, whipping a brown paper parcel from under the counter and slapping it on the counter. 'Here we are! One christening robe guaranteed to fit King Kong or Baby Neill.'

I could have kissed her. Instead, I ran up to the house with the parcel. Dad was at work but Rosie was sitting at the fireside with the baby on her lap. She looked downhearted but tried to smile when I burst through the door.

I held the parcel aloft. 'One christening robe, Rosie.'

Her eyes were bright as she laid the baby in his cot. With trembling fingers she opened the parcel. Lying wrapped in tissue paper was the most lovely robe we had ever seen. Although I was no expert on such garments, even I could see how beautiful it was.

Rosie quickly undressed the baby and placed the robe over his downy head. It fitted perfectly. He squinted comically at his mother and we both burst out laughing.

Rosie said, 'Here I am thinking what a bonny bairn he is in his lovely robe and he's putting on a funny face.'

Still, there was no denying that he looked a picture.

When I left the house, Rosie was beaming with pleasure. And as I made my way back to the shop, her words were still ringing in my ears: 'You're a great lassie for working miracles, Ann – I've always said that.'

I had pointed out it was all Connie's doing but Rosie said, 'But you're the mover, Ann. You make things happen.'

For some obscure reason, these words filled me with a warm glow until I remembered how far away I was moving from Greg.

The days to the christening seemed to fly by and Rosie, Alice and Granny plus Lily and I managed to put all our ration books together and get the necessary food for the event.

Mrs Pringle kindly offered to bake a small cake and this offer was accepted with an almost indecent speed.

Hattie, however, was unhappy about the Hilltown flat as a venue for the party and the Salvation Army as the place for the christening. 'Why don't you hold the party in my house, Rosie? I've got lovely china and a super white damask tablecloth. And, as for the christening, what about that lovely church Maddie and Danny were married in?'

Rosie was delighted by the tea party suggestion but not the change of service and she told her so. But when she mentioned the conversation to Dad he almost burst a blood vessel. 'Bloody cheek! Does she think we live like some lower form of life? Does she think we'll give our guests their tea in jeely jars? And, if we want wee Johnny christened in the Citadel, then that's our business. She's aye trying to change folk's arrangements to suit herself.'

Rosie shook her head. 'No, Johnny, she's just trying to be helpful and it would be a big help to have the christening tea at her place. I really don't think I've got enough cups and saucers for about twenty folk.'

Dad merely shook his head in amazement. 'Women – I'll never understand them. You know what Hattie's motives are, don't you? She doesn't want the Pringle family or that new man in her life to see how the other half live. She's aye had these delusions of grandeur. She wants everyone to think we have the same gracious lifestyle as she has.'

But it was all settled. The tea party would now be held at Hattie's house in the Westport. Not that it was much bigger than Rosie and Dad's house but the contents were definitely much grander. The flower-sprigged china and white damask cloth had won the battle.

It was planned that Dad, Rosie and the baby plus Lily and I would all leave the Hilltown together for the Citadel where we would meet up with members of the family and the guests.

Maddie had brought the small cake over the previous night and Rosie had made up the christening piece – a small bag which held some little cakes and a silver threepenny piece. Rosie was delighted with the cake. Not that it was anything grand and the icing looked a bit watery but this was wartime and we were grateful for it. Mrs Pringle had even managed to find a small blue cradle which looked so impressive on the anaemic-looking creation. Rosie was delighted with it.

The cake was taken to the Westport and it now took pride of place on the snowy-white damask tablecloth.

John Alexander Young Neill was now ready to be carried forth to his christening. Meanwhile, Lily was beside herself with excitement because she was going to be carrying the christening piece.

It wasn't a bright day but thankfully it was dry and we all set off down the stairs and on to the street which was reasonably busy. Lily had been instructed to give the christening piece to the first female we met. When she asked why, Rosie explained. 'It's aye a woman or lassie who gets the piece if the baby is a boy and a man or laddie if it's a girl.'

'But why do that, Rosie?' asked Lily.

Rosie looked perplexed for a moment before answering, 'It's just a tradition Lily but don't ask me why.'

Now that the big moment had arrived, Lily was obviously going to do her duty properly. There was a group of three women standing outside Connie's shop and Lily became agitated.

'If there's three women, Rosie, who do I give it to?'

Rosie was unsure and I could well imagine her worry. This was her first baby and she wanted the day to be perfect.

I inwardly prayed for the group to break up before we reached them but I had no sooner said these mental words when a scruffy little girl suddenly darted in front of us. She looked about seven years old and, to my mind, this was manna from heaven. I called out to her and she stopped in mid stride. 'I cannae stop missus because I've to get the paper for my dad.'

Rosie explained about the christening piece and the girl's eyes grew wide with wonder. Lily duly and solemnly handed it over and we went on our way with a new spring in our steps.

The Citadel was full of people and music, and the service was lovely. I was a godparent and I found the service uplifting and I was filled with a sense of timelessness. Countless babies were maybe being christened on this day and they were all entering a dark and uncertain time, a future filled with worry and war, but, in some unknown way, I felt no worry for them and, although I wasn't a religious person, it seemed, on that day, as if some unknown hand was at work. I felt inwardly that the world would go on in spite of the doom and gloom on the war front.

The baby behaved perfectly until the last hymn when the tambourines suddenly filled the air with their jangle of musical noise. John, who was half asleep at this point, awoke with a start and began to howl. Rosie was distressed but the congregation seemed to enjoy the twin noises. As someone said afterwards, it's a lucky baby who cries during his christening.

Then it was back to Hattie's house. A small pile of brown-paper-wrapped christening presents lay on the sideboard and Rosie could hardly wait to open them. Lily and I had given John a silver rattle and a silver teething ring while I also added a silver bangle which I sent in Danny's name. When the war was over, Danny would be the baby's other godparent but, until that far off and unknown day, I would do his duties by proxy.

Maddie and her parents arrived soon after us and they were full of praise for the lovely service. 'It's such a cheery service and the singing and the Salvation Army band is wonderful,' said Mrs Pringle. 'I couldn't stop tapping my toes to the music,' she confessed.

Then the families from Lochee arrived. Ma Ryan couldn't come said Kit and, although Hattie expressed her regret at this, I could see she was relieved. To give Hattie her due she had put on a lovely buffet and her silver cutlery and china looked so well on the table. The only thing missing was Hattie's new man.

Kit sat beside me as we tried to juggle a cup, saucer and plate on our laps. Kit laughed quietly. 'I'm not used to such grandeur, Ann. We never use saucers, only the cups.'

I felt I had to defend Hattie. 'Still it's good of Hattie to put herself to all this work for Rosie, Dad and the baby.'

Kit's eyes were full of mischief. 'Och, I'm not running her

down, Ann. In fact, look at my man and Lizzie and Bella over there. You would think they hadn't seen food for months the way they're stuffing themselves. No, what I want to know is, where is the new man friend?'

I shrugged. Kit wasn't alone in wanting to see this new man. I was also keen to see him, as was Bella – I could tell by her comical looks in my direction.

Fortunately Bella was behaving herself but I knew Granny had given her a warning prior to arriving at the house. 'Now remember, Bella, no asking Hattie about her private life.'

Bella had snorted with derision but Grandad had also given her a parting shot at Hattie's door so she seemed to be on her best behaviour. She was standing beside Rita and Nellie, our old neighbours who had been so good to us after Lily's birth. Thankfully they had money coming into their houses now that their men were in full employment and it showed on their faces. What a difference a war makes I thought cynically. Mass unemployment for two decades and then, when we were on the verge of extinction, everyone had a job.

I was a bit worried about Grandad as he looked tired and thin. Not that he was ever fat but he now seemed so spare looking. He was busy chatting with Mr Pringle and I hoped he would put on a bit of weight when summer arrived.

Granny and Alice were dressed up in their Sunday best frocks as was Hattie and Mrs Pringle but Rosie stole the show. Although quietly dressed in a plain blue frock and a tiny hat, she seemed to have a radiance about her these days. And I wasn't the only one to notice this as Dad couldn't take his eyes off her. Good for you, Rosie, I thought.

When I said Rosie stole the show, that wasn't quite correct because the star of the show was the baby. He smiled serenely at everybody, the earlier tears forgotten and we were all enchanted with him. Rosie and Dad were bursting with pride when we all commented on their lovely son in his gorgeous christening gown.

I managed to escape to where Maddie and Daniel were sitting. She was chatting to Minnie but there was no sign of Peter. He was busy playing with the children from next door, she said, so she had left him with her mother.

Maddie laughed. 'Your dad looks so happy, Ann, and I think Rosie will burst with pride very soon.'

Then we all became serious as we talked about Danny and Peter who were both still away – Danny in a hospital somewhere and Peter fighting somewhere in Europe.

'When will it all end?' asked Maddie.

I shook my head as I looked at them both.

'Now that the Japs have captured Singapore,' said Minnie, 'it'll go on forever or until the Japs and Jerries capture every country and maybe then it'll stop.'

I stayed silent because what could I say? What did I know about warfare?

Then Connie came over and that stopped the topic of war.

Kit, George and her sisters were all saying their goodbyes and they were followed soon after by the Pringle family, Connie and Minnie. They were no sooner out the door when Hattie's friend appeared – Mr Graham Todd.

Bella was so astonished that she forgot to close her mouth while the rest of us tried to appear nonchalant. Lily was the only one who stared without shame.

Over the past few weeks I had tried hard to visualise this new man in Hattie's life but I hadn't come within a hundred miles with my thoughts. I had visualised him as tall, debonair and aesthetic-looking – a cross between a monk and a professor.

Mr Graham Todd, however, looked like a refugee from the variety theatre and the only words I could use to describe him were glossy and brown – like a russet brown chestnut.

From the top of his shiny bald head to his brown suit and glossy brown shoes, he resembled a taller version of Arthur Askey. His face was full of laughter lines and his brown eyes twinkled with mirth. He was an inch or two taller than Hattie – about five feet nine inches.

I half expected him to start entertaining us with a string of jokes but, when he spoke, his voice was very cultured and soft.

He shook hands with us all and I saw very clearly what Hattie had seen in this man that had been lacking in every other man she had known.

I could see Granny and Bella were smitten with him as was Lily. As for me, well, I thought he was wonderful and just what Hattie needed.

Hattie explained his late arrival. 'I was a bit wary of Graham meeting Kit and her family. I was frightened what they would think – you know, Mum, because they're Pat's family.'

Granny said she understood although she did say the Ryan family were all glad for her happiness and she shouldn't leave any future meeting too long. 'Let Graham meet them as soon as possible, Hattie, because they'll be as pleased with him as we all are.'

Hattie looked radiant and gazed over to where her new man was chatting to Bella. Bella saw her and called her over. 'I like your new man, Hattie. I just wish I was twenty years younger and you wouldn't get a look in against me.'

Graham laughed.

Meanwhile Lily was playing with the baby as a bemused Rosie and Dad could hardly take their eyes off Mr Todd.

Lily was holding the certificate of baptism and was reading it aloud. She said, 'John Alexander Young. That makes his initials J A Y – I think I'll call him Jay Neill.'

Rosie looked at me. 'What a braw name, Lily. If your Dad doesn't mind, then that's what we'll call him – Jay Neill.'

Dad laughed. 'Jay's fine with me.'

As if liking his new nickname, the baby smiled at us and it was time to go home.

Afterwards, in the house, Rosie gently removed Jay's lovely gown and lovingly wrapped it in its tissue paper. 'Ann, will you give this back to Mrs Chambers and say thank you very, very much for the loan of it. It's the bonniest christening gown I've ever seen. Tell her we'll pay for the cleaning of it.' Her eyes were moist as she handed it over.

Lily piped up. 'Maybe you should keep it for a wee while longer, Rosie. It can always do the next christening.'

Dad, who was drinking a cup of tea, almost choked.

Rosie smiled. 'We can aye borrow it again, Lily, if we need it.'

She glanced over at me and her look said it all – at my age, I don't think so.

6

Kit's letter arrived out of the blue. This was something she had never done before and, although it was more of a note than a full-scale letter, it urged me to pay her a visit as soon as possible.

Lily wanted to come with me and, as I didn't want to alarm her, I agreed. There was a touch of late summer in the air as we set off to catch the tramcar the following Sunday. Lily's head was full of the qualifying exams which would take place in the early part of next year.

'I'm hoping to get good marks, Ann, so I'm studying really hard.'

That was true – she spent hours with her homework every night while I listened to the wireless. We were both still savouring the peace of the flat and I felt as if the war could quite easily pass us by. I was also aware how grown up she was becoming – her lovely childish ways were now a passing memory and I mourned them. She was a child no longer.

I asked her, 'Are you looking forward to going to the secondary school, Lily?'

Her face lit up. 'Aye, Ann, I am and I hope to be an artist when I grow up – just like Joy.'

Joy, Maddie's sister, being born on the same day as Lily was also looking forward to leaving the primary school behind but in her case she was going to the secondary section of the High School and not changing schools like Lily. Lily would soon leave

Rosebank School behind and move on to Rockwell School.

As usual, Atholl Street was full of people and they were all enjoying the warm sunshine. I couldn't but help notice the change in the atmosphere in the street. Although all the young men were away fighting in the war, the remaining families were now all in jobs and there was a more prosperous feel to the area. Kit and her family were certainly better off. George was still working at the foundry while Patty was doing an apprenticeship at the Caledon Shipyard. Kit still looked after Kitty while Kathleen went to work. When we arrived, Kit seemed so pleased to see us.

'Lily, would you like to take Kitty for a walk?' she asked.

I got the impression Lily would rather have stayed and listened to the gossip but she took the little girl's hand.

'Don't go too far, Lily – just up the street and back,' said Kit.

I was now beginning to be really worried – first the unusual letter and now the request to get Lily and Kitty out of the house. I looked at her. 'What's the matter? Is there anything wrong, Kit?'

Kit looked harassed as she put the kettle on. 'Och, it's Kathleen.'

'What's wrong with her?'

She ran her hand through her hair, making it stand up on end. I had noticed on my last trip that she had cut her hair short and it suited her.

'Kathleen's left her job at Hunter's Store, Ann.'

I was bewildered. Surely leaving a job wasn't the end of the world. Maybe it had been during the long years of the depression but not now. I said so.

'No, it's not that. It's just the new job she's got that's the worry.'

By now, I was totally perplexed. Why did Kathleen's new job warrant an urgent letter?

Kit placed my cup of tea on the table and gave me a worried look. 'She's got a new job with that photographer chappie who took Maddie and Danny's wedding photos. You must remember him? He's got a posh studio on the Perth Road.'

'But surely that's a good move, Kit – a step up in her life? Is she learning the photography side or is she a receptionist?'

Kit's eyes slid away from me and her cheeks reddened. 'Well, she is a receptionist. She takes bookings that come in but that's not all.' Kit stopped and gazed painfully at me, deciding whether to continue while I stayed silent. 'No. She also does modelling work for him. It's all high-class stuff but it's still modelling.' She made it sound like a dirty word.

I said, 'Surely it'll just be facial photographs he's taking.'

'She says it is but you know what a bad name some of these pictures get – you know . . . if she's hardly got any clothes on.'

I could see Kit was on the verge of tears and I tried to re-assure her. 'He's a very high-class photographer, Kit, and, if Kathleen tells you it's all above board, then you have to believe her. She is a beautiful girl after all and he's probably struck with her lovely face.'

Kit looked relieved. 'That's what he said when he came here to offer her the job and I don't think Kathleen would tell lies.'

I was puzzled. 'So you've met him, Kit.'

She nodded. 'He's very professional and he seems like a nice man but Maggie is going on and on about it.'

Maggie, I might have known – Sammy Malloy's mother.

'She's going on and on about how Sammy will react when he comes home from the prisoner of war camp. She says he'll go mad if he finds out his wife is a nude model.'

I almost burst out laughing but stopped when I saw how distressed Kit was. I was also annoyed at Maggie. Did she think her precious Sammy was ever going to get back with Kathleen after the beating he gave her before leaving for the army?

I told Kit this and her face darkened at the mention of the beating. She remembered the incident well.

Then, to speak of the devil, Maggie appeared. She looked as if she had been dragged from the kitchen as there was flour all down the front of her apron. She saw my eyes on it and she wiped some of it away with an impatient hand.

'I'm just making doughboys to put in my mince.' She looked at Kit. 'Now have you managed to talk your lassie out of this job, Kit? It's not the kind of thing we would want in our family.'

I was incensed. Her family consisted of men who regularly

drank themselves into oblivion and daughters-in-law who were run down with pregnancies, money worries and men who treated them like drudges. Then I thought of Kathleen and despaired that she had ever married into this family – even although Kitty was on the way when she did. I thought how brave she was to get out of this never-ending struggle to make ends meet and, if her beauty helped her along the way, then so be it. But I stayed silent – after all, this wasn't my affair.

Kit glared at Maggie. 'Kathleen does have a mind of her own and, if she likes the job, then that's fine by George and me.'

'But modelling in the nude, Kit? Have you gone out of your mind?'

'She's not modelling in the nude, Maggie. It's all professional facial shots and all very high-class work.'

Maggie snorted. It sounded like a steam train. 'My man Mick was telling me that photos like that were seen during the last war and they were all taken by high-class photographers.' Her thin face was pinched with annoyance at the thought of any photos of her daughter-in-law being touted around the army barracks. She stood up quickly. 'Well, I cannae wait here any longer, Kit, because my doughboys will be like gold balls but I've said my piece about Kathleen and you know how we all feel.'

I thought Kit would explode but Maggie swept out of the house like a whirlwind to rescue her dinner.

'Don't let her bother you, Kit. I think Kathleen is right in making a step upwards for herself and for getting out of the clutches of the Malloys. Sammy is such a wee creep and I could never understand what Kathleen saw in him.'

For the first time since I arrived, Kit smiled. 'Well, you have to admit he's a handsome wee creep.'

I nodded. It would seem that good looks won every fair maiden – Kathleen included. But now she had the sense to make something of her life and not be bogged down with a husband who treated her like dirt, plus maybe a handful of children. There would be no escape then.

Lily and Kitty arrived back home. Both were laughing and Kit and I were glad of this lighter mood. Maggie's appearance had put Kit under a cloud but now the cheerful chatter from the children made her smile. She looked more like the Kit I remembered – even with the grey strands that were now showing through her red hair.

I suddenly thought of Danny. How did he look now? I wondered. Still as handsome with his bright auburn hair? Or was he now a broken man? I sincerely hoped not.

Kit said, 'I almost forgot, Ann. Ma wants to see you. She says to go round to her house. You know where it is? It's in the same close as Lizzie and Belle.'

'What does she want, Kit?' I knew I sounded anxious but I couldn't help it.

Kit shrugged her shoulders. 'I don't know, Ann. She knew you were coming here today so she asked me to tell you to pop round and see her.'

I left Lily with Kitty and set off down the street towards Ma Ryan's close. Her single-roomed flat was on the ground floor which must have been a great help to her. Lizzie lived on the first landing while Belle had her head in the clouds on the third floor.

I was taken aback by the spruce appearance of the house. In spite of the lovely weather, a small fire was burning in the brightly black-leaded grate. All her brass ornaments were polished to a high sheen as was the furniture and the brown linoleum on the floor.

Ma was sitting in a high backed chair with a lovely crochet shawl over her knees. A small tray with cups and saucers and a plate of biscuits lay on a tiny table at her elbow. The kettle was boiling on the gas cooker while the teapot had spoonfuls of tea in its base.

Ma looked pleased to see me. 'Just put some boiling water in the teapot, Ann, and come and sit beside me.'

I did as I was told and sat opposite her with another cup of tea. I would be waterlogged before the end of the day, I thought.

'How are Maddie and Daniel?' she asked.

My heart sank. Did she know something bad about them?

Having the sixth sense as she so often said could be a curse instead of a blessing.

In spite of the tea, my mouth was dry. 'They're fine, Ma. I saw them last week and Daniel is getting quite big. Maddie is missing Danny so much and just wishing this war was over.'

Ma nodded. 'And what's the news of your young man, Ann. How is he?'

Where was all this leading? I wondered. I gave her all the latest news of Greg as received in my last letter from him.

'You'll be wondering why I asked you over here?'

I nodded.

She gave me a curious look. 'I did debate about telling you this but the feeling is so strong that I feel you should know.'

My eyes were like saucers and my heart was thumping in worried anticipation. It was another of Ma's warnings. She had warned me once before while I was working at the Ferry with Mrs Barrie and that had come true. This new warning could only mean some sort of danger. Otherwise why ask me over to her house like this?

She leaned forward. 'The feeling is a bit patchy, Ann, but very, very strong. Watch your step, that's all I can say. Watch your step very, very carefully.'

I was perplexed. 'In what way, Ma, do I have to watch my step? Is it in everyday life? Something I do every day?'

'I'm sorry, Ann, but I can't tell you because I don't know. I just keep thinking you've to watch your step because there's danger of some sort.'

Oh, no, I thought. Was my life always going to have this dangerous element? Surely I wouldn't meet another Miss Hood – the housekeeper at the Ferry who had tried to kill me.

I made a mental note to look extra carefully when crossing the road and to make sure I never went up a ladder. I told Ma I would take care and went to pick up Lily. Kit seemed a bit more cheerful and I told her not to worry about Kathleen or Maggie.

Lily chatted all the way back in the tramcar, stopping only to gaze down on the streets now and then. She loved the top deck of the tramcar. We soon reached our stop and my mind was full of Ma's warning. What did it mean?

Lily went downstairs ahead of me but, halfway down the metal spiral stairs, my heel caught and I was suddenly thrown forwards. I think I screamed but there was no sound as far as I could recall and I saw Lily's wide-eyed stare as I hurtled past her.

Suddenly, a strong arm grabbed me. It was the tramcar conductor. 'Watch your step, love. You almost fell out on to the road.'

Lily was almost crying when we stepped on to the pavement.

'It's all right, Lily – I'm not hurt,' I told her.

Reassured, she set off towards the flat with me following her. I was shaking a bit with the fright and my legs felt numb with the shock of the incident.

Ma had been right about her warning. I should have watched my step. Surely this was what she meant, wasn't it?

7

Grandad was ill and Granny was worried sick about him. It was also clear to the rest of the family that his bronchitis, which was a yearly winter affliction for him, was getting worse. But he wouldn't listen to anyone when we told him to stop smoking his pipe with its dark, foul-smelling slivers of Bogey Roll tobacco stuffed into its bowl.

'I've been smoking since I was sixteen and it's never done me any harm,' was the usual statement when Granny or I chastised him.

Granny sighed. 'He'll not listen to anybody, Ann, and I'm really worried about his breathlessness – he could hardly climb the stairs the other night.'

This was true and, to make matters worse, the weather was now cold and foggy which made me cough, never mind Grandad with his bad chest.

It would soon be New Year and the war was still as savage as ever but there had been good news with the glorious victory at El Alamein. Then there was the Battle of Midway where the Americans had pushed the Japanese into retreat plus the Russian Army had broken through the German line at Stalingrad.

Joe was full of this news. 'What a great victory over the Afrika Korps, isn't it Connie? Monty fair sent Rommel scuttling back to Berlin. And the Americans are finally getting the upper hand with the Japs and the Russians will soon send the German Army packing. Aye, it'll soon be victory, Connie.'

Connie, who was usually tired of listening to Joe's ramblings on the war front, was enthusiastic at the latest news from Stalingrad. 'Aye, it certainly is good news, Joe. Maybe the war will be over soon.'

I mentally echoed this sentiment. Then Greg, Danny and Peter could all be home once more with their families.

Joe was still chatting. 'Another bit of good news is the British Army have pushed the Japs from the Malay peninsula and shoved them back to Burma. Aye, they'll find it's not so easy to beat us – even with their Emperor Hirohito.'

Meanwhile I was becoming more worried by the day about Grandad and I hoped he would see sense and give up the smoking. I had made up my mind to enlist Hattie's help on this.

That evening, when I went to her house in the Westport, Graham was there and he was dressed in a smart suit.

'Hattie is getting dressed,' he said, nodding towards the closed bedroom door.

I was puzzled.

He explained. 'We're going to the Christmas dance in the Queen's Hotel.'

Then Hattie appeared and she looked surprised to see me sitting by the fire. She looked beautiful in a long satin dress in a lovely shade of bronze. She wore long brown evening gloves and her shoes matched her handbag. She looked like the Queen. It was easy to see that the clothes rationing wasn't a big issue in her house. But then I realised I had seen that dress before – a good few years ago.

Her face went white when she saw me. 'It's not Grandad, is it?'

I mentally kicked myself for arriving on her doorstep unannounced but I said, 'He's not any worse, Hattie, but can you make him give up his pipe? He'll not listen to Granny.'

Hattie made a little snorting sound. 'And you think he'll listen to me, Ann?'

Before I could answer, she went on. 'I've told him time and time again to give up that pipe. In fact, you've heard me yourself and will he listen? No he won't.'

I noticed Graham had taken a cigarette from an elegant silver case but he now put it back. Very diplomatic, I thought.

'Look, Hattie, I've come at a bad time. You're on your way to a dance but will you think about having a talk with Grandad. I'll also have a word with Dad and maybe, between the two of you, Grandad will listen and see sense.'

Hattie nodded. 'All right, Ann, I'll speak to him tomorrow but don't raise your hopes too high. I've been going on about that smelly pipe for years and you know it. As for your father . . . what do you think he'll manage to do? He smokes as well and many a word I've had with him about this.'

Graham now slipped the cigarette case back in his pocket with a rueful look at me. Thankfully, Hattie was gathering up her bag and she didn't notice it.

Hattie was right when she said Dad would be no help. He never listened to anyone either – just like Grandad.

When Hattie reached the door, she said, 'And another thing. Has your father gone back to the doctor for a check-up on his head wound?'

I shook my head. 'He says he's going next week but he says he's feeling fine.'

Graham smiled. 'How are Rosie and little Jay?'

'They're fine, Graham. Jay is getting bigger every day and, although he's not walking yet, he's crawling all over the floor and getting under everyone's feet.'

I could see that Hattie was impatient to be off to her dance so I made my escape.

Lily was sitting with Granny and they both looked subdued. Grandad was lying asleep in the big bed by the fireside and his breath was coming out in sharp gasps.

I went over to him and looked at him. 'Tomorrow, I'm getting the doctor to have a look at his chest, Granny,' I said to her.

She looked as if she was about to resist but she said, 'I think that would be for the best, Ann. He's not getting any better.'

Lily looked unhappy. 'Grandad will be all right, won't he, Ann?'

I tried to look cheerful. 'Of course he will, Lily. It's just a matter of getting him to realise he can't keep smoking – especially in this cold, murky weather.'

Lily looked at Granny. 'He was smoking his pipe before he went to bed and he'll not listen to Granny.'

Granny got up and put the kettle on. 'Never you mind, Lily. He'll listen to the doctor – that's for sure.'

But I saw her face as she turned towards the stove and her look belied her convincing words. I also knew she was worried about the outcome of Dad's medical. He hadn't been going to the Home Guard meetings since his accident although he had taken his share of fire-watching on a few nights during the past few months.

To take our minds off Grandad, I mentioned the Christmas dance and Hattie's lovely outfit.

'Aye,' said Granny, 'she's had that frock since 1936 but then she's aye kept her trim figure so she can still wear all the clothes she had before the war – lucky her.'

Lily was busy getting the cups from the cupboard. 'Will she get married to Graham?'

Granny almost choked. 'Och, I've no idea, Lily. Maybe she will. I suppose it all matters on how long this war is going to last. After it's over, he'll probably go back to Clydebank and his business there.'

I looked at Lily. 'Would you like to see them married?'

Her face lit up. 'Oh, I would and I could be a flower girl at their wedding – just like I'm going to be at your wedding, Ann – when Greg comes home, that is.'

For some reason her statement left me feeling sick. Would there ever be a wedding? I thought. I was certainly not getting any younger and at this rate I would qualify as one of the oldest brides in the city.

Granny brought us both back to earth. 'Well, I'd better have a word with Hattie and Graham – just so they don't get married on the same day as Ann and Greg. We can't have you missing out on being a bridesmaid twice, can we, Lily?'

Lily was munching a huge slice of toast and she nodded.

As I looked at her, I marvelled at her talent for coming out with an important statement, only to totally forget it when faced with food.

We could still hear Grandad's noisy wheezing as we left. I said, 'I'll call the doctor from Connie's flat tomorrow, Granny, and I'll pay his bill.'

I was a bit late in arriving at the shop the following morning. Even although we were staying at Roseangle, Lily was still a pupil at Rosebank School. This time next year she would be in the secondary school but, till then, our routine never varied. She normally arrived at the shop with me and stayed until it was time to go to school. This particular morning, we'd overslept and we were hurrying up the Hilltown. It was another grey, dank and foggy morning and the air felt cold and wet. It was like a thousand wet drops against our faces.

Connie's shop was blacked out because of the regulations but it was cosy inside. The gas mantle was a golden glow against the stack of newspapers and the paper girl was just beginning her paper round.

I explained my mission to her and she said to use the telephone when Lily went to school. I had become quite fond of her doctor and had got to know him well over the year or two since I first called him out.

Lily turned to me as we set off. 'Grandad's going to be all right, isn't he, Ann? The doctor will give him some medicine to make him feel better.'

I watched her as she set off down the road, calling out to her friends as they emerged from the dark entrances on to the cold street.

Connie's flat was still over-furnished and I smiled at her refusal to throw away her parents' things. Still, it was hard to let go of the past but some people managed it better than others. I loved the large black telephone. There was a similar one at Roseangle which I never used – apart from the one time when Maddie went into labour with Daniel.

Despite Connie's protestations, I always paid for my calls – I would hate to think I was abusing her kindness.

I slowly dialled the doctor's number and very carefully gave the address in the Overgate and a brief account of Grandad's symptoms. I knew Granny would be ready for him and I also knew she would be edgy about keeping Grandad in the house. He could be thrawn when it suited him, complaining that getting the doctor was women's meddling.

I also knew she would have stripped the bed and put on clean sheets and pillowcases and that would alarm him. He would know exactly what was being planned and he would try to make his escape.

I could barely wait for the morning to go in, wondering what the doctor would say about Grandad.

Connie noticed my agitation. 'We're not very busy this afternoon, Ann. If you want to go and see how your grandad is, then just go.'

I threw her a grateful look and put my coat on. It was very cold outside and although it was still wet, the bitter wind promised snow before nightfall. Granny had a big fire on in the grate when I arrived and Grandad was asleep. She placed a finger against her lips and I tiptoed over to sit beside her.

We spoke in whispers. Granny looked upset as she described the doctor's visit. She glanced over, every now and again, towards the bed in the corner, making sure Grandad was still asleep.

'The doctor says his lungs are not working right, Ann. He didn't say they were knackered but that's what he meant. When Grandad worked in the coal yard years ago, the coal dust irritated his lungs and that, combined with his heavy smoking over all these years, hasn't helped him. The doctor wants him to go into hospital for a check-up but he almost went mental and said the hospital is the last place he'd end up in.'

I didn't know what to say. All morning, I had harboured the notion that a few days in bed and giving his pipe a rest would see him on the road to recovery but now, judging from Granny's face, the news was bad.

I recalled the years he had spent as a coalman and the awful black dust that forever hung in the air in the coal shed in Ann

Street. But surely this wasn't enough to cause an illness years later? I said so.

Granny just shook her head gently. 'It's just a matter of time, Ann. His lungs are damaged and there's no medicine that can help him now.'

We listened to his laboured breathing and the tears rolled down my cheeks. Grandad was facing death and I just couldn't believe it. I didn't *want* to believe it.

Granny, as strong as ever, said, 'The doctor said someone should sit up with him through the night in case he chokes.'

'I'll do that, Granny – you have enough to do during the day.'

She nodded. 'I'll also ask Hattie to help out.'

'Lily and I will come to live here. We'll manage in the wee room in the lobby. That way I'll be here to look after her as well.'

Granny gave me a sad look. 'Poor Ann – you're aye looking after somebody else and never yourself.'

I had to get time off from he shop but I could still work the afternoons and early evenings.

Connie was very understanding. 'Och, just come in when you can, Ann. I'll do the early morning shift and you can maybe do the later shift and I'll get a rest then. Will that be fine?'

Actually at that moment I didn't know what would be fine or not. It was going to be a question of settling into a routine with me sitting up during the night to let Granny get a sleep.

I tried to pass all this off lightly when I picked Lily up from the school. Her eyes widened in pain but I explained it was only for a short time until Grandad got better and she believed me – thank goodness. Although I hated telling her a lie, I knew I could never tell her that her beloved Grandad was dying.

Rosie and Dad were very upset when they heard the news and Rosie immediately offered to help out with the nursing – an offer I knew she couldn't possibly fulfil.

'You have Jay to look after so you have enough on your plate as it is, Rosie.'

This was true because Jay, who was almost a year old, was now crawling and he seemed to get into everything and into all the corners. Rosie was forever picking him up. In desperation, she would place him in the playpen but he viewed these wooden bars like some criminal in prison and would pull himself up and shake them violently, crying so hard that Rosie relented and let him crawl around the room in freedom.

The first week wasn't too bad. Grandad seemed to rally and he got out of bed and sat on the chair by the fire, filling his pipe with tobacco and sucking on the stem like a man dying of thirst instead of a man dying by degrees.

To begin with, I tried to persuade him not to smoke but Granny said that, at this late stage, smoking couldn't do him any more harm. The damage had started years before and had slowly grown worse with time. So I sat and read while he smoked.

One night he laughed out loud. I looked at him, puzzled. 'What are you laughing at, Grandad?'

'I'm just thinking what a big lassie Lily is now.' He chuckled. 'I'm thinking about the time I brought yon muckle pram home from Jumpin' Jeemy's Emporium and the look of horror on Hattie's face when she saw it.'

I smiled at him. 'I remember how you threw the door open like some conquering hero, Grandad, and how Granny scrubbed it till it was shining.'

Grandad laughed again. 'Och, aye, I mind that. When I'm feeling better, I'll have to take young Jay along the Esplanade. He'll enjoy that.'

I had to look away, my eyes full of unshed tears.

It was time to get him back to his bed. I noticed how thin he had become and his striped pyjamas now hung from his body. His neck was so thin that I was sure I could encircle it with my two hands.

Luckily, Granny was sleeping in the spare bed in Alice's house. It was just to let him get a good night's sleep, she told him – which sadly, as the days went on, became increasingly rare.

Hattie arrived one night with Graham but, when she saw him coughing, his body racked with the effort of it, she ran from the house, crying. Graham gave me a pitying look as he went out after her. She never came back again at night although she did visit during the day.

Much to Grandad's delight, Dad would pop in every evening with Rosie and Jay. Lily would read the newspaper out loud for him as he didn't have the energy to hold it and she would add her own comments which could be hilarious. This made Grandad laugh and Lily was so pleased because she thought this meant he was getting better.

One bit of good news was Dad's medical. His skull fracture had healed completely. The doctor had said, 'You've got good strong bones, Mr Neill' and he'd praised Granny's good food when he was growing up.

Granny laughed when Dad told her this medical snippet. 'Aye, you and Hattie were fed on good Scots fare when you were bairns.'

Hogmanay was looming but there was little anticipation of a celebration. The war was still going on and there didn't seem an end in sight – just like Grandad's illness.

We had all decided not to celebrate the end of 1942. Even Connie, who always kept so cheerful, seemed tired and drained of energy. She had been listening to Joe who went on and on about the Italians coming over to the side of Allies, forsaking Mussolini and the Germans.

During the afternoon of a day that was particularly dark and wintry and very depressing, she said to me, 'I suppose it's good news – the Italian Army siding with the Allies. It must mean we're winning although it certainly doesn't seem like it. Queuing for this and queuing for that – it fair makes you mad.'

She was right. The rations had been slashed still further and it was getting more difficult to keep a family fed. Thank goodness for potatoes and bread, I always thought.

'Speaking about the Italian Army, Connie, they're ordinary folk like us and I bet they're as sick and tired of this war as we are. And the German people as well.'

Connie nodded. 'Aye, you're right, Ann. It's just the dictators and governments that want to see it go on and on – just for their own glory and a wee mention in the history books.'

Greg's letter arrived the next morning. Instead of being over-joyed by the sight of it, I was suddenly plunged into a panic.

He wrote, 'I'm getting another short leave and will be home for the New Year with a special licence in my pocket. It's time to tie the knot, don't you think, Ann?'

I had spent a long hard night with Grandad as he didn't sleep very well because of the cough and pain in his chest. I was feeling so tired and, afterwards, when the damage was done, I realised I wasn't thinking straight. Of course, it would be great to see him but to get married? Not yet, I thought – especially with Grandad so ill.

I sent a letter away immediately saying Grandad was very ill and could we postpone the wedding till later but also saying I was looking forward to seeing him.

His letter arrived on Hogmanay and it was short.

I think we should part company, Ann. I'm sorry to hear about your grandad but your life is never your own. The family all seem to come first and I'm a poor second. I've become friendly with a girl down here and, although we are just friends, I want you to know about it as it wouldn't be fair to be seeing someone else while we are engaged. That's why I'm breaking the engagement to let us both have some time to think things through and to lead our own lives.

I sat for ages with the letter in my hand and tears streaming down my face. In my heart, I knew I couldn't blame him for wanting to go out to dances and social occasions, which he often mentioned in his letters, but another girl – that was something else.

Thankfully, I had opened the letter in my small cupboard of a bedroom just before grabbing some sleep before setting off for the shop. Granny and Lily were bustling around the kitchen and I didn't want them to see me upset. Granny had enough to worry about without my added problems. I managed to get into bed and tried to weep silently. It wasn't easy. I thought of all the years Greg and I had known one another but now we were just another two casualties of this dreadful conflict. Daniel was growing up without a father, as was Peter. And, as for me . . . well, it looked as if I would never have children of my own – or a husband.

Later, as I made my way to Connie's shop for the last afternoon in another year, I managed to hide my distress and put on a face. Granny gave me some strange looks but I said I was tired – it was nothing else but exhaustion.

Then, at midnight, we sat with a small glass of sherry and listened to Bella as she gave us a rundown on her latest illness. 'It was the flu, Nan, and I really thought I'd had it. In fact, I'm still so weak my legs can hardly hold me up.'

Granny and I were so tired we could hardly keep our eyes open never mind give an answer to Bella's flu. Grandad then took another bad fit of coughing and we hurried over to help him while Bella lapsed into silence.

Then Hattie and Graham arrived. They had been to a New Year's dance and Hattie was dressed in a lovely blue evening gown. She looked so out of place in the kitchen with Grandad coughing and a silent Bella.

She sat on the edge of the bed and took Grandad's hand. 'You'll be fine, Dad. Just wait till the better weather is here and you can get out for your walks along the Esplanade.'

He gave her a weak, watery-eyed smile. 'Aye, Hattie, I will,' he said before lying back on the pillow with a sigh.

Hattie and Graham left with Bella. Graham offered to see Bella home and she accepted with a gracious smile – much to Hattie's annoyance.

Thankfully, Lily was staying with the Pringle family while Dad, Rosie and Jay had all paid a visit earlier that afternoon. Everything was quiet in the close as all the neighbours knew of Grandad's illness. Sometimes a short burst of sound carried up from the street but it was short-lived. Grandad drifted off into a fitful sleep while Granny and I gazed at one another in dismay.

I think Granny knew something was wrong with me but she said nothing and the two of us brought in another New Year in silence and misery. Both of us on the verge of losing the men we loved.

8

Granny was resilient and she took Grandad's illness in her stride while I was quietly disintegrating by degrees. One thing was clear – he was getting worse with each passing day and, although we were now in the warmer days of spring, it didn't help his cough or his breathing.

The only thing he still enjoyed was his cup of tea but it took him ages to drink it. He managed to sit up for a short time before collapsing back on to the bed, looking absolutely drained and breathless.

We were still in our routine of sitting up every night with him and Granny and I still took it in turns to do this. I was managing only a few days at work but Connie said she understood and that I was to take as long as I needed off.

I had to admit that I enjoyed my few hours away from the sickbed, catching up on all the Hilltown gossip and I was even listening with a different ear to Joe.

He seemed pleased by the way the war had turned. 'I told you, Connie, didn't I, that the German Army would have to retreat from Russia and look what's happened. They've been defeated at Stalingrad. Hitler seemingly told the army commanders they were forbidden to surrender but they did surrender. It's all right for his nibs in his cosy command room to forbid anything but it's not him standing up to his oxters in snow – and starving as well.'

Connie and I were hopeful that the end of the war could now

be in sight but it still rumbled on and on. It was as if all the victories and defeats in different parts of the world were still not enough to bring about the peace we all longed for – not just in our country but everywhere. Then there was the rationing, and food supplies were being cut further and it was difficult to keep going – especially for those with big families.

Grandad sometimes enjoyed a small piece of toast with his tea and Granny added a cup of hot Oxo to his menu. Its beefy aroma seemed to perk him up while Granny swore by its health-giving benefits.

We were hardly ever in the flat in Roseangle now. While I stayed with Granny, Lily was now living with Rosie, Dad and Jay. This was a big help as it saved us cooking for her which was a big consideration when one of us was up all night. Also, Lily was spared the worst of witnessing Grandad's bad bouts. When she visited us, he was usually sleeping and quite peaceful-looking which was a blessing.

However, it was becoming clear that Grandad needed a lot more care and the doctor advised Granny to let him admit Grandad to the hospital. This was something she was totally against so we carried on, taking one day at a time. But we did have some help. Maddie offered to sit up at the weekends and let us have a rest – an offer we accepted so swiftly that we were both ashamed of ourselves.

Granny had been dubious to begin with, however. 'You've got wee Daniel to look after, Maddie. He's now at an age when he's into everything and you'll need eyes at the back of your head just to look after him.'

Maddie nodded. 'Oh, yes, he can be a little monster at times but my mother will look after him to let me help out. After all, he'll be asleep during the few hours I'm here.'

As I said, we accepted with speed.

Hattie also did two days a week which was a big help because it let me get to my work and I was grateful to them both because it also let Granny catch up on some badly needed sleep.

I would stay up with Maddie for a couple of hours when she

did her stint and we'd sit by the banked up fire, holding hot cups of tea in our hands.

Maddie, being a nurse, was excellent with Grandad. She was able to make him eat a tiny breakfast before leaving in the morning. Then she gave him a blanket bath some mornings and this seemed to settle him for the rest of the day. He was now sleeping quite well during the night because Doctor Bryson had given him a big bottle of medicine and we were grateful he wasn't suffering from the racking cough and pain he had during the earlier days of his illness.

One lovely night in early June when it hardly seemed to grow dark, Maddie and I sat by the side of the bed and chatted quietly.

'I just wish that there was a cure for Grandad,' I said, looking at the thin figure under the blankets.

Maddie gave me a sympathetic look. 'You'll all have to steel yourselves for the fact there will be no betterness for him, Ann. I'm sorry.'

I nodded. 'Aye, the doctor warned Granny right at the start that his lungs were damaged beyond help but he's had bad doses of bronchitis before and I keep hoping against hope that there will be a miracle cure.'

She said nothing.

'Granny hasn't said any more to me about his condition, Maddie.'

Maddie slowly sipped her tea and gazed at the embers of the fire. 'Perhaps she doesn't want to worry you. She knows you always get all the family's problems and she's shielding you from this extra worry.'

Looking back on that night, I've often wondered why I wasn't totally shocked by the thought of Grandad's imminent death. It was as if I had accepted this fact over the many sleepless nights during the past months.

One night I told Maddie about Greg's letter and the broken engagement. 'I've put the ring back in its box, Maddie,' I confided, 'and I'll send it to him when this war is over. I don't like to send it through the post.'

Maddie was silent and I knew we were both remembering when Danny had broken his engagement to her – that awful time when he couldn't forget how his late father had been part of a firing squad that had shot and killed a young deserter in the Great War. How Danny had anguished over that before finally coming to his senses and getting back with Maddie.

'Is he really serious about this girl he's met?' she asked.

'I don't know, Maddie.'

'But you were always such a lovely devoted couple – everyone said so.'

I tried not to sound bitter but it somehow crept into my words. 'Well, it just goes to show how appearances are wrong. He couldn't have cared for me very much if a simple letter asking him to put the marriage on hold for a while because Grandad is ill is enough to make him break our engagement and throw him into the arms of another girl.'

Maddie looked unhappy. 'Write to him to explain how bad your Grandad's illness is – he'll understand.'

I was horrified. 'What? Plead with him to have me back? Oh, I don't think so, Maddie.' I'd uttered brave words but I felt far from brave – in fact, I was almost on the verge of tears.

Maddie gave a loud sigh. 'When is this terrible war going to end, Ann? Daniel is growing up and he's never seen his father. Maybe Danny doesn't even know he has a son.' She was tearful as well.

I took her hand. 'Danny knows he has a son, Maddie – I'm sure of that.'

Her face brightened up. 'Oh, I do hope so! Do you feel that in your mind, Ann?'

I nodded. I did feel close to Danny some days but I was now wishing I had held my tongue. Why did I persist in coming out with statements based on thin air? At this rate, I should be sitting on the end of a pier with a crystal ball in my hand, charging sixpence a time for fortunes told.

Suddenly, Maddie laughed.

'What are you laughing at?' I asked.

'I'm thinking about Hattie and Graham.'

I smiled. 'She seems to be dotty about him. Granny says she's in love.'

Maddie became serious. 'Does she know anything about him Ann?'

'Only that his house and office were both bombed in the Clydebank Blitz but surely your father knows something about his background?'

She shook her head. 'He knows him professionally but knows nothing about his personal life.'

I smiled. 'Och, well, as long as they're both happy . . . I think we should all grab our chance of happiness if we get offered it during these dark times.' I was thinking of Greg when I said this. Was he grabbing his chance of happiness with someone else?

I took the two cups over to the sink and washed them. It was time to go to my bed in my tiny room in the lobby. I had promised to do the early morning papers for Connie, to give her a Sunday off and a well-earned rest.

Granny and Alice appeared about six o'clock that morning and I left them with Maddie. It was a glorious morning as I quickly walked to the Hilltown. The sun had risen over the river as it met the North Sea, turning the water and the sky into a golden glow. I wished Grandad could see it with me.

Once again I marvelled at such peace in a world torn apart by warfare. The streets were almost deserted on this quiet Sunday, most of the workers no doubt having a long lie in after a busy working week.

Joe was waiting for the shop to open. Suppressing a feeling of irritation, I smiled.

'How's your grandad, Ann?' he asked, lighting up one of his homemade cigarettes and coughing harshly from the smoke.

'He's still the same, Joe – no change.'

He followed me into the dim interior of the shop and gave me a hand to lift the bundles of papers on to the counter.

'I'll have my *Sunday Post* and *Sunday Pictorial* as usual, Ann,' he said, throwing his cigarette end out of the open door. 'I see the Allies are winning the U-boat war in the Atlantic – that'll send them packing back to their own waters.'

Quite honestly, I was tired of hearing about the war but I tried to be polite and listen to him. I knew he was a lonely old man and he liked nothing better than a good chat with Connie every morning and I was her stand-in today so I was getting the chat.

I nodded vaguely while writing the customers' names on the corners of various papers. The paper boy was late but I was a bit slower than Connie so I was grateful for the extra time.

I found myself wishing that Joe would go away but he seemed quite happy standing there and spouting about the headlines in the papers. 'Aye, it's just like I said – Allied shipping losses down to 18,000 tons last month and seventeen U-boats sunk – that'll learn them.'

I wanted to tell him that the world was losing sons and husbands, no matter which country they belonged to. But I thought Joe would be shocked if I showed the tiniest bit of sympathy to those boats lost at sea. It didn't matter what nationality – if you were drowned, then that was that. What a world.

Joe finally left and I managed to get well ahead before the paper laddie came in. He was rubbing his eyes when he appeared. 'Sorry but I slept in.'

He picked up the canvas bag and dragged himself out of the shop into the brilliant morning sun, muttering about the weight of the bag – a complaint I totally ignored because the bag wasn't as heavy as it used to be because of the restrictions on paper. He would have had something to complain about before the war when the papers were much thicker.

Then Lily appeared and she wasn't looking very happy. When I asked the reason for her solemn face, she said, 'It's Jay. He throws his porridge all over my frock and I have to get changed.'

'So Jay's learning to feed himself?' I said, trying to keep a straight face.

Lily nodded glumly. 'I wish we were back at Roseangle, Ann. It's not that I don't like being with Rosie and Dad and Jay but I would rather be with you.'

'When Grandad's better, Lily, then we'll go back to Roseangle. I promise.' I didn't mention that there was no getting better for poor Grandad.

To cheer her up, I said, 'What about taking Jay for a trip on the tramcar to see Kit?'

Her face lit up. 'I'll run up and ask Rosie if we can take him this afternoon.' She was gone in a flash only to reappear a few minutes later, slightly out of breath. 'Rosie says we can take him out later, Ann.'

'Right, then, I'll see you at three o'clock.'

The shop normally closed early in the afternoon every Sunday so I just had time to hurry back to the Overgate and help Granny with the chores and Grandad's dinner.

Dad, Rosie, Lily and Jay arrived soon after and we set off for our trip to Lochee. We left Rosie and Dad sitting by the bed, trying to have a conversation with Grandad – which wasn't easy because he kept dropping off to sleep.

We left the sad faces behind and headed with the toddler towards the tram stop. Jay was excited when he saw the tramcar and he kept twisting around in my arms. Trying to see everything and everyone. It put me in mind of Lily when she was that age. Now she was growing up and would soon be at the secondary school after the summer holidays. She had passed her qualifying exams with flying colours and now Rockwell School beckoned along with a new chapter in her life.

As usual, Kit was pleased to see us and I was both surprised and delighted to see Kathleen. She was looking as lovely as ever in a soft powder blue jumper and smart navy blue skirt. There was no sign of Kitty.

Kit explained, 'George has taken her out for a walk. What a pity we didn't know you were coming with Jay. He could have gone as well.'

Jay, however, was quite content to toddle around, picking up Kitty's books and thrusting them into Lily's hands.

'All right, Jay, I'll read you a story but you have to sit down first,' she said cheerfully.

We left them in their corner and sat down with our tea at the table which I noticed Kit had now moved to the window. A shaft of sunlight fell across its surface and I also noticed the room was much smarter than during the bad old days of unemployment. What a difference a couple of wage packets made to people's lives.

We were having a great gossip until we saw Maggie on the street. By the way she was hurrying, it was clear she was heading for Kit's house.

Kathleen groaned out loud. 'For heaven's sake, not another lecture.'

But Maggie was more irate than that as we were about to discover. She flounced into the room and, barely taking time to draw breath, she rounded on Kathleen. 'What's this I'm hearing about you giving up your house in Louis Square, Kathleen?'

A momentary glint of anger appeared in Kathleen's eyes but her voice was quiet when she spoke. 'So you've heard then, Maggie? Gossip fair gets around this part of the world.'

Kit looked embarrassed but said nothing.

Meanwhile Maggie was furious. 'I've heard you've got a flat from that photo fellow and that he's setting you up like some kept woman.'

At this point, Kit exploded. 'Look here, Maggie Malloy, let's get one thing clear – Kathleen is trying to get a better life for herself and Kitty and not end up like you and me. She's not any kept woman but just a young mother earning a living. And another thing – she's paying rent for her flat. She's no' biding in it for free.'

This was all news to me and I was puzzled by all the accusations flying around, as was Lily. I wished she hadn't been in the room but it was too late to do anything now. Her face was a picture as she tried to read to Jay but look at the warring women at the same time. Maggie's tirade won and even Jay fell silent.

Maggie didn't look convinced. 'Well, that's not what I heard, Kit.'

Before Kit could answer, Kathleen said, 'Well, Maggie, I really don't care what you've heard.'

Maggie went white and I thought she was going to choke. Kit also looked shocked.

Maggie turned to Kit. 'Do you hear her, Kit? She's shameless and I just wished my Sammy was back here to sort her out.'

Kathleen went pale but it became apparent a few moments later that this was with anger and not fear of Sammy Malloy.

'If what you've heard is that I've got a lovely flat above the studio for Kitty and myself then that's true, Maggie, and that's all it is – just a new flat with my new job – a business arrangement.'

Maggie snorted. It was a cross between a steam engine and a sledgehammer. 'A business arrangement, my arse! I've heard about men like him that seduces young lassies – takes their photos and gives them posh flats.' She stopped for more breath – or more venom. 'There's a special name for somebody like you Kathleen and as a respectable married woman I wouldn't like to use it.' She glanced over at Lily and Jay. 'Especially not in front of bairns.'

Kathleen coolly picked up her cardigan which hung on the back of the kitchen chair and looked Maggie straight in the eye. 'I'm going to say one thing before I go, Maggie. My boss is about sixty years old but if he ever did say one word of romance to me then I would feel it was a privilege and I might just respond. He's oceans apart from your precious Sammy who thinks it's a great idea to beat me up before going off to the army, just to leave me with his little message of who's boss. Well, I'm not having him back – no matter where I work or where I live. So think that over and don't come running back here every few days and spout about how wonderful your Sammy is. As far as I'm concerned he's a wee thug and I rue the day I ever met him, let alone married him.'

There was silence in the room. Maggie looked as if Kathleen had physically hit her and Kit's face went bright red with annoyance.

Maggie, who still had her Dinky curlers in her hair and was wearing her old slippers, tried to look undefeated, but failed.

'Well, I've said my piece, Kathleen, and, if you make your bed, then you'll have to lie on it.' On that note, she opened the door and walked out.

Kit was furious – not with Maggie but with Kathleen. 'That was a terrible thing to say to your mother-in-law. She didn't deserve that.'

Kathleen looked chastised. 'Well, I didn't mean to say it, Mum, but she just got on my nerves. It's Sammy this and Sammy that – anybody would think he was the King of Britain.'

'He is her son, Kathleen, and it's natural for a mother to think he's wonderful.'

Kathleen spread out her arms in an appeal to her mother. 'All I want is this chance to work with a great photograper and the flat goes with the job.' She turned to me. 'You'll have to come and visit us, Ann. It's a lovely flat and it's got some really nice furniture in it. The only thing I've got to do is put in a bed for Kitty. I'm only wanting to better myself and give Kitty a better chance in life as well – not like these Malloy wives who are forever pregnant or hard up for money. Maggie seems to glorify their lifestyles but it's not for me – or for Kitty.'

I said I understood and looked at Kit but she merely shrugged her shoulders. No doubt she had also spoken to her lovely head-strong daughter and lost – just like Maggie.

It was time for us to leave but not before promising to visit Kathleen's flat the following Tuesday evening as this was one of my nights off from nursing Grandad. Lily was also invited and she could hardly wait to see the place.

As we travelled back in the tramcar, I was feeling quite weary from all the arguments I had just witnessed. On the one hand, I could understand Kathleen's point of view but on the other I also sympathised with Kit and Maggie. They could see their old way of life changing and I don't think they very much cared for this change. Oh, I knew they didn't have wonderful lives with their husbands and children and money worries but it was the way it was always done. Childhood, marriage, motherhood and old age were the way their lives were mapped out. But now Kathleen and thousands of young women like her were challenging the old order – not for them the drudgery of a dead-end life.

Then I thought of myself. A future old maid if ever I saw one and that filled me with a black cloud of depression. Kathleen had at least tried marriage and had a lovely daughter as a result but what had I achieved? Nothing. Was a bad husband better than no husband at all? Quite honestly, I had no answer to that.

Grandad was still the same when we arrived home. He was sleeping most of the time which was a blessing. Dad and Rosie were still there, waiting to take Jay home, and, after they left, Lily told Granny all about the arguments at Lochee.

'Maggie was really angry, Granny, but she was funny as well. I thought she would explode but she didn't. Her Dinky curlers were jumping all over her head as she flounced in.' Lily burst out laughing and I could hardly keep a straight face as Granny looked at us with her eyebrows raised.

I explained the situation and wasn't surprised when Granny sided with Kit and Maggie. 'She is a married woman with a husband in a prisoner of war camp and folk like to gossip. But I wish her well in her new job.'

On the Tuesday evening, Lily and I set off for Kathleen's flat in the Perth Road. It was a few hundred yards past Roseangle and Lily gave a wistful glance down the road as we passed. I didn't want to promise her a quick return as it all depended on Grandad's health so it was better not to say a word in case of disappointment.

The photographic studio and shop had a very expensive look to them. The flat was up one flight of stairs in a very posh-looking close which was painted with a grey gloss paint – very grand looking.

Kathleen opened the door. She was wearing a different blue cardigan and the same navy skirt. The flat was tiny but beautiully furnished and decorated. I never thought of myself as an envious person but I suddenly wished we had somewhere like this to stay. Maddie and Danny's flat was every bit as grand but it wasn't mine – not like this place which belonged to Kathleen.

Kitty was sitting on the settee and Lily went to read her a story. The bright blue damask curtains framed a large window which also had a good view of the river. The setting sun was going down in the west and the room was bathed in a translucent glow. It was simply beautiful.

Kathleen laughed. 'Maggie can't understand why I prefer this flat to yon dark hole at Louis Square.'

'I think she's maybe a bit worried about your reputation, Kathleen. It's understandable, I suppose, in someone her age and maybe she doesn't mean it personally.'

Kathleen gave me a direct look. Something I had noticed she did a lot. 'Right then, Ann, I'll apologise next weekend.'

We sat at the window and looked at the ever-changing river until the kettle whistled cheerfully in the tiny scullery which led off from the living room.

'Do you often think about Danny, Ann?'

I was taken aback by her direct question but I nodded. 'Aye, I do – all the time.'

'So do I and I think he would approve of me trying to make a better life for us.'

'Well, he certainly didn't like you getting married to Sammy,' I reminded her.

She nodded. 'Aye, that was a big mistake but I really thought I was in love with him.'

'And you're not?'

She shook her head and her long auburn curls swung around her pale neck. She looked like a model from a Raphael painting and it was no wonder her photographic boss was enchanted by her.

She leaned closer to me and gave a quick glance over to where Lily and Kitty were still engrossed in their story. Her voice dropped to a whisper.

'I love my job here and I've just met Chris. He's Mr Portland's son and he's a photographer with the War Office in London. Oh, you should see him, Ann! He's really tall and good-looking – a bit like a young Leslie Howard.'

If that was a true description, then he was a very lucky man to have so much going for him.

'Is he married, Kathleen?'

Her eyes filled with mischief. 'No, that's the best part. He was almost married before the war but his girlfriend married someone else. Imagine that – turning down this Greek god!'

I was a bit doubtful about this description. At my time of life, I realised one rarely met someone presentable, let alone a god – Greek or otherwise.

'Mr Portland's really great to work for and Chris was telling me that, after the war is over, he'll be coming back to work with his father.' Her eyes took on a faraway, dreamy expression and I was suddenly worried about her.

'You'll watch your step, won't you, Kathleen?'

As she nodded, I realised I had repeated Ma Ryan's warning to me to watch my step.

9

Grandad died at the end of June. It was a warm sunny Friday morning. Thankfully it was a peaceful passing. One moment he was sipping a drink of water and the next he was gone. Lying back on the pillows with a final sigh.

Granny was by his side and she gently covered his face with the white sheet while I stood in shocked silence by the side of the bed, the water glass still in my hand. She turned to me and, although she wasn't crying, her eyes were glazed with unshed tears.

'He's passed all his suffering now, Ann. Go and get Hattie and your dad.'

I went to the Westport first, hoping Hattie would be at home. She was and she looked shocked at the news even although we had anticipated this moment for weeks.

'I've to go and get Dad, Hattie.'

We walked to the Overgate together and I left her to go to the warehouse to see Dad. When I got there, I found him sitting in the tiny dusty office with its small grimy windows which let in shafts of filtered sunlight. As I entered, I could see he was busy with a pile of paperwork. He was bending over a book and, when I saw him, I began to cry.

He looked up in alarm and his face went white. 'What is it, Ann? Is it Grandad?'

I nodded wordlessly and he came over and gave me a hug.

'Come on, I'll get my jacket and have a wee word with Mr Pringle.'

I waited outside. The sun was warm on my face and I felt so sad that Grandad couldn't be with me on this lovely morning – or on any other morning.

Mr Pringle came to the door with Dad, his face full of sympathy. 'I'm very sorry to hear about your grandad, Ann – so very sorry.'

Again, I just nodded, unable to form words in my mouth. Then Dad took my arm and we set off for the Overgate.

Hattie was sitting by the side of the bed and she was crying. Granny, as usual, was bustling around being busy and making tea.

Dad made her sit down beside me and we made a grieving semicircle around the bed and I suddenly thought how Grandad would have laughed at us all. Sitting with our sad faces. Then I realised I would never see or hear from him ever again and tears ran down my face.

Hattie gave a huge sob. 'How many times did I tell him to give up that awful pipe? But he wouldn't listen.' Her voice was harsh with grief.

Granny took her hand. 'Shush, Hattie. Dad's at peace now and there's no use in recriminations. You all knew what he was like. He enjoyed doing his own thing.'

Hattie just shook her head.

The rest of the day passed in a blur of visitors. Rosie and Jay arrived as soon as they heard the news and they were followed by Alice. The doctor came and wrote out the death certificate. He said a few words of comfort to Granny before leaving and he passed Bella who was coming in as he was going out.

Bella looked upset and, for once, didn't comment on her own illnesses. She slumped down on the chair beside me. 'Your poor grandad, Ann – at least he's not suffering any more.'

I nodded again. I felt my head must surely fall off my neck by the amount of nodding I was doing but it saved me speaking and breaking down in a flood of tears in front of the visitors.

It was almost time to go and fetch Lily from the school. This was her last week at Rosebank School and I know she was a bit sad about leaving even though she was looking forward to the adventure of a new school in the autumn.

Lily had been staying at the Overgate for the past week as Granny thought we should tell her how serious Grandad's illness was. I had explained as gently as I could about the finality of his life. I was amazed by how grown-up she had become and what I had failed to realise during Grandad's illness was the fact that Lily had suspected how ill he was – we just hadn't spoken of it.

So, every night, Lily had sat at the side of the bed and read the evening paper out loud to him. Sometimes he opened his eyes and looked at her which made her so happy. When this happened, she chattered on about her day at school but I didn't have the heart to tell her he wouldn't hear a fraction of it.

Now, standing at the school gate, I was unsure how to tell her. As it turned out, she guessed the truth from the look on my face.

'It's Grandad, isn't it, Ann? He's dead?'

'Aye, he is, Lily. I'm really very sorry.'

Because Rosie and Jay hadn't stayed too long at the Overgate, Dad had said to take her to the house and Rosie would look after her. As we walked towards the house, we both tried to keep the tears at bay until we reached the safety of Rosie's kitchen.

Rosie was sitting at the table and she wiped her eyes as we entered. Jay was toddling around the kitchen, playing with his toys and singing a nursery rhyme. Normally we would have laughed at his antics but not today. As if sensing our grief, the song died away but thankfully he started singing it again when Rosie picked him up and hugged him tight. I made some tea and we sat around the table, speaking about our memories of Grandad.

Rosie recalled the episode of Lily's pram and we smiled at the memory of it. Lily recalled her walks along the Esplanade with him and how he would buy her an ice-cream cone afterwards. As for me . . . well, the memories came flooding back. I particularly remembered how strong he and Granny had been after Mum's death and I was suddenly filled with a deep sense of sadness at our loss and all the old thoughts that had filled my mind during the long dark years after Mum died came rushing back. Was this what life was all about? This vale of tears?

Lily wanted to come back with me to the Overgate but I explained there simply wasn't enough room at the moment. Actually that wasn't true but I didn't want Lily to see Grandad. I wanted her to remember him as he had been in life – the centre of her existence.

I went to see Connie before heading back. She didn't know what to say but what could anyone say? Grandad had had a long life. It had been a hard-working one, just like the majority of people, and now it was over. This was something that happened to us all but that didn't mean it was a painless process. In fact, I felt I was falling apart with grief and sadness.

Maddie was in the house when I arrived and she came over and put her arms around me. This simple sympathetic gesture was something I would never forget.

She said, 'I know it sounds cruel, Ann, but your grandad is at peace now. He would have suffered more and more as time went on, believe me.'

'I know, Maddie.'

Granny was sitting with a box on her lap.

Maddie nodded towards it and said softly. 'Your granny is looking at all the old photos. She's had a good deal of comfort from that.'

We went over and Granny held out a faded sepia-tinted photo of a stiff-looking couple standing beside a huge potted palm. It was her wedding photo. Grandad was extremely young and good looking and Granny looked no more than a lassie. He was wearing a dark and severe-looking suit while Granny was in a long dress and an enormous hat.

She suddenly laughed out loud. 'I mind fine how much he hated that hat – said it hid my bonnie face.'

Maddie took the photo from her shaking fingers and we gazed at the image of a happy event from another age. 'It's a lovely photo, Mrs Neill, and you both look so handsome.'

Granny sighed and put it back in her box. 'Aye, he was a real handsome fellow was your grandad, Ann.'

Maddie said we would both stay the night with her but she shook her head.

'No, you two go away back home. I'll be fine on my own.'

But Maddie wouldn't hear of it and she made Granny go next door to Alice's house. 'Ann and I will stay here tonight. You go to bed and try and get a good night's sleep. You need it.'

For a brief moment she looked as if she would reject this idea but she slowly made her way next door.

Maddie and I sat in the long twilight of the summer night, as we had done on other nights over the past weeks. We talked about Lily, Danny and Daniel, Rosie and Jay and Minnie and Peter – as if concentrating on the young and healthy would somehow dispel the overwhelming feeling of death. Of course this talk of the young and living didn't truly dispel the sadness but it helped a little bit.

Then, in the morning, the undertaker arrived and we left him with Granny, Dad and Hattie.

The funeral took place at Balgay. Grandad was being buried beside Mum which I thought was very poignant and all the terrible memories of another day spent here were once again raised, like a suppurating sore.

There was a large gathering at the graveside. A lot of Grandad's old friends and neighbours were there as well as Maddie's father and uncle. Then, to my surprise, I saw Greg's parents amongst the crowd. It wasn't that I was displeased to see them because I had always got on so well with them both but I was dreading meeting them afterwards. Had Greg told them our engagement was over? Then I realised they would know because Greg wouldn't leave them in the dark over something as serious as this.

I stood with Maddie and Lily. I hadn't wanted Lily to come to such a sad occasion but she had insisted so I gave in. Alice was looking after Jay and one of Maddie's aunts had Daniel.

I didn't know the minister who was conducting the service.

Hattie had taken everything in her stride after Grandad's death and we were grateful to her. It let Granny have a rest.

Granny . . . I looked over to where she was standing with Hattie, Dad and Rosie. Although I knew she had shed tears over Grandad's death, today she was dry-eyed and standing very straight. Only the sadness of her face belied her widowhood. She was from the old school that taught stiff-backed dignity in all matters and I marvelled at her resolve.

It was a stiflingly hot day and I couldn't help but recall how Mum had died on a day such as this. Her funeral, however, had been held during a thunderstorm but there were no ominous black clouds today. The sky was bright blue with tiny wisps of white cloud scoring the vast expanse of sky. I felt the heat of the sun beat down on my head.

Kit and George stood beside Nellie and Rita, our old neighbours, and I wondered if they too were remembering Mum's death. They had been such a great help to us then and I was glad to see they were looking smarter and better nourished than during the bad old days of unemployment.

Ma Ryan was missing but I didn't expect her to be here although she had sent us a letter of sympathy. I looked over at Granny again. Would I be able to be like her in these circumstances? I doubted it.

The minister's words sounded like the drone of some dozy insect and his solemn words seemed to hang in the stillness of the air. There was a strong perfume coming from the many flowers which had been placed on some nearby graves and I felt almost drugged with the heat and the scent. I also felt as if I was on the outside looking in. Beyond sadness. Never to see Grandad ever again or laugh at his many antics. I was bereft and it was as if I had lost an arm or a leg, the pain was so intense.

Even Hattie looked shattered. Hattie, who always looked so self-reliant and confident, was now weeping silently, a white handkerchief held against her mouth.

But all things pass and, when the funeral was over, we all made our way to Hattie's house. I thought Dad may have been annoyed at her making all the funeral arrangements but he had said she wanted to do this last thing for her father. It was cathartic, she said, as if it had cleansed her soul. We all knew what she meant. Although deeply fond of her mother and father, she had, over the past few years, lived a totally different life from them but now she was coming home.

Graham wasn't at the funeral or at the house. Hattie said he would be there later as he had an important appointment with a client in Glasgow. He was hoping to catch an early-evening train back to Dundee.

Then, to my dismay, I saw the Borlands, Greg's parents, coming in the door. Maddie gave me a warning glance but I took a few deep breaths and went over to see them.

Barbara Borland gave me a hug while her husband said, 'We're so sorry about your grandad, Ann.'

'Thank you for coming all this way – it's such a long journey.' I was kicking myself for being so formal but I was dreading hearing any news of Greg – news like his engagement to his new girlfriend or, even worse, his marriage. 'How did you manage to get away from the farm?'

Barbara said, 'We've got a neighbour to feed the animals but we'll catch an early train back to Struan so we won't be gone for too long.'

I knew their farm was run mostly by themselves except for some extra help at lambing time or during the harvest and it was really very kind of them to come to see us on this sad day.

I took them over to meet Maddie and went to get them some tea and sandwiches. When I returned, I noticed Lily had joined them.

'You'll all be devastated about your grandad, Ann – he was such a big part of your lives,' said Barbara.

I nodded, unable to speak.

Lily said, 'How is Paddy?' Paddy was their collie dog and Lily had loved going up the hill with him.

Dave Borland smiled. 'Still running up the hill and chasing the sheep, Lily. You must come and see us soon as Paddy misses you.'

I threw her a warning glance but she didn't notice it. 'Oh, that'll be lovely.' She turned to me. 'Can we go and visit Paddy soon, Ann?'

'Of course, Lily, but we'll have to stay with Granny for a while. She'll need us.'

Lily's face became sad and I was furious with myself for making her feel like this. What was wrong with me? Just because a man had dumped me it was not an excuse to snub his parents or make my own sister feel sad like this.

I tried to smile warmly. 'Of course we'll visit you soon, won't we, Lily?'

Lily nodded happily.

Barbara leaned forward and said quietly, 'We do understand, Ann, but, as always, you're both very welcome to come and stay any time.'

Maybe Lily was, I thought sourly, but surely I wasn't popular with them, having strung along their only son on so-called false promises.

Maddie saved the situation. 'I had an aunt who stayed at Struan. She had a small holiday cottage there before the war but she's given up the lease because of all the restrictions on travel and also because she's getting older.'

The Borlands said they knew Maddie's aunt and I left them chatting about mutual acquaintances.

Thankful to escape, I went to sit beside Granny and Bella. They were praising Hattie's sandwiches. 'She's aye been good with pieces,' said Bella, pushing the last morsel of a dainty sandwich into her mouth. I also noticed she had a large glass of sherry.

Granny looked so tired and I was suddenly worried about her. She'd had so much worry during the past few months but she assured me she was fine when I asked her.

'It was so good of Hattie to deal with everything, Ann. It's a big load off my mind, I can tell you. I can just sit here and remember your grandad and all the braw years we had together. I keep telling myself how lucky I've been to have had such a good man by my side and I've got lots and lots of happy memories to keep me going.'

'Oh, Granny, I'm so happy you feel like that,' I blurted out. I also had loads of happy memories but that wouldn't make up for the loss of Grandad. In fact, I didn't know how I would cope with the thought of never seeing him again.

Kit and George came over with their condolences. Afterwards Kit said to me, 'We've had some good news, Ann.'

'Is it Kathleen?'

Kit shook her head. 'No she's still working and living above the studio and Maggie is still going berserk. No, my good news is about Patty. He's been exempted from the forces because of his asthma and also because of his job at the shipyard. His apprenticeship's finished now and we were worried that he would be called up but seemingly miners, farmers and some other workers are looked on as doing war work and the shipyard jobs fall into that category.'

I was so pleased for them and I said so.

The Borlands came over to say their goodbyes to Granny. I knew it would be bad manners to move away so I tried to compose my face into a smile although my mind was seething with emotions. I saw them to the door and thanked them again for coming.

Barbara turned and took my hand. 'I know how you're feeling, Ann. You've lost your beloved grandad and we also know that you've split up from Greg. We were really very sorry to hear that because we always thought that ...' She hesitated. 'Well, you know what I mean?'

Yes, I did know what she meant but they probably would soon have a daughter-in-law – only it wasn't going to be me.

'Greg is going to write to you – he didn't realise your grandad was as ill as he was. Also will you consider coming to visit us with Lily?'

'Aye, I will, Barbara. I'll drop you a note when we can get away.'

She gave me a searching look. 'You promise?'

I nodded. 'I promise.'

I felt terrible afterwards when I walked home with Maddie. 'I promised to go and see them and I've no intention of going. What a fraud I'm turning into!'

Maddie was sympathetic. 'You're not a fraud, Ann. You've just had too much to do for most of your life and now you're tired of it. Greg obviously didn't realise how much your family means to you or how much they've always relied on you. Which is a great pity because you have always divided yourself into little pieces for everyone and he should have been happy to share you.'

As I walked back along the streets which were still warm from the earlier heat, dark clouds hovered above me. They matched my mood. I thought about Maddie's words but was too tired to analyse them. Greg had either loved me or he hadn't. It was as simple as that. Or was it?

I was almost at the Overgate when the rain came – heavy thundery rain that streamed from the sky and, within a few moments, I was totally soaked. I had my head down and was running as hard as I could when a familiar voice called my name. Looking up, I saw Graham walking towards me and he was carrying a big black umbrella. He held it over my head and we hurried up Tay Street. He spoke about the funeral and said he was sorry he couldn't manage to put his client off. I glanced at his face and was dismayed to see it had a tired and strained look. A small nervous tic flickered at his eye and his mouth looked tense.

'Are you feeling all right, Graham?' I asked, hoping another worry wasn't looming large.

He gave me a startled look and tried to smile but the smile didn't reach his eyes. 'Just a bit of a headache, Ann. I've had a tiring day and a long frustrating journey but seeing Hattie will soon cheer me up.'

So it was love, I told myself. Well, good for them!

He insisted I stay under the umbrella until I reached Granny's close. As I ran up the entrance, he said, 'I'll be round to see your gran later, Ann. Will you tell her?'

This bit of news pleased Granny. 'Och, he's a really fine man. I just hope Hattie is happy because she deserves to be.'

Lily was listening to the wireless. A sad look was on her face. 'Do you ever get tired of listening to all this news of the war, Granny?' She fiddled around with the dial and suddenly some cheery music blared out. Glancing quickly at Granny, she turned it off.

'Switch it back on, Lily. You listen to your cheery music and enjoy it because your grandad wouldn't want to see moping and sad faces, now, would he?'

Lily switched it back on. Granny's words made her feel less sad. She had always been Grandad's special wee girl and she would always remember that.

I had decided to stay at the Overgate as long as Granny needed me. I didn't want her living on her own but to my astonishment she said it was time for Lily and me to go back to Roseangle. 'You've done enough here, Ann – not just for Grandad but over all these years and now it's time to get your life back together.'

I knew she was referring to Greg. I hadn't told her about the broken engagement but I planned to tell both her and Lily some-time – just not at this moment.

I tried to protest but she was firm. 'No, Ann. I'll have Alice in and out for our usual gossip and Hattie and Graham are coming over later so I'll be fine. Now don't you worry about me.'

I was still not sure but she was adamant. I said I would continue to come over to do the heavy washing and chores and this seemed to please her so, after our tea, Lily and I headed for the flat.

It had an unlived in feeling and I realised we had been absent for a few months. I soon had a fire going. Not that it was cold but I felt it cheered the room up, especially since the rain was still heavy. Even though it was twilight, we drew the blackout curtains. We listened to some dance band music on the wireless. Later, as we lay in our settee, I listened to the steady rhythm of Lily's breathing and thought I would never sleep again, such were the conflicting emotions going round in my head.

It had been a terrible day of sadness and loss – not to mention meeting the Borlands and leaving Granny on her own. Then there had been that feeling of foreboding I had felt when meeting

Graham. Was he ill? I sincerely hoped not. Yes, it had been some day. Meanwhile, Lily slept like an innocent baby – a sleep that was deep and free from worry but that was as it should be.

I made a mental note to go and see Connie the next morning. There was no reason now why I couldn't do my usual hours and I also wanted to thank both her and Joe for coming to the funeral. They had been at the cemetery but, as they hadn't come back to the house, I didn't get a chance to talk to them. I also wanted to see Nellie and Rita and planned to see them when I visited the Hilltown.

I was just dropping off to sleep when Graham's face came to mind with its tense, strained look and the nervous tic. A headache? Well, it could have been, I suppose. I had the impression he looked haunted. I mentally scolded myself. What was I turning into? Some kind of fool who made a drama out of everything?

The next morning, before Lily and I could go and see Connie, a letter arrived from Greg. My heart started to pound and I wished Lily had been at school instead of it being the long summer holiday. I tried to look casual. 'Lily, will you run down for a newspaper please?'

She set off cheerfully. I gave her one of my sweetie coupons to buy some sweets if they were available because sometimes they weren't. Anyhow, she would be gone long enough for me to read the letter in private. Greg's letter was full of sympathy:

Mum and Dad have written to tell me about your grandad's death, Ann, and I can't begin to say how sorry I am to hear this awful news. Hattie wrote to them to let them know and I hope they managed to go to the funeral. I'm sorry I wrote that letter to you but it was done more in annoyance than in reason and I didn't know your grandad was so ill. Please forgive me.

There was more of this sentiment before he signed it.

Well, that was one little mystery cleared up. I had wondered how his parents had heard about the death but it was Hattie who

116

had written to them. She didn't know the engagement was over so she thought she was doing the right thing.

I was sitting with the letter in my hand when I heard Lily's footsteps on the stairs. Screwing it into a tight ball, I went over to the fireplace. The ashes were still in the grate from the night before and I had been in the process of cleaning it out when the postman called. After dropping Greg's letter into the ash bucket, I then scooped three lots of grey ash on top of it.

Well, that is that, I thought. But, for some reason, instead of feeling triumphant, I was overwhelmed by a flood of sadness and tears weren't far away. But I couldn't cry – not in front of Lily.

10

At the end of the summer holiday, Lily and I set off for her new school. It was a dismally overcast and misty day, very still and mild but with a hint of autumn in the air, and the grey smoke from countless chimneys rose into the sky like an army of ghosts – a multitude of grey wraiths intent on departing from their earthly homes.

Rockwell School was a large building. Red-bricked and imposing, it was so different from the primary school. It was quite a long journey every morning from Roseangle but, because all of Lily's classmates were going to this school, we decided the extra journey was justified. Another consideration was the fact that the flat wasn't ours and I had a niggling feeling that I should start very soon to look for somewhere else to rent. When Danny returned, Maddie and Daniel would want to move back in right away to welcome him home.

According to Joe, the war was on the turn. The Allies were capturing more and more ground and the American Army had recently captured Palermo in the Sicily landings. Joe had been almost ecstatic with joy when it was announced that Mussolini, the Italian dictator, had been deposed and had been replaced with King Victor Emmanuel.

'Aye, it's just a matter of time before Hitler is deposed as well,' he said to Connie.

Still, all this talk of war and the worry of looking for another flat was at the back of my mind as we stood beside the large entrance of this new school. Lily's friend Janey was with us as her mother had been unable to come with her. Janey had started primary school on the same day as Lily and they had been great friends since those early days. She lived in Dallfield Walk and came from a large family. In fact, another baby had just been born which was the reason she was with us.

Janey had chattered on as we walked to the school. 'The baby is to be called Kenneth. It's after my uncle Kenneth and he's in the army fighting the Nazis,' she informed us with a great deal of relish.

It was a well-known fact that Janey's father hadn't been passed fit for the army because he had a deformed foot. But Connie had said years ago that they were a very happy family and he managed to provide for his large brood, giving them a decent lifestyle from his rag-and-bone round. He was a familiar figure on the streets with his pony and cart, collecting old rags or scrap – in fact, anything that could be turned into money.

Janey and Lily looked with apprehensive eyes at their new school.

Janey said, 'I didn't think it would be as big as this, did you, Lily?'

Lily merely shook her head and looked at me. For a brief moment, I almost whisked them away back to the warm, familiar surroundings of their old school. Yet I realised I couldn't protect Lily or Janey from the world forever.

We walked towards the gate. By now, groups of pupils were streaming through the entrance and into the very large playground.

I said, 'Come on – you'll be fine when you get used to the size of the place. Anyway, most of your class are here so you'll not be on your own.'

Janey almost wailed, 'But we're no' in the same class, Ann. I'm going into domestic science and Lily is going into French/Commercial. We'll be in different classes, won't we Lily?'

Once again Lily nodded unhappily.

Faced with two unhappy twelve year olds who looked as if they were about to bolt into the blue yonder, I realised I had to make some sort of stand here. I said firmly, 'You'll still have one another at playtime and you'll be arriving and leaving together so you're not on your own, except for the short time during the lessons.'

This seemed to calm them down and I gently ushered them through the gates. They both turned before they reached the playground and the miserable look on their faces made me want to cry out loud. Instead I waved cheerfully and they turned hand in hand into a new episode in their lives.

Then I heard someone calling their names. A small group of girls, all dressed in similar gym tunics, called them over. For a moment, I was anxious until I recognised the girls as classmates from Rosebank. I had no idea what classes they would be in but the odds had to be in favour of some of them sharing either Lily or Janey's classes. I had told the girls I would pick them up at four o'clock and that they had to wait by the gate.

As I walked back to Connie's shop, my heart felt weighed down with sorrow. What kind of world would these children inherit when they finally left school? Would we still be at war?

As usual Connie cheered me up. 'Yon fruit shop just down from the Plaza has got a consignment of apples from Canada. Nip down, Ann, and get some.'

Apples? What a treat! We hadn't seen apples since the start of the war but then there were loads of foods no longer available – bananas, butter, oranges and real strawberry jam to name a few. They were things I had to admit we didn't have a lot of before the war due to lack of money but nevertheless they had been in the shops for those who could afford them.

When I reached the tiny fruit shop down from the Plaza picture house, I couldn't believe my eyes. The queue stretched almost to the bottom of the Hilltown and it seemed as if the entire population of Dundee had heard about the Canadian apples. Scores of women stood in the mist, their coats tightly belted against the greyness and clutching message bags close to their bodies. Most of the women were wearing colourful turbans on their heads. These headsquares, tied around the hair and knotted in front with the ends tucked in, kept the hair reasonably clean. Especially helpful now that women were working, not only in the jute mills but as conductresses on the trams and in scores of other jobs left vacant by the men who were now fighting all over the world.

I joined the end of the queue which, by the time I reached it, had turned the corner into Victoria Road.

A group of women ahead of me were muttering in annoyance. 'Half the fowk here dinnae live in this area,' said one woman to her neighbour. 'See that woman ower there? Well, she bides in Strathmartine Road.'

Her neighbour looked reassuringly shocked. 'Bloody cheek!'

I tried not to smile. I knew Strathmartine Road wasn't exactly local but it wasn't situated on Mars. It would seem that waiting in queues every day for basic foodstuffs was a chore most women put up with but, when it came to exotic Canadian apples, the women were certainly turning into territorial creatures.

As it turned out we were all to be disappointed – the stranger from Strathmartine Road included. Long before we reached the fruit shop, the owner closed the door. A large sign stated that all apples were sold out. Well, that was life during these difficult times.

Because I was in the area, I hurried up the road to Burnett's bakery where another long queue had formed – probably from the remnants of the apple queue. Fortunately, bread and rolls weren't on the ration which was a huge blessing to large families who relied on bread and potatoes to fill the hungry stomachs of their children.

When I reached the counter, I bought two loaves – one for Rosie. The assistant handed over the bread which had a grey look. The national loaf it was called but, as we had no choice, we had to forget about the great white bread in the days before the war. In fact, this was becoming a popular pastime. 'I mind afore the war when we got ice cream.' Or, 'The pre-war tatties tasted better than these watery ones.'

Connie didn't seem to be too disappointed about the lack of apples. 'To be honest, Ann, I hardly ever ate an apple before the war but now, when you can't get them, well, I have this craving for them. Strange isn't it?'

'No, Connie, it's not – it's just a case of wanting what you can't get.' Like Greg, I thought bitterly. Had I been too complacent about him? Was that why he was now with someone new? He had written about forgiving him but had that been just kind words to a lonely old spinster? Me.

Connie was speaking and I realised I hadn't heard a word. 'Sorry, Connie, I was thinking about something.'

'I'm just asking if Lily and Janey liked their new school.'

I looked dubious. 'It's certainly much bigger than we thought, Connie, and I'm not sure how they'll get on.' I wanted to protect Lily from all the unfairness of life and I suddenly wanted to wrap her up in warmth and love – to keep her away from anything harsh.

Connie laughed. 'Och, don't worry about Lily. She's a tough wee lassie – just like you. And Janey is the same – they have to be.'

Was that how Connie saw Lily and me? Tough? But, somehow, because of this statement, I felt a great deal better about the school. However, at four o'clock, my stomach was doing cartwheels as I waited by the gate. The large windows that overlooked the road gazed back at me with their sightless, desolate panes of glass. Then I saw boys passing in front of them and the tall figure of a teacher and the place seemed to become a bit more human-looking.

Then the school came out and I was astounded to see hundreds of children of various ages emerge from both the boys' and girls' playgrounds. For one terrible moment I thought I would miss the girls in this throng but they saw me and it was with a feeling of relief when I saw them running towards me.

I felt sick with worry. What if Lily hated this new school? What if she cried every morning? I didn't think I could cope with her unhappiness. I was almost afraid to speak to them but Janey and Lily began to talk at once. They stopped and laughed.

Janey went first. 'Och, it was quite good, Ann. I've got Marlene and Jean in my class and I used to sit beside them at Rosebank.'

'Oh, that's great, Janey,' I said, looking at Lily. 'And what about you, Lily?'

Her eyes were shining. 'Like Janey said, it's great. I've got Alice, Cathy, Robert and Jimmy in my class and we all like it. We get different lessons in different classrooms and although we've got a registered teacher, we get a different teacher for every period.'

In a cheerier frame of mind, we set off for home, dropping Janey at her close in Dallfield Walk.

'I've not got any homework tonight, Ann, but I'll have a lot later this week.' She sounded a bit worried.

I gave her hand a squeeze. 'You'll manage fine, Lily.'

As the weeks went by, she sat at the table by the window and, after her tea, she studied her books and wrote long screeds in her jotters. Occasionally, she would give a long drawn-out sigh and when I looked over she would be resting her chin in her hand like a juvenile Einstein and she'd mutter darkly about science and the French language or trial balances and shorthand. It all sounded highly educational and far above anything I had been taught at school.

'I sometimes wish I had taken the domestic science course like Janey,' she said one evening. 'She gets to bath a dolly and pretend it's a baby or else she bakes tattie scones or cleans a wee classroom made to look like a house.'

I didn't answer on those occasions as she seemed to be happy with her lot.

In November, I got a letter from Jean Peters. She lived in Broughty Ferry and had been the cook at Whitegate Lodge when I worked there for Mrs Barrie. She hadn't managed to come to Grandad's funeral. She had broken her leg a week before he died but now she said it was better.

Although we had corresponded over the weeks since the funeral, I hadn't managed to pay a visit because of my job and the travelling to Lily's school – plus the chores I did for Granny. It left me with little spare time but, when I received her latest letter, I decided to pay her a call.

Lily and I went to see her on the Sunday. She looked perky

enough and her leg had mended but she still needed to take things easy, she told us. However, she managed a gentle stroll to the beach.

'You have to stay off the sand,' she said. 'It is all fenced off with barbed wire in case the Germans land.'

We walked slowly along the esplanade with a bitter east wind blowing in our faces. The sky and sea were the same shade of steel grey and they seemed to merge into each other on the horizon. It was similar to the day I first arrived at the Ferry all those years ago.

'How is your granny coping?' Jean asked.

'Oh, she's amazing, Jean. I thought she wouldn't get over it because they had been together for so many years but she says she's got so many happy memories to keep her going.'

This was true. Over the months since Grandad's death, I had visited the Overgate most days and, although she needed help with the heavy chores like the washing and bringing in some messages from the shops, she was coping well.

Jean nodded. 'I can understand that, Ann. And she's always got you and Lily and your Dad and the rest of the family.'

We sat down on a bench while Lily ran ahead. I gazed at the distance to try and catch a sight of Whitegate Lodge but it was much further along the road.

As if reading my mind, Jean said, 'The house has been sold, Ann. A retired couple bought it a few months ago and they asked me if I could work a few hours a week for them but I said no. Then this happened.' She indicated her leg. 'I tripped over a broken pavement and fractured my leg again. Who says lightening never strikes twice?'

She was referring to her first accident at Whitegates when she broke her leg while feeding the blackbirds in the courtyard. How my life had changed from that moment on. Ma Ryan's warning to me about danger from a blackbird had sadly come true but not in the context I thought.

'Jean.'

She looked at me.

'Ma Ryan has given me another warning. What do you think about it?'

She looked thoughtful. 'Well she was right the first time, wasn't she?'

I nodded unhappily.

'What did she say?'

'It's difficult to put into words,' I said, trying hard to remember what Ma had said. 'She said I was to take care.' I stopped. 'No, that wasn't it . . . It was to watch my step. That's right, it was to watch my step.' I recalled the day I got the warning. 'The strange thing is, Jean, on that day, I almost fell off a tramcar and, if the conductor hadn't grabbed me, then I would have been badly injured. Maybe that was the meaning of the warning and the danger is now passed.'

Jean took my cold hand in hers. 'Well, let's hope so, Ann. Now what is the news of Greg?'

My face told her the whole story.

'Och, don't tell me you've broken up?'

I nodded. 'I'm afraid so, Jean. You're looking at a frustrated old maid. Nobody wants me.'

She laughed. 'Don't be so daft. If it's no' Greg, then there will be some other lucky man, believe me. You're a great catch for any man. Sensible, hardworking and aye doing your best for everybody but yourself.'

Lily was running back so I said cheerfully, 'Well, I hope you're right, Jean.'

Lily said, 'What do you hope, Ann?'

Jean laughed. 'She hopes you still have your appetite for my scones.'

Lily had and, as she sat at the cosy fire with a cup of tea in one hand and a floury scone in the other, she looked a vision of contentment.

Meanwhile Jean was apologetic. 'Sorry I've no jam or butter Lily. We've all got to get used to this awful margarine. It's the one part of the rations I hate and so does my man.'

I also hated margarine but Lily didn't mind it. I always spread it as thinly as possible on the grey slices of the national loaf. What a life.

Jean nodded to me and pointed to the back room. 'Just you eat up, Lily. There's something I want to say to Ann.'

Lily was quite happy to help herself to another scone and I followed Jean into the bedroom. It was a small room which was dwarfed by a huge double bed and a solid looking wardrobe which filled one entire wall. A tiny dressing table stood in front of the window and successfully eclipsed any light that may have filtered through.

Jean went over to the wardrobe and brought out two parcels wrapped in newspaper. 'You know my man is a joiner, Ann, and, although he's retired now, he still likes to make the odd thing or two. In fact, he lives in that workshop of his.' She placed the two parcels in my hands. 'This is a wee present for Jay for his Christmas when it comes and also a wee present for Lily.'

I was overwhelmed. Jay's present was a beautiful wooden train and carriages. Each filled with small wooden people. Jean showed me the catch that opened the doors and the tiny passengers could be removed. It was lovely.

Lily's present was smaller but still beautifully handcrafted. It was a large wooden pencil box with her name stencilled on the lid.

'Oh, Jean, these are lovely. Lily and Jay will be thrilled with them and delighted to get them at Christmas. I'll get Lily to write and thank you both later.'

Jean beamed. 'Well, as long as they like them – that's all that matters.'

Liking them was an understatement. Toys, like everything else, were in short supply and the toys that were available had the utility label which everything from clothes to furniture now had stamped on them. Although such things were adequately made, they were always a bit skimpy – not like these two glossy, hand-made toys that spoke of a better time before the war.

Jean brought out the large message bag I remembered from our days together and she laughed. 'You remember this bag?'

'Yes, I do.'

She put the parcels into its cavernous depths and we went back to Lily who gazed at the bag with round eyes.

Before I could think up something to say, Jean said, 'It's just a wee present for Jay's Christmas, Lily. You'll no' say anything, will you? We want him to think it comes from Santa Claus but you're a big lassie now and you know better.'

'Oh, no, Jean – cross my heart.'

We set off for Dundee and, as we made our way back, Lily said, 'Jean's a lovely woman, isn't she, Ann? Imagine giving something to Jay from Santa.'

My mind went back twelve years to my time at Whitegate Lodge and what a great friend and ally she had been to me during my traumatic time there. I also thought of the lovely Mrs Barrie. They had been my two saviours. A lot had happened in my life since then but Jean was still a good friend to both Lily and me.

'Yes she's a great woman, Lily. A very special person and we're lucky to know her and have her in our lives.'

Lily nodded. 'Aye, we are.'

Rosie was looking forward to Christmas. Jay was two years old and able to understand the meaning of the day. Granny, on the other hand, was dreading it. This was her first Christmas and Hogmanay without Grandad.

Rosie was also over the moon with Mr Peters' gift. She ran her hand over the polished wood and marvelled at how smoothly the wheels turned round. 'He's a lucky wee laddie to be getting this wonderful gift, Ann.'

I had hidden Lily's present at the Overgate and I just knew she would be delighted with it. The box would hold all her pencils and crayons – her own art box with her name on it.

Rosie had asked us up on Christmas morning to see Jay unwrap his four presents. Granny, Lily and I had bought him a picture book with letters of the alphabet printed in it and Dad and Rosie had got him a little tinplate car while Alice gave him a set of building blocks with four different pictures on them. He certainly was a lucky little boy.

His face was a picture when he saw the three presents beside his stocking and I wished we could have captured the moment forever. He sat on the floor making vroom-vroom noises with the car then chugging noises with the train.

Dad sat and looked at him with pride in his eyes and I silently blessed Rosie for giving them a secure loving home.

I couldn't help but remember that awful time when Dad had been married to Margot and how unhappy we had all been. Thankfully, it was a bigamous marriage and Dad had been able to escape her clutches. Now he was happy with the lovely, homely Rosie – he definitely knew a lot more about happiness than I did. Would I ever meet another man? Somehow I doubted it. I just never seemed to mix with any eligible males – and certainly not in Connie's shop where the youngest male customer was about fifty. Still, it was Christmas and I tried to be cheerful – if not for myself then at least for the family.

Then it was time to go to work and I set off down the Hilltown with Dad. Joe was already in the shop but Dad only had time to give him a brief greeting as he didn't want to be late for the warehouse.

'I never see your dad these days, Ann. Is he keeping fine?'

I nodded happily. 'Yes he is, Joe. He's a family man again and that's what he needs.'

'Well, that's another Christmas and we're still at war,' moaned Joe. 'But never mind – it'll soon be over, we hope.'

Connie looked up from her pile of papers. 'And so say all of us.' She gave me a wink. 'Did Jay like his toys?'

'Oh, Connie, you should have seen his wee face. It was a picture.'

She handed over four small parcels wrapped in brown paper. 'Just a wee thing for Lily and Jay plus a wee thing for yourself and Granny.'

I was overcome with her generosity. 'Oh, Connie, what can I say except thank you? You're always so good to us.'

Connie looked modest. 'Well, you're such a good worker and you help me a lot.'

I put the parcels in my bag. 'We're going round to Hattie's

house tonight. She's invited us because this is our first Christmas without Grandad. We'll open the presents then but I'll take Jay's present up to the house when I finish work. Rosie has asked her mother to stay with them today.'

After work, I went back up to the house. Jay was now building his blocks but they kept falling down so he resorted to chewing them.

'No, no, Jay,' said Rosie, taking it from him. 'Don't chew them – you'll have no pictures left.'

I handed over Connie's gift and Rosie and Alice handed it to Jay. 'Here's another present from Santa.'

Jay's chubby little fingers soon made short work of the parcel. Inside was the shiniest red apple I had ever seen. It looked as if Connie had polished it with Mansion furniture polish. There was also a small picture book which Jay opened with delight.

Rosie took the apple. 'I'll cut this up for your dinner, Jay.' She smiled at me. 'Are you all set for Hattie's meal tonight?'

I nodded. 'We've all put our meat coupons towards a steak pie but no doubt Hattie will dress it up beautifully – especially as Graham is going to be there.'

Rosie looked mischievous. 'Will there be a wedding do you think?'

'Well, I think Hattie is hoping for that, Rosie.'

Granny and Lily had already left for home so I set off alone for the Overgate. Lily pounced on her presents with glee while we unwrapped ours very carefully. Granny always saved the paper so we smoothed our wrapping paper out.

Granny got a lovely floral apron while Lily was delighted with a set of colouring pencils which were obviously pre-war and good quality. I got a jar of Ponds cold cream and a jar of vanishing cream – no doubt to make myself attractive.

I actually considered giving Granny the pots of cream in exchange for the apron until I realised what an old misery I was turning into. Then, when Lily opened Mr Peters' present, she burst into tears. I was taken aback but she said the present was so lovely that she cried with joy.

We left her transferring all her pencils and bits and bobs into the wonderful box and I noticed she traced her name with her finger. Thank you, Mr and Mrs Peters I thought, for giving two children such wonderful presents – and I was sure they would treasure them for a long time.

Granny was making a pot of soup for our dinner and the rest would be taken to the Westport later. 'Hattie said we're having our meal at teatime because Graham has had to go to Clydebank on business,' she said.

I stood and looked out the window. The street was abuzz with noise as children played with whatever toy had come their way. Most of these looked home-made but the children were shrieking with delight and it was a pleasure to listen to. Toys, like every-thing in this wartime world, were in short supply and it was a case of making do and mending.

At five o'clock, all dressed in our best frocks, we made our way to the Westport. Hattie's house was a delight. She had put up paper garlands and, although they were a bit frayed in places because they were years old, they made the room cheerful.

A tempting smell emerged from her tiny scullery and the table was lovely with her best white cloth and sparkling china dishes.

There was no sign of Graham.

'Oh, he shouldn't be long now,' she said when Granny asked.

Hattie, who was always so elegant, had surpassed herself that night. She looked incandescent in a blue crêpe-de-chine frock and a floaty blue scarf. She kept touching this scarf and I wondered if it had been a present from Graham.

She had managed to get a bottle of sherry from goodness knows where and a bottle of raspberry cordial for Lily. I went into the tiny scullery to give her a hand.

She turned and looked at me, a glowing expression on her face. 'Can you keep a secret, Ann?'

I didn't know what to say. What did she mean? A secret? I nodded dumbly.

She lowered her voice. 'I think Graham is going to ask me to marry him.'

I was so pleased for her. 'Oh, Hattie, that's wonderful! Congratulations!'

She whispered, 'Don't mention it yet. I'll let you all know tomorrow.'

We were sitting with our sherry, trying to feel cheerful. Granny, Lily and I had all shed a few tears before leaving the Overgate – tears of remembrance for Grandad.

Then Graham appeared and once again I was shocked by his appearance. Hattie, however, didn't seem to notice and he smiled at us all.

'You're just in time, Graham – the soup and steak pie are ready,' said Hattie, looking fondly at him.

We all sat round the elegant table, trying desperately not to spill a drop on the snowy white cloth.

Graham now seemed to have recovered from his journey and he was chatting to Granny. 'Yes, although my office was demolished in the bombing, I still have clients in Clydebank who like me to go and see them personally – you know what some old people are like. It's so difficult to travel but I get the train and then walk to their houses to see them. A lot of the houses on the outskirts weren't hit so they are still habitable.'

At that moment two things hit me with suddenness. If the outskirts of the city were still standing, why had he not looked for an office nearer to his old one? And was I imagining a wariness in his eyes every time he mentioned the city? Oh, God, I hope not, I thought silently.

Hattie was now serving the steak pie and we all laughed when we saw how little meat it held. The entire pie was filled with vegetables.

Graham laughed. 'Let's have a "guess the amount of beef" competition!'

Hattie gazed at him with so much love that I was suddenly afraid. Of what I didn't know and, quite honestly, I didn't want to know.

But the evening went well. Granny put on a brave face for our sakes but I knew she was grieving for Grandad on this first

Christmas alone so I think we all were glad when it was time to go home. Hattie and Graham saw us off and I could see Hattie was also glad we were leaving.

Would he propose tonight? I wondered. I sincerely hoped so but there was a little niggle of doubt in my mind and the worst thing was I couldn't put my finger on what was wrong. Graham had been cheerful all evening but I was sure there was something.

Lily and I had decided to stay at the Overgate and, when we reached the house, the first thing Granny did was put the kettle on. 'One thing Hattie can't make is a cup of tea – no' the way I like to make it.'

Lily laughed. Granny's tea was legendary – it was so strong and black and not at all like the weak amber liquid served up by Hattie. We sat with our cups of tea while Lily went upstairs to her friend's house as she wanted to show her the great pencil box.

When she was gone, Granny asked me, 'What do you think of Graham, Ann?'

It was such an unusual question that I almost dropped my cup. 'Graham?' I said.

She nodded. 'Aye, Graham.'

'I think he's great and just what Hattie needs,' I said truthfully. 'Why do you ask, Granny?'

She shrugged. 'It's just that you were sitting at the table and you looked like you were summing him up – like there was something you couldn't figure out.'

I tried to pass it off. 'Och, Granny, I just think he looks like Arthur Askey and I keep thinking he'll come out with a string of jokes.'

Granny seemed satisfied with my answer and, to be honest, so was I. Was it this discrepancy between his looks and his manner that was confusing me? Then another thought came to mind. Had he asked Hattie to marry him? On that note, I went to bed but I didn't sleep. As usual there were too many thoughts whirling around in my mind – Greg and Granny, Hattie and Graham, even Maddie who had visited us on Christmas Eve.

'That's another year almost over, Ann,' she had said. 'Another year older for Daniel and he still hasn't seen his daddy.'

She sounded down in the dumps and I had tried to cheer her up. 'Joe says the war will be over by this time next year and Danny will be home with you both.'

She shook her head, her blonde curls swinging. 'What does Joe know? He's just guessing.'

'Well, that's all anybody can do, Maddie – just look to the future and hope.'

I think I fell asleep around three o'clock but my dreams were full of whirling images. Greg was walking towards me with his hand out but, before I could reach out and take it, another girl stepped in and they both walked off together, leaving me alone and feeling foolish.

I was glad when the morning came. At least I was back in the normal everyday world full of war talk and shortages and not in some surreal dreamworld with its sad images materialising from the subconscious. No, in this normal world, I could block out the image of Greg and another woman.

Hattie appeared later that day and I saw by her face that the proposal hadn't happened. I opened my mouth to speak but she stopped me.

'Not one word, Ann – I don't want to speak about it again,' she whispered furiously.

I recalled her incandescent look last night and was suddenly saddened. What a world we all lived in – Maddie and Minnie's children growing up without their fathers; me growing older and heading for a life alone when Lily grew up; and then there was Hattie and Graham but no wedding ring in the near future.

Even Joe seemed subdued when he called at the shop. He had been full of the Italian armistice which had been signed in September but this euphoria had seemingly worn off. 'I see Eisenhower's to be the chief bummer in this war,' he said sourly. 'The Americans come in at the last minute and then they take over.'

Connie said crisply, 'Does it matter who's in charge, Joe? As long as this war is over, I don't care who's the chief bummer. The Archangel Gabriel or Lucifer – it doesn't matter a fig.'

Joe was shocked. 'You don't mean that, Connie. Surely it's got to be the good guys that win. We don't want the devil taking over.'

Connie laughed. 'Just kidding, Joe. Let's hope it's Gabriel.'

And so the year ended with long queues at shops and everyone making do and mending and Granny trying hard to keep a cheerful look on her grieving face.

The only two bright spots were Lily's success at Rockwell and the happy family that was Dad, Rosie and Jay. Somehow they made up for all the rotten bits.

II

The papers were calling it D-Day, 6 June 1944. The Allies had landed on the beaches of France and were now poised to overrun Europe. Surely it would only be a matter of a few weeks before the war was finally over?

Joe was almost speechless with joy and, to be honest, Connie and I were also ecstatic with this news.

'Did I not tell you that the end was in sight, Connie?' Joe said, looking smug that his continuous optimism had finally been proved right.

'Aye, you did, Joe, and it now looks as if we're going to win this awful war. Mind you, I think Eisenhower might take all the credit for it.'

Joe's face went a deep puce colour. He said darkly, 'He'd better not. We were fighting this war all on our own and it's only because we held Hitler and his hordes at bay to let the Americans come into the picture – carrying on like a platoon of Errol Flynns and John Waynes.'

'Och, I'm sure the ordinary American soldier is just as frightened of the war as our lads are,' I said.

Joe snorted and muttered something as he left the shop.

But the good news was everywhere. The women standing in the queue at the grocer's shop were full of it. One tall gaunt-looking woman was telling the assistant as she put her rations in her bag, 'Och, aye, it'll be jam and butter and roasts of meat at

Hogmanay this year now that it looks like the war will soon be over.'

The thought of plentiful food again and no more queuing, coupons or rationing cheered us all up. What bliss! I felt so much more optimistic, as was Maddie. She could now envisage a future with Danny and Daniel.

Minnie, however, was less sure. 'Quite honestly, Ann, it's been such a long time since I've seen Peter that I'm worried about our reunion. He's bound to have changed after all these years and what if we don't get on?' She gave me a worried look. 'To tell you the truth, I can't even picture his face. I try hard to visualise him but the harder I try, the more his face becomes vague and I have to look at his photo to remember him. Do you think that's right? Am I the only woman that can't remember what her husband looks like?'

I tried to reassure her. 'You'll be all right, Minnie. You're bound to have these worries after all these years and I don't think you're alone with having these feelings but, once Peter comes home, you and wee Peter will be so glad to see him that your worries will disappear.'

She nodded but didn't look convinced.

Then all this euphoria evaporated when the papers started to report the latest weapon from Germany – the V-1 flying bomb, nicknamed the buzz bomb or the doodlebug. These terrible weapons, which crashed when they ran out of fuel, were being unleashed all over the south of England and London, bringing terror to cities and the countryside alike. Everything that lay under the flight path of these pilot-less planes was at risk of destruction and this corridor was called 'Bomb Alley'.

Joe knew all about them. 'You're safe if you can hear its engine but, when the noise stops, it just crashes down on the streets full of folk or on houses, hospitals and schools. It's terrible and I just hope this doesn't turn the war in favour of the Germans again.'

Connie was distressed, as I was. 'That's barbaric, Joe. Imagine going to school or your work one day and one of these doodle-bugs falls out of the sky. I can well imagine the terror it brings to folk living under its flight path.'

In spite of myself, I couldn't stop shivering.

Joe said, 'Well, it's one blessing of living so far north – the buzz bombs will never reach us.'

I heard myself saying something and I realised it was a little prayer of thanks at this huge blessing.

Then, at the end of June, I got a letter from Greg – actually it was more of a note than a proper letter but its contents were distressing:

> You remember the girl I wrote about last year Ann? Well we plan to get married soon. I wanted to tell you myself and not let you hear it from someone else. I had hoped to hear from you but as you never answered my last two letters I can only hope you are well, as are Lily and Granny and Rosie, Jay and your Dad and also Maddie and Daniel.
> Regards, Greg

Well, that's that, I thought. Greg was now a million miles away from me and soon to marry another woman. I hurriedly sent off an answer – one as terse as his letter had been.

> Congratulations on your forthcoming marriage. Best wishes to you both for the future. Lily and Granny also send their good wishes.
> Ann

Actually the last bit had been a white lie because I hadn't told either Granny or Lily this news and, in fact, I was in two minds whether to tell anyone.

After posting the letter I sat by the window and looked at the river. A scene that always made me feel calm but, on this particular occasion, my mind was in a turmoil. Greg hadn't mentioned a date for his wedding but it had to be soon, I thought. I couldn't imagine him writing to tell me of this event if it was to take place in the far distant future. I reckoned the nuptials would take place within a month or maybe even earlier and I inwardly dreaded living through the next few weeks. It would be on my mind all the time – I just knew it.

Another problem was the looming school holidays and I would have to put on a brave face for Lily's sake. She had been at the secondary school for almost a year and I often wondered where the time went. Days seemed to merge into one another. It was as if we were all holding our breath, waiting for something to happen. Then in July it did. Alice, Rosie's mum, fell down the stairs and fractured her ankle. Granny had sent for the doctor and Alice was now lying on the couch with her ankle in a white stookie plaster. Rosie was spending her days between the Overgate and the Hilltown and Granny and I did what we could to help.

I was in the shop a week later when Rosie rushed in, her face flushed red and her hair uncombed.

We were taken aback but, before I could speak, Connie said, 'What's the matter, Rosie?'

'Ann, can you come up and look at Jay? He's not well and I'm really worried about him.'

Connie nodded to me to go and I followed Rosie up the hill. 'What's the matter with him, Rosie? Has he been sick?'

She was almost crying. 'No, he's lying on the floor and he looks terrible. My neighbour next door is looking after him until I got you.'

By now I was really worried. It didn't sound like Jay. He was normally so full of life and mischief and running around with his wooden train. Thankfully, we soon reached the door and I saw the neighbour kneeling on the floor beside him. She was a small elderly woman with a thin face and sharp dark eyes.

When we entered, she stood up. 'I think your bairn has the measles, Rosie.'

Rosie was upset. 'But I don't see any spots on him, Ina.'

Jay was dressed in a short-sleeved shirt and short trousers. Ina lifted his arm and we saw the telltale spots on the inside of his arm. Ina left and I helped Rosie lift Jay's floppy little body on to her lap while I went to fetch his pyjamas from the bedroom. By now, the red spots were all over his back and he opened his eyes and cried.

'I'll go and get the doctor, Rosie. I'll use Connie's phone.'

I hurried back to the shop and told Connie the news. Thankfully, she had a telephone in her flat and this had proved to be such a lifeline over the years.

Doctor Bryson appeared an hour later and confirmed Ina's diagnosis – it was measles. By now, Jay was in his bed in the room I used to share with Lily. The sun was streaming in through the small window.

The doctor immediately pulled the curtains shut and, because they were blackout curtains, the room was almost plunged into darkness. 'You must keep the light from coming in this room,' he said. 'Measles can sometimes cause complications and the eyes are one thing you must keep protected. Keep him in this dark room until he feels better. Also, if you take him into the kitchen, keep the gas lamp shaded.'

Rosie was beside herself with worry. 'What complications, Doctor?'

He closed his bag with a loud snap. 'Measles is part of growing up, Mrs Neill – a childhood complaint that the majority of children recover from but, now and again, a few children get eye and ear complications from the disease. Also don't let other children in the house as it's highly contagious.'

Rosie was appalled. 'We were at the park this morning, Doctor, and there was lots of children playing on the swings.'

The doctor smiled. 'That can't be helped. It's difficult to protect children from these infectious diseases. Your little boy caught it from someone.' On that note he left.

Rosie sat down beside the little patient who looked so quiet and ill. His beloved toy train lay at the bottom of the bed but he had shown no inclination in playing with it.

'What did the doctor mean by complications, Ann? I hope Jay doesn't get any.'

I had to be optimistic for her sake. 'Och, Jay will be fine, Rosie. He's a healthy laddie and the doctor told you the measles happens to all bairns at some time during their childhood.'

I made Rosie a cup of tea while she pulled the cover around the little prone figure in the bed.

'Honest to God, Ann, worries never come singly, do they? First my mum falling down the stairs and now Jay being ill like this.' She sounded so weary.

'Would you like me to stay the night, Rosie? I can sit up with Jay while you get some sleep. Although Lily has had the measles I think I'll let her stay with Granny. What do you think?'

Rosie looked grateful. 'You don't mind?'

'No, Rosie, I don't mind. I'll have to go to the Overgate and tell Lily to stay with Granny and maybe Connie will give me a couple of days off.'

As it was, Connie was once again decent about me taking time off but I offered to do the early morning shift for her if she was busy.

Back in the house, Jay had become fretful in his bed and Rosie had picked him up and carried him through to the kitchen. He was lying in her arms, almost asleep when I arrived back. The curtains were shut and the room was as dim as the bedroom.

Rosie whispered, 'We'll have to keep the gas lamp turned right down at night and also be very quiet going around the house. The doctor did say that.'

When Jay was finally asleep, Rosie carried him back to his bed. She looked really distressed when she came back. 'He looks very ill, Ann. I hope the complications that the doctor mentioned don't happen to my wee laddie.' Tears were running down her cheeks.

I went over and made her sit down. 'Jay's a big healthy laddie, Rosie. I suppose the doctor mentioned the bad bits because some bairns are maybe not so strong so try not to worry.'

I recalled how worried I had been when Lily took this disease but fortunately she had recovered with no ill effects.

Rosie became flustered. 'Och, I've just remembered I've not got my messages yet.'

I put on my jacket. 'Give me the list and I'll go.'

I was taken by surprise when I emerged into the street. The

sun was warm and bright and I was amazed how quickly I had become used to the gloom in the house.

Rosie had very little left on her meat ration so I used some of mine and bought half a pound of mince at the butcher's shop. I then filled the bag with potatoes and turnips from the fruit shop and bought two loaves from the baker. My heart sank when I saw the large queue at the grocer's. I had no option but to join the end of it and be content to edge slowly forward.

The two women in front of me were discussing the D-Day landings. 'Oh, Eh hope that means the war will be ower soon, Lizzie,' said the first woman who was short and dumpy and dressed in a brown swagger coat with a floral headsquare covering her hair.

Lizzie was a bit taller with a white podgy face and prominent teeth. Her coat was tightly belted and looked as if it could repel a snowstorm. She was also a cynic. 'Och, Eh dinnae think so, Dot. Thae Germans are no a pushover, you ken. The allies are maybe in Europe but they were there in 1940 and look what happened at Dunkirk.'

Dot gasped. 'Oh, Eh hope that disnae happen again – just when it looks like it'll soon be ower.'

Lizzie gave her friend a sharp glance. 'All Eh'm saying is this – the war will last a while langer. You mark my words!'

Thankfully, they reached the counter together and all further talk of war ceased but to say I was depressed was an understatement. Like Dot, I had also assumed the end was in sight. Still, maybe Lizzie was wrong. After all, I hadn't seen a crystal ball in her hand.

When I reached the counter, I managed to get a treat – a bag of broken biscuits. Although they didn't look great, these biscuits tasted just like the perfect ones and the bag also had the advantage of sometimes holding more than the statutory half pound.

Rosie could put them aside for when Jay was feeling better. It would have been great to have found an apple or an orange for him but the fruit shop had only the root vegetables plus some cabbages on display.

Rosie was in the bedroom when I reached the house. Jay was fretful again and he was tossing and turning in a half-awake sleep. The quilt had fallen on to the floor and the sheets were rumpled.

'I'll make the tea, Rosie,' I said, putting the mince in the pan to brown. With all the vegetables added it would make a meal that would last for a couple of days at least.

Rosie stayed in the bedroom and I heard her softly singing some of Jay's favourite nursery rhymes.

Then Dad arrived home and he gave me a quizzical look. 'Ann? How nice to see you . . .' His voice trailed away when Rosie appeared.

'Jay's got the measles, Johnny, and he's really ill,' she said, her voice thick with tears.

Dad rushed through to the bedroom. Jay was still restless and he began to cry when he saw his dad. Dad sat beside him and smoothed his hair. 'Don't cry, wee lad. Daddy's here.' After a few moments Jay fell asleep.

Dad came through to the kitchen. 'When did this happen, Rosie?' he said, sounding puzzled.

'After you left for work this morning. He woke up and I thought he looked pale so I took him to the park to get some fresh air and when we got back he was worse and looked really ill. I went for Ann and the doctor says it's the measles. We have to keep the room dark and quiet.' She sounded tearful again.

'You mind when Lily had the measles, Dad,' I said. 'She was ill for a while but she got over it.'

Dad did remember but he was now facing the same thing with his precious son.

We all had a very restless night. Dad sat with Jay until midnight then Rosie took over till three o'clock. There was hardly any darkness and dawn had already arrived by the time I woke up to take my turn. Jay's bedroom was dim and quiet and I sat alone with my thoughts. I wondered if Rosie would ever open the curtains again, she was so worried about the light.

Then there was Greg. Was he married by now? Or were they

still at the planning stage? Not many marriages in these war-torn days were elaborately planned. It was now a case of a quick wedding and a few snatched days for a honeymoon if you were lucky. No one knew what lay ahead of them in these strange times and I realised Greg was right to try and snatch some happiness but I always thought it would be with me, not someone else.

Dad and Rosie appeared in the morning, looking tired and dark-eyed. They sat with Jay for a while as they drank hot tea. I managed to get Jay to sip some water but he certainly didn't look any better.

Dad was in two minds about going to work but Rosie persuaded him to go. 'Ann's got some time off and she'll stay here with me. We'll both look after Jay.'

Dad gave Rosie a quick peck on the cheek. 'Aye, I know, Rosie. He's in good hands with the two of you.'

While Rosie sat with her son, I tidied up the kitchen. It was then that I noticed Dad's sandwiches for his dinner time break. In his worry over Jay, he had forgotten to take them.

Rosie was upset. 'He'll have nothing to eat, Ann and it's not as if any of his workmates can give him something because most folk just have enough for themselves.' Then Jay began to cry and she hurried back into the room.

'I'll run down to the warehouse with them, Rosie.'

She looked so grateful. 'Oh, that's good of you. I do worry about your dad getting his meals.'

I knew this was true and, like hundreds of houses in the city, theirs was a home where most of the meat went to the man of the house and the wives and children shared out the rest.

I hurried off down the hill and it was good to feel the warm sun on my face. It was another lovely day and I'm sure I would have been happy if it wasn't for Jay's illness.

I quickly popped into the shop. Connie was having a quiet spell and she sat at the counter with a cup of tea and a news-paper. 'Do you want a cup?' she asked.

I shook my head and explained my mission.

'And how's wee Jay?'

'He's still quite ill, Connie – very fretful and restless and he's now covered in spots.'

Connie was sympathetic. 'Aye, the measles is a rotten disease but most bairns catch it and they get over it.'

On that note, I hurried down to see Dad. The streets were busy because of the school holidays and the children were all playing in the sunshine. I wondered if these children had all had the measles – if they had, then they had all recovered from it.

I was turning down the lane at Dock Street to the warehouse when I saw her. Because my mind was filled with thoughts of Jay, the figure of the woman didn't register to begin with. She was walking away from me and was almost at the far end of the lane where it met Yeaman's Shore but I knew her – Margot.

I stood still. I was so shocked for a brief moment that I almost leapt into one of the narrow doorways that lined this lane but she didn't turn round. Her high-heeled shoes delicately clacked against the uneven paving stones and she looked as if she was being careful of the road surface. She was wearing a grey suit. It was very plain and so unlike the clothes I remembered from her days with Dad.

What was she doing back in the town? My mind was whirling with all the possible reasons for her return. She had been charged with bigamy and also theft from the job she had after leaving Dundee and Dad. Now it seemed as if she was free and back to her old mischief.

I was determined to find out the truth from my father and I made my way to the warehouse entrance. One of the workmen called Dad out and he emerged smiling – especially when he saw the piece box.

'How is Jay? Is he feeling any better, Ann?' His face was all innocence. 'Thanks for bringing my sandwiches – with all the worry about Jay I forgot them.'

I opened my mouth to mention Margot but then I decided not to. Anyway, he would probably lie to me about seeing her but he honestly didn't look like a guilty man or a man who had just confronted a ghost from the past – his bigamous marriage to a glamorous woman. So I decided to remain quiet – at least for the moment and until Jay got better.

My mind was in a turmoil as I walked home and, on seeing Rosie's worried face when I opened the door, I was really angry with Dad. I could barely look at him when he came home that night and I elected to stay with Jay while Rosie and Dad had the remains of the shepherd's pie I had made during the afternoon. Thankfully, no one thought this odd and I had my meal later.

During the evening, I listened to the wireless while Dad and Rosie sat with Jay and I could see Dad through the open door of the bedroom. I studied his face as he sat by the side of the bed, trying to read any guilty thoughts that might somehow appear on his face but he looked and acted quite normally. I was really and truly perplexed.

The next morning, Rosie, who was also worried about her mother, asked me if I could pay her a visit, just to set her mind at rest. We knew Granny and Lily were there to help her out but I said I would go to reassure her all was well.

Instead of going straight to the Overgate, I made a detour to the warehouse. If Margot was once again paying a visit, then I wanted to tackle her and ask her what she was playing at. But I was disappointed. The lane held nothing more dangerous than a couple of horse-drawn carts that slowly trundled towards Dock Street and a few old-looking men who appeared briefly from one of the many doors that lined this busy thoroughfare. There was no sign of the femme fatale.

Granny was sitting with Alice at the open window. They were having a late breakfast of tea and toast and enjoying the sunshine.

Alice looked alarmed when I appeared. 'It's not bad news about Jay, is it, Ann?' she said, her face white.

I shook my head. 'No, Alice, he's still not well but he's not any worse.'

I explained my mission and Alice laughed. 'Och, tell Rosie I'm fine apart from my busted ankle. Lily is very good. She goes for the messages for your granny and me.'

Granny nodded. 'That's where she is now – away for the paper and the milk.'

I wanted to speak to Granny on my own but I could see no way of doing this without being rude to Alice. I made up my mind to keep the Margot incident to myself but, as I stood up to leave, Granny said, 'I'll walk with you as far as the end of the close.' She turned to her neighbour. 'You'll be all right till I get back, Alice? Will I fill up your cup before I go?'

Alice laughed. 'Och, I'm not a complete invalid, Nan. I'll be fine.'

Grateful for this chance to share the worry about Margot with Granny, I immediately blurted it out on our way down the stairs.

Like I had been, Granny was shocked. 'Are you sure it was her, Ann? Maybe it was someone else because it can be difficult to make someone out when the sun's in your eyes.'

Now that Granny had planted this seed of doubt I was suddenly unsure of what I had seen. The sun had been in my eyes and maybe it was some other elegant-looking woman walking delicately along the grimy lane. And, looking at things logically, why would Margot come back? Surely not to see Dad? It wasn't as if they had been legally married and Dad had hated her at the end – of that I was sure. Had my eyes played tricks? The sunshine had been bright and I hadn't slept much the night before.

I was grateful to Granny for setting my mind at rest. 'Of course it couldn't have been her. I must have made a mistake thinking that the back view of some well-dressed woman was Margot. What an idiot I've been!'

'Rosie has enough to worry about at the moment,' said Granny. 'Margot coming back to get in touch with your dad would be the last straw for her.'

I shuddered at the thought. On my way back, I almost went via the warehouse again but changed my mind. Granny was right about the mistaken identity and the woman could have been anyone. Yet I could have sworn it was her.

As the week went on, Jay got a little better every day and was now eating small meals and lying on the couch in the kitchen.

At the end of the week, Rosie said, 'Would you like to go home, Ann? I know you've got your job and Lily to look after. You've been a great help but I'm worried about your Granny having Lily during the holidays.'

'What about Jay?'

Rosie, who was looking a lot better, smiled. 'I think he's over the worst now and the doctor was pleased with him yesterday.'

That was true. The doctor had called at Dad's request, just to check all was right and it was. Jay was still a sick little boy but thankfully he was on the mend.

So Lily and I went back to Roseangle and it was heaven. We spent our first night back at the flat having our tea by the window with my favourite view of the river. The sunshine rippled over the surface and it was like diamonds exploding from the water.

Meanwhile, Lily stayed at the Overgate during the day to do her Florence Nightingale routine for Alice. She was quite the little helper, said Granny, so I was able to go back to the shop and get all the news bulletins from Joe. The Allies had liberated Rome and Connie said the war must surely be over soon.

Strangely enough, Joe was a bit dubious. 'Well, Connie, I don't think it'll be a walkover. The German soldiers will be well dug in and able to stop any advances. The Allies have managed to drive them back from the Normandy beaches but it's a long way to Berlin. And another thing – these buzz bombs are getting worse and I hear that women and bairns are being evacuated from the worst places in London and the south coast.'

Connie looked disappointed and, to be honest, so did I. Still, one bit of good news was Jay. He was much better and playing with his train and eating normally which was a big relief to Rosie and Dad.

On the Sunday, Lily and I were at the Overgate when Rosie came to visit her mother. Alice was still hobbling about and, as it was another lovely day, Lily asked if she could take Jay for a walk. Rosie decided to come with us when Granny appeared with a pot of tea, all set for a wee gossip. We set off for Riverside with Lily holding Jay's hand. The Esplanade was busy on this sunny

Sunday with families out for an afternoon walk and it was pleasant to walk in the warm sunshine with the gently lapping river in the background. Jay kept running over to the sea wall but Lily made sure she kept a tight hold of his hand.

Rosie's eyes were shining as she looked at her son. 'You know, Ann, we were really worried about Jay when he had the measles. Some bairns end up blind or deaf after catching it but we've been lucky, thank goodness.'

We were almost at the Tay Bridge and the crowds had thinned out at this end of the Esplanade. Suddenly Jay took off and ran ahead. Without thinking I ran after him, passing Lily and Rosie who had also sprinted after him.

I caught his arm and he laughingly tried to run away again. 'No, Jay,' I said, my voice quite stern.

He stopped when he realised I wasn't playing with him and it was because of his stillness that I noticed the woman sitting on a bench about fifty yards away. She was sitting with a man but I couldn't see his face, merely his legs. They were sitting in deep conversation and I realised with a shock that it was Margot. She was dressed in the same grey suit that she had worn on the day I spotted her in the lane.

I could hear Rosie and Lily's voices behind me and, for a moment, I was immobile with shock. The figures on the bench didn't turn round but I dreaded Rosie seeing them.

Suddenly Jay turned round to face his mother and ran towards her, laughing with his arms stretched out. Rosie caught hold of him and spun him around. It was a moment of unsurpassed joy on their part and total relief on mine. Also this spin meant they were facing the opposite direction from Margot and it seemed an ideal time to head home.

As we walked back, I was puzzled. There was no longer any doubt that Margot was back but who was the mystery man? I knew Dad had gone out earlier – Rosie had said so – but I didn't think the hidden figure had been him.

We all knew she had entered into a bigamous marriage with Dad and had also stolen money from her employer when she had

had the housekeeper's job. Her crimes had landed her in prison but maybe her jail sentence was over and she was now a free woman? But why come back to Dundee? As far as I knew, she had no friends or relations in the town so why make the move back? I hoped and prayed she wouldn't cause any more trouble in our family. I was grateful Rosie and Lily hadn't seen her – that was one blessing.

Afterwards, back at the Overgate, when I was alone with Granny, I told her of this new sighting. She sounded worried. 'So it was Margot you saw the other week, Ann.'

I nodded unhappily.

Granny said hopefully, 'Maybe she's just passing through. And you didn't know who the man was?'

'No, Granny, I only saw his legs. He was leaning back on the bench and Margot had her body turned towards him but I know it was her.' I relived the scene in my mind – the man's legs stretched out but his body hidden by Margot. He must have said something to her that annoyed her because she turned her head away and I saw her profile. Had it been my imagination that she had been angry by his remark? The more I thought of it, the more I became convinced she had been angry.

Then Hattie arrived and we didn't say any more – the fewer people who knew about her homecoming the better. Hattie looked morose. Not a word about the non-event of a proposal at Christmas had ever been mentioned again but I suspected she regretted telling me. Still, her secret was safe with me and maybe Graham would propose this year.

'What's the matter with your face, Hattie?' Granny asked. 'You look like a wet Wednesday.'

Hattie sighed. 'Oh, we're all down in the dumps at the moment – even the Pringles. We all thought the war would be over by now but it seems to be getting worse with these awful buzz bombs that are killing people all over the place. Nobody's safe. Maddie and I were counting the days till Danny's return but now she thinks she'll never see him again.'

Granny tried to be cheerful. 'Well, we'll just have to hope that it'll be over soon, one way or another.' Then, changing the subject, she asked, 'How's Graham?'

Hattie gave me a quick look but I didn't catch her eye. 'Oh, he's away back to Clydebank on business but he hopes to be back tonight.' Although the words sounded light and carefree, I got the impression she wasn't happy.

Bella then appeared. Hobbling forward, she threw herself into the best chair by the fireside. 'My feet are killing me,' she complained loudly.

Hattie gave her a sour look but Bella was too busy inspecting the insides of her shoes. 'I don't think shoes are as well made as before the war, Nan. These shoes say a size five but they're fair nipping my feet. I've got a big blister on my heel and it's fair thumping with the pain.'

Satisfied that we had all got the message on the feet front, Bella now turned her attention to Hattie. 'I see you're still single, Hattie. I would have thought your fancy man would have asked you to marry him before this.'

Hattie glared at her but Granny stepped in. 'Well, maybe Hattie and Graham are planning something Bella but they're keeping it quiet from nosy parkers like us.'

Hattie gave Granny a grateful look and said, 'It's time I was away back home. I've got Graham's tea to make. He'll be back between six and seven o'clock.' On that crisp note, she swept out.

Bella scowled at her retreating back. 'Damn strange set-up she's got with her fancy man. He's getting all the comforts of home without the responsibilities.' She gave me a sharp glance. 'What do you say, Ann? Do you think it's a strange set-up? Do you think he's got a guilty secret?'

As a matter of fact, I was worried about Hattie's relationship with Graham and the way it seemed to be heading but there was no way I would voice my suspicions to Bella. An answer like that would be food and drink to her and, within a couple of hours, it would be common knowledge to people within a mile radius of the Overgate. Anyway, I was too worried about seeing Margot and the unknown man. From my vantage point on the Esplanade,

I had only caught a glimpse of his trousers and well-polished russet brown shoes. Although Dad owned a pair of brown shoes, he never cleaned them to this russet brightness. The only other pair of shoes I had seen like this belonged to Graham.

I moaned softly and Bella gave me another sharp look. 'What's the matter with you?' This was uttered in the manner of making sure I didn't have anything wrong with me. At least not in the company of the queen of hypochondriacs – namely Bella.

Granny looked concerned. 'Oh, it's just something I forgot to do.' I hurried to the door. 'I'll see you later, Granny. Cheerio, Bella.'

As I was closing the door, Bella's voice boomed out, 'She's becoming another strange lassie, Nan. It's because her fella has also not proposed and we ask ourselves why.'

Granny was annoyed at her. 'That's great, Bella, coming from the likes of you that's never been married herself.'

Lily had gone home with Jay and Rosie so I hurried up the Hilltown to pick her up. My mind was whirling around with worry. Then I wondered if I was getting into a panic over nothing. Thousands of men in the town probably owned highly polished russet brown shoes so why did I jump to the conclusion that this particular pair belonged to Graham. I stopped and gazed in the Easifit shoe shop window. It held a display of men's shoes in shades of black and brown and I suddenly felt an attack of the giggles coming on.

One thing was clear – this fertile imagination of mine was working overtime just now. What did it matter if Margot was back in town and what did it matter if she sat on a bench with a man in brown shoes? She was obviously a free woman now and as long as she didn't bother us, then her presence was of no concern to us.

I had reached the close when I realised the stupidity of my reasoning. What if Rosie should run into her? Or Lily? And even worse, what if she tried to charm herself back into Dad's life. Would he let her? And if the brown shoes did belong to Graham then that was Hattie's problem. Much as I sympathised with her, this was something she had to sort out herself.

12

Kathleen and Kitty came to visit us at Roseangle one Sunday at the end of October. I hadn't seen Kathleen in ages and I was worried by her appearance. Her normally pale face was now white and drawn-looking and she had dark circles under her eyes. I thought she may have been crying recently but maybe I was wrong.

Before I could say anything to her, she nodded towards Lily and Kitty. She obviously didn't want to speak in front of them. I went to the sideboard drawer and took out my ration book. 'Lily, there's some sweetie coupons left. Take Kitty down to the shop and get something for both of you. That's if they have any sweeties left.'

Lily glanced at Kathleen. She was growing up so fast and I guessed she understood that we were wanting her out of the house but she took Kitty's hand and opened the door.

'Mind and hold tight of Kitty's hand and don't let her near the road,' I called after them.

I made some tea and Kathleen sat by the window. 'This is a lovely flat, Ann, and you get such a good view of the river.'

'You've got a nice place as well, Kathleen. Your flat above the studio is marvellous and it's also got a river view.'

She suddenly burst into tears. 'I'm not living there now, Ann.'

I was shocked. Did that mean she was no longer working at the studio?

She wiped her face and tried to smile. 'Sorry about that – crying like a big bairn.'

I was almost frightened to ask, 'Have you given up your job?'

She shook her head. 'No, I'm still there but I've given up the flat. I'm back living with Mum and Dad at Lochee and Kitty goes to the school there.'

'Did Mr Portland need the flat for someone else?'

'Oh, no! It was all the fault of Mick and Maggie Malloy. They kept coming to the flat at night and making a big scene. I could put up with that in the evening in the privacy of the house but Mick then kept turning up during the day and he had a big row with Mr Portland.'

I could visualise the scene and felt so sorry for her. 'That's terrible, Kathleen. What did your boss say?'

'Oh, he was very good about it – said it wasn't my fault – but I decided I had to give up my independence and go back to Lochee. That way I can still work at the studio but for how long I don't know.'

'What does your mum think about this?'

She shrugged her shoulders. 'She sympathises but says it's maybe for the better. I'm still a married woman with a husband in a prisoner of war camp – Sammy the hero.'

I didn't know what to say to her.

She turned her head and gazed at the river. 'I just wish Danny was back. He would stick up for me.'

Danny. There wasn't a day went by but I thought of him and I echoed Kathleen's sentiment.

'The worst thing is Maggie's looking for a house for Sammy and us for when the war's over. She keeps running to the factor and asking him if there are any empty houses nearby for Kitty and me and her precious son, Sammy. He was bad enough before the war but what will he be like now after five years of living in a camp?'

I knew it was none of my business but I knew Danny, should he be here, would have said the same thing. 'You have to think of yourself and Kitty. Don't give in to Maggie or her man. Just tell them straight that you're not going back to him.'

'That's what I tell Mum but she says women don't get divorces. We have to put up with marriage for better or worse – no matter what.' Kathleen was on the verge of tears again.

I was shocked by this. I had always imagined Kathleen's mum, Kit, to be a feisty, enlightened woman but now she seemed to be looking backwards. Then I realised this was her way of life as it was for countless women now and in days gone by. This culture had been accepted without question – not only by Kit and Maggie but by all their little community.

'Well, Kathleen, what are you going to do?'

She said she didn't know. 'Maggie says once Sammy's home and we're back living together then everything will turn out fine. I can give up my job and Sammy will look after us.'

I had this dismal mental picture of Sammy and his little family. It wasn't a pleasant thought and I could see that Kathleen was thinking the same.

Suddenly she said, 'Let's change the subject to something cheerier. If I tell you something, Ann, will you promise to keep it a secret?'

I wasn't very sure but I nodded.

'Do you mind I told you about Chris, Mr Portland's son? Well, he took me out to a very grand evening in Edinburgh last week. He's got this wee car and he drove us there. Petrol is rationed but he keeps some back for when he's home. Oh, you should have seen the grand house, Ann, and the women were all dressed in super frocks and jewels and I felt such a frump. But Chris said I was the most beautiful woman there. I think he's wonderful and I'm sure he likes me.'

A worry festered away in my brain. 'You will be careful, Kathleen, won't you?'

She tossed her lovely red hair. 'I hope you don't think I'm a toff, you know, liking grand houses and bonny frocks but that's got nothing to do with it. I could live in a shed with Chris but could never live in a palace with Sammy. That's the truth.' By now, her eyes were sparkling and she seemed so unlike the woman who had entered the house a mere few moments ago.

'Is Chris a photographer like his father?' I asked.

'Aye, he is but he's a war photographer. He's with Pathé News and he captured the D-Day landings on film. After this short break at home, he's going back to the front line to photograph the action as the Allies make for Berlin.'

It all sounded so adventurous and I sincerely hoped that Kathleen would grasp any happiness with both hands. But I also knew it was difficult to go against a way of life that had been in operation for generations. No doubt countless women like Kathleen had tried to escape the clutches of childbearing and drudgery, only to be sucked under by tradition.

We heard Lily and Kitty at the door. They had managed to get some sweets but not what Lily had wanted. 'The shop only had Spangles, Ann, but we bought them.'

It wasn't as if she disliked these fruit-flavoured sweets – it was just that there was no choice in some of the small shops. Oh, the joys of wartime shortages!

After another cup of tea, Kathleen got up to leave. As we stood on the landing, she said, 'Come and see us at Lochee if you can manage.'

I promised we would go on the following Sunday. After she left, I couldn't get over all the problems that lay in Kathleen's path and I hoped that she would surmount them all.

On the following Sunday, Granny said she would come with us to Lochee. 'I haven't seen Kit and her family for ages,' she said. So the three of us set off to catch the tramcar.

Atholl Street was as busy as ever on this grey and misty, autumn Sunday afternoon. Although Kit was expecting Lily and me, she was delighted to see Granny.

'What a big surprise, Nan! Ma is coming over later and she'll be pleased to see you. I often think she doesn't get the same good blethers these days and she misses it. Everybody is out at work and it's not like the bad old days when the whole street was jobless.'

Kathleen appeared. She had been out for a walk with Kitty and she was out of breath when they came in.

'Where did you go, Kitty?' asked Kit.

Kitty said nothing but looked at her mother. Kathleen said lazily, 'We went to Balgay Park and Kitty played on the swings.'

Kitty nodded happily. 'I had a great time, Granny.'

Kit smiled at her. 'Well, you go with Lily and get a drink of lemonade and cool down – your face is all red.'

Kathleen gave me a direct look and my heart sank. She had obviously been up to something and I dreaded hearing what it was. Fortunately, Ma Ryan arrived at that moment and she went over to sit beside Granny, a look of delight on her normally impassive face.

'Do you fancy a wee stroll, Ann?' Kathleen asked, an innocent look in her eyes. 'You don't mind if we go for a walk, do you, Mum?'

Kit shook her head and joined in with the conversation with Granny and Ma.

Outside in the street, Kathleen took my arm and fairly propelled me along the street, casting glances behind her as we went.

By now I was really alarmed. 'What's the matter Kathleen? What's happened?'

'I'll tell you if you'll keep it a secret,' she whispered.

'Oh, Kathleen, it all depends what it is,' I said – I didn't want to make a promise I maybe couldn't keep.

'Och, it doesn't matter about secrecy. I'm so happy I don't care who knows it. Chris is leaving after his leave and he met me in the park. We just chatted while Kitty played on the swings but he wants to take me for a drive in the country tomorrow. We can't go far because of the petrol shortage but he thought we could have a meal somewhere. He keeps the car in his dad's garage and gets the train back. That way he keeps some petrol in it. He says it's for taking me out. It's so romantic.'

My worries for her well-being returned with a vengeance. I tried to choose my words carefully and tried to think what Danny would say to her if he was here instead of me. 'Does Chris knows you're still married?'

She nodded. 'Obviously his dad told him about my situation

when he gave me the job but I told him about Sammy right from the beginning and I also told him I'm not going back to him when this war's over.'

'What if you've no choice Kathleen? What does the Catholic Church say about divorce?'

She gave me a direct look again. 'I don't care. I only know I'm never going back to Sammy. And I tell you something else, Ann. In one way, I wish this war was over for Danny's sake but, in another way, I just wish Sammy would stay out of my life forever.'

I was shocked but tried not to show it. 'Why on earth did you marry him, Kathleen, if you feel like this?'

'I didn't want Kitty growing up without a father and I didn't feel like this at the time. I really thought I loved him and that we would be happy for the rest of our days. I'll tell you something, Ann. Do you mind before he went away to the war and he gave me that beating?'

I nodded, remembering all too clearly the day it happened – the day Danny and I found her and the baby in the little dark one-roomed house that had been their home. I recalled also how furious Danny had been and how, if he had found Sammy, he would have tackled him and given him some of his own medicine.

'Well, that wasn't the first time he'd hit me. He used to punch me every day but he made sure he didn't hit my face. He told me nobody would believe me. Then, to make matters worse, on the day you and Danny found me, he made it crystal clear that this was going to be my life from now on.' She turned her anguished face to me. 'That's what's waiting for me when he comes back. That and the fact he's planning a half dozen kids to knock the spirit out of me – his words, not mine.'

I put my arms around her. 'Oh, Kathleen, that's terrible. I've always thought you should make a new life for yourself and now you've just reinforced that idea in my mind. And I think Danny would say the same thing.'

She gave me a grateful look and we walked back towards the house. But, before reaching the door, I took her arm and said, 'Just be careful, Kathleen. Please.'

She nodded. 'I'll try to be but I'm so happy that I don't care one way or the other. I'm enjoying my life.'

As answers went, it didn't do a lot to calm my fears for her safety but I knew there was nothing I could do or say that hadn't been said or done before.

Granny was putting her coat on when we arrived back and Kit was chatting to her. Ma Ryan was sitting alone by the fireplace and I went over to say goodbye to her.

Her dark eyes seemed to bore into mine. 'Mind what I told you, Ann. Watch your step. You're in great danger.'

I was speechless. Surely my near accident on tramcar stairs was what her warning was about but it now seemed as if I still had to watch my step.

She took my hand. 'Mind, now, mind what I said.'

There was one thing I couldn't understand. There was Kathleen with all her problems and Ma was busy warning me.

'What about Kathleen, Ma? I'm worried about her. Will she be all right?'

She seemed to give this some thought but, when she spoke, her eyes didn't meet mine. 'Ah, Kathleen . . .'

I waited for the rest of the statement but that was all she said. Her face resumed the inscrutable look that I recognised and I realised I would get nothing more from her.

Granny was full of the gossip as we made our way back home. 'That was a great afternoon, Ann. I fair enjoyed myself with Ma and Kit. Did you enjoy yourself Lily?'

Lily nodded. 'I just wish I could hear all the grown-up talk though. I aye seem to end up with Kitty.' She pulled herself up to her full five foot two inches. 'I am grown-up now, Ann.'

With a shock, I realised she was.

My mind was full of thoughts of Kathleen and Chris. I knew they would only have a short time together while Kitty was at school but that didn't settle my mind.

Still, I had my own problems with working, shopping and doing Granny's chores. I also did her shopping and washing which took up quite a lot of time but most women had this problem. The queues at the shops seemed to grow longer with each passing day and we all lived in hope of the war ending soon.

Then, in December, Joe arrived at the shop full of woe. 'I see the Jerries have surrounded the Allies at Ardennes. Their armies have taken the same route that they used in 1940 and I only hope they don't cause another Dunkirk.'

Connie and I were worried. She said, 'Surely the war will be over soon, Joe. I mean the Allies are in Europe and the German Army will be defeated.'

Joe seemed unsure. 'Well, Connie, we were in Europe in 1940 and look what happened there. The Jerries are sly buggers. They have this pincer movement and they come round and behind the Allies' front lines.'

I suddenly thought of Kathleen. Would this setback please her? The fact that Sammy would still be a prisoner of war? No, I thought, it wouldn't please her – not with Danny being in the same boat.

Then, one day, she appeared out of the blue at the shop.

Connie hadn't seen a lot of her but she was also enchanted by her loveliness. 'That's a braw-looking lassie,' she said later.

Kathleen hoped I was nearly finished at work and I was – just finishing off a few small last-minute jobs. Afterwards, we walked down the Hilltown, her arm through mine.

'Oh, I've got to tell someone about my day out with Chris. I'm almost bursting at the memory of it!' she said, her red hair streaming out behind her as she turned her head and her eyes glowing.

It seemed I was to be her confidante. 'How did it go Kathleen?'

She squeezed my arm. 'Oh, Ann, it was wonderful. We went for a wee run up the coast road – not too far because of the petrol. Because we weren't sure about getting a meal somewhere, we took a picnic and ate it in a lovely sandy cove overlooking the sea. It was so romantic.'

I was pleased for her and she seemed to glow with health and beauty. She was like the sun beside my pale and dismal moon.

'Is he away back to London?'

'Aye, he is. He's got a small flat on the outskirts of London but he was saying that the city has been terribly damaged by bombs dropped during the Blitz and also the buzz bombs. And it's not just London but lots of other cities as well. He was saying we're lucky in Dundee not to have been bombed as well.'

'Is he employed by Pathé News, Kathleen?'

She shook her head. 'He works for them but he's a freelance photographer. He takes loads of pictures and sells them. And he's had photos in the *Picture Post*. He was saying, when the war is over, he's going to take a picture of me for the *Picture Post*.'

I was impressed. The *Picture Post* was one of my favourite papers and I had no doubt in my mind that Kathleen would make a stunning model. I told her so.

'Of course,' she said wistfully, 'it'll be after this war is over – whenever that'll be.'

I left her at the tram stop. 'I must get back and pick Kitty up from the school. I'm just working part-time for Mr Portland at the moment but hopefully I'll get back to full-time soon – when the war is over.'

But, by Christmas, the Battle of the Bulge, as it was called, was still raging on and we all wondered what lay in store. The optimism that had sprung up on D-Day was still evident but it was slowly eroding as time went by. With the never-ending queues for food and other essential things, the euphoric mood was beginning to evaporate like an ice field on the equator.

Meanwhile, Rosie, Maddie and Minnie all tried to put on a brave face for their children's sake at Christmas.

Joy, who was at the High School, invited Lily over during the school holidays. They sat for ages discussing their futures. 'We can go to art school in Glasgow, Lily, and be famous artists,' said Joy matter-of-factly.

Lily, her eyes bright with enthusiasm, agreed. 'Oh, aye. We'll be the best artists that there's been for years and years.'

One dark spot during this time was Hattie's relationship with Graham. I couldn't help but compare this Christmas to the one last year – the one when Hattie, her face flushed and with a bright-eyed look, had confided in me her hopes of a proposal from Graham. What had gone wrong? I wondered. But Hattie had made it quite clear that nothing else was to be said on the subject. Then it turned out that Graham was to be absent this Christmas.

I had debated about telling the family about Greg, wondering when the right moment would come. Perhaps it was cowardice on my part that I hadn't mentioned it earlier but, before Christmas, I decided to come clean on my engagement. Granny and Lily were together when I spoke. 'I have to tell you both that Greg and I are no longer engaged. In fact, he'll be married to someone else by now but he didn't mention the date so I'm not sure what the situation is.'

Granny was shocked and Lily burst into tears.

'It's all right, Lily – these things happen when couples are apart and we're all living in strange times,' I said as I tried to comfort her, adding that I hoped we all had a merry Christmas.

I was kicking myself for choosing this moment to be the bad news messenger but I didn't want another year to end with this hanging over me. It was just too difficult, what with the family asking me all the news from him and with me having to fob them off with vague platitudes.

Hattie spent Christmas Day with Granny, Lily and me, only leaving for home when Bella arrived in the evening. I didn't tell Hattie my news as she seemed preoccupied with her own personal cloud and I also said nothing to Bella – I didn't feel strong enough to share my abandonment with half the community. No doubt the news would leak out as all bad news eventually did but, until then, I wanted to keep it within the close family and Connie and Maddie. I planned to tell Connie the following day and Maddie the next time I saw her.

Granny had asked after Graham but Hattie had been terse, merely saying that he had business in Clydebank. They were, however, going to a dance at the Queen's Hotel on Boxing Day, she said, fingering the gold brooch which had been a gift from him.

Why, I asked myself, was she so lacklustre? Her hand kept straying to her lovely brooch but I felt her mind wasn't on this costly gift but somewhere far away. Still, if she didn't want to confide in me, there was nothing I could do for her – except to say a silent prayer that all would turn out well for them both.

What a worrying world it was where fears for the future mingled with all the domestic problems. I thought about Kathleen and Kitty and then there was Maddie, Minnie and their boys plus Dad, Rosie and Jay and Granny and Lily. What would become of us all? I tried so hard to shift this jumble of emotions from my mind but it wasn't easy. Then I remembered the sightings of Margot. Thankfully I hadn't seen her again so maybe she had moved away again. I hoped for Rosie's sake that she had.

For some reason Connie wasn't taken aback by my announcement. This didn't surprise me as she seemed to read everyone like a book. 'I knew there was something up,' she said. 'But I'm still so very sorry about it all. You didn't deserve this, Ann.'

When I asked her how she guessed, she said, 'You stopped speaking about him. Before it was all "Greg said this" or "Greg did that", then suddenly his name never passed your lips.'

How wise she was, I thought. Not much escaped her sharp eyes or keen ears.

Then, just before Hogmanay, Sylvia, Edith and Amy appeared in the shop for their cigarettes and sweeties. Edith got her sweeties but the other two girls were disappointed because Connie had no cigarettes in the shop.

Sylvia and Amy were desperate. 'Will there be another shop on the Hilltown with cigarettes, Connie?' Amy asked.

Connie shook her head. 'I don't think so, Amy, but you can aye ask.'

They turned to me. 'We're going to the Locarno Dance Hall tonight, Ann. Do you want to join us?'

Before I could say no, Connie butted in. 'What a great idea, Ann! That'll be a night out for you. I used to love the dancing in my young days.'

Sylvia said, 'That's fine then, Ann. We'll pick you up at the

Overgate, at your granny's house, and we'll head for a bit of fun in this awful cigarette-less world.'

All day, I thought of some excuse I could give them when they arrived but Granny didn't help by echoing Connie's sentiment. 'It'll do you a world of good to have a night out. I'll look after Lily for you.'

So I had no choice but to get dressed in my best frock which was a flower-sprigged cotton summer creation. I was a bit cold for wearing this thin dress but I planned to wear my thick tweed coat and woollen scarf.

The girls arrived a few minutes later and they chatted to Granny. Amy said, 'We sometimes go the Progie on a Saturday night but there's no dancing there this week.'

I was thankful for small mercies. The Progress Hall on the Hilltown was actually a church hall I thought but dances were held there on a Saturday. I had never been inside so perhaps I shouldn't act like some critic but, on one occasion, when I had been passing, a very drunk man, with a cap on his head and a *Sporting Post* newspaper in his back pocket, had staggered out in front of me. He tried to dance with me and, when I backed away, he proceeded to dance with himself, prancing up and down the pavement and swaying in between people who were out for a walk or heading to the chip shop. It had been very funny at the time but I didn't relish the thought of being cooped up with a crowd of like-minded dancers.

Sylvia was speaking. 'But we like any dance hall, Mrs Neill. They're usually aye packed with eligible men and there's a lot of Polish men about.'

I could see Granny was regretting her earlier enthusiasm for my night out but I had no option but to make my way towards Lochee Road and the Locarno Dance Hall. I tried hard to match Sylvia and Amy's high spirits but I felt I had more in common with Edith who was always the quiet one in this trio.

Amy laughed as we headed along the road. 'We'll find you a click tonight, Ann. The place will be heaving with servicemen. You'll be able to take your pick.'

Wonderful, I thought sourly, but I smiled at her. After all, they were only trying to make me enjoy my life more. No doubt they had heard about Greg and I breaking up – not that it was common knowledge but young girls like themselves usually heard all the news through the local gossips.

We soon reached the Locarno and I was a bit disappointed by its outward appearance. There was nothing flashy about it but then we still had the blackout restrictions which meant all buildings looked the same in the dark. Inside, however, was another matter. The interior was full of people, the noise was deafening and there was the acrid smell of cigarette smoke.

Amy laughed. 'I see some folk have managed to get cigarettes, Sylvia. Maybe we can cadge some from the soldiers.'

She saw the look on my face and laughed. 'Just kidding, Ann.'

Edith whispered in my ear, 'That's what she says.'

We deposited our coats and scarves in the cloakroom. Amy took out her small powder compact and put a thick layer of creamy-coloured powder all over her face. She had good skin and I felt this addition was unnecessary but it made her feel grown up, she said. Pleased with this adornment she then dabbed some Californian Poppy scent behind her ears and handed the small bottle to Sylvia who did the same.

They then handed the bottle to me. 'Try some of this, Ann. It's supposed to make you irresistible to men. They seemingly love its smell.'

Amy laughed loudly and inspected her face in the mirror. She took out a small case of black mascara and spat on the strip of black. She then began to lather it on to her lashes. I dreaded her giving me some of this but she snapped it shut and placed it in her handbag. I could only think she was almost out of her mascara and wanted to keep it for as long as possible.

With both girls now pleased with their faces, we emerged into the dance hall. The cigarette smoke was really thick in there and blue spirals of smoke danced upwards towards the ceiling, looking slightly fluorescent in the coloured lights.

The band was loud and the floor was crowded. Sylvia gripped

my arm and Edith followed. 'Come on, let's stand over there.' She indicated a part of the floor that seemed to hold a hundred dancers.

I felt myself being propelled by the throng of humanity. There was a strange mixture of smells – talcum powder, cheap scent and carbolic soap all vying to be chief aroma.

I tried to get into the spirit of the evening but there were just too many people in this small arena and the smoke was making my eyes sting. I knew I had to escape but how? Then I saw two ruddy-cheeked men coming towards us and Sylvia and Amy gave a squeal of delight.

'It's Vlad and Slav,' said Amy, turning towards me. 'That's not their names but that's what we call them. They're Polish and such a good laugh.'

Looking at their round, ruddy-cheeked faces, I didn't doubt it but a good laugh was a million miles away from my thoughts and I wondered if I would ever laugh again.

As the two girls went off to dance with their Polish friends, I squeezed through the crowd and went to the cloakroom. As I retrieved my coat, the attendant gave me a puzzled look but said nothing.

Outside, I took in large breaths of cold fresh air. Suddenly I was aware that someone was standing beside me and a feeling of panic gripped me. I felt my throat constrict like someone had grabbed me in a throttle-hold. Was it one of the ruddy-faced men? To my relief, I saw it was Edith. She was wearing her coat as well.

'Oh, Edith, there's no need to come outside with me. It was just the smoke – I couldn't stand it.'

She tucked her arm in mine. 'It's not just that, Ann, is it? You still miss your friend, Greg.'

I thought how perceptive she was. 'Yes, I do, Edith. It's not that I've anything against the dance hall and maybe, in a few months when I get over him, I'll enjoy coming here – but not tonight.'

She laughed. 'Och, I don't think so, Ann. I've never enjoyed

166

coming here – ever! It's just that Sylvia and Amy enjoy it so much that I come along with them. But they're both sociable girls and they love to laugh and dance and sing and, to be honest, I envy them but it's not me. I don't think I'll be coming back either and I've told them. They did say they understood but Vlad and Slav hurried them on to the dance floor again so they've probably forgotten all about us . . .' She smiled. 'With a bit of luck!'

We walked back in companionable silence until we reached the tram stop in Tay Street. I stood with Edith until we saw the tram coming around the curve from Westport.

'We'll be a couple of old maids at this rate, Edith, if we don't go out and enjoy ourselves. Granny always said no one ever got a man by sitting at the fire knitting.'

'At least we're true to our natures, Ann – you and me. And what's wrong with knitting? I love to knit.'

She waved from the misted-up windows and I slowly retraced my steps to the Overgate. Then I thought of all the explanations I would have to give Granny and Lily if I went home at this time so I set off for Roseangle.

It was a crisp, clear night but very cold. The stars were so bright that I felt I could reach up and touch them. It wasn't as dark as I first thought. Some subdued lights were now being allowed on the tramcars, now that the threat of invasion was over. The entrance to the close, however, was in total darkness. I was halfway up the stairs when a dark shape loomed down on me.

Without thinking, I gave a muffled scream and a deep masculine voice said, 'Oh, I'm sorry, I didn't mean to frighten to you, lass. I'm looking for Wullie Burnett's house. Do you know where he lives?'

My voice came out in a terrified squeak which made me feel ashamed of myself. 'No, I don't know him – sorry.'

'I'll try the next close and sorry again for frightening you.' Then he was gone.

I reached the flat but didn't pull the curtains. The river glinted like a silver ribbon and the silence was therapeutic after the clamorous noises of the Locarno and the terror of the last few moments.

This was Ma Ryan's fault, I thought grimly. Her warning of danger had made me terrified of every little fright – her insistence to watch my step. Then I began to worry again. Where had the man come from? Had he shone a torch on all the nameplates in order to search for his friend? Or was his mission a criminal one? A burglar or worse?

I hurried to the door but the lock was fully in place. I glanced out of the window and saw him walking up the street with another man. I breathed a sigh of relief. He had found Wullie Burnett by the look of it.

My heart stopped thudding and I sat looking at the river, my mind reviewing the night's events. Why was I such a strange and lonely person? Most women would have given a lot to have a good night out with their friends. For months, I had tried so hard to put all thoughts of Greg from my mind but, on this beautiful cold night, I couldn't stop thinking about him. He was probably married by now and good luck to him, I thought bitterly.

Memories from past years invaded my mind and I recalled how happy I had been. But had he been happy? Obviously not. Although, I knew now that it couldn't have been easy for him to try and inhabit my crowded and worried world. A wave of self-pity engulfed me and I burst into a flood of tears, laying my head in my arms and completely shutting out the view of the river.

Much later, I made my way back to the Overgate. I had bathed my red puffy eyes in cold water before leaving the flat but although Granny noticed them she didn't say a word.

'Oh, my eyes are all red from the smoke at the dancing, Granny, but I really enjoyed myself. What a good laugh we all had.'

Granny smiled and said nothing but I knew she didn't believe me. She wasn't daft.

13

The war was almost over. Joe kept us informed every day, much to Connie's amusement. 'That man thinks we never read the newspapers,' she said one day.

'Aye, the turning point was beating the Jerries at the Battle of the Bulge. Now the Allies have crossed the Rhine and are almost in Berlin. But the Russians are hoping to take the city before the Allies.'

This was wonderful news and we all rejoiced in it. Peace was at last being predicted for the not-so-distant future. Maddie was almost beside herself with joy at the thought of Danny's homecoming and we were all looking forward to welcoming him home again after all these years.

One worry lay on my horizon – the house at Roseangle. Now that the war was almost over, I knew Maddie and Danny would resume their life in their own home which meant Lily and I had some serious house-hunting to do. It wasn't an easy task as there seemed to be no empty houses in the city. Granny said we could stay with her and, although I had mentally rejected this offer, it now looked as if we would have to move to the Overgate.

Even Connie, who was often a great source of help on lots of things, couldn't help on this big issue. 'It must be because of all the folk that have been bombed out of their houses in other parts of the country, Ann. I heard it could be as much as a million homes that have been damaged or destroyed and maybe they've all moved to places with little damage.'

This was disheartening news and it didn't bode well for the future – not only for us but for all the poor people with no homes left. In fact, the carnage all over Europe was devastating and it seemed as if the entire world had been destroyed. Pictures of people with young children pouring out of bombed cities made my heart ache and I had to stop looking at them.

Then Mussolini along with his mistress, Clara Petacci, was shot by the Italian partisans. Both were hung up by their heels in front of a jeering crowd.

Joe was beside himself with this story. 'I see Mussolini has been shot. It's the best thing that could have happened to him, the heel-clicking bugger.' He stopped and gazed at Connie. 'Mind you, they didn't have to kill his mistress.'

To be honest, we were all becoming inured to all the horrors unfolding before our eyes but, a few days later, Joe almost fell into the shop.

'Hitler's shot himself in his bunker in Berlin.' Joe seemed to know all about it – almost as if he had been a fly on that same bunker wall. 'Aye, Eva Braun took poison but Hitler shot himself. Good riddance to him I say.' He stopped to light his cigarette. 'And all the poor wee Goebbels kids were also poisoned by their parents. What a dreadful thing to do.'

Joe had tears in his eyes when he said this and Connie and I were almost crying as well. What other horrors lay ahead of the Allied world? I wondered.

Then it was all over – at least in Europe. The Far Eastern forces were still fighting the Japanese forces but, here at home, we had peace at last.

Joe, as usual, was still talking about the carnage. 'Did you see yon awfy pictures of the concentration camps, Connie? Auschwitz and Belsen?' He shook his head in dismay. 'How anybody could do that to another human being is beyond me. The papers are saying that millions of Jews and other folk have been killed in the gas chambers.' He wiped his eyes and looked so sad. 'I saw some awfy sights in the trenches during the Great War but this is something far more evil.'

Connie and I agreed with him. We had both been shocked, as had countless others, by the revelations about the concentration camps and, in fact, there were quite a lot of nights when I couldn't go to sleep with the images of these atrocities still fresh in my mind.

Lily and I spent the first week of peacetime unwrapping Maddie and Danny's wedding gifts from their dark imprisonment in the large trunk which had resided in the lobby cupboard for almost five years. We then spent an energetic couple of hours cleaning the flat and it now shone with all the hard work and furniture polish. We then placed all the ornaments in their original positions and put all the crystal glasses and expensive figurines back into the display cabinet.

I remade the bed with Maddie's own bedclothes, gathered all the bed linen and towels and stuffed them into the wicker basket, all ready for the wash-house in the morning. Our small pram lay at the end of the close, in preparation for its job of holding the basket on its way to the wash-house.

For the last time, Lily and I gazed out the window. The river was bathed in sunshine. Lights glinted from its dappled surface and I knew it was a scene I would never forget, no matter where I lived – now or in the future.

Lily was quiet as she stood beside me and when I looked at her I was dismayed to see her crying. I put an arm around her shoulder and realised with a pang that she was almost as tall as myself. 'We'll come back and see Maddie and Danny. We can aye look at the river then.'

She wiped her face. 'But it'll not be the same, Ann. It'll not be like when we were living here and had the river all to ourselves. It'll not be the same.'

I knew what she meant but it wasn't our house. Maddie had been very generous in letting us stay so long, especially as it was rent-free but it was now time for her and Danny to return.

'Come on, Lily – time to say cheerio to it.'

Although I had tried to be practical, I also had a lump in my throat at the thought of saying goodbye to this lovely flat.

Lily wiped her eyes with the back of her hand and gazed wistfully at the room. She whispered, 'Cheerio, Roseangle. Cheerio, River. I'll aye remember you.'

On that sad note we carried the washing downstairs and placed it on our pram. Lily pushed it up the slight slope to the Perth Road and we made our way to the Overgate in silence.

Granny had made our tea and Lily cheered up. The wireless was playing lively music interspersed with good news.

Granny said, 'I'll have to look for the flags. Alice was saying that we should dress the windows with bunting.'

This cheered Lily up even more. 'Can I look for the flags Granny?'

'Of course you can Lily and you can also look for Alice's flags. She's got a big trunk in her lobby cupboard, just like me.'

I was grateful to her for putting a smile on Lily's face.

She came over and put the table cover on the wooden table. 'And what can I do to put a smile on your face, Ann?'

I gave her a rueful grin. 'A miracle, I think, Granny.'

It was a cheery meal. Everything was still rationed but surely, from now on, everything would get easier? We would get our own place and food would be plentiful again – no more coupons and no more ration books.

The street was abuzz with people out celebrating the peace. The city councillors had put on a variety of events to commemorate VE day and it seemed as if the city was out in force.

Lily and I went to a couple of events – a street party and a small private party put on by Maddie's mum. Lots of the streets in the town held their own parties but we went to the one on the Hilltown. We had been asked by Connie who was donating some sandwiches and home-made cakes and what a great day we had with all the children from the top of the Hilltown down to Stirling Street.

Lily sat beside Rosie and Jay while I helped Connie and some of the women to serve the party fare. Jay's eyes were large as he surveyed the plates of fairy cakes with their thin trickle of icing but he didn't want one of the spam sandwiches when the plate was passed around. He wanted a cake with pink icing and Lily plucked one from a plate and handed it to him. He sat gazing at it and, at the end of the party, it was still clutched in his little hand. 'I'm keeping it for Daddy,' he said, proudly carrying it home while Rosie looked at him with pleasure.

'Och, you're a really good boy to think of your Daddy.'

By now, the cake was squashed out of all recognition and looked nothing like a fairy cake but, later, Dad ate it with his cup of tea – much to Jay's satisfaction.

Meanwhile, the party at the Pringle's house was every bit as enjoyable if somewhat less boisterous. It was held on a cool but sunny Saturday in June. The entire family had been invited – Granny, Bella, Dad, Rosie and Jay as well as Minnie and Peter plus the Lochee crowd.

We all turned up in high spirits now that the war was over. Minnie said how wonderful it would be if Danny and Peter should turn up at the door – all the way from Europe. But this was reality and not some scene in a picture or a novel.

Minnie was still a bit doubtful about Peter's return. 'The reason Peter took the job in Clydebank was to get away from my mother. She was aye interfering in our marriage so what's he going to say when he turns up and sees I'm back living near her.'

Maddie was sympathetic. 'Oh, I expect he'll be so glad to see you both safe and well that he'll not bother about your mother.'

Minnie didn't look convinced. 'It's not as if it's easy to get another house. There is nothing to rent in my part of the world – at least not to my knowledge.'

I agreed with her. 'I've been going round all the factors in the town but they've got nothing on their books – well, that's what they're saying.'

When we were on our own, Maddie said, 'You should have stayed on at Roseangle, Ann – at least for a while longer.' She sounded upset. 'Does Minnie have any idea when Peter will be demobbed?'

I said I didn't think so. We sat in silence and looked at the river. The sun had gone in and it looked grey and sluggish, almost as if it was going nowhere or, worse, it had nowhere to go – a bit like Lily and me.

Lily had gone off with Joy the minute we arrived – to paint, they said. Now they reappeared, clutching their sketchbooks close to their chests. Lily was much taller than Joy who had kept her small fragile-looking frame. She had a heart shaped face framed with blonde hair which gave her an angelic appearance – a look that was belied by a stubborn glint in her blue eyes. They came bounding over, eager to show us their pictures.

Both had painted a river view as seen from the bottom of the garden but I noticed how different their styles of paintings were. Joy had filled her painting with the precise shapes of the houses across the water and also the river. It looked almost like an architectural drawing. It had a colour and preciseness that was pleasing to the eye and both Maddie and her parents loved it.

Lily, however, had done hers in a freehand style that had vitality and a fluid movement and, although it could have been painted anywhere, we all knew somehow that it was the scene at the bottom of the garden, at the foot of the path that meandered between rows of vegetables that had been planted in place of the flowers of an earlier pre-war age.

Both girls were obviously talented but I was gratified when Mr Pringle looked at Lily's painting for a second time and gazed after her as she went into the house with Joy to get a drink.

Then Hattie came out into the garden with Rosie and Jay. Dad hadn't managed to come and, because George was ill, Kit and the family hadn't come either. Rosie was worried that Jay might damage something in the house or in the garden so she kept him near by her and stayed close to Hattie who, with her stern eye, could make him stay quiet. This was a family joke and Bella often said it was this sternness that had kept the gregarious Graham at bay but I never laughed when Bella trotted out this assumption on her visits to the Overgate.

I somehow knew the situation was more complex. Graham had certainly changed since I first met him – that time when I thought he looked like Arthur Askey. Now he looked haunted and I didn't know what had caused it and nor, I suspected, did Hattie.

The sun came out again and Maddie turned her face upwards. 'What a wonderful feeling it is to feel the sun on your face and know the war is over.' She gazed over to where Daniel was playing with Peter. Jay had been allowed to join them and they had two large tinplate trucks which they kept filling with earth before transporting it to another patch of earth where they duly tipped their loads on to a giant mound. The boys were grubby but obviously happy.

Maddie turned away from the sun. 'Minnie, Peter knew his son before he went away, didn't he?'

'Aye, he did. He was just a wee bairn then but his father was there.'

Maddie looked worried. 'Danny doesn't know about Daniel – at least I don't think he does. I wonder how Daniel will be when they meet?'

Minnie said, 'Och, he'll be fine, Maddie. They'll soon get to know one another.'

Just then, a cloud passed over the sun and I shivered. Please God, I prayed silently, don't let anything mar Danny's homecoming. Thankfully, Mrs Pringle called from the open door to come inside for our tea and we all trooped inside while Maddie, Rosie and Minnie took their boys off to the bathroom to clean them up.

A long trestle table covered by a couple of white cloths was laid with plates of sandwiches and small cakes were displayed along its length but taking centre stage in the middle was a glass bowl filled with pear slices. As luxuries went, this was the tops. We all gazed at it with wide eyes, wondering who had brought this luxurious item. Mrs Pringle, wiping her hands on her apron, said, 'I've been saving this big tin of pears until the war was over. I bought it in 1940 but I think the pears will taste all right.'

Granny said, 'You should have kept them, Mrs Pringle – rationing isn't over yet.'

Mrs Pringle laughed. 'No – we're eating them today, to celebrate the war's end.'

Even though there was just a mouthful for each person, they tasted delicious and three lucky boys all got a bit more. This was a taste from the days before the war and hopefully a taste of things to come.

We sat and talked of our hopes for the future. How we would spend our time when there were no longer any queues for anything. Oh, the joy, we said. During this happy chatter, my mind drifted off to our homeless state. Granny didn't really have the room for us now that Lily was growing up and I couldn't think where else to look for a house.

I caught sight of Hattie and I realised she was also away in a world of her own and, judging by her expression, these thoughts were similar to my own – uncertain and unhappy. I must have a word with her, I promised myself. Then she saw me looking at her and she gave me such a glare that I cancelled my last thought. Whatever was bothering her was obviously a secret known only to herself. Well, I didn't blame her. We were all living in worrying times – and for some folk it was worse than for others.

I gladly turned my attention back to the world of rationing. Mrs Pringle was hoping the shops would now keep food that had long since vanished from the shelves. Foods like butter, jam and real eggs hadn't really vanished but had been in such short supply that they were severely rationed. However, bananas, apples, oranges and onions had all but disappeared.

The day was such a success that it was over too soon and we all made our way homewards. Minnie was unhappy. 'My mother will be moaning about getting Peter into his bed.' She looked me straight in the eye. 'Och, Ann, do you ever wish you were a thousand miles away?'

I said I did but it didn't help to wish for the unattainable.

'When Peter gets demobbed, Minnie, you'll be happy. Maybe Lipton's will give him another shop to manage – somewhere that hasn't suffered bomb damage.'

She gave a mirthless laugh. 'Like the Hilltown or Overgate branch.'

I didn't want to lie to her or raise her hopes. 'Would that be so awful?'

'No, it wouldn't matter where he worked as long as we could be miles and miles away from my mother but that doesn't seem likely, does it?'

There was nothing I could say to that so I sensibly stayed silent. Maybe a miracle would happen, I thought. Peter would get a small branch in some town that had escaped the Luftwaffe's bombs – a place like . . . My mind gave up. I wasn't an expert on the bombing map of Scotland except to know Dundee had been a lucky city. Everyone said so. Maybe other places had also been as fortunate as us.

Before Minnie left to climb the Hawkhill, Granny said, 'I know houses are like gold dust, Minnie, but try and get something as far away from your mother as possible.'

And I'll take your small poky flat Minnie, I thought. Mrs McFarlane wouldn't bother me. The afternoon had turned really cool and we were glad to be indoors. I asked Lily to show me her painting again and once more I was struck with its luminous quality.

'Mr Pringle said when he got Joy's painting framed he would get mine done as well, Ann, and I want you have it.'

When we got back, Granny went through to see Alice so I knew she wouldn't hear me. I didn't want to hurt her feelings by talking about another house. 'We'll put it on the wall when we get a place of our own,' I promised her. 'But, until then, we'll put it on Granny's wall.'

As the summer days progressed from the high hopes of May, it was becoming clear that things weren't getting better but worse.

Then, in August, came the news of the Japanese surrender but at a terrible cost. Even Joe was shocked by the dreadful atom bomb devastation of Hiroshima and Nagasaki. He shook his head in dismay when the papers printed the full horror of this terrible new weapon devised by the Americans.

Connie said that an irretrievable step towards the destruction of the world had been taken – words that made my heart grow cold. What kind of a place would it be for Lily and all the children growing up in this new peaceful world? What on earth would they inherit?

The atom bomb was on everyone's lips. People had seen the suffering of people as portrayed in the papers and on the cinema newsreels. I always thought of Chris Portland when watching these. Was he still taking photographs of all the devastated cities both here and abroad?

I hadn't seen Kathleen for some time and I promised myself I would visit her soon. The food queues seemed to grow longer and the potato shortage earlier in the year hadn't helped the housewife's constant quest to make healthy, tasty meals from hardly anything.

People had grown used to queuing during the war but now that it was over, folk thought the rations should be scrapped. The faces in the daily queues got longer and more disgruntled as the summer wore on. The women stood with empty baskets and were grateful for a couple of slices of corned beef along with their meat ration. One small consolation was the increase in the tea ration from two ounces to two and a half ounces.

There was still no sign of Danny or Peter. And, thankfully as far as Kathleen was concerned, Sammy was also in the vast throng of soldiers waiting for their release day. Servicemen were being demobbed every week and they arrived at the railway stations, wearing their new dark, pinstriped suits. Granny said they looked like the American gangsters we saw in the films at our weekly visit to the pictures.

Maddie was becoming downhearted. After the euphoria of VE Day and the victory party at her house that was now becoming a distant memory, the days passed in a blur of waiting. All over the country, families were being reunited but not, it seemed, in our small corner of the world.

Then, at the end of September, Peter arrived in his gangster suit to be reunited with Minnie and his son. She came to see us the next morning with her news. Seemingly, Peter had gone to Clydebank and found the whole area demolished. 'Luckily he met our old neighbours – the couple who made us go to the shelter the night of the bombing – and they told him we had come back to Dundee to live.' She sounded out of breath with all her rushing around to spread the good news. 'Peter says it's quite all right to work in the Dundee branch of Lipton's but he's hoping for another transfer in a year or so. When I mentioned my mother's interference, he said he would sort it out.'

I was so pleased for her and I knew Peter would be glad to be home at last from the horrors of the war.

Granny said, 'Have your old neighbours got a house in Clydebank, Minnie?'

She nodded. 'Aye they were lucky and managed to get another place but there's loads of folk still homeless.' She turned her face and she looked so happy that I almost cried. 'Oh, we're so happy to have him back – Peter and me. His dad said they would go to the next football game and do lots of things together to make up for all the lost years.'

On that ecstatic note she hurried towards the door but, before she reached it, she said, 'I really hope Danny will be home soon, Ann. Maddie is getting very worried, isn't she?'

I nodded unhappily. Maddie had convinced herself that something had happened to Danny. Had he succumbed to his wounds? she asked. After all, as she said, no more word had reached her after that initial letter saying he was in hospital and would end up in a prisoner of war camp.

So the flat at Roseangle lay empty and forlorn and she often said that we should have stayed longer and not be cramped into the small space at the Overgate.

The city certainly had a festive air as married couples headed for the town centre every Saturday morning and the cinema was once again packed with couples – both married and courting. Still, 1945 was a strange year with not everyone celebrating the end of the war. Lots of families had lost loved ones on the battlefields or in the bombing and they mourned while the rest rejoiced.

Personally I mourned not the dead but the living. Greg. I often wondered where he was and what his wife looked like but usually these remembrances led me to despair so I tried hard not to think of him too much. But the mind has a life of its own and I found little things or certain places triggered my memory so I decided to throw myself into my work and looking after Lily. I tried not to allow myself the luxury of mourning a lost love.

Another blot on my horizon was the lack of housing and I had been unsuccessful in finding another home. But then so had a thousand other families.

One night, Bella arrived and she was moaning. 'I've got squatters in my close.'

Granny was surprised and so was I. 'How can squatters live in a house if folk are already in it?' she asked.

'Well, the old wife up the stairs died suddenly and the minute the house was empty and before the key could be handed back to the factor, squatters moved in. Mind you, they're a nice young family but, as they were homeless, they said they had no option but to break the law.'

I was a bit annoyed although I didn't say anything. I didn't want Granny to be upset at my obsession with finding new accommodation. Why hadn't Bella warned me about the empty house? Then I realised it didn't matter because the squatters were now in residence and the poor old woman was hardly cold in her grave.

Bella was still harping on about the horrors of homelessness – as if I didn't know it myself.

'The police say they will evict them but the man said he fought in the war and now they have no place to stay. "It's a bloody disgrace", he told them. They originally lived in Dundee before moving to the west coast but their house was bombed and they've nowhere else to go.'

'I've heard that Dundee Corporation are planning to build prefabricated houses,' said Granny.

We had all heard that but there was no definite date set for their construction, at least not to our knowledge.

Granny and I had taken down the blackout curtain at the end of May so she now decided to use some of her coupons on a new pair of curtains. 'It'll cheer us up when the nights draw in. We'll be fine and cosy, sitting listening to the wireless. We can shut out the winter weather.'

As it was only October, she was certainly looking ahead but we spent the following Saturday afternoon at Cyril's curtain shop in the Westport. He didn't have a huge selection. 'The war might be over, missus,' he said, 'but everything's in short supply. I was reading that Churchill hasn't the money to buy extra food because all the commodities are bought by the mighty dollar and this country doesn't have enough dollars. And the countries in Europe have so many starving people that America is concentrating on feeding them. They are also trying to save the lives of the concentration inmates with all the milk that's available. Still, there are some that can't be saved, the poor souls.'

We only came in for some curtain material, I thought with amusement, and now we were leaving with a potted history of the world. Still, it was true what he said about the starving millions in war-ravaged Europe. Some church groups in Scotland were organising food parcels to send to these poor people. Maddie and her mother knew someone who was organising these supplies to be sent away and I had given her a few precious tins from my small store cupboard. We didn't have that much to eat but we weren't starving – not like the poor inmates of the horrendous concentration camps. It was unthinkable what fiends could do to fellow human beings – not to mention the huge populations of the Netherlands and other countries under the heel of the Nazi regime.

Granny spotted some dark maroon chenille material lying at the back of the shelves.

Cyril, if that was his name, extricated the roll with a great deal of huffing and puffing. 'Oh, aye, missus, you've got a great eye for lovely material. This is left over from the days before the war but there's not much left. That's why it's back here but for your wee windows it'll be fine.'

Granny's windows weren't actually that small but, because the curtains only came down as far as the sink and the coal bunker, this amount left over from before the war would be sufficient.

Granny was pleased with her purchase and she set off for the house while Lily and I walked towards the High Street. The shop windows were still pretty bare but at least we had the feeling that the land of plenty wasn't too far away so, for the moment, we were content to dream.

We were passing the La Scala cinema when we met Kit, Kathleen and Kitty and they weren't looking very pleased although Kit smiled when she saw us.

'Is there something wrong, Kit?' I asked. 'You all look down in the dumps.'

Before Kit could answer, Kathleen piped up. 'I'll tell you what's wrong, Ann – Sammy is back.'

I was surprised. 'When did he get home?' I asked lamely.

'Oh, just the other day,' snapped Kathleen. 'But Maggie is running around looking for somewhere for us to live. She's shouting all over Atholl Street that it's not right for a married man to be biding with his mother while I'm biding with mine.'

I noticed Kit was holding on to Kitty's hand and she stayed quiet.

'Well, one thing's for sure, Kathleen, houses are thin on the ground at the moment and Maggie will be lucky if she finds one,' I said.

Kathleen grinned. 'Thank the lord for that.'

I was curious about Sammy. 'Did he say anything about Danny? I mean were they in the same camp?'

She shook her head sadly. 'He said they were in the same hospital after Dunkirk but Sammy says he was taken away to a prisoner of war camp while Danny stayed at the hospital. He was very badly injured and Sammy never saw him again. Now he's strutting around like some big war hero. Telling all the stupid lassies what a big man he was in the war. They hang on his every word but he's just a toerag as far as I'm concerned.'

Before they left, Kit said, 'You must come and visit us at Lochee. We're all very worried about Danny – especially when every other serviceman seems to be getting demobbed.'

I said we would go and visit the next day, Sunday. Although I put on a smile as I left them, I felt miserable with worry. Why wasn't Danny home? Sammy the toerag was back and I thought, not for the first time, what an unfair world it was.

I dreaded meeting Maddie these days. She had an air of desperation and I knew her parents were worried about her and Daniel. Maddie kept telling him about his daddy coming home and he was becoming confused by it all. Every time Maddie mentioned his daddy, Daniel expected him to appear like a magician's rabbit. And, of course, when he didn't, he got upset.

I knew Mrs Pringle had enlisted the aid of the Red Cross in trying to trace Danny's whereabouts but, so far, they had been unsuccessful. The whole of Europe was in a chaotic mess and families had been separated by the fighting. Entire cities had been devastated and Connie and I were heartbroken by the sight of so many people picking over the ruins of their homes. So much for Hitler's dream of a thousand years of the Reich.

It was quite a blessing to get back to domestic chores and, on the Saturday afternoon, Granny and I sewed the curtains on Alice's treadle sewing machine. Afterwards, I stood on the bunker and hung them from the curtain pole.

Granny stood in the middle of the room and supervised until I got them to her liking. 'That's great, Ann. They look really cosy and rich looking and they make the room seem warmer somehow.'

Because of the coal rationing, this was a bonus. Keeping the fire burning was becoming a difficult task.

'I wonder when the government will take things off the ration?' she asked. 'Surely it'll not go on forever?'

I wasn't so sure. Judging by the comments from the women in the queues and the shopkeepers, things could be very black for some considerable time.

The next day, Lily and I set off for Lochee, leaving Granny and Alice admiring the new curtains. It was a cold blustery day and, as the tramcar passed Dudhope Park, we could see autumn leaves lying in great mounds on the paths and grass edges. It would soon be winter, I thought sadly. Another year was almost over and still the same old problems persisted, plus the new big one – Danny. I made a mental note to try and speak to Ma Ryan – maybe she could shed some light on Danny's non-appearance – but, when we reached Kit's house, Maggie was there. Standing in a dowdy-looking frock with the flour-streaked apron tied like a sack around her thin waist.

Kitty wasn't there but Kathleen was getting the rough edge of Maggie's tongue. 'You can aye come and bide with us. After all, a wife's place is with her husband and Sammy is getting fed up living on his own without his family.'

Kit swept past her to come and speak to us while Maggie resumed her tirade. 'If you don't want to bide with us then Sammy can come and live here with you and your parents.'

'Heaven forbid,' whispered Kit and I had to give Lily a sharp glance when I heard her muffled laugh.

Kathleen, however, was having none of this happy-family togetherness. 'Maggie, I'm telling you for the last time. I'm not going back to your son – not now or ever.'

Maggie was outraged. 'Your man was away in the war fighting for you and his country and this is the thanks he gets? A wife that'll not bide with him the minute he's back from the horrors of the war. You're a fine wife, I can say.'

Kathleen was stung by this rebuke and she turned away to look at her mother.

Kit was also annoyed. 'Don't give us all that war hero stuff, Maggie,' she said, with a dangerous sharp edge to her voice. 'Your Sammy spent the war sitting on his arse in a prisoner of war camp. Although it wasn't a pleasant experience, I bet there wasn't a great deal of fighting going on in there.'

Maggie opened her mouth to reply then thought better of it. She stomped from the room and we heard her clattering away down the stone steps.

Kathleen burst out laughing. 'That's telling her, Mum!'

Kit gave her daughter a stern look. 'No, that's not telling her, Kathleen. I've said it before – you are a married woman and Maggie is quite right in pressing you to return to your husband. You should never have married him in the first place.'

Kathleen elegantly shrugged her slim shoulders. 'I know. It was the biggest mistake of my life.'

'Well, what are you going to do about it?' asked Kit.

'Just live from day to day, Mum. There's no room at Maggie's house for Kitty and me and it's the same here. As long as this situation lasts, then it'll give me some breathing space.'

We sat with our cups of tea with me hoping Ma would put in her usual appearance but I was to be disappointed. Kit said she always kept away from Maggie and Kathleen's problems. Given Ma's talent for seeing into the future, I thought this was strange but Kit always said that Ma never gave any advice to the members of the family. If she did sense something bad, then perhaps she would say something – otherwise she liked to stay silent.

I mentioned Danny and Kit's face clouded over. I said, 'I just wish he would come home soon, Kit – mainly for Maddie and Daniel's sakes but also for us as well. It's such a worry wondering what's happened to him and I imagine all the worst things possible.'

Kit nodded. 'Aye, so do I.'

We then spoke about the scarcity of houses. Maybe this worked in Kathleen's favour but Lily and I were outgrowing Granny's house. Another thing was that Granny liked to have the place to herself – just as I liked having my own corner.

Kit was lamenting about the rationing still being in existence. 'I could swear things are getting scarcer, Ann. And we're not getting as much for our coupons. George and Patty are working hard and they're aye hungry when they come in at night. Thank goodness the bread's not rationed although I have to say it's a queer grey colour, isn't it?'

I agreed but thankfully a few slices helped to fill an empty stomach. Then it was time to go home. We had chewed over the inequalities of life and found there was nothing we could do to change things or plan new recipes on the small rations allowed. However, it was good to have a moan.

That night I had a vivid dream about Danny. Maybe it was because we had been talking about him and he was on my mind but, whatever the reason, the dream was disturbing. We were in this austere-looking building and he had a white bandage around his leg. He held out his hand to me but, as I approached him, he disappeared and was replaced with a heap of rubble. It was so alarming and became even more so in the morning when I recalled it clearly.

Connie and Joe were still talking about the atom bomb when I appeared in the shop and I wished they would talk about something a bit more cheerful. 'You mark my words, Connie,' said Joe, 'this atom bomb will keep folk like the Jerries and the Japs in their place in the future. They'll be too frightened to start another war in case the Americans drop another mushroom cloud on them.'

Oh, yes, I thought, civilisation had come a long way from the Stone Age. Or had it? After all, we were still killing people but instead of clubs we were now bombarding whole cities with an atom bomb and all because some genius of a scientist had managed to spit the atom – something that had been regarded as impossible. Why couldn't some scientist invent food to feed the starving masses or make instant homes to house the homeless? Now that would have been a challenge worthy of a Nobel Prize.

When I got home from the shop, Maddie and Daniel were waiting for me. I could see by her face that there was still no news of Danny.

'We're trying the Red Cross records but nothing has turned up. It's getting to be very worrying – especially since Sammy Malloy has been demobbed from the prisoner of war camp.'

I tried to cheer her up. 'Aye, Maddie, but Sammy wasn't in the same place as Danny and I believe him when he says he's no idea where they took Danny after his stay in hospital. Sammy has been demobbed because his camp was liberated by the Allies just after VE Day.'

Granny said, 'That's right, Maddie. Maybe Danny was put somewhere further away and it's taken a while to sort everything out.'

Maddie nodded, her blue eyes full of worry and pain.

Daniel looked at us. 'I'm going to see my Daddy soon – Mummy says so, don't you Mummy?'

Maddie knelt down in front of him. 'Of course you are. It won't be long now and you'll see your daddy before you go to school.'

With a pang, I realised Daniel was almost five years old and he had never seen his father – and, just as bad, his father had never seen him.

When Maddie left to go home, I went with her. It was a lovely but blustery autumn day. Leaves from the trees in the gardens of Perth Road were scattered all over the pavement until they were caught by the breeze which swirled them over our heads like multicoloured confetti. Daniel walked ahead of us, his shoes scuffing against the leaves.

Maddie said sadly, 'What if Danny doesn't come home, Ann? What if he died of his injuries? Would I ever get to hear about it?'

Everyone knew Europe was in a state of total chaos. The news-papers were full of the carnage and destruction left behind by the armies. The Germans, Americans, British and Russians had all left their deadly fingerprints on the countries that had been under German rule. Danny could be anywhere in that vast heap of broken cities. A lot of them had been reduced to rubble.

Then I remembered my dream and I felt dismayed once again by its clarity. Had his camp been bombed by one of the hundreds of aircraft that had systematically destroyed so much? I decided not to mention my dream or the fact I had been hoping to speak with Ma Ryan. Maddie had enough to cope with without me adding to her worries. When we reached the top of Roseangle, we both gazed wistfully down at the close.

'You should have stayed on in the house, Ann,' said Maddie.

I didn't want to mention that I thought Danny would have been home by now. 'Och, well, it's all ready for you and Danny when he comes home.'

'Promise me that you'll go and live there this winter if Danny doesn't come home.'

My head ached. What should I say to her? Was she looking for confirmation that Danny was all right? Or had she made up her mind that Danny wasn't coming home? Ever.

I gave her arm a squeeze. 'Don't be so daft, Maddie. Danny will be back home long before the winter comes.'

She looked relieved. 'Do you honestly think so, Ann?'

If I had to be really truthful, then the answer was no. I didn't know what had happened to him but I had to be positive for her sake. 'Of course I think so. I would never have said it if I didn't believe it.'

'Oh, I do feel so much better now, Ann. You're normally right with your assumptions and I do believe in you.'

A hundred yards ahead, we parted and I watched as she made her way along the road, holding Daniel's hand. There seemed to be a spring in her step, as if I had allayed her fears. However, there was no spring in my step when I made my way back to the Overgate.

Why did I always seem so sure in my assumptions? I should have stayed silent but then Maddie would have gone home full of misery. I had at least given her a few more days of peace. After that, should there still be no word of Danny, then I would have to review my policy of happy-ever-after endings.

One bright spot amid all this gloom was Lily's academic success. She was outstanding at her studies and enjoying the school very much. She still wanted to go to art school with Joy but it was comforting to know she could perhaps do something else should she change her mind.

The picture she had painted at the VE Day party was now framed and we hung it on Granny's wall, above the fireplace. Granny was so proud of it and everyone who visited her was told all about her wonderfully talented granddaughter which, of course, she was.

Over the next few weeks, I met up with Maddie three times a week but, in spite of the searches by the Red Cross, nothing was heard of Danny. By now, we were all really worried.

Kit and George went to see her one Sunday and came in to see us on their way home. Maddie had been very distressed and Kit was vexed that there was nothing she could do to help her.

'It's just a matter of waiting. That's what I said to Maddie but it's not easy – especially with wee Daniel always asking where his daddy is.' Kit was almost in tears when she told us this.

George was angry. 'Every time I see that toerag Sammy strutting about it makes my blood boil. Not that I wish him any harm but he's been demobbed like thousands of other servicemen and Danny is still missing. And he's still pestering Kathleen to go and bide with his folks – as if they haven't enough room for themselves, never mind a wife and a bairn.'

I was almost frightened to broach the subject but I was at my wits' end with worry. 'Kit, can Ma tell us where Danny is?'

Kit shook her head. 'I've asked her but she says she can't see the future to order. Things just come to her and she says she can't tell me anything about Danny.'

I mentioned the earlier vision she had seen years before – the one I had overheard a snatch of and had asked Ma about when Danny first went missing in 1940. She'd said then he was all right but now there was nothing. It didn't bode well.

'Well, Ann, Ma still sticks to her story of that earlier vision but she says she never had another one regarding Danny. But then she hardly ever gets any feelings about her family and, if she does . . . well, she never mentions it.'

I wanted to know something. 'Did Maddie mention Ma?'

Kit gave this some thought. 'No but I got the impression she wanted to say something but Hattie was there as well as her mum and dad and she wouldn't have wanted to upset them. Not everyone believes in Ma's second sight.'

'How was Hattie?' Granny asked.

Kit looked sad. 'Putting on a brave face but she's suffering as well. After all he's her laddie as well as being Maddie's husband.'

After they were gone I was left with a feeling of depression which even Lily's chatter about her schoolwork couldn't lift. Perhaps it was because of the high hopes we all had on VE Day when we thought everyone was going to come home from the battlefields and POW camps. After all, the war was over and we'd imagined we could all settle down to enjoy the peace. Now, as the euphoria of that wonderful day in May slowly evaporated, I could see our worries for the future weren't going to be over for a long time yet – if they ever were to be over. Like the rationing, things were getting worse instead of better.

Connie had stopped asking about Danny as had Rosie and Dad. They knew by my face that no news was forthcoming. Even Joe stopped speaking about the war, at least when I was in the shop, although Connie said he was as bad as ever when I wasn't there. Still, I appreciated his small gesture.

The snow arrived in a blizzard of white flakes, leaving the pavements covered in a white carpet that soon changed to a pile of melting grey slush which seemed to penetrate the seams of my sturdy shoes and seep into my depressed soul.

Granny looked out a pair of old galoshes to put over my shoes but I found they were too slippy in the slushy streets. People no longer stood and chattered on the street corners. They were too glad to be indoors in front of their fires, albeit tiny ones because of the coal rationing.

Customers came into the shop all muffled up, their grey pinched faces peeping out from under woollen scarves and headsquares. Some lucky people had the luxury of owning furry gloves – huge items that made the wearer resemble a refugee from a bear park in Canada.

In all, we were a motley population, perpetually cold and totally fed up with queues and rationing with not enough coal to keep warm or enough food to eat on some days.

The government was still trying to keep up our wartime spirit with chirpy slogans and informative films at the cinema but, to be honest, it was the Hollywood films with all their glamour and escapism that cheered us up as we watched life as it was lived in the land of plenty where the sun always shone on seductive film stars in expensive apartments with their glamorous clothes and fabulous jewels. Watching these scenes always made Granny, Lily and I drool and Granny could never understand why they sat down at a table laden with food but never ate a thing.

'Can you imagine that happening here, Ann? The food on yon table would have disappeared like snow off a dike. It would resemble a flock of vultures descending.'

We had laughed then but this couple of hours of glamour didn't last long. For another dose of pleasure we had to wait till the following week's picture from that utopia, America.

Then, one morning at the end of November, Kathleen arrived at the shop. She had taken Kitty to school before catching a tramcar for the Hilltown. I could see she was distressed and had been crying and Connie also noticed it. She took her key from her bag. 'Go round to my house and make yourselves a cup of tea,' she said.

I gave her a grateful glance and ushered Kathleen along Stirling Street towards Connie's flat. Once inside I noticed the large bruise under her eye – a blue streak that extended right down her cheek. She had kept the hood of her coat up in the shop and we hadn't noticed it.

While I was putting the kettle on, she told me about her bruise. 'Sammy caught up with me this morning, Ann, but, because I wouldn't listen to him about going back to him, he gave me a punch right in front of Kitty and now she's away to the school crying. I told her it was just an accident and she's accepted that, thank goodness. I don't want her teacher to know.'

I was shocked but, before I could reply, she went on, 'I'm telling Mr Portland that I can't work for him any longer. In fact, I'm going there shortly.'

I sat down beside her and put a hot cup of tea in her still shivering hands. I was so angry that I was afraid to speak. I walked to the cooker to pour out my own tea and took a few deep breaths.

'You mustn't give up your job, Kathleen. You love the work.'

Tears ran down her cheeks. 'Oh, aye, I do but Sammy's father came to the shop last week and threatened to thump Mr Portland – said he was a dirty old man for taking photos of a young lassie.

What else can I do, Ann? Mr Portland was very nice about it but I can't let the awful Malloys break up his business.'

That was true but it didn't make me feel any less angry.

Kathleen stood up and walked across to the mirror which hung above the fireplace. She inspected her bruise. 'If I put some pancake make-up on it it'll not be so noticeable.'

She rummaged in her handbag and brought out the make-up. The thick foundation certainly covered the mark but I suspected it couldn't cover her bruised heart.

'What about Chris?' I asked. 'Have you seen him recently?'

She shook her head sadly. 'Not since the day we went for the drive and the picnic. He's been in Germany and I got a letter from him a fortnight ago.'

I gave her a startled look and for the first time since her arrival she gave a rueful laugh.

'Oh, it came through the shop, Ann – he knows not to send anything to Lochee.'

I nodded. 'So you're looking for another job?'

'I suppose so. Maybe I'll apply again to Hunter's department store where I worked before Mr Portland asked me to work for him.'

She re-examined her face in the mirror and we then left Connie's flat to make our way back to the shop.

In the street, she stopped and looked at me directly. 'I'll not walk back with you Ann but thank Connie for the use of her house and the cuppie.' She pulled the hood of her coat over her bright hair and I noticed fresh tears in her eyes. 'I just wish Danny was here. He would know how to deal with Sammy and his father. I often lie awake at night and wonder where he is.'

'We all think that, Kathleen. If only we had some word of his whereabouts it would be such a big relief to Maddie and to us all.'

Before we parted, I said, 'Tell your dad about Sammy punching you. He'll soon put a stop to it, Kathleen.'

Once again she smiled ruefully. 'Och, Dad would kill him if he ever found out. Now promise me you'll not say a word, Ann.'

'But what about the bruise? What will they think has happened to you?'

She gave this some thought. 'I'll make up some story about banging my head against a door or something like that.'

Then she was gone. I was quite bemused by her excuse. How many women had come into Connie's shop since I started with this excuse or a variation of it. There must be lots of women in the city who were accident prone with doors.

Back at the shop, Connie gave me a questioning look. I explained what Kathleen had told me because I knew Connie would keep the information to herself.

She just shook her head in anger. 'You would think that young man had seen enough violence in the war to fill a lifetime. Still, maybe he sincerely loves her and wants her back. Maybe he can't live without her.'

I smiled. 'Maybe you've been reading too many of your own books from the lending library, Connie.'

'Aye, maybe I have.'

The year slowly dawdled to a close. The weather was terrible and people became grumpy and totally fed up. One woman in the butcher's queue said what we all thought. 'This is not living. This is just getting up in the morning and if you're still breathing then you're still alive.'

No one applauded this sentiment but the ripple of agreement that ran through the large queue summed up all our feelings.

Still, we had our Saturday nights at the pictures to give us some colour and glamour in our grey lives. Just before Christmas, Granny, Lily and I went to the Plaza cinema for our weekly fix of escapism. The Pathé News burst on to the screen with its usual blast of frenetic music. I was looking at it with half my mind, wondering about Chris Portland and waiting for the main film to come on. Suddenly the commentator was telling us about the prisoners of war in a Russian hospital. I grabbed Granny's arm. In the corner of the ward, a figure lay on his bed and, although it was a grainy picture, I could swear it was Danny or someone very like him. Then the image faded to be replaced with another news item. Without waiting for the main film, we hurried out of the cinema.

'Do you think it was Danny?' I asked

Granny and Lily both said yes but Granny said, 'I'm almost sure it's Danny, Ann, but, if Maddie sees it, maybe she'll confirm it.'

So Lily and I hurried to Perth Road. Hattie wasn't there and Maddie and her parents were surprised when we almost burst in. We must have appeared half demented with our red faces and breathless appearance. I told them what we had seen and Maddie jumped up. 'The Pathé News will be on all the cinemas,' she said as she grabbed her coat and, along with Mr Pringle, we all hurried to Green's picture house in the Nethergate.

We had to wait for the first house to finish and it was hard trying to sit in our seats patiently waiting for the second house showing. Luckily the Pathé News was on first and the same footage was shown.

Maddie almost leapt from her seat. 'That *is* Danny! I'm sure of it. I wonder if we can see the film again?'

We followed Mr Pringle to the manager's office but he said he was sorry but the answer was no. He had to put on the full programme for the hundreds of patrons who now occupied the seats. He did, however, say the family could come back the following morning and he would show the news once more for them.

Back at Perth Road, Maddie couldn't settle, especially as the commentator had hinted that prisoners in the hands of the Russians could be held for years. The Pringle family would see the film in the morning and, if they were sure it was Danny, Mrs Pringle said she would get the Red Cross to investigate the sighting.

All these things were set in place but Christmas came and went and there was still no news of Danny. Maddie and her parents were convinced the soldier was Danny but everything was in such a state of chaos that they had to remain patient while the Red Cross did all they could to help.

Then came some bleak news three days after Christmas. The Red Cross reported back that there had been a disastrous fire in the hospital and two wards had been burned with no survivors. There were Polish and German survivors from the two other wards but Danny had not survived. Of course, Maddie was inconsolable, as we all were.

I wished we had stayed quiet about the sighting. That way, Maddie would never have known the terrible news. She told Daniel about his daddy and the wee boy took it pretty well but then he had never known his daddy. For him, he was merely someone in a photograph in a frame.

Maddie wasn't sleeping and Mrs Pringle asked me if I could come and stay for a few nights just to be with her.

Maddie's sadness was terrible to see and she grieved over the fact she wouldn't be able to bury him. 'You know the worst thing, Ann? I won't be able to go and put flowers on his grave.'

On these occasions I just held her close and listened to her heartbreaking crying. Hattie tried to put on a brave face on this awful news but she wasn't coping very well either.

She also confided to Granny that her relationship with Graham was almost over. 'He's changed so much since we met,' she said. 'I really thought he was in love with me. In fact, I'm sure he was but there's someone else in Clydebank. I'm positive about that.' She gave a huge sigh. 'And now that Danny's dead . . . well, I feel that life's not worth living.'

Granny became firm with her. 'Now listen to me, Hattie. Thinking like that will do you no good. We're all grieving for Danny and God knows how we'll all manage without seeing him again but talking like that will not help you.'

Hattie shook her head. 'I lost Pat in one war and now I've lost my son in another.'

Granny said she knew how much she was grieving for both the men in her life – three if you counted Graham. Later, Hattie left the house still weeping.

The family at Lochee were also grief-stricken, especially George, Kit and Kathleen and, although they didn't voice it, I knew they were comparing Sammy's homecoming with Danny's death. Ma, however, was as stoical as ever.

On Hogmanay, nobody felt like celebrating the first New Year of peace and we went to bed early. The Pringle family had to go and visit a sick relative who lived in Fife. Maddie, who didn't want to go, finally agreed when the old lady said she wanted to see Daniel. Maddie said it would have been cruel to deprive her of this small bit of pleasure. They would be away all day on the 1st January 1946.

Granny and I awoke early in the morning and made some tea. Sitting by the side of the dying embers of the fire, I couldn't describe the sadness we felt. It felt like a heavy iron chain around my neck and I wondered if anyone of us would ever feel happiness again.

It was still dark outside and a strong wind was blowing flakes of snow. It would be another cold day both inside and out.

Kit had invited us to Lochee but I knew I wouldn't be going. What was the point now there was no Danny? I remembered all our times together when he had been a tower of strength to me during my time at the Ferry and also afterwards. I recalled his bright blue eyes and brilliant red hair, his laugh and his merriment. Suddenly the tears started to flow and I cried and cried. Sobbing harshly into Granny's shoulder, my tears turned the sleeve of her flannelette nightgown into a sodden mass.

She let me cry for what seemed ages then said it was time to go back to bed. 'Get some sleep, Ann. Our troubles will still be the same in the morning but there's nothing we can do. It's just a matter of getting through each day as best we can.'

We both went back to the large bed in the corner of the room and, in spite of myself, I soon fell asleep. My dreams were so disturbing and they were all about Danny.

It was daylight when I awoke and Granny was sitting by the newly lit fire darning one of Lily's school stockings. Outside, the weather was grey and miserable-looking.

She saw I was awake. 'Just you stay in bed, Ann, and I'll bring you some tea and toast.'

We didn't wish one another a happy new year because whatever 1946 brought us it wouldn't be happiness. I sat up in bed with my tea, waiting for Lily to wake up. She was missing Danny so much – just like the rest of us.

Before we went to bed the previous night, she had said, 'I'm glad we saw Danny on that newsreel but I wish I had said cheerio to him in the Plaza.'

In time would Maddie feel like that? I wondered. Would she look on it as a sort of goodbye to him?

There was a knock on the door. Granny sounded annoyed. 'I hope it's just Alice and not some drunk first-foot.'

She went to open the door with the darning still in her hands and I gazed listlessly at her. She opened the door and there stood Danny. I leapt out of bed, spilling tea all over the quilt while Granny stood as if in shock, still holding Lily's stocking and the darning needle.

We both burst into tears and Lily, on hearing the commotion, also began to cry when she saw him.

Danny seemed taken aback. 'Well this is a great way to treat your first-foot, Granny,' he said. 'I went to Perth Road and there's nobody there. What's going on?'

We would tell him later but not just now. This was the moment to savour his safe return.

I said, 'Maddie and her family are away to see her aunt in Fife, Danny.'

I quickly got dressed while he had some breakfast. I hurried from the house. For some obscure reason, I remembered the telephone number of Maddie's aunt. In the telephone box I placed my pennies and when I heard a voice, I pressed button A. When Maddie came to the phone, she sounded apprehensive. I was crying with joy. 'Maddie, it's wonderful news. Danny is here at the Overgate. He's looking ill but he's alive. Get here as quick as you can.'

While I was phoning, Lily had run up to Hattie's house to give her the wonderful news and she rushed down to the house. A coat over her nightgown which in my bemused mind was another first for her. When she saw Danny, she threw her arms around him and started crying as well. We were all weeping and Danny seemed nonplussed.

197

Later, I heard that Mr Pringle had driven at great speed and Maddie, Daniel and the family finally arrived to a joyous reunion. Afterwards, Dad, Rosie, Jay, Alice and Bella joined us plus all the family at Lochee.

We were all crying and Danny said it was like visiting the Wailing Wall in Jerusalem. Still, I noticed his eyes were bright with unshed tears when he saw Daniel. He hadn't got the news of his son's birth and he was overcome with emotion.

Was 1946 going to be a good year? I wondered.

14

Danny was really ill. His leg hadn't healed properly and his face was gaunt and haunted-looking. His hair was still as red and his eyes still blue but they now seemed to have faded to a paler version. On his arrival at New Year, I had quickly noticed the washed-out effect that his eyes seemed to have.

Maddie was just so pleased to have him home and Danny . . . well, he was quite overcome when he heard he had a son, Daniel.

Unfortunately Daniel wouldn't go anywhere near him. He kept saying he wasn't the man in the photograph and that his daddy had died – Mummy had said so. Maddie tried to explain to him that she had been wrong but he still ran away when Danny went near him or came into the room.

Although he was terribly upset by this, Danny told a tearful Maddie that it would all come right soon. It just needed time. We were all anxious to hear Danny's story and, when he told it, it was really upsetting.

'I was sheltering with a group of my comrades in a house at Dunkirk when it was hit by a shell and I landed with a broken leg. The order then came for us to make our way back to the beach but, as I couldn't walk, I thought I would have to stay where I was. Then this big burly chap put a rough splint on it and put me over his shoulder and carried me towards the beach. He had been a rugby player before the war and he said my weight was nothing new to him. Then the next thing I remember was waking up in a field hospital, not knowing who I was. I had been in a coma for ages with a head wound seemingly and I was really confused. One day this big lad came to see me and it was the rugby player. He was also injured and he told me we had both been hurt by shrapnel and we hadn't made it to the beach. Then, still not knowing who I was, I was transferred to a German hospital. It was ages before I got my memory back. Then one day Sammy appeared. He had also been injured but not so seriously and he was being transferred to some prisoner of war camp. The German doctor was wonderful. He told me that not all the German people were Nazis. Anyway, he got in touch with the Red Cross with details of all the injured servicemen in his hospital and that would be when you got word about me still being alive, Maddie.'

She went over and gave him a huge hug. 'That's what kept us all going, Danny – that letter.'

'I'd no idea where Sammy went to and the doctor didn't know either but the Red Cross were told he was all right. The doctor tried to keep a lot of us in hospital but one day these SS guards arrived and we were all taken to a camp. We seemed to travel for ages and it was at least four days that we were in this cramped and overcrowded train and, when we arrived, the camp was full of Russian and Polish prisoners. We later found out the camp was on the Russian border.'

'But we saw you on the newsreel, Danny,' said Maddie.

Danny nodded. 'I seemed to have bad luck when it comes to breaking my leg. The Russians were advancing and the camp guards rounded us all up and placed us in this block which was then hit by a shell. We were all buried and . . .' His voice was full of emotion and tears filled his eyes.

I looked at him. 'Don't go on with the story, Danny. Leave it for another time.'

He shook his head. 'No, it's better to get it off my chest now and then I'll try and forget the whole thing.' He stopped for a moment, trying to get his emotions under control. 'As I said, the entire block was demolished and most of the men inside were killed or very badly injured. My leg was broken again but I was saved by this big Polish chap who managed to lift a wooden beam from my leg. He saved my life and thankfully he also survived. Then the Russians arrived in the camp and we were all carted off to a Russian-run hospital. Sadly a lot of the injured men didn't make it. I kept telling the doctors I was a British soldier but they didn't seem to understand me and just kept telling me to lie down, lie down. One morning this French camera crew arrived. I later found out that they were filming the destruction and horror of the thousands of displaced people who were now refugees without homes or a country.

'I didn't get the chance to speak to the film crew as they were only in my ward for a short time but soon after this filming, the doctor in charge of this small, makeshift hospital told us that the war was over. All the Russian prisoners who had been with us in the camp had been taken away by the Red Army and it was only Polish and German soldiers in the hospital. I was the only British soldier. Of course we were all overjoyed and hoping to be sent home in the not too distant future. Then ten days later the tragedy happened.' He stopped speaking and wiped his eyes.

'Don't go on Danny,' said Maddie, clearly distressed.

'I must finish the story Maddie and then perhaps I can try and forget all the horror and carnage of this futile war.

'One night I couldn't sleep and I kept thinking of all my family. Ma Ryan's voice kept popping into my head and I couldn't stop thinking she wanted to tell me something. My bed was next to the window on the ground floor so I decided to slip outside for some fresh air and to think things out in my mind. I went and stood by the fence that overlooked a forest. The moon was full and it was a beautiful frosty night with huge stars in the sky. I kept thinking how peaceful it was and surely it would only be a matter of time before I was sent home.

'Then I heard the explosion and saw flames shooting out of the window of my ward. I tried to hurry towards the building but by the time I reached it the whole side of the building was well alight. There was pandemonium and chaos with patients jumping from windows, and the hospital staff trying to do their best to get everyone out. They managed to save the lives of patients in two wards but my ward and the one next to it were totally gutted. Everyone had died in their beds.

'The next morning was even more chaotic. A couple of the doctors and some nurses also died in the fire and no one noticed that I had survived. But to be honest I was still in shock at the tragedy. Then we were all herded onto a truck to be taken to Poland but when we reached the Polish border the truck broke down. The men were all ill with breathing in the smoke and some had injured themselves in the evacuation from the building. We were all in dire straits.

'Then out of the blue an American patrol turned up and they loaded everyone into their vehicles and transported us to some large town in Poland. I can't remember its name but we were taken to a hospital where my leg was treated and dressed. I told the American captain I was British and he said I would be taken to Berlin and transferred to the British Army sector. But when the plane arrived it was scheduled to come to England so that is where I ended up. The American soldiers on the plane had a whip-round for me, they bought my train ticket in London and I arrived back in the sorry state you saw me in. They were my guardian angels along with Ma Ryan. If I hadn't been thinking so strongly of her I don't think I would have gone outside and I wouldn't have survived the fire.'

Granny asked, 'What caused the explosion Danny?'

Danny shook his head. 'We never found out but some of the men said it was the old heating boiler. The hospital was an old army hut that was being used for casualties and when the fire started it spread rapidly. The boiler was in a room behind our ward and I can only think that was why the two wards caught fire so quickly. And the walls were wooden so that must have played a part in the terrible scenes we all saw that night.'

He looked totally drained and I was almost crying myself. He looked at Maddie. 'The roads were full of people travelling with whatever they could carry on their backs, Maddie. It was awful.

Most of the towns were bombed and even small villages had been devastated.'

Danny was still not able to go back to work as he had to attend the hospital to get his leg checked out. He was told it would take time for his leg to heal completely. The first injury had healed but the second one hadn't, not properly, and he was told he would probably walk with a limp for a long time.

However, Maddie and Danny got ready to move back into their flat the following week but, before they did, Danny came to see me in the shop. He had just been to the infirmary and was on his way home.

Connie and Joe were delighted to see him but I knew he was worried about something. Connie had got into the habit of going home for a couple of hours in the late morning. I realised she wasn't getting any younger and this was confirmation of my thoughts.

Joe was eager to hear Danny's story but thankfully he knew he would have to wait till Danny was a lot stronger so they both wished him well before leaving the shop. After Connie left, I made Danny sit down on the chair. He still had a tired and ill look and I knew he was suffering from a lot of pain in his leg. I wondered why he had made the trip to see me.

He quickly came to the point. 'We don't think we can move back to Roseangle, Ann.'

I was totally surprised by his blunt statement. 'But it's your home, Danny.'

He passed a hand through his hair and I saw with remembered tenderness how it stood up like a small boy's ruffled look.

'It's Daniel – he's now screaming if I go near him. Maddie and the Pringles have told him I'm his daddy but he'll not accept it.' A spasm of grief showed in his bright but tired-looking eyes. 'Mind you, I can't blame the wee lad. After all, he never knew me till I turned up out of the blue. The photo he keeps looking at is a wedding picture and I look like a different person on that.' He tried to smile but failed and instead he had a dejected look which broke my heart.

I had to agree with Danny about the photograph. He had lost his vibrant colour but then so had thousands of men. They had left this country in 1939 as young boys and returned as war-weary men – all except Sammy, it had to be said. He had returned as if he had never been away but then he hadn't suffered a broken leg – and not just once but twice – nor had he been a prisoner of the Russians who spoke no English.

'So what are you going to do, Danny? Stay with Maddie's parents?'

He nodded. 'We feel it'll be better for Daniel to be in his familiar surroundings.' His voice registered the deep grief he was feeling at Daniel's rejection of him. Maddie had never envisaged this treatment. She had always thought Danny's homecoming would be glorious, especially after the long anxious wait.

There was nothing I could say to him. No words that would comfort him. It was just a matter of letting Daniel get used to having his father back home – however long it took.

I felt so sorry for them. I was naive in thinking the war was over. It may have been on the battlefields but, for some of the returning servicemen, the war was still carried on their shoulders like an unwelcome raincoat in a heatwave.

I put my arm around him. 'I hope everything works out for you all, Danny. It's been such a long terrible time not knowing how you were and now all this worry over Daniel.'

He sighed and tried to smile. 'Well, at least I'm back home and we're all together – not like lots of people who have lost all their families. And I never got to say goodbye to Grandad. Did he have a long illness?'

I nodded, sadness washing over me at the memory of that time. 'Maddie came and helped out and she was a great comfort to us, as was the doctor. Still, Granny said it was a blessing when he died because the pain would have got so much worse. In fact, it would have become unbearable and that would have been terrible for him.'

I was crying but then I always did when I thought of Grandad. I missed him terribly as did Granny and Lily and all the family.

Danny was upset as well. 'Maddie also told me about Greg. We're sorry it's turned out like this for you, Ann.'

I tried to look unconcerned but my heart was hammering. 'Och, well, it's just one of these things that happen, Danny. He met someone else and they're married now I expect.'

He looked at me as if he wanted to say some more but maybe thought better of it. Instead he said, 'I can't believe Dundee looks just the same as when I went away. The river and the bridge and all the buildings – exactly the same. There's been such devastation in the world, Ann. I came through London on my way home and it's razed to the ground in places. As for Europe, well, there are millions of displaced people and so many cities have been ruined. It's a damned disgrace that one megalomaniac like Hitler could cause such devastation and mayhem.' He sounded bitter.

I agreed with him. We had been lucky in our small corner of the world while others weren't but, to change the subject away from the world's woes, I tried to be cheery as I asked him, 'Will you be going back to Lipton's shop soon?'

'Yes, I will but can I say something in confidence, Ann?'

I looked at him with apprehension. I hoped this wasn't going to be another secret worry.

'Well, I would really like to own a shop instead of working in someone else's. It's something I've always dreamed of and, if there's anything this awful war has taught me, it's to make up your mind to chase your dream. Looking at the poor people in the camps and the hospitals has made me realise that life is too short and that life can be snatched away at any time without warning.'

I was intrigued. 'What kind of shop are you looking for, Danny?'

He gave it a bit of thought. 'Something like a general store. I've spoken to Maddie's Dad and he agrees with me that once the rationing ends, the shops will take off in a big way. Folk have some money now and they'll be keen to buy all the things that have been missing from the shelves for years.'

'Will Mr Pringle help with the money side?'

He nodded. 'He says he'll get me a loan to start off with and

I have my eye on a shop in the Hawkhill. The owner is retiring and he's not asking for a huge sum for the business because he let it run down during the war and the rationing. I think it has great potential.'

I was glad for him. When he was telling me about this new venture, I could see glimpses of the old Danny shining through.

'But, until I get everything sorted out, I'll return to Lipton's.' He didn't sound morose, thankfully.

He was on the point of leaving when he turned back suddenly. 'I almost forgot the main reason why I came to see you, Ann. Maddie wondered if you and Lily would go back to live at Roseangle until we get Daniel sorted out?'

'But, Danny, you'll all be wanting to stay there yourselves in the near future so it'll not be long empty till you and Daniel get together.'

'Well, until then, will you stay and look after the place? Maddie likes to keep it aired and lived-in so she's hoping you and Lily can move back in again – but just if you want to. Maybe you've found a flat for yourselves?'

The thought of returning to the lovely flat was tempting. I knew Granny would never put us out of her house but she was getting older and she liked the place to herself although she would be the last person to admit it.

'All right, Danny, we would love to move back. Will the weekend be fine?'

He gave me a grin that was so like the old Danny that it gave me hope for his well-being. 'That'll be great, Ann. Maddie will be so pleased.'

If Maddie was pleased, then Lily was ecstatic. 'We're going back to live there?' she said with joy. 'After us saying cheerio to it as well!'

'Well, I'm sure it'll not be for long, Lily. It's just to keep it aired until Maddie and Danny get organised.' I didn't want to mention Danny's problems with his son.

We moved in that weekend and, once again, put all the wedding presents away. Lily sat on the settee. 'Hullo, bed settee,' she said, 'we're back again.'

This time we didn't have to put up any blackout curtains and we sat at the table by the window to have our meals in the company of the river. It was as if we had returned to an old friend.

Back at work, Connie seemed to get tired quickly and she spent most of the day at home, leaving me to run the shop. It meant longer hours but, now that Lily was almost fifteen, she was able to look after herself most of the time.

Joe kept popping in to give me the usual rundown on the world's events. 'I see Churchill has warned the world that the Russians have pulled down an iron curtain over the countries they control. That Stalin is as bad as Hitler – just another bloody dictator. And have you read about the Nuremberg trials with Hitler's henchmen trying to pretend they're bloody innocent. Innocent? Innocent?' he spouted. Spittle landed on his lips and he wiped it away with a huge hankie. 'Innocent when they murdered all those poor Jews and Gypsies and loads of other folk? I know what I'd like to do to them,' he said darkly.

However, I wasn't to know what his solution would be because Rosie and Jay appeared.

Rosie looked flustered. 'Your dad has gone away to work without his dinner-time pieces, Ann. Do you think you can hand them in to him on your way home?'

I was just about to tell her I couldn't leave the shop when Connie appeared. Joe, who was on his way out, quickly retraced his steps back into the shop. He looked like a faithful dog and, if he'd had a tail, he would have wagged it.

'I'm just telling Ann about the Nuremberg trials, Connie.'

Connie gave me a look that said she wished she had stayed at home but it now meant I could go home for a couple of hours before coming back to do the evening papers.

I couldn't get over how big Jay was becoming. He was starting school later in the year and it was unbelievable how fast the years had gone in. The warehouse was now fully back in business with its fruit and vegetables. Bananas had been imported into the country but they were still in very short supply. Dad, however, had managed to get one for Jay who had gazed at it for ages before eating it. It was something he had only ever seen in his picture book and it was such a treat for him.

All these thoughts were going through my mind as I hurried to the warehouse with Dad's sandwiches, feeling a bit annoyed that he would sometimes hurry out of the house without them. He must have something on his mind, I thought.

I was almost at the warehouse door when I saw the figure emerge from the exit further up the lane. To my astonishment and horror, I saw it was Margot. It was so like my previous encounter with her in this same lane that I experienced a feeling of déjà vu. I stopped and gazed at her retreating figure. What was she doing here? Surely she hadn't come to see Dad.

Then, to my dismay, a few minutes after she disappeared, Dad appeared out of the same door with a barrow-load of boxes. He was whistling cheerfully. Thankfully he didn't see me as he pushed his load over to the building across the lane and went inside.

My mind was in a whirl. It had to be Dad that Margot was seeing but surely he wouldn't be so daft to start anything with her again? Would he? I wasn't so sure. Then I had another thought. What if Rosie had brought the sandwiches to him? Was this the reason for his forgetfulness? Margot?

I headed for the main warehouse and met Bill who worked with Dad. I handed over the box and asked where Dad was, trying to keep my voice even and unemotional.

'He were up in the other store a few minutes ago, Ann,' he said, pointing with a gnarled finger towards where I had seen Dad and Margot both emerge. 'I've no idea where he is now but I'll give him his pieces when I see him.'

I walked slowly down the lane but neither Dad nor Margot appeared again. To be quite honest, I had almost forgotten about seeing her last year. Where was she staying? I wondered. And was she hankering after a reunion with him? Oh, God, I hope not, I said silently. She had caused enough trouble in our family during her short reign and she was the last person I ever wanted to see again. And as for Rosie and Jay . . . well, it didn't bear thinking about.

I walked quickly to the Overgate and told Granny about this new sighting. 'She must have been talking to Dad. She came out the same door a few minutes before him. He must have seen her and he's the only reason she'll be hanging about there. And maybe she has been going to see him all this time. I mean, I don't often go down with his dinner box.'

Granny sounded thoughtful. 'I wonder if it's money she's after?'

'Money,' I said. 'Where would Dad get any significant money? I know I gave him Miss Hood's money but that was years ago and he used some of it to pay the household bills when he had his accident in the Home Guard. He might have some of it left but not in the amounts that matter to a woman like Margot.'

Granny said not to worry. It would all come out in the open soon enough and we would cope with it when it did. However, I didn't want Rosie and Jay to be distressed by Dad's secrecy and I sincerely hoped it would never come out. Maybe Margot would disappear in a puff of smoke but these things only happened in children's fairy tales and not in real life.

On leaving the house, I bumped into Danny. He was on his way to the infirmary to get his weekly check-up on his leg. I decided to accompany him. It was dry but there was a cold breeze and I was glad I had worn my tweed coat to work that morning.

We made our way up the steep brae to the Dundee Royal Infirmary and the main door. The last time I had been there had been the night of Jay's birth – that awful breathtaking time of waiting in the darkness for news of Rosie's delivery and the way Mum's death had seemed to hang over Dad and me and how we had been convinced the same thing would happen to Rosie.

I recalled Greg and how annoyed he had been to start with but it had all come right in the end. Or had it? Had the seeds of his discontent been sown that night? Now I would never know.

I sat on a bench in Barrack Park, which was across the road from the infirmary, and waited on Danny.

He wasn't long and he looked happy when he joined me. 'The

doctor is pleased with my leg. It's finally healing like it should and my limp will soon be a thing of the past.'

'That's good news, Danny,' I said.

His smile disappeared. 'I just wish it was good news on the home front, Ann.'

'Daniel?' I asked.

He nodded, his face grey with worry. 'He'll still not come near me and he'll be back at school in a few weeks' time. What will all the other fathers think when it comes out that he doesn't want anything to do with me?'

I didn't know what to say. Instead I changed the subject. 'Danny, what would you think if you knew Margot was back in Dundee?'

He gave me an amazed stare. 'Margot? Back here?'

I nodded unhappily.

'Well, Ann, that has me stumped, I must say. Was she not put in jail for stealing yon money from the retired judge? The one she went to work for?'

'Maybe she's got out on good behaviour or whatever term is used in the jail,' I said. 'But she's certainly back here and what's worse is that I've seen her twice coming out of the warehouse where Dad works.'

Danny gave a low whistle. 'That's bad news. What does your Dad say about it?'

'Oh, I haven't mentioned it to him. Granny says to keep quiet and maybe the whole thing will blow over.'

He gave this a moment's thought. 'Well, Granny's advice is usually sound, Ann.'

We sat in silence for a moment, looking at the peaceful view. The park was almost empty except for a few women pushing their prams. Like me, they were well wrapped up in their thick serviceable coats. Everything was still on the ration and clothes coupons had to go to the children who soon grew out of their things.

Suddenly, Danny mentioned Kathleen. 'Is she going back to live with Sammy?'

'No, Danny, she's not.' I didn't want to mention Chris.

'Kit said she's given up a good job in Mr Portland's photographic studio.'

'Yes, she has.' I was still in a quandary about speaking of Kathleen's private life. I felt it was up to her to tell Danny the whole story.

Danny was puzzled. 'I can't understand why she gave it up. Kit says she loves the work and it's a good job with prospects.'

'Well, Kathleen told me that Sammy's father went to see Mr Portland and was very aggressive. Kathleen decided to give the job up rather than let the business suffer. You know what big mouths the Malloys have.'

He nodded grimly. 'Why she ever married that wee thug is something we'll never understand.'

We sat and looked at the view in silence. After a few moments he said, 'What a strange world it's turned out to be, Ann, hasn't it? Who would have guessed that a few years ago the world would be turned upside down with the carnage and horror of another war? And now look at us – I'm married with a son who won't be with me and you've lost Greg because you've been too dedicated to your family. Maddie is unhappy at Daniel's behaviour and my mother has something hanging over her, I'm sure of that. The only two people full of life are Lily and Joy who are delighted to be going to the art college next year. They at least are happy.'

I took his hand. It was very cold. 'Everything will work out for us Danny – if we're patient. Is there any more news about your shop?'

He shook his head. 'No, the owner hasn't retired yet but that's fine with me. The more money I can get together, the better it'll be.'

He stood up. 'Heavens, it's chilly for June.'

I had to agree. I couldn't feel my toes.

As that strange cool summer wore on, one bit of good news was Danny's return to Lipton's shop. It also took him out of the house and all the unhappiness of Daniel's denial of his father. I honestly didn't know what to say to him and I knew Maddie was becoming more desperate about the situation.

Daniel went back to school in August but it was Maddie who took him to the gate of the Harris Primary. He looked so smart in his wine blazer, white shirt and grey short trousers but, afterwards, when he had left, Danny confessed to me that he had cried like a child when he saw his son go away into the wide world.

Hattie was also worried about her grandson but she had other problems on her mind – namely Graham. He had returned to Clydebank and managed to rent an office and was now back in business as a solicitor in his home town, after the few years of being with Mr Pringle.

Granny told me that Hattie had tried to forget Graham, saying she had merely been a diversion for him while he was in Dundee but I didn't believe this. Like Hattie, I had also thought he was truly smitten with her and something had happened over the years. But, whatever it was, Graham wasn't saying a word.

There was also a war going on in Lochee between the Ryans and the Malloys. Sammy had insisted that his wife stay with him – or else.

Kit was furious at the 'or else' statement. One Sunday Danny, Maddie and I had gone to see them and we walked into a war zone.

Maggie was screeching in Kit's kitchen. 'I've put an extra bed in the room and Kathleen can bide with us. Kitty can sleep with me.'

Kathleen gave Danny a beseeching look but he obviously didn't want to interfere in their married life – at least not at this early stage in his homecoming. Meanwhile, Sammy sat in the corner, a dark surly look on his face. He glowered at his mother and at his estranged wife. As for Kitty . . . well, she didn't get a second look.

Maggie looked more demented than usual. Her hair was uncombed and she had stains on the front of her blue jumper. She was bare-legged and her thin, fire-scorched legs were thrust into a pair of tatty old slippers. Sammy, on the other hand, was smartly dressed and still as good-looking as ever.

He glanced at his mother, his face showing annoyance. 'Listen, Ma, if she doesn't want to come back to me . . . well, let's forget about it.'

Maggie was stunned into silence as we all were, especially Kathleen.

'Just leave it alone, Ma. I don't want her back. She bores me. No, I've found another lassie that thinks I'm the bee's knees and, when I get my divorce, I'm going to marry her.'

I thought Kathleen was going to strike him but she turned and went out of the door, taking Kitty with her.

Maggie howled at her son. 'You can't get a divorce, you daft bugger.'

On that note they both went outside but we could hear Maggie's voice berating her son as they made their way home.

Kit sat down. 'I feel as if I've been in the war, never mind Sammy. What a mess everything is these days.'

We didn't stay long. It was obvious the Ryans had a lot of worry and, as Maddie said on our way home on the tramcar, hadn't we all.

I gave a furtive look at Danny and he looked shattered.

At the end of October, the old man who owned the shop in the Hawkhill finally retired and Danny, Maddie and I went to see it. It was quite a large shop with a big window. Inside, the interior was roomy and there was also a decent-sized back shop. It had a dark dismal look, as if it hadn't been painted from the previous century, and most of the walls were covered with cardboard adverts that looked as if they dated from the Great War. They were all advertising products that had long disappeared from the wartime shelves.

Danny, however, was optimistic. 'When the rationing finally ends and we're able to stock the shelves, I think we can do a roaring trade here, Maddie. What do you think?'

I thought Maddie looked pale and tired but she smiled. 'I think you'll make a go of it, Danny, and it'll be our very own business.'

They both looked at me and I nodded. Although there was a

lot to do to make the shop bright and cheerful, I knew, if anyone could do it, it was Danny. He was getting stronger every day and his face wasn't as gaunt as it had been when he first arrived home. His eyes, however, were still sad. Daniel, although he no longer screamed when he saw his father, was still distant and cool with him.

I put Maddie's paleness down to the strain of having the two most important men in her life not getting on with each other.

The following week, Danny put in his offer for the shop and it was accepted. Work would start at once and I offered my help should it be needed. Danny was really exited about his new venture and Maddie and I smiled at the change in him. Every day he was becoming more like his old self.

He told us, 'When the rationing ends, I'll stock lots of products and the shop will have its shelves full.'

But the rationing didn't end. In fact, the government put bread on the rationing – something which hadn't even been done during the war. The women were becoming more militant as the queues grew longer each day. 'It's a bloody disgrace that we won the war but we're still having to stand like the Three Stooges in these queues for a sliver of meat, a wee bit marge and two ounces of tea,' was the general consensus of the population.

Another bone of contention was the fact that milk seemed to turn sour more quickly these days. 'I blame yon atom bomb for this,' said one wee woman who was never at a loss for words. A situation that had been remarked on early in the war years when a neighbour of hers had whispered to her pal in the queue, 'It's a pity they haven't put her tongue on the ration then maybe we would get a bit of peace.'

Anyway, the atom bomb was being blamed for everything from the weather to bread not lasting as long as it used to.

Then one day, Jean Peters arrived at the shop, her face red and sweating as if she had run up the hill. I was surprised to see her. Normally Lily and I went to visit her at the Ferry and I couldn't recall her ever coming to the shop.

Thankfully I was on my own. Jean was so puffed out that she

had to sit down in the back shop in order to catch her breath. I put the kettle on the small gas ring and placed another tiny bit of coal on the fire. Fortunately the back shop was small so it soon warmed up.

When I was seated across from her with our cups of tea, I asked her what was wrong.

'Och, there's nothing wrong. I mean not really and terribly wrong but I was in the town this morning and I decided to go into a small cafe at the bus station and who did you think I saw?'

My heart sank and I knew what was coming.

'I saw Margot. She was sitting as bold as brass in the corner but still trying to look as if she didn't want anyone to see her. But it was her, Ann, I'm sure of it.'

She saw by my face that I believed her.

'You believe me, don't you?'

I nodded. 'Was she with anyone, Jean?'

Jean looked disappointed. 'No, she was on her own.' Jean stopped for a moment before continuing. 'But I got the impression she was killing time before she had to go and meet someone. I was going to follow her, just like the old times, but I was desperate for the toilet and, when I came out, she had disappeared. Damn it.'

I knew where she was going – to the warehouse. Although I couldn't help it, I found I was crying and Jean looked unhappy.

'I should never have come here, Ann. I should have had more sense.'

I assured her it wasn't her fault. 'I've seen her a couple of times at Dad's work and I can only assume he's back seeing her.'

Jean was distressed. 'What can I say, Ann, except I'm really very sorry – for you and Lily but also for Rosie and Jay.'

I thought of Jay. He was now no longer a baby or a toddler but a small schoolboy and I felt a murderous rage in my heart at both Dad and Margot. After all, what were a pretty face and fashionable clothes against a lovely wife like Rosie and a great son?

By the time Jean had left with the promise of a visit from Lily

15

Maddie was expecting another baby. Danny was thrilled because this was one child who would know his or her father. He'd be there right from the start – not like it was when Daniel was born. Maddie, however, wasn't keeping very well. She had terrible morning sickness and I was taken back to those terrible months with Rosie so I could well sympathise with her and all the family.

Danny had tried taking Daniel to school in place of his mother but he had resisted this – much to Danny's unhappiness. Still, he had his shop to take his mind off Daniel's rejection of him.

I went over in my spare time to help out and Mr Pringle gave a hand at weekends. Everything was still in short supply, including paint but Mr Pringle knew a retired painter who still had some tins of paint in his shed. These turned out to be a dingy shade of cream but it brightened up the dark-coloured walls and gave the shop a clean and spacious look.

Danny remarked as we brushed this on to the walls, 'This colour will do for the time being, Ann, but, when this awful rationing is over, I'll get a bright colour and repaint the walls.'

It wasn't only Danny who was glad to have this bolthole to keep his mind off his problems – I was glad of it as well. I still hadn't got up the courage or found the right time to tackle Dad and I only hoped he wasn't still seeing Margot. I was also glad to have this time with Danny and we usually worked in a harmonious manner, talking a lot of small talk and keeping away from the big issues.

There was also a big change in Connie's shop and she now let me run the business from early morning to three o'clock in the afternoon when she would take over for the evening papers. It was a suitable arrangement for us both and it gave me some extra wages. I was now able to save some money every week in Lily's art college fund. It was a big help not having to pay any rent but this would all change when Maddie had her baby. Surely then they would want to move back to their own home?

I said as much to Maddie on one of my visits. It was a bad day for her as it turned out. She lay on the couch, pale and tired-looking. Her hair was still shining but she had dark circles under her eyes and she seemed to have lost her sparkle. But she was still able to chat to me. 'I'm really lucky, Ann, I get my sickness first thing in the morning and not like poor Rosie who had it all the time. That's why I can't understand being ill like this because I didn't feel as bad when I was expecting Daniel. It's worse on some days, like today.'

I got ready to leave as I didn't want to tire her out. She was at home alone because her mother was at a Red Cross meeting and Hattie was due in later. But, before I left, I broached the subject of her flat. 'Lily and I had better get packing, Maddie. You'll be wanting to move in before the new baby comes.'

She shook her head. 'Oh, no, I don't think so, Ann. We'll think about moving when the baby comes and Danny has his shop up and running. I'm not due till next June so we have plenty of time to get our problems with Daniel resolved.' She didn't sound very sure.

I tried not to let my relief show. Houses were still hard to get even although the Corporation had started to build prefabs at Glamis Road and Blackshade. I would have loved one of these compact houses but they were only being allocated to families. Lily and I were a family but I was minus one huge sticking point – a husband.

Life still continued to be a struggle. I had to juggle work with standing in long queues for food. Once a week, I also had to do Granny's washing as well as our own. Lily was a big help. She normally cleaned the flat every Saturday and she helped out with Granny and Bella's shopping.

Bella had fallen on the pavement and injured her wrist. It wasn't broken thankfully but it was still too sore to carry her message bag. I met up with her at the Overgate and I couldn't help but smile when I saw her sling. It would have supported a two-storey building.

Strangely enough, for such a seasoned old hypochondriac as her, she was reluctant to mention her fall. 'You see, Nan, I had on these shoes with slippery soles and the pavement was wet. One minute I was standing and the next I was sitting on my backside. A couple of young laddies helped me up but I'm fine now,' she said.

Granny wondered if she had been drinking from her medicine bottle but she normally only did this in the house or at the Overgate. So nothing was said and that had to be a first as far as Bella went. For years, she had been spouting about all her imagined ailments and now, when she'd had a genuine accident, she seemed to want it hushed up. It was a queer world we were all living in.

I was so tired at night that I fell into the bed settee and was asleep within minutes. Lily had a lot of homework to do and I realised she would soon be away from home – both her and Joy. This made me so sad but, in some perverse way, I was also glad that she would be out in the wide world and be independent.

Then the grocer shop on the corner of Perth Road and Step Row offered her a few hours' work on Saturday afternoons and she was over the moon at the thought of having her own money.

I went in one day and she was behind the counter. Wearing a long white apron and a serious expression, she was serving a small woman with two children.

'And how are you, Mrs Smith? Are your husband fine and the children?' She gazed at the two small toddlers who were standing wide-eyed at this white-clad apparition.

Mrs Smith chatted back and explained her lack of sugar coupons. 'My man likes three spoonfuls of sugar in his tea, Lily, and I'm a bit ahead with the coupons. I've tried putting condensed milk in his tea and that helps a bit but he still needs two spoonfuls.'

Lily nodded sagely as if she also had this problem with a sweet-toothed husband and she went off with the ration card to the owner. Unfortunately he wasn't as accommodating as Lily and he warned Mrs Smith that her husband had better curtail his sugary tea in future or until the rationing ended.

Mrs Smith passed me as she left the shop with her two toddlers. She bent down to speak to them. 'What a pity Lily doesn't own this shop! She kens what I'm speaking about – no' like the crabbit man that owns it.'

I had to laugh afterwards. Lily had this chatty manner and she always sympathised with all the women and their lack of coupons. Much to the owner's annoyance, I imagined.

Still, she was able to open her post office account and place her wages in it. It was her art college fund, she said.

Years later I was to remember these months as a peaceful hiatus, a calm before the storm – or storms as it turned out.

As with all the biggest storms, it started quietly enough. I was leaving Danny's shop one late afternoon when I saw Margot again. She looked distracted and she didn't see me so, on impulse, I decided to follow her. I had a half-formed idea as to what her destination was and I was proved right. She made straight for the warehouse.

I hung about the lane, skulking like some third-rate spy. Thirty minutes later, she reappeared and hurried up the narrow lane that led to Dock Street. It went through my mind then and I was surprised I hadn't thought of it before – I could maybe follow her to where she was staying.

Keeping a good bit behind her, I decided to keep following her. She walked quickly up the Nethergate and my heart beat more quickly when we passed Mr Portland's studio. I thought about Kathleen.

Margot obviously didn't know I was behind her because she

never once looked furtively behind her or even stopped to look in any shop window. This was obviously one lady with a lot on her mind.

By now, we were at Perth Road and I was becoming more puzzled. Where was she going? Then, as if in answer to my unspoken question, she turned up the short path of a large house. I was taken aback. Surely this wasn't her house? I knew I couldn't go any closer in case she saw me from a window but I made a mental note to come back again later that night.

I was annoyed to realise how near she was staying to us at Roseangle. It was a miracle I hadn't met her on more occasions.

I made up my mind to visit Dad and Rosie that night after seeing what I could find out about Margot's house. Fortunately Lily had a lot of homework that night and she was happy to stay at home and wade through it.

I tried to sound casual. 'I'm just away to see Rosie and Jay. I'll not be long.'

I set off up the street. It had turned out to be a misty night but quite mild for the time of year. I was grateful for the cover as I could walk silently up to the house and look to see if there were any names on the door. After that, it would be time for Dad. I knew I would have to get him on his own – at least to begin with as there was no point in upsetting Rosie at this stage.

I pulled the collar of my coat up over my ears like Ingrid Bergman in *Casablanca* and hurried towards the house. Quietly opening the gate, I walked up the short path. There were a few lights in the upstairs windows but the lower windows all had their curtains pulled.

The street seemed to be deserted but, now and again, a ghostly figure walked past. Perhaps because I was feeling guilty, I assumed these people would view me with suspicion but they merely hurried past, too intent on their own business to notice mine.

When I reached the door, I saw the sign. It was a small plaque on the wall that stated this grand house was 'The Greenside Hotel'. So Margot was living in a hotel . . . That should have meant her visit wasn't permanent but she had been in Dundee for some considerable time. I tried to remember the first time I had seen her, but the sound of footsteps behind the closed door made me run down the path and through the gate.

As I hurried up the Hilltown, my mind was in a whirl. Margot must have a large sum of money to be able to stay in a hotel for months.

I reached Dad's close and was making my way up the stairs when a stranger came up behind me. I was suddenly afraid but he merely smiled as he passed me. I couldn't make out his features in the dim gas-lit staircase. That's why it was such a surprise to see him at Dad's door. Rosie answered his knock and the look of surprise on her face when she saw she had two visitors was almost comical.

The man asked after Dad and Rosie and I went inside to get him. She gave me a quizzical look when Dad went to the door and we strained our ears to try and catch some of the conversation.

Then Dad came back into the room with the stranger who apologised to Rosie for calling so late.

'What can I do for you Mr . . . ?' asked Dad.

'My name is Victor Jones,' he said.

We all gazed at him with apprehension. He was well dressed in a dark woollen suit and a cream-coloured raincoat. He placed his hat and gloves on his lap and surveyed his small audience. Jay, thankfully, was in his bed.

I was holding my breath and I couldn't think why.

Victor Jones hesitated for a moment before making up his mind. His voice was cultured and his accent hard to place. One thing was clear – he wasn't from Scotland.

He confirmed so at once. 'I've just arrived from Portsmouth, Mr Neill,' he announced.

Afterwards, I thought he must think we were all goldfishes with our open mouths as we gaped at him.

'Portsmouth?' said Dad, in a puzzled tone, while Rosie and I merely looked blankly at each other.

'Yes but I have business to do here in Dundee. In fact, I was hoping to visit sooner but the deal I'm involved in hasn't moved as fast as I would have liked – all these wartime restrictions.' He gave Dad a nervous and embarrassed glance. 'My visit is about someone you used to know – your ex-wife Margot Neill.'

Rosie gasped out loud and Dad gave her a concerned look. I sat like a wooden statue. As the saying went, a whole can of worms was about to be opened up.

Dad looked puzzled again. 'Margot?'

Mr Jones nodded.

'Well, I'll make one thing clear, Mr Jones. Although I was married to Margot, it was a bigamous marriage on her part and I haven't seen her since she left years ago.'

I gave a loud gasp and Dad gave me a sharp look.

Mr Jones sighed. 'My interest in her is this. I married her in Portsmouth two years ago but it wasn't a happy marriage. I gave her a job in my Edinburgh branch a year ago and now the auditors have discovered she's embezzled five thousand pounds from the firm and I want to find her.'

Rosie said bitterly, 'I bet you do.'

Dad turned to his visitor, his face a picture of innocence. I was struck by his cool handling of this revelation. He had been meeting Margot secretly for months and now he sat there like a man without a guilty secret in his whole body. I couldn't remember him ever being such a good actor but perhaps Margot had been giving him lessons.

'Why do you think she's in Dundee?' I asked.

'I employed a private investigator and he tracked her movements here. Also I found papers she left behind when she disappeared. They had this address and one in Edinburgh. There was also a hotel bill made out for a Mr and Mrs Neill with a hand-written note on it which said, "Our honeymoon hotel".'

Dad looked embarrassed. 'I wrote that when I paid it, Mr Jones.'

He looked at Rosie but she turned away.

'Call me Victor,' he said. 'I only want to find her to get a divorce. I certainly won't prosecute her.'

Rosie said bitterly, 'I wouldn't be surprised if she married you bigamously as well, Victor. She seems to make a business of it. And as for your money . . . well, I reckon you'll never see it again.'

'I'm not worried about that, Mrs Neill. I just want to face her and ask why she had to embezzle the money in the first place. It's not as if she didn't get enough money during our short marriage. Even though we were separated, I let her run my Edinburgh branch and she had a good salary.'

Dad, no doubt worried by Rosie's bitter tone, said, 'There never seems to be enough money for Margot. She has to have more and more. It's the way she is.'

'Yes,' said Rosie, 'a ruddy crook.'

Victor didn't want any tea and he stood up to leave. 'If you do hear from her, please let me know.' He handed over a small card with his name and address printed in gold lettering.

Very classy, I thought. Trust Margot to marry into a classy life. What a puzzle she was.

As he walked his visitor to the door, Dad said, 'You're the second husband I've had at the door looking for her.'

For the first time since he arrived, Victor looked nonplussed. 'The second husband? How many has she had?'

Rosie answered for Dad. 'God only knows. At least two before Johnny and who knows how many since then?'

As Victor left, he was shaking his head. I wondered if he was wondering about the gullibility of these Scottish men who had been fooled but, there again, he was also a victim of the infamous Margot. A sophisticated, wealthy man of the world from the prosperous south of England, he'd been taken in and robbed by a pretty face and a good line in clothes and charm.

At the door I quietly asked Dad for a quick word. He gave me a surprised look but called back to Rosie, 'I'll walk down the stairs with Ann and get some cigarettes. I'll not be a minute.'

When we were out of earshot of the house, I rounded on him. 'That was a great display of innocence, Dad.'

He gave me a blank stare. 'What innocence?'

'When you told Victor that you hadn't seen Margot since she left you years ago.'

'That was the truth – I haven't seen her.'

For a brief moment, I could have sworn he was telling the truth but I had seen her with my own eyes.

'Dad, I've seen Margot coming out of the warehouse at least three times over the last year.'

For the second time that night, he gave me a sharp look. 'Margot? Coming out of the warehouse? When was this?'

Now I was on the spot. I hadn't noted down the dates but I had followed her yesterday so I told him. 'The last time was yesterday.'

He sat down on the cold stair. As if all the power had left his legs.

He said, 'Yesterday?'

I said, 'Yes,' and added, 'and I know where she's living.'

He sounded angry. 'Why did you not tell Victor Jones all this, Ann?'

I was perplexed. 'I didn't want Rosie to know about Margot's visits to the warehouse.'

Dad laughed and I was shocked. 'Do you not worry about Rosie's feelings?'

He became serious. 'Of course I do. I never want to hurt Rosie or Jay. Margot might have been visiting the warehouse but she didn't come to see me – cross my heart.'

By now, I was becoming more puzzled by the moment. 'Why would she have gone to the warehouse if it wasn't to see you, Dad?'

He shrugged. 'I've no idea but I'll tell you this. I'm letting Victor Jones know where she's living. He can sort it all out.'

'I'm sorry, Dad. I just thought if she was back in Dundee, she was seeing you.'

He gave me a look I'll never forget and I was suddenly ashamed of myself.

'Well, I'd better get back home,' I said in an embarrassed voice. 'She's living at the Greenside Hotel in Perth Road.'

He nodded unhappily. 'Now I suppose I'll have a devil of a job convincing Rosie this has nothing to do with me.' He sighed loudly.

'I'll come back up to the house with you and support you.'

He scowled at me. 'No thanks – you've done enough with getting the address. We'll have to nickname you "Sherlock Holmes".'

So I trudged homewards, feeling tired and downhearted. Why hadn't I shown more faith in my father? I thought. Then it suddenly struck me that I had, over the years, been a hundred per cent right in my assumptions about my father. The fact that he had changed was down to Rosie's influence – and Jay's.

One thing was clear, however. Margot's arrival was bad news – if not for Dad, then for some other poor man. I hoped that Victor Jones would cart his errant, embezzling wife back to Portsmouth or Timbuktu and far away from us. But, as I walked home that misty night, I could never have begun to envisage the trouble she would cause. That would come just before Christmas and, like all trouble, it didn't come singly.

16

Danny confessed to me that he wasn't a happy man. He was worried about Maddie who was still suffering from morning sickness and this meant extra work was put on her mother's shoulders. Mrs Pringle had landed the job of taking Daniel to school every morning and, although she didn't seem to mind this, Danny was upset by it.

He appeared at Roseangle one night, a couple of weeks after Victor Jones's visit. His face was white but I could see he didn't want to say anything in front of Lily.

'I'm thinking of doing some work at the shop tonight, Ann. Can you help me?'

I gave him a sharp look. It was dark and he hardly ever worked in the shop this late at night. Still, Lily didn't think this was odd so we set off for the Hawkhill. I was surprised when we reached the Overgate and he headed towards the High Street, going in the opposite direction from the shop.

'I just mentioned the shop as a cover, Ann. I've got to go and see your Dad and Rosie.'

I opened my mouth to ask a question but he said he would explain everything when we were at the Hilltown. We walked in silence for a few minutes until I asked him about Maddie and Daniel.

He reinforced what I already knew. 'Maddie is still sick every morning and Mrs Pringle has to take Daniel to school. Things are getting so chaotic, Ann. I never thought I would come back to this. I always harboured dreams that our life together would resume where we left off.' He gave me a lopsided smile. 'How naive of me I guess.'

I tucked his arm in mine. 'No, Danny, you're not naive. I'm the same with Greg. I always thought he would wait till Lily grew up but one thing I've learned during these war years is to never assume anything. Just take what you want now and don't wait. You've got your shop and you'll be a father again soon. As for Daniel . . . well, it'll just take time, I'm sure of it.'

He said softly, 'I look around me and the streets and buildings are still the same as when I left but I'll tell you something, Ann, nothing is the same. It's as if the world has been carted off to another galaxy. We all look the same but we're not. People are becoming more demanding and asking questions. The women who come into Lipton's are becoming more militant about these awful ration restrictions and I don't blame them. It's almost eighteen months since the end of the war and rations are being cut instead of increasing and people want to know the reason for it.'

I nodded in agreement. I had noticed the tendency myself while standing in the daily queues. 'I know, Danny. A few women were shouting at the butcher last week because the meat ration hadn't been increased and, although the bread rationing isn't as bad, it's still a case of first come first served and sometimes the baker doesn't have much left. And it's much darker bread than the wartime loaf so we wonder what's in it.'

'There's a world shortage of food and the government has spoken of a world famine. Then there was a bad wheat harvest and that hasn't helped. Seemingly, there are thirty million Germans to be fed because of all the damage to their agricultural system and you can multiply that right across the world – everywhere except America.'

'Still, you can't blame the women for getting frustrated at the rations still being so small. It's almost as if we're still at war,' I said with feeling.

By now we had reached the house and all the talk of world shortages stopped. Rosie answered our knock and she was surprised to see us, as was Dad who looked up from his paper. Jay had gone to his bed.

Danny didn't mince his words which surprised me. 'I hear that a Victor Jones has been looking for his wife Margot?'

Dad looked gutted while Rosie said, 'That's right, Danny, but we didn't think it was common knowledge.' She gave me a look but I shrugged my shoulders to let her know this news hadn't come from me.

Danny sighed. 'Oh, I wish it wasn't.' He turned to Dad. 'Ann gave him her address in Perth Road and, when he went there to tackle her, she just laughed at him. Seemingly, she has another man in her sights and she told Victor Jones to get lost. Well, he lost his temper and called the police the next day. He wanted her arrested for embezzlement but, when the police arrived, she had vanished.'

Rosie was puzzled. 'But what's this got to do with us, Danny?'

Danny was white-faced. 'The other man – the one she was hoping to go off with – was Maddie's uncle.'

Dad gave an agonised groan. 'My boss at the warehouse?'

Danny nodded. 'The whole family are up in arms over it. She was seemingly getting money from him. She threatened to tell his wife about a so-called affair they were supposed to have had a few years ago – before Maddie and I got married.

'Although he confessed earlier, he was scared Margot's reappearance would be construed as a new affair. Margot could tell lies so convincingly that John was afraid.'

Of course, this wasn't news to me or to Rosie – or to Jean Peters. Jean and I had seen them in the lounge of the Royal Hotel.

'He's admitted to the police that he was foolish for giving her money but the worst thing is the fact that his marriage to Dot is over. She was wild when she heard the story.'

I always knew Margot had the soul of a mischief maker and now it was proved once again. She had almost destroyed Dad and now she was doing the same to Maddie's uncle – not to mention Victor Jones.

Danny was still talking. 'The worst part is she doesn't need any more money. She has a house in Edinburgh and was coming back and forth from there to get more money out of Mr Pringle.'

Dad was speechless but Rosie summed up what we were all thinking. 'She's a wicked woman, Danny, but she'll get her come-uppance.'

'Well, I hope so,' he said. 'As it is, Dot has asked John to move out of the house and he's living in a rented house in Blackness Road. Maddie's parents are trying to get them to patch things up but it's a mess.'

There was something I wanted to say to Rosie. 'It's true that I first saw Margot some time ago but I never said anything because I didn't want any more trouble from her. Tell me, Danny, has she been arrested by the police?'

He shook his head. 'No, she hasn't. She disappeared after Victor Jones visited her at the hotel. But not before confronting John and Dot and telling her all about her affair with her husband and also about the money he was giving her. She also said John was planning to go away with her and start a new life together. That's something John denies – he says it's a pack of lies. He says he felt sorry for her because she was Harry Connor's widow and she came to him with a hard-luck tale of money problems. He denies saying he would go away with her. It did start with him feeling sorry for her but Margot manipulated his kindness and he was always a bit daft over a pretty face. But hopefully the police will catch up with her when she goes back to her house in Edinburgh. They'll catch her then.'

Danny and I then left Dad and Rosie to their own thoughts. I was so relieved that Dad wasn't involved but I still felt very sorry for John Pringle. He had been a good boss to Dad and I only hoped the business wouldn't go under with all this domestic pressure simmering away.

As we walked back through the cold dark streets, Danny seemed to be lost in his own thoughts so I remained silent. We were almost at Roseangle when he said, 'Come back to the house and see Maddie.'

I was worried about leaving Lily for so long and I said so.

Danny was apologetic. 'Of course – I forgot she was in the house on her own. Maybe you'll manage to see Maddie soon, Ann?'

He looked so worried and I knew Lily was capable of being on her own for one evening so I said I would go but only for a short visit.

Perth Road was quiet at that time of night. White frost was beginning to lie on the garden walls with their iron stumps that had once been iron railings. They had all been cut down early in the war to be used as metal salvage.

Danny said, 'I can't believe all this trouble has all started up again. What has that woman got against this family? First your dad and then John Pringle. Maddie's parents are really worried about the whole thing and they are urging Dot to patch things up with her husband. As it is, she's on the phone every night, crying.'

There was nothing I could say to cheer him up. If I came out with some well-worn platitude, he would see it for what it was worth – only words. And he didn't know about Margot's earlier affair with John. With hindsight, it was now clear that she had set her sights on him years ago and had been trying to get him to leave his wife for her. She had also been quite willing to leave Dad as well, if her plans had gone well.

'How is Maddie coping with all this?' I asked.

'I think everything is getting her down, Ann – what with her being sick every morning and Daniel just tolerating me. That's why I wanted you to come and see her tonight. She always listens to you and says you're a very wise person.'

I had to smile inwardly at this description. If I had been so wise, why was I not married to Greg by now? It had been my stupidity that had sent him packing into the arms of another woman.

We were now at the gate and the house looked so welcoming as always. It was a house I loved ever since the first time I saw it in 1931. I always thought it was such a peaceful place. That is until we went inside. Like Lochee a few weeks ago, it was a war zone.

231

James and Fay Pringle were in chairs by the fireside while John and Dot sat at either end of the large settee, like bookends. Sitting in a chair by the window was Maddie. She looked downright miserable.

Danny's face went white when we entered and I was embarrassed. I turned to leave. Maddie jumped up and came towards us. She led us up to their room which, in an earlier life, had been hers. A small box room next door was Daniel's bedroom and he was fast asleep.

'Maddie, I'm sorry. I shouldn't have come at a bad time like this,' I said.

Suddenly she grinned and I was taken back to the very first time I ever met her. She had grinned at me like this on that far-off day in 1931.

'Oh, don't be sorry. You've saved me from the battlefield, believe me.'

Danny went down to the kitchen to make some tea. Maddie was beginning to put on weight around her tummy and it was clear she was expecting another baby.

She patted her tummy. 'Do you remember how huge I was with Daniel? Well, I think this one will make me even bigger. I'll resemble an elephant and Danny will emigrate to Canada to get away from me.'

He appeared at the door at that moment and laughed. 'No, Maddie, it'll be Australia.' He became serious. 'What's the news on the battlefront tonight?'

Maddie sighed. 'Oh, just the usual recriminations, Danny. Dot believes every word Margot said to her but we all know what a liar she is.' She looked at me. 'Especially you, Ann – you had to live with her in your life when she married your father.'

I nodded as all the unhappy memories of those distant days now came flooding back. To push them from my mind, I asked, 'How are you keeping, Maddie?'

She made a face. 'As sick as a dog every morning. Danny doesn't believe I was like this with Daniel, do you, Danny?'

He smiled. 'Of course I believe you.'

None of us mentioned Daniel again. Danny was still too hurt by the way his son kept his distance from him. Instead we were all laughing about our dressmaking attempts with the camiknickers and Maddie was telling Danny how she'd made them especially for him.

'That was when I was trying to get you to notice me,' she told him.

Then James Pringle knocked on the door. He smiled when he saw Maddie and Danny laughing. 'You always make people feel better, Ann.'

I was totally thrown by this statement but even more confused when he continued. 'Can you come downstairs for a moment?'

Maddie and Danny looked as puzzled as I felt but I followed him downstairs. The atmosphere in the room was icy, in spite of the glowing fire.

Dot looked tearfully at me while John gazed at his feet as if he had suddenly developed eleven toes. I noticed the highly polished russet brown shoes that I had last seen by the bench at Riverside.

Fay Pringle smiled and asked me to sit down. She came straight to the point. 'James and I were wondering if you could tell Dot what kind of woman Margot is.'

Dot continued to look at me and I was momentarily speechless. What did Maddie's mum want me to say?

Noticing my hesitation, she said, 'Just tell Dot the truth, Ann.'

And I did. I held nothing back. I told her about how callous she had been over her late husband Harry's death – a death that put her within reach of Dad. I told them about her stealing my money from the savings jar and also the horrible abuse of Lily at her hands. I mentioned her treatment of a husband who had turned up at our door a few years ago. How she had spent all his money before disappearing and how she had treated her latest husband, Victor Jones, by embezzling five thousands pounds and how good he had been to her, providing her with a house and job in Edinburgh. What I didn't mention was the short affair John had had with her or the conversation Rosie, Dad and I heard at Maddie and Danny's wedding. He had been foolish but then so had a lot of men, Dad included. He had been truly hoodwinked by her.

'She's nothing but a common criminal,' I told them. 'She's a bigamist, a liar and a thief, albeit a pretty one. The only reason she married my father was because he was daft enough to mention my inheritance from Mrs Barrie. He never mentioned how much so maybe she thought she would get her greedy little hands on a lot of money. Well, she was sorely mistaken.'

Suddenly James Pringle burst into laughter and we all looked at him. 'I can see she was mistaken in taking you on, Ann. You were more than a match for her.'

The mood in the room seemed to lift and Dot, who had stayed silent all through my tirade, now smiled. She said quietly, 'So what my husband says is true? She's a wicked woman?'

For the first time, I laughed. 'It's not only your husband, Mrs Pringle, who'd say so but also my sister Lily and my dad and his lovely wife Rosie. No doubt, if we all had enough time, we could maybe dredge up a few more names but why bother? Rosie says she'll get her comeuppance and I hope she does.'

Dot thanked me and I left the room but, before I reached the door, I turned. 'This conversation will be in confidence and I'll never mention a word about it. Margot has caused so much mayhem that it's a shame to let her continue to do so in her absence.'

I left soon after that and it was another week before I met up with Danny again. We were both doing some work at his shop and he said, 'John and Dot are back together again. We've no idea what you said to them but things are back to normal, thank goodness.'

I was busy washing the floor of the back shop and I was on my knees beside the bucket. I looked up at him. 'That's good news, Danny, but I only told them the truth.'

He looked at the big clock which was a leftover relic from the previous owner. 'Maddie wondered if you could maybe pick Daniel up from the school, Ann. she has to go to a Red Cross meeting with her mum.'

I stood up. 'On one condition only, Danny.'

He said, 'What's that?'

'That you come with me.'

He shook his head. 'I don't want the other parents at the school gate to see Daniel upset. He'll be looking for his mum or his grandmother.'

'Well, I'm only going if you come as well,' I said, giving him no option but to agree.

Snow had started to fall earlier in the day and there was a thick covering on the ground. As we slowly trudged towards the school, Danny looked more and more apprehensive. By the time we reached the gate a few minutes before the school came out, it had started to snow again. We joined the group of people who stood waiting patiently on the pavement, all of us huddled up against the snowstorm.

Then the doors opened and the children poured out, their hats and scarves making a bright splash of colour on this grey, snowy day. We saw Daniel and I called over. For a moment he stayed still as his eyes scanned the playground in search of his mother or grandmother. He walked slowly forward but kept his eyes averted from Danny.

Suddenly Danny picked up a handful of snow, formed it into a ball and threw it at his son. Daniel's eyes widened in shock as he gazed at us both. For one horrible moment, I thought he was going to burst into tears but then he bent down and made a big snowball and threw it at Danny. His father then made an even bigger ball and launched it at his son where it spilled all over his school coat. Running across the playground, Daniel scooped up more snow and threw it at his father. Danny chased Daniel over the deep snow and when he caught him they both fell down and rolled in the snow, laughing as they gambolled in the deep drifts.

When they finally stood up, Daniel's eyes were shining. 'That was great fun, Daddy. Can we go sledging after we get home?'

I saw tears in Danny's eyes as he gazed at his son. Then he smiled as he put his arm around his shoulder. He said cheerfully,

'Yes, we can and we'll also make a huge snowman and use your Grandad's golfing hat and his old pipe.'

Later, I was to remember that day and bless the sudden snow-storm for breaking the stalemate between father and son. And I knew Maddie and her parents thought the same.

17

It was the middle of March and it was still snowing. The streets were thick with brown, wet slush and there were mini mountains of dirty snow piled up at the kerbs. Even the children who had initially greeted the snow with joyful exuberance were now also tired of the relentless heavy snow that fell from the sky, endlessly.

Danny had opened his shop at the beginning of the year and, after a slow start, it was now beginning to get more trade. People commented on his bright cheery shop and its helpful owner but he thought the growing trade came mainly from the closures of two other small grocer's shops further up the Hawkhill. The customers from these shops changed their ration books to Danny's shop which helped him increase his takings.

He was quite content to let his business grow slowly but steadily because, as he had said, once the rationing was over, people would be desperate to buy all the longed-for items that had been denied them during the war years.

Still, during the long, dark, snowy days of March, we were all struggling to survive. Because of the icy cold weather, the coalmen couldn't get the coal out of the railway yards and there was now a shortage of fuel which added to the other shortages and made life difficult.

Lily and I were worried about Granny. She hadn't seen her coalman for three weeks. One night, during a blizzard, we carried over some of our coal to the Overgate to make sure she had a small fire. Her kitchen wasn't very warm but she had gone to bed with a hot-water bottle and she was sitting up reading her book. We had filled two message bags with coal and we deposited it in the coal scuttle.

'We'll bring over some coal every night, Granny, just to make sure you have a fire every day,' I said.

Granny was worried. 'But what about yourselves? Have you got enough?'

We assured her we had which wasn't the truth but we could also go to bed and snuggle up together in our bed settee.

Meanwhile, Connie was hardly ever in the shop during this wintry weather and I was running it myself which, I had to admit, I liked. I missed her company but I still had Joe every morning who was, as usual, the oracle.

'I see the farmers can't dig the tatties and neeps from the ground because it's frozen. There's going to be a shortage because of this awful weather.' He gazed morosely through the window at the curtain of snow that fell from a leaden sky.

'And nobody has any coal. I'm burning all my dross but, when that's finished, there's nothing left. We'll all freeze to death and what does this government say about it? Damn little.'

I tried not to encourage him to get on to the subject of the government. It was a well-known fact that he didn't support any of the political parties but that didn't stop him being scathing about whoever was in power. He had been particularly venomous about the Labour Party landslide the previous year.

'I see Manny Shinwell has nationalised the coal mines and now we can't get any coal from the railway yards. Bloody disgrace!' he said, rolling up a cigarette in his little Rizla machine before giving it a huge lick to stick it down.

I was always fascinated by his huge tongue and how delicately he could lick the strip of glue on the cigarette paper.

'Never mind, Joe,' I said, 'life can only get better.'

He gave me a sour look. Optimists were people he disliked. Better to always look on the gloomy side of life and you would never be disappointed was his motto.

Well, I thought to myself, maybe he's right. We'll either freeze to death or starve. Potatoes and turnips were the great fillers in our diet as was bread which was also rationed. Yet how much better it was to smile and hope the worst was over. We had survived the war and the Margot affair although things were still strained in the Pringle marriage – a least that was the story according to Dad. Danny and Maddie kept a discreet silence about the whole sorry episode.

'Put on a cheery face,' I told Joe.

He gave me a doleful look and pointed with a large, bony hand towards the outside world. 'Cheery? What is there to be cheery about?' He sounded shocked by my frivolous request.

'Well, I like to look on the cheery side,' I said, with as much conviction as I could muster.

A week later, I was to remember my words and was grateful I hadn't offered to eat them at the time. Kathleen dropped her bombshell and cheery faces were thin on the ground. Danny was the one to break the news to Granny, Lily and me after Kit and George had sent an urgent summons to him to come to see them at Lochee.

'Kathleen is taking Kitty and going away to live in London,' he said, as we sat at Granny's meagre fire. 'She's going to live with a man called Chris Portland who's the son of the photographer she worked for.'

I gasped and Danny gave me a sharp look. 'You knew about this, didn't you, Ann?'

I had to admit I did but I added, 'I never thought she would go and live with him in London.' And that was the truth.

'Well, she leaves at the end of this week and nobody but us and Kit's family know about it so keep it quiet. Kathleen is frightened that if Sammy gets to hear about her plans he'll stop her.'

'What does Kit think about her running away like this to live with another man, Danny?' I asked. I was as shocked as the family and I couldn't ever recall anybody doing such a drastic thing.

Danny looked sad. 'She doesn't like it at all and neither does her father but Kathleen has made her mind up and that's that.'

He looked at me with his direct kind of stare and I realised anew how alike he and Kathleen were in looks. 'She's coming to see you tomorrow night. She wants to explain her actions and her side of the story.'

After he left, Granny said it was all very sad. 'She should never have married Sammy. That was her biggest mistake but, unlike most women who make the same mistake, she's not putting up with it. I have to say she's either very brave or terribly stupid to run away like this.'

Amen, I thought.

Lily was agog at this news – this strange adult world that she was on the verge of entering. I warned her to keep quiet but I knew she wouldn't say a word.

Kathleen appeared the following evening at Roseangle. She looked like a snowman when I answered the door and I felt terrible about the meagre fire but no doubt it would have been the same at Lochee. Snowflakes glittered on her red hair and her cheeks were glowing – either from the weather or love, it was difficult to say. She glanced at Lily, unsure about discussing personal matters in front of her. Lily noticed this and went into the bedroom to do her homework. A move I felt sorry for because we never used that room and it was freezing cold in there.

Kathleen came right to the point at once. 'Chris has asked me to move in with him at his flat in London, Ann. I'm going and I'm taking Kitty with me.'

I was still unsure what to say but it didn't really matter what I said as she had made up her mind weeks ago. Still, I had to say it. 'Do you think that's wise, Kathleen? I mean do you really know him that well?'

She shook her head and became thoughtful. 'How well do we ever know anyone, Ann? You have to take your chances in life, I think. Make up your mind, grab your opportunities and make the decision.'

'But what about Sammy? Will he not want to see Kitty? He's going to make an awful fuss when he finds out.'

For the first time that evening, she laughed. 'Well, I'll be hundreds of miles away so it'll not matter.' She became serious again. 'If there's one thing this war has taught me, it is that life's too short to be miserable all the time. Every minute I spend with Chris is wonderful and we get on so well together. He also adores Kitty so there's no problem there. Since we got married, I haven't spent one happy moment with Sammy – not one. If I told you that, would you believe me?'

I nodded.

'I don't want the Malloys to know where I am because they will make Mr Portland's life a misery and he has a successful business to run. But he knows all about us and our decision and he's fine about it. But, there again, he's seen a lot of the world and how other folk live. He says lives shouldn't be lived in precise wee boxes that turn into prisons – unlike Sammy who thinks he can go off to the pub every night then come home and knock me about and yet expect my undying love.'

There was nothing I could say. In private, I agreed with her but it was a very big step to take – to leave your husband and go and live with another man in a city that had been badly bombed as well. I told her this.

'As I said earlier, Ann, Chris's flat hasn't been damaged and we'll live there for the time being. Chris has been offered a job with a newspaper as a photographer and he's thinking of accepting. He says his days of roaming around the world are over and it's time to settle down.'

She stood up to go and at the door I gave her a big hug.

She said, 'Will you come to the station on Friday night, Ann, to see me and Kitty off?'

I promised we would. Lily, I knew, would want to be there.

It was blowing another blizzard on the Friday night but this one was whipped up by a wild cold wind that blew the snow into deep drifts across the pavements. The railway station was bleak on that snowy night and we all felt as grey as the weather. Granny had stayed at home but she had said her goodbyes to Kathleen in a letter.

When Lily and I arrived, Danny, Maddie, George and Patty

were all standing by Kathleen's side and Kit was holding Kitty's hand. Kit was tearful and Kathleen was trying to cheer her up. 'London is not that far away, Mum. You and Dad can always come for a holiday in the summer and, once this all blows over, I'll bring Kitty and Chris up to see you.'

Kit went white. 'Oh, the Malloys will be wild when they find out, Kathleen. Maggie will go mental and we've no idea how Sammy and his father will react.'

Kathleen said nothing but, there again, what could she say? Kit was correct in her assumption of how the Malloys would react to her going.

Kit went on, 'Ma sends her love, as do Belle and Lizzie. They didn't want to come and say cheerio to you as they said it would be too upsetting.'

We then heard a voice announce the imminent arrival of the London train and slowly it steamed into the station. Kitty was almost jumping with excitement, poor wee lass. It was all a big adventure for her but she wouldn't have to live with the aftermath should this romantic venture go wrong.

Kathleen's face, however, was glowing and I prayed it would all end happily for them all. Maddie and Danny were saying their goodbyes and Kathleen was issuing invitations to us all to come and visit her in the far distant future.

It was when Danny said his goodbye to her that she started to cry. He held her close and wiped her eyes with a spotless white handkerchief. 'You'll be fine, Kathleen, but just remember you always have us all to fall back on if things don't go the way you planned them.'

She smiled through tearful eyes. 'Thanks, Danny – and you too, Maddie.'

George picked up her large suitcase and a small bag which held sandwiches and drinks for the journey.

Kathleen took my hand. 'You're the only one apart from Danny who understands this move, Ann.'

I nodded. 'Just you grab your dream when you get it, Kathleen, and, if it doesn't turn out the way you hoped, then at least you've tried. You're on your way to a new life and, honestly, I envy you. You're not a stick-in-the-mud like me.'

She gave me a strange look. 'Oh, you're never that, Ann. Too many folk depend on you – believe me.'

I said, 'Your mum and dad will get the brunt of the Malloys' anger but I'll help out as much as I can and so will Danny.' I handed over Granny's letter. 'Just a few words from Granny.'

Then, just as she was about to step into the carriage, she whispered in my ear, 'Sammy has a secret but it'll soon come out, Ann. Mum will have no bother with the Malloys later on – maybe to start with but not later on.'

The train began to steam out of the station and our little group stood silent as it disappeared into the dark night and out of our lives.

Kit was crying again but no one tried to stop her tears. After all, she had just said goodbye to her daughter and grandchild and there was no guarantee when she would see them again.

Danny suggested we go into the railway buffet – to gather our thoughts together, he said. The place was dismal but it was reasonably warm. The windows were steamed up with condensation but that didn't matter because the weather outside was foul.

The tea was weak and tepid but it seemed to cheer Kit up. 'Kathleen's right – London's not that far away and we can save up and maybe go in the summer to see them. I've never met this Chris. Have you, Ann?'

All eyes turned on me. 'No, but I've seen his photo.'

Everyone seemed to give a collective sigh and I knew we were all hoping everything would turn out fine for this new venture.

After the tea, we all set off for home. Lily and I waited at the tram stop with the Ryans. Danny also wanted to wait but Kit said to take Maddie home and out of the rotten weather. She was certainly looking tired but she was six months pregnant now and it showed. She was much larger this time than with Daniel but she joked it was going to be a much bigger baby.

I think Kit was hoping I could shed some light on Chris and his character but I couldn't. I only had a scant knowledge of the man and, anyway, our opinions didn't count with Kathleen. She was in love and that was the end of the story.

The snow was still falling and we were grateful to see the Lochee tram come into sight, looking like an oasis of warmth and light on this atrocious evening.

As they boarded the tram, Kit said, 'Come and see us next Sunday. Danny and Maddie have promised to come as well. Maybe we'll have some word from Kathleen by then – just a postcard to say how she's settling in.' Her voice trailed off and tears weren't very far away. Patty took her arm and we waved as the tram set off.

When we got back home, Lily and I jumped into the bed settee with our two hot-water bottles and two cups of piping-hot cocoa.

Lily thought it was all so romantic – young lovers running away together to live out their dream in the glowing sunset.

I didn't tell her that those scenes were usually based on Hollywood films and were pure fantasy. Still, maybe Kathleen and Chris would have a Hollywood-style life . . .

I fell asleep and dreamed of the Malloys, their faces red with rage. When I woke up, I remembered Kathleen's words. What secret did Sammy harbour? And why was Kathleen whispering to me?

I was dreading our visit the following Sunday. I imagined an irate collection of Malloys, old and young, but, when we arrived, all was peaceful.

Kit couldn't believe it. 'It's been like this since last Friday. I hope this is not a false calm.'

Danny and Maddie were as surprised as Kit and so were we. Danny laughed. 'I thought Sammy would be here, shouting and threatening everybody in sight.'

I was glad to have this chat with him. I wanted to ask him if he had heard anything from Ma Ryan on Kathleen's decision to leave. He said he hadn't but we all knew Ma's reluctance to use her psychic powers on her own family.

'Ma told me a while ago that I was in danger, Danny. She said I had to watch my step and it was just like the time when she gave me the warning about the Ferry. Still, I think the danger is over now.'

He looked alarmed.

'I almost fell from a tramcar on the same day she warned me so I reckon that was why I had to watch my step.'

He looked worried. 'What a lot of trouble we're having just now, Ann – first it was Margot and now it's Kathleen. Let's hope that's the end of it.'

I echoed this sentiment. Things might be quiet today but the storm would erupt sooner or later and Kit and George would be in the front line – of that I was sure. I mentally envisaged Maggie on the warpath and it wasn't a pleasant thought. Still, we could all breathe a sigh of relief and enjoy today and our time together.

It was when we were on our way home that Maddie and Danny brought up the subject of the flat at Roseangle. I immediately said we could leave in a couple of days but that wasn't the plan they said.

'We were thinking of selling the flat Ann and buying a house with a garden. It would be much better for Daniel and the new baby,' said Maddie.

My heart sank at the thought of handing the flat over to a stranger.

Maddie went on, 'Danny and I were wondering if you would like to buy it from us?'

I almost collapsed with amazement. 'Buy a house Maddie? I couldn't afford it.'

Danny said, 'We've spoken to Maddie's dad and, if you go to see him this week, then he'll give you some good advice.'

Lily hadn't come with us. She had stayed with Dad and Rosie and Jay and I didn't want her to find out about this – at least not for the time being. She would be thrilled if she thought the flat could be ours but how could I possibly buy it? I didn't want to raise her hopes only to dash them when I discovered I couldn't afford it.

Danny and Maddie got off the tram before me and I spent the rest of the journey thinking about the offer. There was no way I could afford it, I thought. I was halfway up the Hilltown to pick Lily up when I decided there was no harm in going to see Mr Pringle. He would obviously put me right about the exorbitant costs of buying a house.

However, the next morning I got such a lovely surprise that I forgot about our recent worries or buying a house. When the three girls came into the shop for their cigarettes and sweets, Amy and Sylvia were unusually quiet. Joe even remarked on it.

'Edith's got good news, Ann,' said Sylvia.

I thought there was a hint of jealousy in her terse remark.

I looked at Edith and she held up her left hand. On her fourth finger was an engagement ring.

'Edith,' I said, totally surprised, 'when did this happen?'

She looked so pleased with herself. 'At the weekend! My fiancé is a friend of my brother. They are both at university but we plan to get married when he graduates.'

'That's wonderful!' There was nothing more I could add. I was speechless.

Joe turned to the two other girls. 'And when are you two humdingers getting engaged?'

The girls perked up at these complimentary words. 'Och, we've no' got any fiancés,' said Amy, sounding miffed.

Joe looked shocked. 'What? Two good-looking lassies like you? You're kidding me.'

'Well, we're going to the dancing tonight so maybe we'll meet the men of our dreams – just like Edith,' said Sylvia. She put the cigarettes in her pocket and turned to leave the shop. It was yet another snowy morning and the girls pulled their headscarves tighter around their heads.

Edith gave my hand a squeeze. 'See, you *can* meet a man by sitting at the fire knitting, Ann,' she said softly.

I smiled. 'Of course you can, Edith.'

If that's the case, I thought, where is my Prince Charming?

Still, that small piece of good news cheered me up as I set off for Mr Pringle's office. I sat in the hard-backed chair in the outer office and watched one woman typing what looked like a novel while the other one was busy putting paper sheets into the many files that were crammed into the wooden shelves.

Mr Pringle came out and I was ushered to a softer seat in his office. He got right to the point. 'Maddie and Danny have told you of their proposition, Ann? About buying the flat at Roseangle?'

I nodded. My mouth felt dry. 'I don't think I can afford it, Mr Pringle.'

He opened a thin file in front of him and studied it for a moment. 'Well, according to your finances, you can buy it. The money you inherited from Mrs Barrie has been wisely invested and you haven't used any of it over the last few years.' What he didn't say was I hadn't touched it since the money I had taken out for Lily when Margot was married to Dad.

'But I wanted that money to be kept for Lily. That's why I haven't been to see you about it for years. I thought, if I just forgot about it, I couldn't spend it. You know she wants to go to art college when she leaves school which will be later this year. I'll need that money to cover her fees and her keep.'

He studied the file again. 'Well, if you put aside one hundred and fifty pounds for that, you still have a balance of two thousand pounds.'

I gasped out loud. 'Two thousand pounds?'

He nodded. 'I did say it had been wisely invested. You can easily afford the flat and the balance of your money will be invested again, hopefully to grow in size.'

I didn't know what to say.

'Well, you think it over, Ann, and let me know what you decide. Remember, however, that property is capital and you can always sell the house at a later date and you'll probably get all your investment back – maybe even a bit more.'

Put that way, how could I refuse? 'I'll think it over, Mr Pringle, and let you know soon.'

Outside in the street, my head was in a whirl. It was similar to the day Jean Peters, Mr Potter and I were told about our legacies from the darling Mrs Barrie. I remembered how we had all been so surprised but pleased by the news.

What would Lily say if she knew? She would be over the moon, of that I was sure. But having my legacy tucked away was like having money for a rainy day. It cushioned Lily and me and I desperately wanted her to have her art college education.

Suddenly Kathleen's image floated in front of me. Her voice was saying take what you want and to hang with the consequences. And it would mean Lily would always have a roof over her head instead of starving in some Glasgow garret.

I went back to the office and Mr Pringle was surprised to see me so soon.

'I've made up my mind, Mr Pringle. I'll buy the flat.'

I decided not to tell Lily until the deal was finalised and I was planning to tell the family at the same time.

The weather didn't improve by the time April arrived and it was still snowing. Kit was expecting trouble any day and it arrived at almost the same time I got the letter from the Borlands. Greg's mum and dad. It was a grey Saturday and the leaden sky seemed to sit on top of the buildings. The letter thankfully was short. 'We would love to see you both during the school holidays. It would be lovely to see Lily before she goes away to the art college. Please write soon and say you'll come.' It was signed 'Babs'.

The next day, the Malloys, realising they hadn't seen Kathleen or Kitty for a few weeks, finally burst into Kit's kitchen. They were demanding to know the truth because they had heard a rumour that Kathleen had done a bunk.

Danny and I heard about it later but seemingly the row could be heard at the far end of the street, Maggie's screeching being so loud. When neither Kit or George would tell them of Kathleen's whereabouts, Sammy's dad had threatened to burst into Mr Portland's studio the next day and sort him out. George told him he could do what he wanted but they wouldn't find Kathleen or Kitty there. They had gone for good and the Malloy family could do nothing about it.

Later, Danny told me how strange it had been that Sammy hadn't joined in the melee and, according to the Lochee grapevine, he hadn't wanted his parents to cause such a fuss.

'I think that's strange, Ann, don't you?' he said.

I wasn't so sure. I was still intrigued by Kathleen's whispered secret. Still, at that time, I was finding life so topsy-turvy that I didn't give it much thought.

I had told Maddie and Danny that I was buying the flat and they were both pleased.

'That will let us look for a house before the baby comes,' Maddie had said.

Yet, with the wintry weather still making everybody miserable, they hadn't the inclination to go and look for somewhere else to live.

'We'll wait until the better weather to look around,' she said, patting her ever-expanding waistline. 'We'll have something sorted out before this bundle arrives.'

I still hadn't answered Babs Borland's letter and, as each day passed, I felt guiltier than ever. After all, it wasn't their fault that Greg had gone off with someone else.

That night, as Lily and I sat at the window with our tea, watching a fierce blizzard blowing from the east, I asked her, 'Would you like to go and see the Borlands before you and Joy go to the art college?'

To my dismay, her face lit up. 'That would be great.'

That was that decided then, I thought. I would write to them that evening and say we would visit them sometime during the school holiday.

I then mentioned the flat. 'Danny and Maddie are going to sell the flat, Lily.'

Her face, which a moment before had been beaming, now became downcast. 'Oh, that means we'll have to leave it, Ann?'

I smiled. 'No, Lily, I'm buying it with Mr Pringle's help so it'll always be here for you and me.'

She jumped up from her chair. 'Oh, Ann, that's wonderful. I've always loved this place and now it's to be ours.' She put her arms around me and gave me a hug. 'Thanks for doing that.'

I posted my letter to Trinafour first thing the following morning before I had a chance to destroy it. Still, I thought, July was a long way off. Maybe we wouldn't have to go. Maybe the Borlands would write back with news of other unexpected visitors and they could no longer put us up . . . or something along these lines.

It was after I posted the letter that I remembered the shop. Who would be able to do it if I was to be away from the Friday till the Sunday or even the Monday?

Connie said not to worry. She would hold the fort with some help from Joe.

'Joe?' I said, taken aback.

'Aye, Joe. He used to help out in the old days and I don't think he ever got over having to give it up when his legs got too bad to stand on them for hours. That was why I advertised for another assistant and you came. But he still misses it – all the gossip and buzz. Why do you think he comes in every morning and evening?'

I had to admit I hadn't given it a lot of thought. I mean, for all I knew, he could have been carrying a torch for Connie all these years but was hiding his feelings under his gruff exterior. I said so and Connie burst out laughing.

'Don't underestimate Joe, young lady. You should have seen him in his younger days. A real good-looker was our Joe but, after his wife died early on in their marriage, he never seemed to bother with anyone else. Which was strange because his wife was a real tartar. She had a tongue that would cut steel.'

I was amazed and began to see him in a different light. Up till then, I had always thought of him as one of Dad's old friends and a bit of a blether. Now it seemed he had had a difficult married life. It made me wonder how little I knew about anyone else.

The world had been turned upside down and if the papers were to be believed, there were still pockets of war-like aggression in the world – and not only in far-off countries. There was also the war at Lochee.

Babs wrote back by return, saying how glad they both were that we were coming for a visit and how much they were looking forward to seeing us again. As far as I was concerned, I didn't share the sentiment. I couldn't bear an entire weekend of hearing how happy Greg was with his wife. In fact, the more I thought of it, the more depressed I became.

18

People were saying it was the worst winter they could remember. The snow, which had started in February, was still falling at the start of April. We had long run out of coal. Hattie was helping Granny out with some from her meagre stock but she was also running short.

The women in the food queues were becoming more and more angry about all the continued shortages and I was beginning to get frazzled myself. Trying to get to the paper shop in the early morning was a nightmare. Mountains of snow were being shovelled up at the side of the kerbs and it was difficult to stay upright on the slippery pavements.

Lily and I had received a postcard from Kathleen. She didn't say much except that she and Kitty had settled in and were enjoying their new life. She had enrolled Kitty at a school near the flat and she was seemingly enjoying it.

Struggling to work the morning after receiving the postcard had made me grumpy. Kathleen was living a happy life while I was miserable. Still, the thought of owning the flat gave me some pleasurable moments – which was more than George and Kit had as Maggie and Mick Malloy were still coming round, shouting the odds.

I kept thinking about our promised trip to Trinafour. It was still weeks away but I was depressed at the thought of going. I kept hoping something would come up to put the visit off. Wishful thinking, I called it.

Joe was waiting for me when I went to open the shop the next morning and I wondered if he ever slept. He was always the first customer and today he was standing in the shop doorway and he was shivering.

'For goodness sake, Joe, you should be in your house instead of standing on a freezing cold step.' I didn't mean to be sharp but it had been one of those weeks – cold outside and cold inside. Thank goodness for hot-water bottles and cosy blankets, I thought.

Joe echoed my thoughts. 'Och, it's just as cold inside my house as it is standing here, Ann. The coal is finished and so is the dross. The bunker is well and truly empty.'

I felt sorry for him but we were all in the same boat.

However, he had some cheerful news. 'The coal is seemingly being despatched from the yards and the coalman said he might have some supplies tomorrow – I do hope so.'

I had long since stopped putting on the small fire in the back shop and the shop never seemed to warm up. There were always customers opening the door and letting all the freezing cold air in.

That night I went to check up on Granny and to see if her coalman had made a delivery. To my delight, he had. Her fire wasn't exactly blazing but at least it was on and that was a blessing.

I made a mental note to get my coalman to call when I would be at home but, failing that, I could always leave my key with the elderly man next door who had proved so helpful to us over our long stay in the flat.

Granny and I were hugging the fire when Hattie appeared. Her cheeks were red with the cold and she looked pleased with herself. Considering how miserable she had been over the last few months, we were both surprised to see her looking happy.

'I've just had some wonderful news,' she said, sounding breath-less from her walk.

Granny and I stared at her, surprise written all over our faces.

'I've heard from Graham and what to you think?'

We gave her a blank stare.

'He's coming back to Dundee to work. He's got an office in the town and he's letting his partner run the Clydebank office.'

Granny spoke first. 'Och, that's great news, Hattie. Does that mean you'll be back seeing him?'

She nodded happily.

I remained silent. Surely this happy, fairy-tale ending hadn't suddenly appeared out of the far blue yonder. What about his strange behaviour before he left for Clydebank?

Hattie saw my expression. 'I know what you're thinking, Ann, but Graham has told me everything that's happened.'

'What's that, Hattie?' said Granny, her face frowning in puzzlement.

'About his strangeness last year. Well, he came to see me last week to tell me about his move back here and also to tell me the whole sorry story. He's not a widower like I thought . . .' She corrected this statement. 'Or as everyone thought. He called himself a widower because, six years ago, his wife left him to go and live with another man.'

My heart lurched. Oh, no, I thought, just like Kathleen.

'Graham was going to divorce her but he never got around to it. He said he hadn't met anyone he was interested in till he met me. That's when he decided to file for a divorce so we could get married. Unfortunately a stray bomb at the end of the war changed all that.'

Granny was still perplexed. 'Why was that, Hattie?'

Hattie smoothed her hair and I recalled this was always a sign that she was nervous. 'I really don't know all the circumstances except that the house where the wife and her man friend were living took a direct hit. The man escaped but Graham's wife was badly injured. She was taken to hospital and the man gave the hospital staff Graham's address in Dundee. He was called urgently to the hospital but his wife was unconscious.'

I suddenly remembered the night I met him – the night when he had that evasive and haunted look in his eyes. It must have been that day when he got the news.

'He's been visiting her every week since then – hoping her

254

friend would come back. But he's disappeared. Graham was heartbroken because he didn't want to deceive me while still visiting his wife. And he couldn't get a divorce while she was in a coma so he was torn between two rocks. That's why he decided to move back to Clydebank and open his office up again.'

One thing was puzzling me. 'Why are you looking so happy, Hattie, if Graham has a wife?'

'His wife has been in a nursing home for ages as she was too ill to go home but she's all right now. Graham didn't want to mention a divorce until now and, although she's unhappy about it, she's agreed to it. Oh, we know it'll take a while but he'll be living and working here and we'll be together. That's all that matters.'

Granny was pleased for Hattie but was also worried about Graham's wife. She said, 'I know she was the one to leave him, Hattie, but what will she do now? Where will she live? I mean she must still be feeling ill and alone and won't she be left homeless?'

Hattie said, 'She won't be homeless, Mum. Graham has given her the flat they used to have before she left and he'll send her money every month until she gets on her feet and gets a job – or another man. She was very fond of men, I believe.'

'Did Graham say that?' I asked, shocked that he would tell Hattie something like that about his wife.

It was Hattie's turn to look shocked. 'No, he didn't. It was Mrs Pringle. Graham told them all about his wife's illness and she went down to see her. When Mrs Pringle entered the hospital room, she was admiring herself in a mirror and the first words she said were that she hoped she would get her good looks back again or she would never get another man. Mrs Pringle was still shocked when she told me about it.'

Granny said sincerely, 'Well, we're all happy for you, Hattie, and you always knew we were all fond of Graham. We hope you'll both be very happy.'

Hattie looked at me and I nodded. Another happy couple, I thought. I seemed to be surrounded by them. Then I immediately felt guilty. It wasn't Hattie and Graham's fault that I was growing into a bitter old spinster.

I went over and gave her a hug. 'I'm really pleased for you both, Hattie. You deserve happiness after all these years without Pat.'

There were tears in her eyes when she got up to leave. 'I never thought I would ever meet another man – not after Pat. But Graham is very special to me and I only wish he had told me all his troubles earlier on. We could have both worked them out.'

After she left, Granny stoked up the fire. She sighed. 'What a strange time this has been, Ann – first the trouble with Margot then Kathleen going off to London and now this happy ending with Hattie and Graham. Things aye come in threes so maybe that's the end of all the dramas in our lives.'

Graham and Hattie appeared the following Saturday. Lily and I were playing cards with Granny, Alice and Bella when they arrived in the kitchen. Hattie was dressed in a lovely green satin evening dress and Graham was looking as proud as Punch.

Bella looked sourly at them. 'Well, is that you away out galli-vanting again?'

Graham beamed at her. 'Indeed we are, Bella. We're going to a dinner dance at the Queen's Hotel.'

With these words and a final swish of her long dress, they left. Bella, who knew all the story of Graham's marital troubles, gazed at her cards and snorted. 'You wouldn't think he had a wife, would you? Gallivanting with Hattie to dinner dances. It's no' right.'

Granny glared at her. 'Just you mind your cards, Bella, or else I might win.'

This threat was enough to make Bella study her hand with intensity. If there was one thing she loved more than her continued ill health, it was to win at cards and scoop all the pennies into her apron pocket.

'Anyway,' said Granny, 'I think Graham behaved like a true gentleman – giving up living here and going to look after his injured wife, at least while she needed him. He should have told

Hattie but, there again, maybe he didn't want to hurt her feelings or promise her something that might not materialise.'

Bella gave her another sour look but then snapped back to attention when Alice unexpectedly won the game.

As the cards were being dealt out again, Bella gave me a pseudo-innocent look. 'And when will we hear wedding bells for you, Ann. Lily will be leaving in the summer for her art college and that means you'll be biding on your own if you don't pull out all the stops to get another man.'

Before I could answer and much to my amazement, Lily said, 'Don't be so rude to Ann! She'll get a great man one of these days. He'll be good-looking and rich and he'll fall head over heels in love with her.'

Granny laughed and the tension was broken but trust Bella to hit the nail on the head with her statement. Lily might make it sound like there were loads of eligible fellows hanging around me but that was just a fantasy in her ever-fertile imagination.

The truth was much bleaker – in the real world, the only man I ever met on a regular basis was Joe.

Afterwards, when Bella went home with the majority of pennies in her pocket, Alice said, 'It's good that Bella's not walking around with her stick any more, Nan.'

Granny laughed. 'Aye, we never got to the bottom of that wee incident, did we? We think the reason she kept quiet about it was because she'd had too much to drink from her medicine bottle.'

We all laughed.

There was some good news around in the shape of Danny's shop. He was steadily building up his trade and I made a mental promise to go and see Maddie soon as I hadn't seen her in over a week. She didn't like coming out on to the snowy pavements and I knew they still hadn't found another house.

Minnie and her son Peter were two other people I hardly saw during those winter days. They had managed to get another house in Albert Street and I promised myself I would go and see them as soon as this awful snow finished. But working the longer hours in the shop left me with little time for socialising. In fact, there were some nights I was in bed and asleep before Lily. When this happened, she would remark, gazing at me with her youthful but solemn eyes, 'You are getting older, Ann, aren't you?'

I would laugh and pretend to throw my pillow at her but she was right. I was certainly not getting any younger. I tried hard not to think of the time when she would be gone. This house would be so silent and empty and I didn't think I could bear it. But did I have a choice? No, I didn't.

The winter seemed to go on forever as we went about muffled up against the snow showers. We were all longing for spring and the sun and Maddie was longing for June and the birth of her baby. It was as if we were all in a world of waiting – a sort of limbo – and we were just putting in the time until the perfect day arrived.

But spring did arrive in May and we were all grateful to feel the warmth of the sun again on our faces. The roads and pavements became black once more as the snow slowly melted.

Lily was doing her final exams at Rockwell and she concentrated on her homework every night. This gave me an excuse to visit Danny and Maddie and on one of these visits they took me to see a house they were interested in. It wasn't too far from the Pringles' house but still far enough away for them to lead their own lives. I had the feeling that Danny was longing for a place of his own although he hadn't said anything.

The house lay basking in the evening sunshine, like a fat contented cat, I thought. Long golden rays spread over the large garden and turned the west-facing windows into molten gold. It was an enchanting house and I liked it straight away. But I remained silent because it wasn't me who would be staying in it.

Danny had been given the key from Mr Pringle who was acting as executor for an old lady who had recently died. Her only son lived in England and he had given the entire sale over to Mr Pringle. The only stipulation he had made was on the price. He knew what it was worth and he wanted the market price for it.

We wandered through the empty rooms. Dust rose as we walked over the bare wooden floors and mingled with the golden beams of sunlight. The living room window overlooked the river but because it lay on higher ground than the Pringles' house, the entire panorama was stunning.

Maddie and Danny loved it. I could tell by their faces.

Maddie said, 'Can we afford it, Danny? Also it'll take more to furnish it. The flat was so small we didn't need an awful lot of furniture.'

That was true and I couldn't visualise their small amount of furniture filling this empty space.

'Your dad will arrange a mortgage for us, Maddie, and we'll just have to take our time with the furnishings. As long as we get this room and the bedrooms done then we can do the decorating slowly.'

Maddie nodded. I could see from her face that she was already planning colour schemes and room layouts.

Later, we walked through the sunlit street and I went straight back to Roseangle. The sale of the flat was almost complete but I had to get Maddie and Danny's belongings packed up for when the removal men arrived.

I too would be without furniture when everything was removed but I had my own plans on how I would like to furnish our flat. Our flat – I liked the sound of that. Lily and I were having great fun looking at curtains and furniture and she had a good eye for colour. I would take her advice when it came to furnishings.

Hattie was only working two days a week now with Mrs Pringle but she was still glowing with happiness. Graham went back to Clydebank to put his divorce plans into action. He was saying goodbye to his old life and he was looking forward to a future with Hattie.

With the coming of the sun, I thought our lives would be smooth and our troubles were surely behind us. Maddie's delivery date wasn't that far away. Another six weeks to go and she was praying for the day to arrive to get it all over with and regain her figure. She was certainly much bigger this time around and she didn't so much walk as waddle. It was getting her down.

Mr Pringle was making the arrangements for Joy and Lily's

accommodation in Glasgow and they were enrolling in the art college in September. With these comforting thoughts, I was happy to go to the shop and get on with all the chores for Granny and myself.

As it was, I should have known never to trust in comforting thoughts. They had a strange habit of turning against me like some jinx. One Sunday, Danny arrived at Granny's door and asked me to go to Lochee with him. My heart sank at this request. What was wrong now?

Danny said he didn't know. Patty had arrived that morning with the message. When we arrived, I was surprised to see Kit and George sitting beside a very quiet Maggie and Mick. For a moment, I thought Kathleen had come home but there was no sign of her or Kitty. I couldn't think what had happened and suddenly felt so afraid.

'What's the matter, Kit?' I asked, my voice sounding strange even to my own ears.

Maggie wasn't looking at anyone. She seemed to find the toe of her slipper a fascinating thing to look at and that surprised me even more – especially after all her recent screeching about Kathleen.

Kit looked embarrassed. She glanced at Maggie and said, 'Sammy has got Jean Martin in trouble – she's expecting.'

Danny gasped. 'But she's only fifteen.'

Maggie looked even more uncomfortable while her husband gazed at the wall. It was the quietest I had ever seen him.

Then Maggie spoke. It was like bullets hitting a brick wall. 'Wait till I get my hands on him. I'll knock him from here to China.'

Danny and I looked at one another. We didn't understand what she meant. When she got her hands on him? Surely he was in the house.

Kit explained, once again glancing at the furious, red-faced Maggie. 'Sammy has gone away and we don't know where he is.'

'He's joined up in the army, I reckon,' mumbled Mick while Maggie glared at him.

Danny asked, 'What's going to happen to Jean?'

'Her parents want Sammy to marry her but, as he's already married, that's not possible – unless Kathleen gets a divorce which we hope she will,' said George.

Maggie opened her mouth to speak but thought better of it. Instead, she stood up and Mick followed her to the door. However, when she reached it, she couldn't help herself. She was so incensed. 'If your Kathleen had been a proper wife to Sammy then this would never have happened.'

Kit wasn't going to let this pass. 'Maggie, your Sammy has been strutting around all the young lassies here since the minute he got back from the war. This has nothing to do with Kathleen but I'll tell you this – she made the right decision when she made up her mind to clear off from all this bother and trouble and all because your Sammy can't keep his trousers on.'

After they left, Danny and I stayed on for a few more minutes. There hadn't been any fresh news from Kathleen and all the conversation seemed to go out the door along with the Malloys so we left.

On the way home, Danny said, 'Can things get any worse at Lochee, I wonder?'

Quite honestly, I couldn't answer him truthfully. It was a tangled mess and now Sammy was missing, Kathleen and Kitty were gone and poor fifteen-year-old Jean was in the family way. I wondered if this was Sammy's secret that Kathleen had mentioned to me.

I said, 'I think Kathleen knew about this pregnancy, Danny. She told me on the night she left that Sammy had a secret and that the Malloys wouldn't bother her mum and dad again.'

'It's terrible that he's got a fifteen-year-old girl in trouble.'

I couldn't agree more, especially when I saw his worried face.

However, he cheered up slightly by the time we reached our stop. 'We've bought the house, Ann. Hopefully we'll get it into shape in time for the baby's arrival.'

I smiled. Maddie didn't have long to go now which was just as well because she was getting bigger every day – like a barrel on legs, she said, and it was true.

Danny was worried about Daniel. 'I just hope he's not jealous of the new baby. I couldn't bear him being upset again – especially after the trouble we had when I came back from the army.'

I tried to reassure him. 'Och, he'll be fine, Danny. You've all got over your problems now.' Yet, as I spoke, I too hoped everything would go well.

I was about to leave when he called after me. 'I forgot to say that Peter has been made manager of Lipton's in the Overgate and Minnie is expecting again.'

That was wonderful news and I made a mental note of either writing to them or maybe visiting them to say congratulations. When I had a spare moment – whenever that might be.

19

'Twins!' I didn't realise my voice sounded so loud until three women at the next table stopped drinking their tea and gazed at me. The woman at the table on our right also looked wide-eyed, her hand frozen halfway to the three-tiered cake stand. 'You're going to have twins, Maddie?' I said, a good bit quieter this time.

Maddie sat across from me and she nodded. I wasn't sure if she was pleased or merely shell-shocked.

'How can it be twins at this late date, Maddie? Why didn't the doctor tell you earlier?'

She sighed and slowly buttered her scone. 'Well, he did suspect it might be twins but he couldn't detect two heartbeats – at least not until a few days ago.'

We were sitting in Draffen's coffee lounge after spending a long morning looking for curtain material for the windows of the new house. Everything was still in short supply and it had been a frustrating few hours. Afterwards, Maddie and I were grateful to sit down and have a cup of tea but then she dropped this bombshell.

'I still have all Daniel's baby things and there should be enough for two babies but I'll have to sell my pram and get a twin one. Of course, with everything in such short supply, I don't think I'll get one before the birth. Seemingly there's a long waiting list for prams and most new mothers order theirs during the first few months of their pregnancy. I thought my old pram was ideal but it doesn't look like it now.'

Her face was flushed with worry so I took her hand and said that things would work out and they always did – Ann the oracle at work again.

'And there's the house to get ready,' she said, looking at me with worried eyes. 'I don't honestly think there's going to be time to get everything ready.'

'Look, Maddie, don't worry about prams and houses. At least you've got Danny here this time to help you with everything. It's not like the last time with Daniel, is it?'

Suddenly she smiled and she looked more like the old Maddie I knew. 'Of course it's not. Even if I have to push one baby in the pram and carry the other one like an Indian papoose, what's the problem?'

'I can help you and Danny with the house if you like – in the evenings.'

She accepted this offer of help with a grateful smile. 'I doubt if I can be of any help in the house, Ann. I could maybe sew the curtains but even then I'm not comfortable sitting in a chair. I just feel so huge.'

So we all mucked in. Mr Pringle was a big help and every evening, during the long hours of daylight in early June, he joined Danny, Lily and me in getting the house cleaned and ready for Daniel and the new babies.

Maddie didn't want to remove everything from the flat. She said, 'It would mean leaving you with nothing, Ann.' So a compromise was agreed. The bed settee, a table and two chairs were to be left behind along with some essentials like crockery and pots. I assured her this was all I needed until I could manage to buy my own things for the flat.

As Danny often said, once the rationing was over, it would become a golden time for the shoppers. Well, that was as maybe but, at the moment, it was still a land of queues and rationing and shortages.

One night, after I was finished in the house, Danny walked back with me to Roseangle. It was a sunny evening but very chilly with the wind blowing cold against our faces as we quickly walked along the pavement.

Danny said, 'Heavens, this wind feels icy – almost as if we'll get some more snow.'

'Oh, I hope not, Danny – not after the winter we've just had.'

There was obviously something on his mind but we walked in silence until we reached my house.

'Come up for a cup of tea,' I said. 'Lily will still be at Granny's, keeping her company.'

He said sadly, 'Granny still misses Grandad, doesn't she?'

I nodded.

'That's one of the things I regret – not being here when he died.'

But he laughed when he saw the half-furnished flat. 'Och, you're worse than us, Ann. I think we've got a couple more chairs than you.' He looked out of the window. 'Did you know that Sammy Malloy has joined the army like his father said?'

I came out of the small scullery. 'No, I didn't.'

Danny sat on one of the two chairs and, when he spoke, he sounded pensive. 'The one thing Sammy was good at was being a soldier so maybe this will be the making of him. But Jean Martin will not think so.'

There was nothing I could say. I didn't know the girl but I sympathised with her predicament. Although she would be sixteen when the baby was born and lots of girls of this age were also pregnant, it was still an undesirable state of affairs.

'Any more word from Kathleen?' I asked, setting the cups down on the window sill.

His face brightened up a bit. 'Aye, she writes to Kit every week and they're getting on fine, her and Chris. Kitty is still enjoying her new school. She was saying that London is one vast bomb site but buildings are being rebuilt slowly.' He sipped his tea. 'It's strange how everything has worked out – lots of lives turned upside down and folk living in places they could never have dreamed of before the war.'

I agreed. 'Kathleen said we should all take our happiness when we find it,' I told him, trying to keep the sadness from my voice.

Not very successfully it seemed as Danny asked, 'Have you had any more word from Greg?'

'No.'

Perhaps the shortness of my answer alerted him to my hidden feelings because he gave me a quick sharp glance and turned to look out of the window.

'I'm worried about Maddie, Ann – the fact that she's having twins. I hope it all goes well.' His forehead creased in a worried frown and there was a slight tremor in his hands.

'Och, Maddie will be fine, Danny. Lots of women have twins or even triplets. I was reading the paper the other day and saw that one woman had one set of twins and one set of triplets and she looked great. She had her picture in the paper with the two toddlers and the three babies and she was positively beaming.'

Danny laughed. 'So what you're trying to tell me is to count my blessings? It could have been three instead of two.'

'Or maybe four.' I rolled my eyes in mock horror and we both laughed.

He set off for home still chuckling but, before he left, he said, 'You're a great help in times of worry, Ann. You always put everything into perspective.'

I still felt the glow from this compliment. Lily arrived home and soon we were snuggled up in our bed settee with our hot-water bottles against the cold night air.

Lily lay awake. 'I'll be really pleased to see the Borlands again, Ann. Are you looking forward to it?'

My heart sank but I couldn't let my feeling show. I couldn't upset Lily now that she was on the home run to the art college.

'Aye, I am, Lily. Let's hope the weather is a bit warmer though.'

As it turned out, the weather did improve and it became warm and sunny again. In later years, I was to remember these weeks as a hiatus – a golden time of waiting for Maddie's twins and Lily and Joy's eventual departure.

Lily also viewed this time as a crossroads. She told me she was going to miss the school and all her friends she had made over the years. I also felt there was a slight hesitancy about her going and I knew she was worried about leaving me on my own.

Then, at the end of June, Granny, Dad, Rosie and I all went to the school to see her getting her leaving certificate. We sat in the large assembly hall with all the other parents and friends, all puffed up with pride as their children walked on to the stage to get their certificates and school prizes.

Lily looked so grown-up and dignified as she climbed the stairs to shake hands with the headmaster. Then, to our delight, she also received the top prize for art. She hadn't mentioned this and wanted it to be a surprise for us which it certainly was. But, like all good things, it didn't last long and it was soon over. I wished I could have held that moment forever – to hold its image in my memory and not let it go. I closed my eyes and tried to savour the moment so I wouldn't forget it – ever.

We stood outside in the playground while she said her farewells to her friends, all of them vowing undying friendships. Their young, shrill voices were floating over the hard concrete and echoing against the red stone walls. 'Keep in touch!' 'Please write!' 'Here's my address!' 'Write your name in my autograph book!' 'Cheerio!' 'Cheerio!' 'Cheerio!' 'Goodbye!'

I saw Janey, Lily's friend from primary school days and was struck by how grown-up she had become. Where had all the years gone? I wondered as I remembered them as two nervous five-year-olds not so many moons ago . . . or so it seemed.

Granny, dressed in her new blue frock, looked on with a smile. 'It's hard to believe she's grown-up now, Ann. It only seems like yesterday when she was born and now she's on her way into the big wide world.'

The memory of that unhappy time was mirrored in her eyes and I felt a lump in my throat. If only Mum could see her now. She would be so proud of how she had turned out.

Rosie and Dad wiped away a tear from their eyes. He said, 'I'm glad I came. I thought it would all be academic and highfalutin.'

Rosie gave his arm a squeeze. 'She's a great lassie, Johnny.'

Alice was going to look after Jay when he came back from

school because we had decided to have a celebration tea in Franchi's restaurant in the Overgate. Lily's eyes were bright with excitement, especially when we got a table at the window and she was able to look down on all the people passing underneath.

'I can't believe I've left the school,' she said breathlessly, 'and, in a few months, I'll be going to Glasgow with Joy.'

We all looked at her with affection. At that moment I said a mental prayer, hoping her young life would always be full of love and excitement and adventure.

Lily scanned the menu and her dark eyes became solemn.

'When it comes to food, Lily always gives it her full attention,' Granny said and we all laughed.

Later, after we had all eaten, I asked her, 'Which painting won the first prize, Lily?'

We had left her art portfolio at Granny's house before heading for the restaurant but she bent down and, from her large bag, she brought out a rolled-up tube of paper tied with a white ribbon. She handed it to me and said, 'This is the winner, Ann.'

As everyone looked on, I unrolled it. It was a watercolour painting of me and I gasped. Lily had caught me in pensive mood and I looked unworldly. The soft tones seemed to enhance my face and the faraway look in my eyes as I rested my chin on my hand. I looked sad and must have been thinking of Greg, and Lily had caught this moment in time and recreated it forever.

'Oh, it's beautiful, Ann!' said Rosie. 'And it's just like you when you're thinking of something.'

Granny and Dad both said the same thing and I felt tears come to my eyes.

Lily looked at it with matter-of-fact eyes and said, 'I wanted to give you something before I left, Ann – to thank you for all you've done for me.'

I wiped the tears from my eyes. 'Oh, thank you, Lily. It's the best present I've ever had. I'll get it framed and put it above the fireplace at Roseangle where I can sit and look at it and remember you. And I'll also remember it won the top art prize at Rockwell.'

We then all went home after a memorable day.

Two days later Maddie went into labour. She was admitted to the nursing home at seven o'clock in the morning. A young lad who was a part-time message boy in Danny's shop arrived at the Hilltown to tell me. Connie was doing the evening papers so, as soon as I finished in the early afternoon, I headed for the Perth Road Nursing Home.

I only meant to look in for a few minutes to see Danny but he asked me to stay. He couldn't sit still and I didn't blame him. Everyone was always saying how giving birth was a natural process but Mum had died giving birth to Lily. But I said to myself that I mustn't dwell on this tragic event. I had to be positive for Danny's sake.

'You were here when Daniel was born, Ann. Was Maddie's labour long then?'

I thought back to that awful night – of how Maddie had cried and cried for Danny and how she had thought he was dead.

I nodded. 'It was, Danny, although I wasn't actually here during the labour. She came here in the evening and Daniel wasn't born till the next day.'

Danny shuddered. He said, 'Mum was here with Mrs Pringle but they've gone home for a wee while and will come back later but I'd like you to stay with me if you can, Ann.'

I said I would because I knew how worried he was. It was the least I could do.

The door opened and a nurse came in with a tray. Along with the tea she had placed a small plate of plain biscuits. She apologised for the biscuits. 'We're supposed to be getting chocolate biscuits sometime but we never see them,' she said with a smile.

This small luxury hadn't been around on my first visit so things were certainly improving. I looked at the magazines and noticed there were some copies of *Picture Post* in the pile.

I said to Danny, 'Kathleen was telling me that Chris sometimes puts his photographs in this paper. He's a freelance photographer.'

Danny nodded. I wondered if he had heard me but it didn't

matter. I was merely making idle chat, hoping to fill this awful void – this waiting to hear of new life.

The sun dipped behind the trees in the garden and long shadows spread over the well-kept lawn. It would soon be night and Maddie had been in labour since seven o'clock that morning. I wondered if I would be allowed to stay for much longer. Did the waiting room close at night? Or did it remain open at all times?

I glanced at Danny. He was sitting with his head down, his hands clasped in a white-knuckled grip on his lap. There was nothing I could say to him. After all, what did I know about giving birth? How could I tell him what was happening when I couldn't even visualise what it entailed? Hattie or Mrs Pringle would have been a better companion for him as at least they were mothers.

I took one of his hands and he gave me a weak smile.

'Are you hoping for boys? Or girls?' After I said it, I felt stupid.

He gave me another weak smile. 'Oh, Ann, I don't care – as long as Maddie is fine.'

By now, the sun had disappeared and the grounds had become mauve with twilight. The nurse came in and pulled the thick curtains over the windows and I felt the entire world was now cut off from us.

She gave Danny an encouraging smile. 'Your wife is doing fine. It won't be long now.'

For the first time since we arrived, Danny looked animated. 'How long, Nurse.'

'Not long. I'll let you know as soon as the babies are born.'

I sat back in my seat and I hadn't realised I had half risen from it. The clock on the wall ticked loudly and I recalled the one in Rita's house the day Lily was born and how merrily it had ticked away the final hours of Mum's life. I had to push these sad memories away. It wouldn't help Danny if I was to become morose so, with his hand in mine, we sat in silence except for the relentless ticking that marked the passing of time. I watched the clock with a perverse sort of fascination. How slow and ponderous the pendulum looked and yet the hands moved over the clock face in a loud tick, tick.

Thirty minutes later, the nurse reappeared. 'You have two baby boys, Mr Ryan.'

Danny leapt to his feet and, for one giddy moment, I thought he was about to kiss the nurse. Instead he grabbed me and said, 'Do you hear that, Ann? Two boys!'

I was so pleased for him and relieved it was all over for Maddie.

'Can I see my wife and the boys?' asked Danny.

The nurse said he could but only for a short visit as Mrs Ryan was tired.

I wasn't allowed in so I went and stood outside in the purple twilight, smelling the sweet aroma of the flowers and grass and feeling a bit weak in my knees. It had been a long wait.

Fifteen minutes later, Danny appeared. He looked ecstatic and I could swear his feet weren't touching the ground.

'Maddie is terribly tired but she's fine and the two wee boys are lovely. One was five pounds and the other was five pound six ounces.'

I laughed. 'No wonder she was like a barrel on legs! She'll be able to see her feet again.'

I left him as he hurried home to tell Daniel, the Pringles and Hattie. I quickly went to see Granny before going home, to tell her the good news. I would tell Rosie and Dad the next day. I hated to admit it but I was exhausted too – almost as if I had given birth as well. All I wanted was my bed.

Lily and I were able to visit Maddie on the Saturday afternoon but only for a short visit as she had so many visitors.

She was in a room similar to the one she'd had last time but the similarity ended there. After Daniel's birth, she had been tearful and depressed but, this time, she was almost glowing with pride. The two babies lay in two small cots and they were lovely. I thought Lily would also explode with pride – just like Maddie.

Maddie said, 'They normally stay in the nursery but they've just been fed.'

Lily kept peeping into the cots. 'Och, they're lovely, Maddie – just like two wee dolls.'

Maddie laughed. 'You wouldn't say that during the night, Lily, when they wake up to be fed.'

Before I could take another look, a nurse came in and wheeled them out of the room.

Maddie laughed again. 'I think the nurses are frightened my visitors will give them leprosy or something equally drastic.'

'Still, it's better to be safe than sorry, Maddie,' I said. 'After all, we could have a bad cold or the 'flu.'

'We're calling them Patrick and James after both their grandads. I know Daniel has these as middle names but we wanted to have them as Christian names for the twins.'

'Your mum and Hattie will be pleased about that,' I told her.

Then it was time to leave but I told Maddie that if she needed any help, she was just to ask.

'Thanks, Ann! You're such a good friend to me. I don't know what I would do without you.'

As we were walking through the grounds towards the main road, we met Hattie with Mr and Mrs Pringle. Coming behind them were Danny and Daniel and they were all hurrying to see the new additions to the families. Daniel looked up at his father and he was laughing at something Danny had said to him. It warmed my heart and we waited a few moments to say hello to them.

After the jubilation of seeing the babies, a dark cloud settled above me. The cause was a letter in my coat pocket. Babs Borland had written to say how much they were looking forward to seeing us and asking if the second week in July would be suitable for our visit. The very thing I had been dreading for months was now almost upon me and there was nothing I could do about it. Lily was so excited about the visit that she had started to pack her suitcase in anticipation. As for me . . . well, I was almost crying. How would I get through this visit? Listening to the Borlands telling me all the news of Greg and his wife. And worse – what if she had also given birth?

Oh, my God, I thought, what could I do?

Then the answer came in a small voice in my head. The answer was nothing. I would have to grit my teeth, swallow my pride and listen with feigned interest to the married lives of Greg and his wife.

20

Lily was darting around the flat like a little bird, packing last-minute things for our journey. She saw me standing by the window.

'Have you packed everything, Ann?'

Without turning, I nodded.

She stopped in the middle of the floor. 'If you don't want to go, then that's fine by me, Ann.' She sounded concerned.

I turned round and smiled at her. 'Of course I want to go. What gave you that idea? I was just admiring the view from the window – as always.'

She came and stood beside me. 'It is lovely, isn't it? And it's all ours.'

Lily had been so excited when the sale of the flat was finalised. I had one small niggling worry. I couldn't help thinking about Dad, Rosie and Jay in their small stuffy flat on the Hilltown with its view of pavements and shops. It was not at all like our airy corner with its river views. Still, putting these thoughts aside, I went into the bedroom and carried out my small suitcase and put it on the rug beside the fireplace.

Lily got up from the chair. 'Well, are we ready to go, Ann?'

I nodded again. 'Yes.'

Lily gave me a look as if she was puzzled by this monosyllabic response from me so I gave her a smile and made a huge show of picking up my suitcase and handbag – an effort that seemed to reassure her.

The train station was busy but it was really no wonder – after all, it was July and people were either going off on their summer holidays or just for a day out. The platform was thronged with people and Lily kept looking down the railway tracks as if, by constantly surveying them, the train would somehow magically appear. I recalled with a smile that this was something she had always done. Personally I hoped that the train had maybe broken down between its last station and here but my mental prayer wasn't answered because it appeared soon after our arrival. It steamed into view like one of the Four Horsemen of the Apocalypse. Within the next few hours, we would be at Trinafour and the Borlands' house, making small talk about the various members of both families.

Lily, however, was full of excitement. She had managed to squeeze in beside a large woman and an equally portly man while I got a seat across from them. Lily winked at me and I had to stifle a laugh as she looked so comical between the two plump people. Then, fortunately for us, two passengers got off at one of the small stations on the line. After that, we were each able to get a window seat and we gazed at the passing scenery on that hot July day.

'I hope the weather stays like this,' said Lily, fanning her face with a copy of a newspaper. 'It'll be great to be in the country if it's this warm.'

To be honest, I couldn't have cared less about the weather. I would just be glad when this ordeal of a weekend was over but I just smiled at her and nodded.

The train puffed its way past green fields. As it left the industrial landscape behind, much to my amazement, I began to relax. There was something soothing about trees and greenery.

We had to change trains at Perth and we sat on the platform for thirty minutes until our connection arrived. Then, with a great deal of pushing and shoving of luggage into the overhead compartments and getting a seat again, we were on our way on the final stage of the journey.

Mr Borland was meeting us at Struan station and he would

take us the few miles to the farmhouse. Knowing this, it was still a surprise when we reached our destination to see him standing beside a smart grey van.

Lily ran up to him. 'You've got a new van, Mr Borland. When did you get it?'

He gave her a smug-looking smile. 'Just a few weeks ago, Lily, but it's come in handy for your visit.'

He took our suitcases. 'It's nice to see you again, Ann. You're looking well.'

I was surprised. Was I looking well? He wouldn't have said it if it hadn't been true.

He then turned to Lily who had always been a great favourite of his. 'My, what a big lassie you are now, Lily! And you're away to art college soon?'

She nodded happily and, at that moment, I envied her. She was starting out on her life and everything was always such a joy to her. If only I could say the same – that everything was joyous.

This new van had seats in the rear and Lily scrambled into one of them while I climbed in beside Dave.

'I like your new van, Mr Borland,' said Lily. 'But I miss sitting on the cushion in the back.'

She was referring to his previous van which only had two seats and a cushion in the back for a third passenger or maybe the dogs.

'I had to get another van, Lily, as the last one almost disintegrated with rust. Still, I had some good years out of it so I'm not complaining.'

The road was just as twisty as I recalled it and it seemed more than six miles to the rough track that led to the farmhouse. Because of the dry weather, dust thrown up by the wheels flew in through the open windows.

'I'll be glad to see some rain,' he said. 'It's been such a dry spell for a few weeks and everything will get parched if this keeps up.'

I looked out of the window and the hills looked green. The fields where flocks of sheep could be seen grazing looked quite lush to my eye but I wasn't an expert on farming.

Then we were at the back door of the farmhouse and Babs was standing waiting for us. She had a white apron over her dark-coloured floral dress and she smiled when she saw us.

'Come away inside. I've got the dinner ready for you as I know you'll be hungry.'

Lily said she was starving and I apologised. 'Lily hasn't changed, Babs – she still loves her food.'

Babs gave her a quick look-over. Standing in front of her, she said, 'You're so much taller since we last saw you, Lily. You're all grown-up and about to go into the big wide world.' She turned to me and I noticed her eyes were wary. 'Ann, you haven't changed much I have to say but you're looking really well.'

I smiled. That was two statements of how well I was looking so things must be improving, I thought. Was I getting over Greg?

Lily and I had the same attic bedroom as before and we carried our suitcases up the narrow wooden staircase.

Lily sat on the bed and sighed. 'Oh, I love this room, Ann, with its sloping roof and window overlooking the hills.'

'Don't forget the owl!' I warned and she laughed.

I had to admit, it was a lovely little bedroom but I couldn't forget that, on previous visits years ago, Babs had said it had been Greg's room. His belongings were no longer there, however, and it could have belonged to anyone. All the character and soul had been removed along with him.

The dinner was substantial as usual. Home-made soup, steak pie and apple crumble. I felt I would never be able to move again. We were lingering over a cup of tea, chatting about nothing in particular and I felt we were all skirting around any mention of Greg.

Dave said that the hydroelectric company had begun to build dams and power stations over at Tummelbridge and Pitlochry. 'The days of the oil lamps will soon be over. Then we'll all have electric light.'

I wasn't quite sure if he was pleased about this new technology or sad.

Babs asked me about the flat. I had mentioned it in my last letter.

I was able to chat about this non-taboo subject. 'We'll need a bit more furniture and household items but we're getting things slowly. I managed to get a sideboard and two fireside chairs. They've got the utility mark on them so they're a bit plain although well made.' Still, if Danny was to be believed, the day would soon come when everything was readily available and generously made.

'And what about Maddie and Danny's twins? How are they?'

Before I could answer, Lily said, 'Oh, they're bonny babies. They've got three boys now and Rosie and Dad have Jay so that makes four boys. When Joy and I were born we were called the Sunday girls by Mrs Pringle. Ann and Maddie and Joy and I were all born on a Sunday so that's how we got our name.'

Babs smiled. 'I know, I've heard that description before and now it's four boys. Were they all born on a Sunday as well?'

Lily had to think about this. 'No, I don't think so. So we're still the Sunday girls, aren't we, Ann?'

I nodded and told Babs about Hattie and Graham and Chris and Kathleen and the sad saga of Sammy and Jean Martin. In fact, I felt I was babbling on and on like some gossipmonger but Babs didn't seem to notice. She seemed glad to hear all our news.

It was almost teatime when I ran out of subjects to talk about and I knew I couldn't put it off any longer. Babs had asked about my family and I hadn't even mentioned Greg.

My mouth was dry and when I spoke I thought my voice sounded squeaky. 'Greg. How is he Babs?'

She looked a bit embarrassed but we both knew we couldn't skirt around the subject of her son all night.

'He's fine, Ann. He's working in a library in Oxford just now.'

I was so taken aback. 'Oxford . . . that's great.'

She nodded. 'He went to London after Bletchley Park but, when this job came up, he applied for it and got it. He loves it.'

I took a deep breath and felt my tongue stick to the roof of my mouth. 'And his wife . . . does she like it there?'

Babs looked surprised. 'Oh, I thought you knew, Ann. He

hasn't got married yet – the wedding will take place in four months' time.'

It was now my turn to be surprised. 'Oh, I thought he got married just after the war.'

'No. The girl, Daisy, came from London and she lost her mother in one of the buzz bomb raids. That happened while they were at Bletchley Park and the wedding was postponed. Still, it'll be in Oxford in four months' time. Dave and I are going down for it.'

I felt a blackness behind my eyes and I didn't think I would be able to get through this weekend. Now that I'd heard Greg was still not married, I wondered if I would have been better prepared if he had indeed got married during the war or just after.

Fortunately we all went for a walk after our substantial tea and the evening was almost over. There was just the next day to get through and then we'd be going home the following day – back home to cry my eyes out and nurse my grief in private. Why, oh, why had I agreed to come here in the first place? Babs was as embarrassed as I was and I should have made up some excuse ages ago.

Later, in the glow of the lamplight, Dave and Lily played cards while I sat beside Babs as she knitted what looked like a huge brown jumper.

'You managed to get away from the shop all right, Ann?'

'Yes, I did.' A happy thought appeared in spite of my glum feelings as I recalled Connie and Joe tackling the early-morning papers. I had helped out for a couple of hours in the morning but how had they coped with the evening papers? And what about tomorrow's?

'It's nice to see you smile, Ann,' said Babs.

I felt myself blush – I hadn't realised I had smiled. 'I'm just thinking about Connie and Joe. They were snapping at one another this morning when I left and I was wondering how they'll cope tomorrow. Connie likes everything done her own way but so does Joe. It's a case of two bosses and no workers.'

Babs laughed and I felt the tension disappear. Was I the only one feeling embarrassed? Dave and Lily were having a friendly argument over some of the cards and they didn't look embarrassed. And Babs was bent over some intricate part of her knitting pattern. I was the only one who felt out of place. Almost as if I'd moved to outer space and found the natives so busy while I twiddled my thumbs and worried about events that were now past history.

Then it was bedtime. Thank goodness, I thought. Now I could stop pretending to be cheery and fancy-free.

Lily tucked herself up in the comfy bed and pulled the patchwork quilt up to her chin. 'Dave's taking me up the hill tomorrow. We're bringing the sheep down to the pens.' She was full of excitement at the thought of this hard work and outdoor air. 'What will you do, Ann?'

I was taken aback by her concern. 'Och, I'll help Babs in the kitchen and maybe go for a walk later. I've no firm plans.'

Satisfied with this ambiguous answer, Lily fell asleep almost at once but I was far from sleep. I sat at the window and looked at the deeply-shadowed hill. Small white pockets of mist hugged the gullies and it promised to be another fine warm day tomorrow.

Lily had wanted to know what I would do the next day. I didn't know that and I wasn't sure about the next week or the years ahead. I felt so alone and down. What did life hold in store for me? Especially once Lily left home. I could only see years of emptiness ahead of me. I tried hard to snap out of this feeling of self-pity. I was a reasonably young and healthy woman with my own flat. Thousands of people would envy me so why was I moping?

I went over to my suitcase and rummaged down the side, finally bringing out the small leather box that held my engagement ring. I had kept it after Greg had broken off the engagement but I knew I had to return it. That was why I had brought it with me. I would give it to Babs before leaving and she could do what she liked with it. Either give it back to Greg or throw it away. Either way, I didn't care, did I?

I didn't sleep very well. My mind was full of jumbled up dreams that were disturbing. I was glad when the sun rose and I was able to get up.

The kitchen was very quiet and empty when I went downstairs. I looked around for a suitable place to leave the ring and had just made up my mind that the small space between the plates on the dresser was the best place. I had the box in my hand when suddenly I heard Babs coming down the stairs. In a panic I shoved the box in my skirt pocket.

She said, 'You're up early, Ann. Let me put the kettle on and we'll have a quiet cup of tea before the other two come downstairs.'

I dreaded having a quiet tête-à-tête with her, much as I liked her. Then, to my relief, Dave came bounding into the kitchen, followed by Lily.

'I thought I'd take Ann and Lily for a wee run before gathering the sheep, Babs – let them see the new hydro scheme.'

Babs nodded as she placed a mound of bacon into the frying pan. I hadn't seen so much food for years. Later, after breakfast, Dave drew up with his little van and we piled in. He drove along the twisty road that wound through the glen towards Tummelbridge.

'The hydroelectric scheme will harness all this water,' he said, as we passed a large stream of tumbling water. 'There's a lot less water there because of the dry spell but, when it's in spate, the water will turn the turbines and all the rivers, lochs and streams will be controlled with dams until it's needed. It's a big undertaking and there are camps for hundreds of workers.'

I glanced out of the window but all was peaceful – just moors, streams and hills. It was a stark contrast to Dundee with its noisiness and bustle.

We drove into Tummelbridge and Dave pointed out the workers' huts although we didn't see many men.

Dave said, 'It's a Sunday so the men will be having a lie in or maybe some have gone home for the weekend. They certainly work hard digging through all this rock.'

Lily and I gazed at the big boulders at the side of the road and we didn't doubt a word of it.

He then turned the van around and we headed back to the farmhouse.

Babs laughed when we arrived back. 'He's like a big kid with that van! He's always running around in it but just up the road and back as usual.'

In the afternoon, Lily and Dave and Paddy the dog set off up the hill to gather the sheep. I watched their retreating figures walk slowly up the grassy slopes. I was wondering how to spend my afternoon. Hopefully it wouldn't be chatting to Babs as I was frightened she would ask me how I felt about Greg's forth-coming wedding and I didn't want to break down in front of her.

She was putting the kettle on when a voice called out in the yard.

'Oh, it's my neighbour, Ann. She sometimes comes in for a gossip on a Sunday afternoon but I'll cut her visit short.'

This was my escape. 'Oh, no, Babs! I'll go for a walk and leave you to have a chat with your neighbour.'

She looked dubious but I insisted. I stayed long enough to be introduced to her friend. When I saw the gleam of interest in the woman's eye when she realised I was Greg's ex-fiancée I knew I had made the right decision to escape.

I set off up the hill, taking the same path as Dave and Lily. The sun felt hot on my head and it was pleasant to be alone with the smell of the grass and earth. I was still climbing when I heard the voices. It was Lily and Dave and they were surrounded by sheep. I waved at them and continued upwards.

After a while I sat down and looked at my bird's-nest view of the valley below. I decided to climb a bit higher and slowly trudged through the rough grass and brown heather. Heather that Dave said would spring into purple splendour in a few weeks' time.

By now the valley had disappeared and I was surrounded by hills. It was so peaceful. I lay down on the warm grass, planning to have forty winks before setting off back down. With hindsight, I can only think it was because of my sleepless night that I fell fast asleep with the warm sun on my face and the smells of the countryside as a soothing balm. A bird called sharply in the distance but I barely heard it.

It was the coolness that woke me up. Thick mist like a wet grey blanket was wrapped around me and I sat up in a panic. For a few moments, I couldn't think where I was then my memory clicked in place and I remembered my walk in the warm sunshine. But where was the sun? I could hardly see a thing in front of me, so thick was the mist. I felt its wetness and my breath exhaled into this fog. And it was cold. I was wearing a thin blouse and cotton skirt. My legs were bare and my feet were thrust into sandals. I was hardly dressed for being stranded on the hills in this thick fog.

I got to my feet and rushed off in the direction I thought was the right one but then I stopped. Maybe I should be heading in the opposite direction? As I stumbled along with only the mist for company, a large shape loomed out of the fog and I almost had a heart attack. Thankfully it was only a large stone but this was a puzzle in itself. I hadn't passed a large stone like this on my upward journey.

I set off in a different direction but because of the limited view I was hampered. In fact, I had stumbled about the hill so much that I was now totally disorientated. Reaching the stone again, I sat down to try and get my bearings. I felt the coldness of the rock through my thin blouse. I listened hard, hoping to hear Lily and Dave's voices but it all was quiet. It was like being in a grey bottomless void.

I knew the Borlands would be worried about me and Lily would be frantic so I decided to choose a path. But which way? I seemed to be on some sort of plateau as I didn't feel I was either climbing or descending. What I had to do was to get on a downward path and I would surely come out at the farmhouse – or at least not too far from it.

Taking confident strides, I set off. Then the mist parted slightly and I could make out a patch of green grass in front of me. The mist was going to rise and I had nothing to worry about. Once I had my bearings I would be fine.

I was walking across the dewy grass when a dark shadow seemed to stretch out before me. I took another step forward and then suddenly stopped. I wasn't thinking about Ma Ryan but her voice came into my head. I heard her warning as clear as if she was on the hill with me. 'Watch your step. You're in danger. Watch your step.'

Almost crying with fear, I sat down and tried to slither backwards to the large stone. It seemed to take forever and I wasn't even sure if I was going in the right direction. 'Watch your step. You're in danger. Watch your step.' Her voice seemed to drill into my brain.

After what seemed like hours, I felt the stone with my hands and I huddled against it. My face and clothes were soaking and I realised I was crying – crying for my stupidity at climbing so far, crying for my lost life and, most of all, crying for Greg who was going to be married in four month's time.

I put my hand in my pocket to get my hankie and my fingers closed round the small leather box. In my anguish I threw it into the grey mist where it must have landed on the wet grass because it made no sound.

I immediately felt ashamed and scrambled to my feet to look for it. Feeling my way over the soggy ground, I dropped down on my knees and searched the ground, my hands outstretched, but it was a futile task. I got to my feet again and moved further away, kicking at the patches of scrubby heather and moss.

Suddenly Ma's voice seemed to scream at me. 'Watch your step. You're in danger. Watch your step.'

Frightened, I scrambled back to the stone. It was the only place I felt safe. I don't know how long I was there. It was an endless time and the mist never rose. It was as if I was cocooned in a grey silent shell.

I must have dozed off and, at one point, I thought I heard voices. I called out hoarsely but no one came and I realised I must have dreamt it. It crossed my mind that I could maybe die on this hill and I would never see Granny or Lily or Maddie and Danny ever again – or Rosie, Dad and Jay. This started a fresh feeling of panic and I thought about getting down from the hill again. I think, if it hadn't been for Ma's warning, I would have made the effort and taken the risk.

The cold air was making me sleepy and I thought this was a blessing – just to lie down and let sleep take over. My mind was full of jumbled-up images – most of them about Greg. If only things had turned out differently . . .

I slept. I had a dream that voices were calling out loudly. I tried to answer them but I couldn't make a sound. It was as if I was struck dumb. The voices came again and this time I struggled to be awake. The mist was still as thick but the voices sounded louder.

'Ann . . . Ann . . . Ann . . .'

I tried to call out, 'I'm over here – by the stone.'

For a moment, I thought the voices were receding and I tried to shout as loud as I could, 'Over here by the stone.'

There was no answer. Nobody had heard me and I felt as if I was doomed to lie there forever. I tried to stand up but I couldn't. My legs felt like lead and my feet were so cold. I had lost my sandals and could only imagine it was because of the scrambling over the rough heather in my search for the ring.

Then the voices came again. 'Ann . . . Ann . . . Can you hear us? Ann . . . Ann.'

'I'm here,' I called out but realised I was only whispering.

Then I saw the dark shape in the mist and my throat constricted with fear. To my relief, I saw it was a human figure but I didn't recognise the man who stood a few feet away from me.

I called out, 'I'm over here by the stone.'

The stranger called out to someone further down the hill and I heard muffled shouts. The man knelt down beside me and took off his thick jacket. He placed this around my shoulders and I realised I was shivering.

Then I saw Dave Borland appearing through the mist, followed by half a dozen men. I was quickly helped to my feet and thick blankets were placed around me. One of the men, a six-foot burly giant of a man picked me up and carried me slowly down the hill.

I was aware that I was babbling. 'I was frightened about the danger. I had to watch my step.'

Dave said soothingly, 'You'll be fine in a wee while, Ann. We've been searching all last night for you and again this morning. We almost gave up searching here because it's a few miles away from where we last saw you.'

The tall giant said in a lilting Irish voice, 'At least it wasn't cold last night so the lass won't have hypothermia.'

I tried to tell him I had been freezing all the time but my tongue didn't seem to work and my mouth was dry. Dave stopped and gave me a sip of water. I felt like grabbing the bottle from his hand and draining every drop but I resisted this urge because I was so stunned and embarrassed. Imagine putting all these men to so much bother. They wouldn't be very pleased with me. Had I heard them wrong when they mentioned being out all night?

I must have become a burden to the young man who initially carried me from the stone because he put me down. His place was taken by another heftily built man who picked me up as if I was a feather.

We seemed to be ages on the hill before the mist disappeared and the sun came out.

I was confused. 'What time is it, please?'

'Just after seven o'clock,' said Dave.

'I've been gone five hours,' I said, thinking I must have been wrong when I heard something about being out all night.

The man who was carrying me said, 'No, it's seven o'clock in the morning, lass.'

I was shattered. All night on the hill – I hadn't misheard.

Then the farmhouse came into view and Babs and Lily ran out.

Lily had been crying but she smiled when she saw me. 'Oh, Ann, are you all right?'

I gave her a weak smile which was all I could muster. 'I'm fine, Lily – just a bit cold and wet.'

Babs filled the tin bath by the fire and left me to soak in its warm depths while the men gathered in the yard. Dave produced a bottle of whisky and they all had a dram before setting off back to where they came from.

Where had all these men come from? I wondered. Probably from the neighbouring farms, I decided.

When I was dried and dressed in warm clean clothes, Babs cooked me a huge breakfast and poured me a large cup of tea. I tried to eat something but my throat felt sore from the cold air and the calling out. The cup of tea, however, was very welcome and I felt it warming me through and through.

'I'm sorry for all the fuss I've caused, Babs. I didn't realise how far I'd walked and, by the time I tried to return, the mist had come down.'

Babs said, 'Everything's fine. The mist can come down on these hills even during a lovely day like yesterday. It wasn't your fault, Ann. You weren't to know how dangerous the hills can be.'

The mention of danger brought back Ma Ryan's warning but, sitting in the warmth of the kitchen, I felt foolish for thinking I was in any danger. Perhaps, if I'd had the sense to get myself off the hill, then I would have been spared all this humiliation of having half the glen searching for me.

'I should have got myself down, Babs.' I didn't want to mention Ma. I didn't know if Babs believed in or knew of Ma's sixth sense – and, anyway, you had to know Ma to believe in her.

Dave came in at that moment. 'It's just as well you didn't try and walk any further, Ann. Just a few yards in the wrong direction from that stone is a two-hundred-foot drop. One moment, you're on terra firma and the next, there's nothing but space.'

Babs nodded. 'It's a right dangerous spot up there – especially if you don't know the area.'

My mouth went dry and I suddenly felt faint. I recalled the dark shadow that loomed out of the mist. Thank goodness I had stopped when I had, otherwise I could be lying at the foot of the gully, dead or injured. If it hadn't been for Ma's warning . . . I shivered.

To shake off this image, I asked, 'Who were all the men who were on the hill?'

'Some are neighbours from the farms near us but the two big Irish men are workers from the hydroelectric scheme. They came off the train last night and were walking back to the camp when they saw us heading off on the search. They insisted on helping out and thank goodness they did because we were looking in a different spot for you when they went off in the direction of the stone. You certainly wandered far off the track, Ann.'

I remembered walking for ages and how I had backtracked, back and forth – no wonder I was totally lost.

Then I remembered the engagement ring and I cried out.

Babs saw my face. 'What's the matter, Ann?'

Tears had started to roll down my cheeks. 'I lost my engagement ring, Babs – the one Greg gave me years ago. I brought it here to leave for him but it's lost. It was in my pocket.'

She said, 'Don't worry about it – Dave will find it.'

She didn't sound too sure and I knew that looking for a tiny box amongst all that undergrowth would be an impossible task.

Babs wanted us to stay for another day but I said I felt fine for the travelling. Lily also looked grateful to be leaving and I was mentally kicking myself for ruining her holiday.

We said our goodbyes to Babs and once more we clambered into Dave's van. Before leaving, I left notes for all my helpers, thanking them for looking for me. I also said to give my best wishes to Greg and his future wife and I really meant it. After having faced death the night before, I realised what a great life I had and the least I could do was to be gracious to the Borlands.

In the train going home, Lily began to cry. 'I thought you were dead, Ann. The men came off the hill last night and said there was no trace of you. Everybody was wondering where you could have got to.'

I was mortified by all the fuss I had caused. 'Don't cry, Lily. I'm fine now and everything is going to be just right. You'll be away in a few weeks and you've got all your life in front of you. You'll be a famous artist – you mark my words.'

She wiped her tears and gave me a watery-looking grin. 'Do you think so?'

I nodded. My head felt heavy and I was dying to reach home and go straight to bed but I had to keep smiling till then. 'One thing, Lily – I don't think we should worry Granny about this incident. So we'll just keep it quiet.'

Lily agreed.

At the end of the week and totally out of the blue I got a letter from Greg. I was so surprised that I opened it without thinking. Babs had told him about my accident and he was worried – or so he said.

That night, still full of shame about the whole unfortunate incident, I wrote back. It was only courtesy, after all. I told him how stupid I had been but everything had turned out well. I mentioned all the family news. The twins, Hattie and Graham, and Lily's imminent departure for art college – everything except how I had lost his ring but I didn't think he would worry too much about that. He had said, at the time, that I should keep it and, now that it was lost, it would make little difference to him during the run-up to his marriage. At the end, I wished them both the best of good wishes on their forthcoming marriage.

Afterwards, in spite of my brave words, I collapsed into bed in a flood of tears. Thankfully Lily was staying with Dad and Rosie that night so I was the sole witness to my misery and grief.

21

It was the beginning of September and Lily and Joy were getting ready to go to art college. It was a heartbreaking time for me as I finally realised I was losing her.

I recalled my first sight of her away back in 1931 on that searing hot July day when she was born – that awful day when Mum died – and I remembered how it had been love at first sight for me when I saw her lovely face and tiny rosebud mouth. All the years that had passed were filled with memories of us both together but, from now on, I would be without her and I was desolate. Not that I allowed these feelings to show.

Mrs Pringle had organised a get-together on the Sunday before the girls left and we all turned up. Granny, Bella, Hattie and Graham came along. Dad, Rosie and Jay were also there, as were Danny, Maddie and the children.

It was a bitter-sweet day and I realised Mrs Pringle was feeling the same emotions I was experiencing. The two girls were full of excitement at their initial step into the world of study and art and this excitement was infectious. We felt as if this step was being taken by us all but of course it wasn't. We were all staying in the same place while the great big world awaited them.

In a couple of days' time, after their departure, I would find myself back at the shop then home to a lonely house. Danny sensed my desolation as he stood beside me. Jay and Daniel were swooping around in the garden, making loud noises.

'You'll miss her, won't you, Ann?' he asked.

Not trusting myself to answer, I nodded.

'Do you mind when you were working at the Ferry and you bought her that pushchair? Mrs Peters lent you the money for it.'

It all seemed like a lifetime ago. I managed to laugh. 'I mind the day Grandad brought the pram home from Jumping Jeemy's Emporium!'

Danny laughed as well but Hattie, overhearing our conversation, said in a whisper, 'Don't mention that flea-ridden thing here, Ann.'

We laughed again. Danny said, 'Mum certainly didn't like it, did she?'

Hattie glared at us but I smiled at the memory.

Danny put his arm around my shoulder. 'We mustn't dwell on the past, Ann. Let's look forward to the future.'

I promised I would. However, it was a promise I didn't think I could keep but saying so out loud wouldn't help so I remained silent.

In two days' time, Mrs Pringle was going to Glasgow on the train with the two girls. Mr Pringle had got them accommodation in a nice flat in Sauchiehall Street which had come with good recommendations.

I had opened a post office account for Lily for everyday expenses and I would pay Mrs Barber, who owned the flat, Lily's board and lodging money every week. Mr Pringle had also arranged this and the money would come from my legacy which he still managed.

I had also saved up my clothing coupons and I used them to buy her some extra clothes. I didn't want her to look dowdy and old-fashioned amongst the students at the college. Granny had knitted her two jumpers and Hattie had given her a lovely woollen skirt to match. Dad and Rosie had also given her some money to spend in Glasgow and a lovely winter dress which was a present from Alice.

Danny was still speaking about Lily. 'She's a credit to you,

Ann. Maddie's parents have always said so and it's true. You've brought her up well.' He gave me a sharp glance. 'Have you had any more word from Greg?'

I shook my head. 'No, just that one letter, after the accident on the hill.' I felt my face go red and realised I still felt ashamed about the incident – even after two months had passed.

Danny said, 'You were lucky. I heard there was a two-hundred-foot drop just yards from where you were found.'

I looked around, frightened Granny might overhear what I was about to say, but she was busy chatting to Rosie. I shivered in spite of the warmth of the day. 'It was Ma Ryan's warning that alerted me to the danger, Danny. Remember I told you she sent for me one day and told me I was in great danger? Well, that night on the hill, I heard her voice as clear as if she was standing next to me. It was her sixth sense that saved me – just like the last time.'

Danny looked sad. 'Miss Hood?'

I didn't answer. Miss Hood was part of the past – just as the incident on the hill had to be. From now on, I would settle down to become a dowdy spinster and spend my evenings knitting or doing whatever all lonely spinsters did in their spare time.

Then Jay and Daniel came running into the room. I was suddenly taken with their different looks and natures and couldn't help but be amazed how like Lily and Joy they were at that age. Daniel was smaller than Jay and he had Maddie's fair colouring while Jay was taller and had dark hair and brown eyes. Daniel was the quieter of the two while Jay had also inherited Lily's appetite. He was holding a huge sandwich in his hand and obviously relishing it while Daniel was more interested in playing with his car.

Meanwhile, the twins lay asleep in their pram – a twin pram that Maddie's mum had managed to get hold of. I peeped in to see them and I thought I saw faint red fuzz on their heads.

Danny laughed. 'I think James and Patrick are going to be red-haired, like me.'

I thought that was wonderful and I said so. 'I've always liked your auburn hair, Danny.'

Then it was time to go home. Lily and I didn't sleep that night. She was too excited and I was too depressed.

As we lay awake in the bed settee, she suddenly burst out laughing. 'Sauchiehall Street, Ann.'

'What about it, Lily?'

'I think I'll saunter down Sauchiehall Street for a sausage roll or maybe some sugarelly.'

I laughed as well. 'Or maybe you can stagger down Sauchiehall Street for a Spam sandwich or a sherbet dip.'

She became quiet. 'I will miss you, Ann. I wish you were coming with me.'

'Och, don't be daft, Lily. You'll be mixing with young people of your own age – you and Joy. You'll soon forget all about me.'

She sounded shocked. 'Oh, no, Ann! I'll never, never forget you.'

On that note we tried to sleep. The next two days would be very busy. We had planned to visit Jean Peters at the Ferry and Nellie and Rita before she left for Glasgow.

On the way to the Ferry, Lily said, 'I'm glad I'm getting the chance to say cheerio to Jean.'

When we reached Long Lane, Jean was already waiting at the door. 'Come in, come in, Lily. I've got your dinner ready.'

Lily's face lit up and we were soon sitting down to hot Scotch broth and cheese scones. I didn't realise how hungry I was and it was great to taste Jean's lovely cooking again. I remembered how much I had enjoyed it at Whitegate Lodge many years ago.

'We've got lodgings in Sauchiehall Street, Jean,' said Lily. 'The woman who owns the house is a widow and she knows the Pringle family so we'll be fine there. I'm a bit worried about the college. I hope my art is good enough and Joy feels the same.'

Jean soon put these fears to rest. 'You'll both be great, Lily. You have real talent and I think you'll both go far – you mark my words.'

Lily beamed. 'Oh, do you think so, Jean?' She turned and looked at me. 'Ann thinks I'm good but she's biased because she's my sister and sisters are supposed to like everything their wee sisters do.'

I laughed. 'You're using the letter S again, Lily.'

We told Jean the joke from the night before. Afterwards, just before leaving, Jean asked me, 'And how are you, Ann?'

I felt my throat constrict and I wasn't sure if I could answer without bursting into tears – something I didn't want to do in front of Lily but Jean seemed to understand and merely squeezed my hand.

'We've got something for you, Lily,' she said instead.

She disappeared into the bedroom and brought out two small folding art easels. 'My man made these for you and Joy so we hope they help you with all your paintings.'

They were beautifully made and we were speechless.

Then Lily said, 'Oh, Jean, they're great! Thank you! I still have my pencil box that you gave me years ago and I'm taking that to Glasgow with me.'

It was now Jean's turn to almost cry and I said, 'And Jay still has the wonderful train he got. Will you thank your man, Jean, for all the both of you have done for us?'

After another cup of tea, we set off for the Hilltown. Jean stood at the door waving until we were out of sight. I promised to go and see her within the next few weeks. After all, I would have loads of spare time, wouldn't I?

The close at the foot of the Hilltown was still as I remembered it. Rita and Nellie, however, were now more prosperous-looking and not so emaciated. What a difference having a working man in the house again made. Rita's son was also working and the two houses were better furnished and the cupboards, in spite of the rationing, had some tins and food on the shelves.

However, the rationing was still the main topic. 'I see Mr Attlee had ordered more austerity cuts,' said Rita. 'The meat ration has been cut by tuppence to one shilling and he warns there's more cuts to come.'

I knew this was true because the papers had been reporting the shortage of dollars and Britain's inability to pay for imports of food. Hadn't Joe been spouting about this austerity crisis for ages?

Still, they were so pleased to see Lily. She told them all about her imminent departure for Glasgow in her cheery manner and they were both duly impressed. 'Imagine somebody from this close going to college!' said Rita. 'We're all so proud of you.'

I noticed, when she said it, she glanced sympathetically at me. 'And what about you, Ann? Will you still work at Connie's shop?'

I said, 'Yes, Rita. It's a job I like and these days Connie is not so able to stand for hours but she's given me three days off this week to see Lily settled.'

I noticed the old clock with the merry tick had been replaced as had most of the old furniture. The women had obviously been to Henderson's furniture shop in the Wellgate and a solid-looking dining room suite was now in residence in both houses. I felt so glad for them as they deserved a bit of comfort and the money now coming into the home had provided it.

'The best news, Ann,' said Nellie, 'is that we're maybe all going to be rehoused into a new house with a bathroom, kitchen and hot water. These old houses are going to be knocked down.'

I was pleased for them and hoped Dad, Rosie and Jay would also get a new house with all the modern comforts.

Rita, however, put Nellie's statement down to wishful thinking. 'That's the rumour, Ann, but we'll believe it when we see it.'

As we were leaving, a heavily pregnant woman came up the stair. She was holding on to the banister like grim death.

Rita and Nellie smiled at her. 'Not long to go now, Mrs McGregor,' said Rita.

The woman grimaced in passing. 'Thank the Lord! I'm getting more and more tired every day.' She glanced at Lily and me and nodded.

At the foot of the close, Rita said, 'Mrs McGregor and her man are the new tenants of your old house, Ann.'

A look passed between the women and myself and I knew we were all were remembering Mum. Thankfully Lily was ahead of me and she missed this silent communication.

'Keep in touch, both of you,' they said as we went on our way.

It was now time to visit Dad, Rosie and Jay. Rosie was bustling around when we entered the kitchen and I got the impression she was also near to tears. Dad looked so proud as he wished Lily well at the college and Jay was wide-eyed at this small domestic scene. Lily had always been close to him and even he felt the change in the air as she said her goodbyes.

As we were leaving, he ran over and hugged her legs. 'Cheerio, Lily.'

She knelt down and hugged him back. 'I'm just going to Glasgow, Jay. I'll be back to see you all often and, in fact, you'll all be tired of looking at me.'

However, I knew she was as near to tears as we all were.

When we got home, it was almost time for bed and I for one felt exhausted. On that note, we tried hard to sleep because we both knew the next day would be a busy one.

Mr and Mrs Pringle turned up with Joy soon after breakfast. They were both dressed in gabardine raincoats as the weather had turned wet. Joy stood beside them in her new royal blue coat that sparkled with raindrops and I was suddenly glad that Lily also had some new clothes to go away with. There was no way I wanted her to look like some poor relation.

Mr Pringle picked her suitcase up and I then realised I hadn't seen Joy's suitcase. I was on the verge of asking when he said, 'We've got a taxi waiting for us, Ann. It'll save us getting wet on our way to the station.'

Lily's eyes lit up. 'A taxi! The last time I was in a taxi was at Maddie and Danny's wedding.'

Joy smiled. 'Well, we're going in another one, Lily.'

We all hurried downstairs and the taxi was at the kerb with the driver standing beside it. He was smoking a cigarette which he quickly threw away and stamped it out with his foot.

When we reached the railway station, it was quiet – just a few bored-looking businessmen and two smartly dressed women who looked as if they were off to Glasgow for a trip.

Fortunately we didn't have long to wait for the train which was a blessing as I couldn't have stood it if we had. The train appeared and Mrs Pringle and the girls quickly got into an empty compartment while Mr Pringle and I helped with the suitcases. He stowed them away on the overhead luggage rack while I stood awkwardly at the open door.

We just had enough time to say a quick goodbye and the train slowly steamed out of the station. Taking Lily to Glasgow and out of my life.

I knew I was crying but I didn't care.

Mr Pringle took my arm. 'Come on, Ann. I'll treat you to a coffee at Draffen's. I don't have to be at the office just yet.'

We sat at the table and the waitress brought our cups. I had managed to wipe my face and hoped that any person, should they be remotely interested in me, would surmise my face was wet from the rain.

Mr Pringle said, 'When we go down to see Joy you can come with us, Ann.'

I stirred my coffee listlessly.

'It's not that far away and the girls will be coming home for the holidays. Joy said they would be back for Christmas and the New Year,' he said kindly.

'I know, Mr Pringle, I know. Lily said the same. It's just that I'll miss her so much. We've been together for so long that I foolishly thought we would always be together.'

'But you know she's going to be a wonderful artist, Ann. She's got a great talent and so has Joy but she hasn't got Lily's artistic touch.'

I felt so proud of her. 'I know and I didn't mean to be so downhearted.'

'You be as downhearted as you like. It's only natural.' He then changed the subject. 'Do you know Hattie is leaving us?'

I didn't know and said so.

'She feels now that Joy is away from home that there's nothing left for her to do. And she now has Graham to keep her happy and busy. He's buying a house in Broughty Ferry and I hear Hattie is giving up her house in Westport to go and live with him.'

I didn't know what to say so I just said, 'I see.'

'Hattie told Fay that she didn't care if Graham got a divorce or not. She was grabbing her chance of happiness now and she didn't give a fig what other people thought.'

I wondered how Granny would react to this news. Then I thought she probably wouldn't give a fig either. If there was one thing this awful war had taught us, it was to make people live for the moment as it could all be snatched away tomorrow.

He walked back to Roseangle with me. The drizzle had stopped but it was still grey and dreary-looking. After he left, I hurried up to the flat. I planned to have a quick snack and then make my way to the shop.

Connie was waiting for me, ready to offer tea and sympathy but, the moment I saw her, I burst into tears. Luckily the shop was empty and she made me sit in the back shop with my tea.

'After you've drunk that, Ann, just you get away back home. You can start tomorrow.'

I was appalled. 'Oh, no, Connie! I'll be fine in a minute. It's just the thought of not seeing Lily tonight. The flat will be so quiet.'

She nodded. 'Aye, it will. Have you thought of taking in a lodger?'

I looked at her in amazement. 'A lodger?'

'A big handsome man with blue eyes and burly shoulders.'

I said, 'Have you someone in mind?'

'Joe,' she said and we both burst out laughing. 'That's better, Ann. It's good to have a laugh and, if there's ever someone to laugh at, it's Joe.'

'Poor Joe! What has he done to deserve this character assassination, Connie?'

She snorted. 'He dropped his cigarette end onto a pile of newspapers and burned a hole right through them. I've had twenty complaints today. The hole was right through the middle of the death column and, if there's one thing the old folk round here hate, it's the thought of missing a dead body.'

This cheered me up but then Connie always did that. She was

on her way home when she suddenly came back through the door.

'Honestly, I've got a mind like a sieve. I almost forgot. Guess who I had in this morning with his new wife?'

My mind was a blank and I said so.

'Davie Chambers.'

'The paper laddie who went into the navy?' I remembered Davie very well. His mother was a widow who didn't have much money. He would appear at the shop on cold mornings with short trousers and red-raw knees. I had got some good clothes that had belonged to Danny and they fitted him so, after I gave them to his grateful mother, at least he had been warmly clad on the winter mornings.

'He's a fine-looking man and his wife is small and very pretty. They've been staying with his mother for a few days. You'll mind she got another house in Tulloch Crescent and a good job in the school kitchen at Rosebank.'

I did remember. It had been Mrs Chambers who had kindly lent the robe for Jay's christening.

'Well, he was asking for you, Ann. He's away back to Portsmouth now. He's still in the navy and they've got a flat in the city.'

I was so happy for him and his small and very pretty wife but, after Connie left, I felt down again. Everyone seemed to be getting married or moving in with their men.

The appearance of Joe didn't help my mood. He was morose because of the earlier mishap. 'Connie was furious with me,' he said. 'I never saw the fag falling on the papers till I saw the smoke.'

'Och, don't worry about it, Joe. Connie was laughing about it before she left.'

His face brightened. 'Was she?'

He stayed for ages, chatting on and on about the state of affairs in the country. But I barely heard him. I was wondering if Lily had arrived at Sauchiehall Street with Joy and Fay Pringle and thinking about how she would cope with all the newness of a big city.

That night, instead of going back to an empty flat, I went to see Granny. Bella was there but there was no way I could back-track through the door when I saw her. I put a big smile on my face and breezed in.

Bella looked sourly at me. 'What have you got to smile about, Ann? Your sister is away and you've no' got a man in your life.'

Granny gave her a sharp look but either Bella didn't notice it or she didn't care.

'And we see Hattie is going to bide with her fancy man. She's giving up her house to live in sin with him – just like Kathleen and her fancy man. What is the world coming to?'

I didn't answer her.

Granny said, 'You can bide here the night if you want to, Ann.'

It was a very tempting offer until I realised I had to get on with my life. It wouldn't be very long till Christmas as James Pringle had said. I would see Lily then and we would catch up with her news. I would get my life's excitement second-hand.

I left Bella with Granny. As usual Bella was complaining of aches and pains, general tiredness and a few other complaints. I felt sorry for Granny but Bella was too much for me at that moment.

The street was still busy and I considered going to see Danny at his shop on the Hawkhill. Then I realised I didn't want to discuss my loneliness with anyone, not even Danny – at least not that night.

I spent another sleepless night and wondered if Lily was also feeling the same. I hoped not.

October came in grey and miserable and it matched my mood exactly. My days were filled with mundane matters. Going to work, going home, going to bed, day in and day out. My only bright spot was Lily's weekly letter with all her news and I devoured it like a starving man. I tried to make my letters cheery and usually wrote about the customers at the shop and any titbit of news that came my way but I have to say there wasn't a lot of that.

Even the river view from the window failed to brighten my mood. It didn't seem like the same view without Lily. Anyway, the curtains were pulled as soon as I arrived back at night and I sat down with only the wireless for company.

At the end of the month, on a Saturday evening, there was a knock on the door. I had just finished washing my hair and, thinking it was my elderly neighbour from next door, I opened it.

I almost fell down in surprise when I saw Greg standing on the doorstep. I was kicking myself for looking like a frump with a towel around my head.

Then remembering my manners I said, 'Come in, Greg. What a surprise!' As he stepped inside, I looked out at the landing, fully expecting to see his fiancée standing there. The landing, however, was empty.

Greg sat down on one of my new fireside chairs and, to cover my confusion, I went into the small scullery to put the kettle on.

I called out from my haven, 'I thought you were in Oxford, Greg.'

He said, 'I am but a job has come up for a chief librarian in Dundee and I've come up for an interview. Whether I get the job is another matter but I'm keeping my fingers crossed.'

'Where is your fiancée, Greg? I hope she's not waiting outside in the rain.' I tried to make my voice sound neutral but I felt the words came out wrong.

He looked serious. 'We've broken the engagement off.'

I must have looked stunned because he said, 'It's not really a big surprise. We were just company for one another when we worked together but, when her mother was killed in a buzz bomb raid, I somehow got into a situation where we both assumed we would get married – hardly the basis for a happy married life.'

'Where is she now?' I asked, aware that my voice was croaky.

'She went back to London and, as far as I know, she's got another man – someone she knew from years ago.'

My head swam with relief. Greg's engagement was no longer looming like a sword of Damocles over my head.

'How do feel about that? Are you sad?' I asked.

He grinned and I almost cried at the sight of the old Greg. 'Actually, I feel relieved.'

301

My mind was still reeling. I mustn't look too keen, I thought. So, trying to sound nonchalant, I turned the subject away from his ex-fiancée, thinking he didn't want to talk about her. 'Lily and Joy have gone to art college in Glasgow. Hattie is going to live with Graham and Granny is keeping well.'

He nodded. 'That's good news, Ann. Lily will be a big girl now. It's funny how quickly time has gone in. And what about yourself? Are you happy about Lily going away?'

'Oh, yes,' I said brightly. 'I've got lots of plans and loads of friends to look up. And I've got my job at the shop and I meet lots of interesting people.'

He nodded seriously while I almost choked on all the lies I had just uttered. But still I babbled on. 'Maddie and Danny have three boys now. Daniel and the twins, James and Patrick. Kathleen has gone to live in London with her boyfriend, Chris.' I was aware I was babbling but I couldn't stop myself. I knew, if I stopped speaking, I would throw myself into his arms and surely, after all this time, he would be embarrassed.

He sat on my utility chair and gazed quietly at me as I scurried from the room to the scullery and back, chatting like some insane person.

Then, to my utter dismay, he said, 'I won't stay for tea, Ann. I've got my train to catch in an hour.'

I tried to hide my intense feeling of rejection. 'Of course, Greg – I forgot you're just here for an interview.' I walked to the door with him, trying desperately to hide my tears which threatened to erupt any minute now.

At the door, he said, 'I'm glad everyone is fine and that the news is good on all fronts. I just wanted to come and see you and check you were all right after your ordeal on the hill in the summer. Mum and Dad said it was a miracle you weren't killed. Another few steps and you would have fallen into that deep gully. It's a dangerous spot.'

Just hurry up and go, Greg, I prayed, before I show myself up.

'I would come to the railway station with you but, as you can see, my hair is still wet.'

He nodded. 'It's all right.' He stood on the landing for a brief moment and then turned towards the stairs. 'Well, cheerio, Ann. I'm glad I've seen you and that your life is happy and I like your new flat – it's lovely.'

'Thanks. Lily and I love it.'

Then, with a final wave of his hand, he was gone. I stood on the landing for ages, still aware of the faint trace of his presence. I was shaking with anger at myself. Why had I behaved like an idiot? I'd rabbited on and on about trivialities when there was so much I wanted to say to him. Still, if he had wanted to say something important to me, why hadn't he done it? No, I thought, his visit wasn't to say anything special to me but merely a social visit because he was in Dundee. Maybe he thought I would get to hear of it and be dejected that he hadn't called.

Well, I wasn't dejected, was I? Oh, yes I was. In fact, I was worse than dejected. I felt totally drained of any emotion and just wanted to crawl into bed and nurse my grief in the darkness.

I should have gone to the station with him. After all, that was the place where I said all my goodbyes to people I loved. Standing on a desolate platform.

The next day didn't bring any relief from my misery and I mentioned Greg's visit to Granny. 'I should have told him how I feel, Granny, and maybe he would have stayed.'

'Well, Ann, maybe he would have but what if he hadn't? What if his visit was a courtesy call and you had poured your heart out to him? Have you thought of that?'

I nodded miserably. 'I have Granny.'

It was back to work on the Monday morning as usual. The streets were quiet as I made my way to the Hilltown. The mill workers weren't on the streets yet but it would all change in an hour or so.

Connie used to do this very early shift but I had being doing it for a while now, picking up the piles of papers and getting them ready for the paper boy and all the early morning workers. Joe didn't come to the shop as early as this now. He had rheumatism, he said, and he liked to stay in bed a while longer on these cold and damp dark mornings.

I was looking forward to my weekly letter from Lily. She was full of the art college news and all the people she and Joy had met up with. It was a life full of interest and happy socialising. The students all seemed to meet up at the weekends and have lively get-togethers to discuss art and the world in general.

I always tried to keep my letters cheery and bright, telling her all the local gossip from the shop and mentioning all the plans I had for hobbies. I was going to start a brand-new life tomorrow with all my interests. The only thing I didn't mention was that mañana never arrived.

Connie came in during the afternoon and I set off for home. The weather was still damp and murky with spells of heavy rain and I hurried along the wet pavements. I was dying to get the fire on and have a cup of tea. Then I'd spend an evening with the wireless or maybe visit Granny or Rosie. Or maybe I would just sit by the fire like a zombie before going to bed. Or I could visit Danny and Maddie. Maybe.

I saw Lily's letter on the mat when I opened the door and I went to read it by the window. The river was invisible on a dull afternoon like this. Damp mist hugged the pavements and it was like looking over a sea of greyness. I had barely read half of it when someone knocked at the door. It would be the coalman, I thought. Once a month he came later in the day and I paid for my weekly bags of coal then. Moving to the door like some middle-aged spinster with my purse in my hand, I opened it.

A young telegram boy stood on the doorstep and handed me a telegram. My heart almost stopped beating with fright. Please, not Lily I prayed. Please don't let something be wrong with her. The boy turned to go and I carried the flimsy missive in my sweaty hand. I knew I was breathing heavily when I sat down by the window, beside Lily's letter. Had something gone wrong between her writing to me a day ago and now?

Taking a deep breath, I tore the telegram open but shut my eyes, like some tiny child afraid of the dark. Then, steeling myself,

I glanced at the typewritten words, 'Sorry I was such a coward the other night. Will you marry me, Ann? Greg.'

For one dazed moment, I stared at the words – Greg was asking me to marry him. I jumped up and, if there had been anyone in the room, I would have kissed them.

'Yes, yes, yes!' I shouted at the wall. 'Yes, yes, yes!'

I rushed out to the nearest post office to reply. I wasn't even going to think about all that had happened over the years. Seize the day, Kathleen had said to me. She had certainly seized her day and I was about to do the same.

After sending off my reply, I rushed up to see Granny. It was an emotional meeting.

'Oh, Ann, I hope you're both happy after all these years,' she said.

'I am, Granny, I am – believe me!'

She was crying by the time I left but she promised to pass on my good news to all the family – Dad, Rosie and Jay and Hattie and Graham.

Meanwhile, I hurried up to see Maddie. She was putting the twins down for a nap when I burst in.

'Maddie, I'm getting married! Greg has just asked me.'

She was confused. 'Is Greg still in Dundee?'

I shook my head. 'No. He's proposed by telegram.'

Maddie tried to keep a straight face but she couldn't. She burst out laughing. 'A telegram, Ann?' She started to laugh again and I joined in with her. It really was a funny way of proposing to someone, after all.

We wiped the tears from our eyes then Maddie became serious. 'I'm really pleased for you both and I know Danny will be as well.'

'I'm writing to him tonight to say we'll get married as soon as possible. I'm not losing him this time, Maddie.'

'Good for you, Ann. It's about time you thought of yourself for a change.'

22

The next few weeks passed in a whirl of activity of plans and excitement. Greg and I decided to get married in the registry office. Danny was to be the best man and Maddie would be my matron of honour. Because Lily and Joy were to be attendants, the date was set for a few days before Christmas. Lily and Joy would be home for the holiday then. Maddie came with me to choose my wedding outfit but, as I had used up most of my clothing coupons for Lily's clothes in September, I didn't have a lot.

Granny and Bella came to the rescue with their spare coupons and I chose a lovely suit in deep pink. It was in the New Look fashion by Dior of Paris and the hem almost skimmed my ankles. I felt like a film star in it. Maddie chose a matching suit in deep blue and I couldn't get over how much had happened to me over the space of a few weeks.

Choosing a hat was more difficult but Connie said she had just the hat for me. It was a cream pillbox style with a spotted veil that reached the level of my eyes. It made my suit look more like Hollywood than Dundee.

But the best news of all was that Greg had got the job in Dundee as chief librarian although he still had three weeks to finish at Oxford. We were planning to spend that time as our honeymoon before heading back north again.

Oh, I was so excited and, for those last few days, I could barely

speak. I had to try hard not to think something would spoil it –
as it had done in the years before. Every night before I went to
sleep, I prayed that everything would turn out fine. And it did.

Our wedding day dawned very cold with a slight covering of
snow but there was a watery-looking sun and a pale grey insipid
sky. The family all turned out at the City Square to see us married
and the ceremony was beautiful if a bit short.

There was one surprising moment. Just after Greg slipped
the wedding ring on my finger, he brought out a small leather
case.

'It's my engagement ring, Greg!' I cried, not believing my
eyes.

He smiled and placed the ring next to the simple gold wedding
band. 'My dad found it not long after your accident, Ann. I was
going to propose to you that night I saw you in the flat. I had
this with me but I changed my mind when you told me how
happy you were. I thought I had no chance of getting you back.'

Oh, my God, I thought. To think how close I had come to
losing him forever. I smiled at him. 'Well, we're together now.
That's all that matters.'

We had planned a small meal at the Queen's Hotel and all the
family and friends joined us there: Dad, Rosie and Jay and Alice;
Granny, Bella, Hattie and Graham and Dave and Babs Borland;
Kit, George and Patty and Ma Ryan; Peter and Minnie and their
son were also there – Minnie had given birth to a little girl recently
but her mother was looking after her for the afternoon; Nellie
and Rita and their husbands plus Jean and her husband were also
there to wish us well.

James and Fay Pringle brought Daniel and they arrived a few
moments later along with John and Dot Pringle. Connie and Joe
came together. Then there was my beloved Danny and Maddie
– my friends throughout the years. We had been together through
such a lot of heartache and joy.

Lily stood beside me. She was taking her duties as an attendant very seriously and even Joy looked as if she was enjoying
the occasion.

Lily gave Greg a big wink and he winked back. 'I always knew you would get married to Ann. There's not another person in the whole wide world as great as she is,' she said.

Greg, bless him, agreed.

Then the speeches were over and we were able to mix with our guests.

Bella came up. She had a large glass of whisky in her hand. 'This is better than yon wee glasses of sherry you normally get at functions like this. Anyway I'm glad you've made an honest woman out of Ann. It took you both a long time, mind you. But better late than never, I always say.'

Greg took this as a compliment and said so. To my surprise she blushed and I gave her a quick hug. 'Thanks for coming to our big day, Bella, and also for the coupons.'

Then I saw Jean. She had been crying but she wiped her eyes. 'Sorry to be so emotional, Ann, but I've aye looked on you as the lassie I never had. When I think back to the terrible time you had under that tyrant Miss Hood I can cry.'

'Well, it's all over now, Jean, and I'm so happy I could cry myself.' Greg gave my hand a squeeze as if to say all my problems *were* now over.

Connie and Joe left early but they wished us both the best for the future. Connie said, 'Don't worry about the shop, Ann. Joe and I will do it together. Just until you get back from your honeymoon and then you can make up your mind if you still want to work there.'

'Of course I still want to work in your shop, Connie. After all, I have to show my thanks for lending me this super hat.'

As we watched them leave, Greg said, 'Do you think there might be a romance between those two?'

I laughed. 'Oh, I hope so.'

Nellie and Rita and their husbands also left along with Connie and Joe.

'Thanks, Nellie and Rita,' I said to them, 'for all your help when Lily was born and over the years. You've been such good friends to us all – especially to Dad.'

Rita laughed. 'Och, it's been a braw day, Ann, and we're really pleased to see you join the happy band of married women.'

'And it's great to see your dad looking so happy with Rosie and Jay,' said Nellie.

Indeed it was and it was something I blessed every day.

Minnie came over with Danny and Maddie. 'I'm so happy myself, Ann,' she said. 'We've got a lovely house in Downfield and Peter is enjoying his new responsibilities as the head manager of Lipton's. Isn't it funny how life turns out?'

I remembered when she had lived at Clydebank with her small son and how devastated we had all been when we thought they had been killed in the terrible bombing there. Now she had another baby and life was looking rosy for them all.

Greg and I then went to sit beside Kit, George and Ma Ryan. I was so pleased she could come to my special day and I told her this. 'You saved my life, Ma, with your warning of the danger. If it hadn't been for you I maybe wouldn't be a bride today. Thank you!'

She gave me a long searching look. 'You've had a lot to bear in your life, lass, but it's all behind you now. You have a great husband who loves you and he always has – in spite of the parting between you. From now on, the sun will shine tomorrow on all your plans. Oh, I'm not saying it will all be smooth and trouble-free but you'll both cope and grow stronger.'

Kit said, 'We're sorry Kathleen and Chris couldn't come but they send you all their love. She would have loved to be here on your big day but Chris is going away on a photo shoot to France and Kathleen and Kitty are going with him.' She sounded so proud of her daughter and the lovely lifestyle she now had – one that was very different to her life with Sammy.

As we got up to move away, she whispered, 'Did you know Jean Martin has had a son, Ann?'

I shook my head. 'No, I didn't know that, Kit.'

'Well, her father has been in touch with Sammy's commanding officer and he has to pay her money for the baby. That will put his gas at a peep for a while. That and the fact he's in the jungles of Malaya. Maggie doesn't know what to say these days. On the one hand she's worried about the jungle but on the other she's dreading him coming back to Lochee to face the music.' She laughed. 'Poor Maggie, I really feel very sorry for her.'

Greg and I then went over to speak to his parents and Hattie and Graham. I still felt the glow from all their good wishes.

Graham was telling them they were going to get married as soon as his divorce was finalised. 'It might take a while yet but it'll happen, won't it, Hattie?'

Hattie simply smiled and nodded.

I thanked Babs and Dave for all their kindness to Lily and me and I also thanked Dave for finding the ring.

He laughed. 'Oh, it was pretty easy to find in the daylight, Ann. I just retraced the steps from that huge stone and there it was – only a matter of feet away. You'll never make a cricketer with your long throws.'

I blushed but he merely patted me on the shoulder. 'Greg's a lucky man to get such a beautiful bride and a lovely wife.'

Then Danny and Maddie joined us and I almost burst into tears. Maddie held me close while Danny chatted to Greg.

Then Danny took my hand. 'We wish you all the best in the world – you both deserve it.'

Jay, Daniel and Peter were running through the guests, making vroom-vroom noises.

'I'm going to be a Spitfire pilot,' said Daniel.

'So are we,' said Jay and Peter together. 'We'll all be Spitfire pilots.'

Fay and James Pringle looked at the boys with affection. 'I remember the first time I saw you, Ann,' she said. 'It was New Year and I remember I called you the Sunday girls. Do you remember?'

I nodded. 'Oh, I do! It was Maddie and me and Joy and Lily. We were all born on a Sunday.'

'Now it's all boys – Daniel, Jay, Peter, James and Patrick.'

Oh, yes, I thought. It was a new generation growing up and we were all getting older.

I glanced over at Dad and Rosie and I saw she had also been crying. She smiled when she saw me and gave a little wave. She was dressed in a lovely dress of gold crêpe de Chine and her still-dark hair was cut in a short fashionable style. I was so glad she had kept up her smart appearance. Dad was still Dad and he would never change. He liked a pretty face around the place.

He was busy talking to John and Dot Pringle and I was pleased that they seemed to be on good terms. Hopefully Margot's poison had been exorcised from their marriage. Where was she now? I wondered. I actually didn't care but I hoped she wasn't still ruining people's lives.

I had noticed the two young lads earlier but I didn't know where they had come from. Lily soon put me right. 'This is Charlie and this is Colin. They're at art college with us and they stay in the boarding house next door to us. They live in Dundee so I asked them along. Is that all right, Ann?'

'Of course it is,' I said. Greg and I said hello to the two boys who both seemed very young. One had a spotty face and they were both thin and immature-looking.

Joy sauntered over and stood beside us while the two boys went over to the buffet table. Lily and Joy watched them going. Lily gave a huge sigh. 'Joy and I are not getting married for years and years and years, Ann. Just like you and Greg, we're going to be old before we get married. Isn't that right, Joy?'

Joy nodded with relish.

Greg and I looked at one another and burst out laughing.

'Do you think you can put up with this geriatric husband, Ann?'

'Only if you promise to love me into my old age which, according to Lily, is now,' I replied.

'Oh, I promise to love you forever and ever – till death us do part.'

I looked over at Granny. Alice was standing beside her and Granny had been crying. Perhaps like me she was remembering my beloved grandad but she might have been shedding tears of happiness for Greg and me on our wedding day. It was a day